T

Sister Gabriel walked slowly towards Mother Magdalene and began to open the buttons running down the front of her habit. In a husky voice she addressed Father Lionheart. 'Father, I want to confess some of my deepest desires. Can you help me with them?'

Father Lionheart smiled wickedly and replied, 'Mother Magdalene and I are your willing vessels. Speak freely and boldly and we will serve you as best we can.'

The spoken word was such a turn-on for her. Her face burned with shame at being asked to allow the whole community to witness her arousal.

The Order

DEE KELLY

BLACK
lace

Black Lace novels contain sexual fantasies.
In real life, make sure you practise safe sex.

First published in 2001 by
Black Lace
Thames Wharf Studios,
Rainville Road, London W6 9HA

Copyright © Dee Kelly 2001

The right of Dee Kelly to be identified as the Author of
this Work has been asserted by her in accordance with
the Copyright, Designs and Patents Act 1988.

Typeset by SetSystems Ltd, Saffron Walden, Essex
Printed and bound by Mackays of Chatham PLC

ISBN 0 352 33652 8

Contents

Part One

Genesis

Chapter One

A few rays of late afternoon sunlight broke through the clouds and set fire to a mane of red-gold hair, creating a halo around the head of a beaming young woman in the crowd. Her vibrant curls, jaunty, bouncing stride and impish grin carried her along on the sea of marchers jostling amiably down Piccadilly. This is the life! thought Margaret, drinking in the bright clothes, wild hair and beautiful faces around her. It was a far cry from the lonesome rocky shore in Connemara where she had grown up, one of eight kids in a typically Irish, Catholic family. Glancing around at the vast array of people proudly flaunting their sexuality, she felt that these past few years, since leaving home at sixteen, had certainly allowed her to broaden her horizons.

Breasts bouncing joyfully in bra-less freedom, Margaret Dempsey strode past a group of shorn men with bare buttocks and cowboy chaps who were bearing a huge Gay Pride banner. Ducking under a 'Lesbians are Everywhere!' flag, she threw her arms around a willowy young man with shoulder-length chestnut hair wearing an 'I'm Just Sexual' T-shirt.

'Richard!'

He turned, tousled her springy curls and wrapped her

in a warm bear hug. Margaret craned her neck and swept her eyes over his fine, angular features and tawny hazel eyes, basking in the warmth of his sensual smile. Over the chants of 'I Will Survive' he struggled good-naturedly to be heard and brushed his full lips against her ear.

'Do you want to come to mine later? Delia, Mack, Savannah – the usual crowd, are all going to bring some food. You know, have a drink, play some music? Do come. Go on, say yes.'

Margaret turned her sparkling grey-blue eyes up to meet his and nodded her assent. She could hardly breathe with excitement. The last time she'd been to one of Richard Dalbeny's little 'happenings', a lot had happened. An unbelievable, motley crew of lovely young men and women had shared food, wine, a few joints, and then each other. She blushed as a memory of Richard waving his impressive erection about sprang unbidden into her mind. And to think he'd done two years in a seminary before deciding that free love and pacifism were far more pressing than his training as a priest. Nonetheless, Margaret was grateful to Richard for still having faith and charity in equal measure. He had a rare talent for soothing her Catholic sensibilities and had deflowered her with loving tenderness, even offering up a prayer for her mortal soul as he did so.

Hyde Park was awash with banners, chanting marchers and a smattering of riot police, looking sheepish rather than threatening. Several nubile young men and women in black leather and chains weaved their way among the officers, sticking condoms and safe sex leaflets into uniform pockets and under badges. The policemen and women smiled grimly, determined to appear tolerant.

Within an hour of the last marchers arriving, most of them had settled down on the grass, where the air was thick with laughter, the chink of bottles, cannabis smoke and snatches of song. Margaret inhaled deeply and felt her head swim. She lay back, head resting on someone's lap, and surveyed the drifting clouds above her. Praying was as natural to her as breathing, and she fervently thanked God for the beautiful day, the trouble-free march, and the generous company of whomever she was lying on.

Shifting a wayward lock of curls from her eyes, she tilted her head back and peered up at the owner of the lap supporting her head. A serene girl, with straight, shiny blonde hair smiled, Madonna-like, down upon her. Margaret puckered up her rosy-red lips into a smile, and was rewarded by a soft, languorous kiss.

'Hi. Hello again. I'm Savannah, remember?' The beautiful girl looked vaguely familiar, but Margaret couldn't summon the energy to place her, and it didn't seem very important anyway.

'I love you,' she slurred.

Savannah laughed like a tinkling waterfall, her hair shimmering in the sun. 'Well, I love you too!'

Later on, Margaret felt a warm, ticklish, but exciting sensation vying with the urge to drift off to sleep as she contemplated a tiny feather-shaped crack on the ceiling of Richard's bedroom. It was late and she was sleepy, but the persistent, tingling feeling grew, forcing her to lift her heavy head and peer down to where the delightful sensations were being generated.

Savannah's silky blonde hair was fanned out over Margaret's thighs and her perfect, retroussé nose dipped in and out of her ginger pubic curls. As she paused for a moment, her astonishing blue eyes crinkled into a smile and she grinned up at Margaret's sleepy, sensual face. 'Hi, Maggie! Thought I'd lost you there . . . Mmm . . . peaches and cream . . .'

Delicately holding the fleshy lips of Margaret's golden-haired pussy apart, Savannah used the point of her moist tongue to lick and explore slowly, sending Margaret's head back onto the pillow as she moaned

5

with pleasure. Savannah's hot, slippery tongue skilfully probed each and every crevice, plunging into her and sweeping up over her clitoris. As Margaret's breathing came faster, Savannah stretched the hood back from her swollen bud and used her elbows to force Margaret's thighs wide apart.

'You're so beautiful, Mags, I've just got to make you come. Open wide for me, come on, let go. Let everything go.'

Savannah's hair caressed Margaret's inner thighs as she concentrated her efforts onto bringing her off. Margaret writhed and moaned as Savannah's demon tongue hit her pleasure spot again and again. Margaret felt an unbearable level of tension in her groin and grabbed fistfuls of Savannah's hair, shrieking, 'No, stop, I can't stand it.'

Savannah mumbled, 'Trust me, baby, just let go, let go.'

Tingling sensations like tiny electric shocks radiated out from Margaret's clit, reaching up into her belly and making her nipples harden and stand on end. She felt as if she would burst but, trusting Savannah's loving touch, she took a deep breath, sighed and spread her legs wider.

The feeling of pleasurable pressure increased as Savannah homed in on her with strong rapid, flicking motions. Suddenly, Margaret felt waves of incredible sensation burst through her body, making her hips jerk and her pussy pulse and spasm. Half sitting, she gripped Savannah's silken head tightly as she mouthed, 'Wow. Wow! Oh my God!'

As the initial spasms began to fade into a blissful, radiant glow, Savannah shimmied up the bed and planted soft kisses, faintly perfumed with her own tangy aroma, on Margaret's face and mouth. 'Who's a clever girl then?' she laughed, delighted to see her companion in such joyful, post-orgasmic shock.

* * *

Unsure if it was still night or already the next morning, Margaret relaxed in a warm, perfumed bath, surrounded by twinkling candles and incense-scented steam. She smoothed her hair and caressed the tender flesh of her body, now replete with food, wine and sex. Yet she felt troubled. Throughout her life, Margaret had devoutly adhered to the Catholic principles instilled in her by her family, her school, and her community. Being in London and experiencing sexual freedom had not changed her feelings at all. She felt torn between her rigid beliefs of right and wrong and the incredible pleasure she now derived from her newly awakened sexual self. How could what she was feeling be wrong? Surely God would not have created such sensual, lustful beings if he did not intend them to give and receive pleasure? What was the point in having the capacity to scale the heights of erotic pleasure if it was forbidden to do so? It was like telling a rose not to exude perfume or a bird not to fly.

Margaret began to pray, pleading with God to shed light on her dilemma. All her life she'd been a 'good girl', with a big heart and a ready smile. Why should her body, made in God's image, torment her like this?

'What's up?' Richard's concerned voice startled her out of her fervent prayers.

'I – I was praying. For guidance. Isn't what we're doing wrong, Richard? You're a confirmed Catholic too. Aren't you afraid you'll be punished? Or that God will turn away from you?'

Her eyes looked huge and sad, framed by damp curls. Richard knelt quickly beside her and squeezed her hand. 'I don't believe that, Mags, I can't believe God doesn't understand. The rules were made by men, by the Church, not God.'

Margaret sat up suddenly and let go of his hand. 'Yes, but the Church is all we've got! I want to be part of a religious community, the way I have been all my life. Now I feel like an outsider.'

Richard sat back on his heels and sighed. He knew

7

exactly how she felt. Once, he had wanted to be a priest, but his time at the seminary had taught him that there was no way around the rules of celibacy for priests, or abstinence outside of marriage for lay people, and the growth of barely concealed homosexuality within the priesthood held no appeal for him. He fervently believed the authorities had got it wrong. Sexual desire was as natural as breathing and suppressing it only caused problems. He turned to Margaret, so sweet and vulnerable in the bath, and decided that they had to find a new way.

'Listen Mags, you and I are both good at praying aren't we? Do you believe that if we really tried, we could find a solution? How about it? A three-day fast and pray?'

'Do you mean like a retreat?'

'Exactly. No food, no sleep, no sex. Just prayer and faith, Mags, we must have faith.'

Margaret looked pensive for a moment, then threw her arms around his neck, showering him with water. 'You're on! It's a brilliant idea.'

The third day after the march dawned bright and cool as Margaret and Richard fought the urge to lie down and sleep. Sweaty, dishevelled and heavy-lidded, they knelt facing each other, hands entwined.

'Richard. Richard. Are you sleeping with your eyes open?'

Richard jolted awake, aware that he had indeed been dozing, and gave Margaret an apologetic grin. 'Sorry, Mags, I'm doing my best. I was dreaming, dreaming about your poor sore knees, and how I'd like to rub them better for you.'

'Richard!'

'And your tired old back, and how it probably wants a good kneading and massaging . . .'

Margaret groaned. She too had found her efforts to concentrate on prayer perpetually distracted by lascivious thoughts about Richard. Did he still have his priest's outfit, she wondered, with the dog collar and everything? Imagine nibbling his neck just above the white collar while her hands slipped inside his smart black pants.

'A penny for them.'

Margaret blushed. 'Actually, I was imagining you as a priest. You'd have looked fiercely handsome.'

'I still do.'

'What do you mean?'

'I mean I still look good in the gear. I can't resist putting it on sometimes. It's supposed to make you feel holy but it only ever makes me feel horny.'

Margaret squirmed with desire and admitted, 'I always wanted a nun's habit. I love the starchiness of them and the hidden depths in the folds of all that black cloth.'

Richard laughed. 'God, you'd be a riot in one. But wait a minute, what's happened to our retreat? Have you come up with anything?'

'Well, I feel absolutely certain now that we are right about God understanding our needs, but I can't think of how I'm supposed to express my sexuality in a Christian way. The Church isn't going to accept our behaviour, so where does that leave us?'

Richard shrugged. 'Couldn't we form our own little group, you know, Catholics and other Christians who want to celebrate their faith together and share prayer and stuff, but without the sex rules?'

Margaret considered for a moment. Slowly, she nodded her head. 'Yes, we could. We could have our own church of sorts. After all, a church is only a community of people sharing the same beliefs, isn't it?'

Richard slumped forward. 'So we're sorted then are we? My knees are killing me, Mags, I've got to lie down!' He collapsed onto the floor and grinned up at her. 'I suppose you're dying for a good sleep now?'

Margaret crawled over to him. 'Oh, I don't know

about that. I was rather fancying having my poor old knees rubbed a bit.'

Richard pulled her down to him and sucked her rosy lips into his mouth. Coming up for air, Margaret stretched out on top of him and regarded him with twinkling eyes. 'I'd give anything to see you in your priest's gear.'

'Would you now? I'll do you a deal. You don a nun's habit over your best stockings and I'll put on the collar for you. Then you can have your wicked way with me, and afterwards, we'll have a nice stroll out for a cup of tea somewhere.'

Margaret was shocked, but turned on. 'You'd never go out in them, Richard? Isn't that sacrilege or something?'

Richard laughed gleefully. 'Oh no. There's no law against it. We could be a "lay" Brother and Sister, couldn't we? And you are such a great lay!'

Margaret pulled his shirt up roughly and rained kisses on his chest and nipples. Straddling him, she whispered, 'You're in trouble the day we do that. I'll have to punish you for being so naughty. I wonder what I'll think up for penance?' Swiftly unzipping him and ripping open a condom with her teeth, she pulled her knickers to one side and hovered over him, feeling the head of his cock bulging beneath her. Very slowly, she massaged the rubber into place.

'Contraceptives, Margaret? Don't you know they're forbidden, you bad girl?'

Margaret thrust herself down onto him and grabbed a handful of his hair. 'Oh, it's all right as long as there's a hole in it, you know. That's official.'

Richard arched his back and returned her thrust, smiling quizzically. 'And is there a hole in it?'

Margaret grinned broadly and wiggled her hips. 'Of course there is – the one at the top that goes over your cock. You're the naughty one for not thinking of wearing one yourself. You'll definitely have to be punished.'

Richard drew back his hand and landed a sharp, stinging slap on her rear, thrusting up deep into her. 'That's where you're wrong, *Sister*. I'll be the one doing all the disciplining – you know I like it.'

Margaret laughed breathlessly and shuddered with delight as she felt another stinging blow land on her exposed cheek. Her knickers were stuck in the crevice of her cheeks and tugged painfully against her anus as Richard bucked beneath her. Whooping, she yanked her top off and pushed Richard's hands onto her hot, full breasts. She groaned with pleasure as he squeezed and kneaded her soft flesh. As his fingers tightened on her erect nipples, Margaret matched his every move, riding wave after wave of ecstasy. Richard kept his vice-like grip on one nipple while his other long-fingered hand lashed her bare bottom in time with his deep upward thrusts. 'You're a bad, bad girl and you'll have to confess. Are you truly, truly sorry?'

'Oh God, oh my God, yes!' Margaret strained backwards, grinding her pelvis against him and rubbing her tingling clit backwards and forwards until she felt as if she was on fire. Her face and body were dripping with sweat as a shuddering orgasm began to course through her. 'Come with me, oh please Richard, come with me,' she shrieked, abandoning herself to sensation.

Richard gripped her hips firmly and pulled her down hard onto him, jerking erratically and moaning in ecstasy. Opening his eyes, he grinned up at Margaret and whispered, 'Come unto me all you who labour, and I will give you rest.' Margaret kissed him softly and returned his grin.

'Peace be with you, Brother.'

'And also with you, Sister.'

Chapter Two

*T*he insistent buzzing of the doorbell separated itself from the bees droning in her head. Margaret sat up and shook Richard awake. 'Richard. Richard, the door.'

Draping a sheet around himself, he stumbled towards the door and opened it a crack. A beaming ebony face peered back in at him.

'You busy or something, man? You going to let me in or what?'

'Gabrielle!'

Richard threw the door open wide to admit a tall, muscular black girl with a dazzlingly pretty smile and a halo of glossy black ringlets. She cast her merry eyes over Margaret appreciatively and wolf-whistled softly through pearly white teeth.

'My, I can see why you're not answering the door. Who's this beautiful creature? Why's she wasting her good self on a scrawny old thing like you?'

Richard gave her a playful shove and cried, 'Hey, less of the old and scrawny, if you don't mind. I'm a young Adonis in my prime, me. Any woman would be glad to have me. Come and meet the lovely Margaret. This here's Gabrielle, Mags. Believe it or not, we used to do Bible study together.'

Margaret flushed rosy pink and pulled Richard's shirt over herself. 'I don't suppose you'd believe that we actually spent the last three days praying and fasting, and that we were sleeping when you rang the buzzer?'

Gabrielle responded with a rich, booming laugh and dropped down beside Margaret. 'Lord, yes. With this dude, I'd believe anything, although it looks to me like the fasting's turned to feasting.'

Margaret and Richard grinned conspiratorially. 'Fair comment, Gabby, but I promise you, we've spent far more time on our knees than on our backs.'

Gabrielle fixed him with a deadpan stare. 'What have you two got going on that means you spend your time fasting and praying when you could be fucking?'

Margaret looked at her earnestly and blurted, 'It's my fault really. I'm having a hard time trying to decide whether I can still be a good Catholic girl and also have a sex life. I can't stand the guilt, but I can't stand going without sex either.'

'Wow, that's a big one. You ain't alone there, honey. Most of the people in my house group tear themselves up over that one. So what did you guys come up with?'

Richard snuggled up next to the girls and sighed. 'Well, I thought we could form our own sort of church, I don't know, a prayer group or something, maybe offer each other support.'

'Support and sex, I suppose you mean?' queried Gabrielle.

'Yes, but we want to be able to look for guidance in the scriptures too,' interjected Margaret. 'I mean, when I last did some study it came up that there is no such thing as a word for "fornication" in the original scriptures, only one for adultery. That's a completely different thing altogether isn't it? Richard and I think that the rules regarding sex are almost all man-made, if you examine them closely.'

Gabrielle looked thoughtful for a few moments, and then asked, 'But who will this benefit? Where's the

Christian ethic in all of this, you know, the caring, sharing bit? Seems to me like you two are just inventing something to please yourselves. Like a little private club for guilty Catholics to get their rocks off.'

Richard sat up looking hurt. 'God, give us a chance, Gabrielle, we haven't even had a chance to discuss the idea properly yet.'

'And why's that?'

'Because after three days' abstinence on our knees, we needed a little light relief.'

Gabrielle winced. 'Three days? Man, I've been on an involuntary fast for three months now, so don't go complaining to me. All that damn social work visiting I do has got me worn out. I've been too tired for sex.'

Richard and Margaret's eyes met briefly and, as if by agreement, they reached out to Gabrielle and began to stroke her face, hair and arms.

'So, you think we're being a bit selfish, do you Gabby?' Richard smiled wickedly.

'Yes, and we should be doing a bit more caring and sharing, isn't that right, Gabrielle?' Margaret chimed in.

Gabrielle laughed and wriggled out of their grasp. 'Wait a minute, I didn't say with me!'

'Come on,' purred Richard, 'all that hard work and no play. Why don't we give you a nice massage? Relax you a bit.'

Gabrielle squirmed uncomfortably, but eventually conceded. 'Oh, all right. But just a massage, right?'

'Whatever you want, we promise,' soothed Richard.

'Yes, we'll offer it up like devotion, Gabby, we'll try to be completely selfless and only think of you. Just leave it to us.' Margaret clasped her hands in mock prayer.

Richard grinned. 'Just put yourself in our hands, and trust in God.'

The massage, as promised, was wonderful, but before long the soft touch of Margaret's skin and hair and the insistent kneading of Richard's long, strong fingers made Gabrielle desperate for more. It had been so long.

'Tell me what you want, Gabs,' whispered Richard, 'please, don't be shy.'

His loving look and warm embraces reassured her, then seeing Margaret's adorable, eager-to-please face, Gabrielle decided to give herself up to pleasure. Softly, she asked Richard to sit straddling her face where she could nibble on the head of his cock.

'Can you reach my nipples?' Richard leaned back and found her large, erect nipples and squeezed them gently. 'Harder,' murmured Gabrielle. 'Will you lick me, Mags?'

Face wreathed in dimples, Margaret ducked her head and kissed her way down over Gabrielle's smooth, chocolate-coloured stomach to her springy black bush. Trailing her soft curls over her abdomen and thighs, she then dipped her tongue into Gabrielle's musky pussy.

With Richard's fat, silky-skinned penis tickling the back of her throat, Gabrielle arched her back to allow Margaret deeper access with her tongue. Then, clutching handfuls of Margaret's beautiful hair, she sucked Richard even deeper into her throat, enjoying the dangerous thrill of almost suffocating on his thrusting cock. As Margaret's wickedly darting tongue homed in on her cherry-like clit, Gabrielle felt fiery hot waves of pleasure pulse through her body. Groaning and writhing, her tumultuous orgasm triggered hot spurts of come from Richard, which he showered over her face and hair. As Richard slid down to lie beside her, Margaret's hands reached up and massaged her voluptuous breasts and bud-like nipples and kissed her pulsing abdomen.

'There now,' breathed Margaret, 'what did we tell you? Wasn't that a grand massage?'

Laughing, Gabrielle threw back her head and cried, 'Oh man, did I ever need that! Praise the Lord!'

Flopping down either side of her, Margaret and Richard twined their limbs around her until she felt cosily warm and cared for and, within minutes, all three of them drifted into a deep, restful sleep.

Two hours later Gabrielle stretched and purred like a sleek cat, her naked, ebony flesh glistening with baby oil and sweat. Peeling one eye open, she caught Margaret's twinkling blue eyes regarding her gravely. 'Why so serious, sister? Don't tell me you're sorry?'

Margaret shook her head, 'Oh no, far from it. Do you know, I enjoyed pleasuring you as much as myself? I really did offer it up as a kind of prayer, and I felt no guilt at all. Do you think if you performed sexual acts for others with love, God would still think it was wrong?'

Gabrielle sat up and took her new friend's hand. 'Richard's always saying that Catholic rules about sex are man-made. Who's to say God ever thought any of it was wrong? Everything about the way we're made is perfect really – our bodies carry us through life, bear children, provide for us. Why would we have such strongly developed sexuality if not for pleasure?'

Margaret nodded. 'Is it possible then that God gave us the gift of sexual pleasure as a kind of reward or bonus, like our ability to enjoy good food or to appreciate beauty? I mean, you can be poor as a church mouse but still feel wonderful if you're able to enjoy good sex.'

Richard stirred, yawned and grinned up at both of them. 'Who's able to enjoy good sex?'

Margaret slapped him playfully. 'Everyone – that's the whole point. Look, I'm beginning to believe that helping someone to feel good sexually is just as valid a form of Christian charity as, say, giving them soup or shelter. Why shouldn't we use our new group to serve the sexual needs of the community?'

Gabrielle sat bolt upright. 'Isn't that a bit radical? I mean, isn't it against the law or something?'

'No', Richard replied thoughtfully, 'no it isn't. Money would have to change hands for that, but if it's between consenting adults, where's the harm? Don't all sorts of adult sex groups exist – S&Mers, couple-swappers, cross-dressers, what have you? We'd be doing it for our own spiritual enlightenment and as a favour to others. There's nothing illegal in it.'

'All right', insisted Margaret, 'there may be nothing illegal in it, but it could be viewed as sacrilegious or even blasphemous.'

'I reckon', said Gabrielle, 'that you'd be better off keeping it secret. Why go looking for trouble? At worst, we'd be thought of as some kind of weird cult, but no-one would know for sure.'

'We?' said Richard and Margaret in unison. Gabrielle grinned broadly.

'Well, sure! You don't think I'm letting you guys have all this fun on your own do you? Besides, I quite fancy myself as "Sister Gabriel". I could be doing lots of special visitations of my own!'

'Wow!' shrieked Margaret. 'We're really going to do it! Well, I'm tired of being Miss goody-two-shoes, so I want to be the Bible's bad girl, Mary Magdalene. I want to become Mother Magdalene. How's that?'

'Spot on,' grinned Richard. 'You can mother me any time you like, and I'm not averse to a bit of toe-washing.' Margaret and Gabrielle both whacked him on his arms, but he laughed gleefully and fought off their blows. 'As one of the founding fathers of this new order, I think I'll take my namesake, The Lionheart, as a role model. Father Lionheart. What do you think?'

The girls laughed hysterically and then mock-swooned beside him. 'Oh Father Lionheart,' cooed Margaret, 'we've this terrible crush on you.'

'Yes', simpered Gabrielle, 'a terrible crush. Are we bad girls, Father?'

Richard kneeled over them and smiled. 'Nothing a bit of special penance won't sort out, Sisters. Bottoms up, please.' More than willing to oblige, Gabrielle and Margaret turned onto their fronts and pushed their bare cheeks up high in the air. Richard dealt each one a stinging slap and intoned, 'Now make a good confession. Repeat after me: Bless me, Father, for I have sinned.'

Gabrielle and Margaret obediently repeated the words in unison. 'Bless me, Father, for I have sinned.'

'And will sin again and again and again,' interjected Richard. Laughing, all three of them tumbled into a comfortable heap together and began to think about the future. Soon, they found themselves addressing the serious issues of what to call the new organisation, how to recruit people, and where to raise funds. It wasn't going to be easy but, for the first time in her life, Margaret felt confident that she had finally found her true calling.

Part Two

Exegesis

Chapter Three

Mother Magdalene walked crisply across the cobbled courtyard, barely suppressing the skip in her step. Her cheeks were flushed a rosy pink in the frosty spring air, but today she could not feel the cold.

Her eyes swept over the beautiful buildings of Mount Olive Priory, glowing warmly in the watery morning sunshine. Warm red and gold herringbone bricks framed sparkling lead-paned windows under charming wooden eaves. In a corner of the rectangular courtyard, complete with cloistered walkways, nestled an exquisite private chapel hung with incense-infused tapestries and scattered with hand-embroidered prayer mats.

Who could believe that The Order would come so far, so fast, in just ten months? She shivered as she recalled the awful community halls and draughty church annexes in which they had first held their meetings. Too often, they had attracted selfish pleasure seekers with no interest in sharing, and they had also seen more than their share of out-and-out weirdos. But Mother Magdalene knew that she and Father Lionheart had been right to persevere and, as they had hoped, they had gradually formed a loving group of Sisters and Brothers dedicated to sexual emancipation.

The Compassionate Order for Relief, or The Order, was now beginning to spread its net far and wide. There were teachers, counsellors, musicians and artists – people from all walks of life who enjoyed furthering their aims of sexual and spiritual enlightenment. Despite coming from such different backgrounds, they had all started out with one thing in common: an inability to reconcile their desires with their own feelings of guilt, or the rules of their faith. Mother Magdalene grinned when she realised that her own days of feeling guilty were long gone.

She craned her neck and stared up at the windows on the first floor, but there were no signs of movement. Her hands felt sweaty and she anxiously rubbed them on her habit as she strained her ears to listen for any sounds of life. The location was secluded and difficult to find, which suited their needs perfectly. Sister Gabriel had been right to insist that The Order's true function remained secret. With the help of her experience in social work, The Order had managed to obtain charitable status for offering help to troubled street people in central London. But away from the practicalities of the Waterloo project, The Order was fully committed to its mission to serve the diverse sensual needs of a much wider community.

Approaching the main house, Mother Magdalene could see that it was much larger than their current needs, but inside there was an air of intimacy created by twisting stairwells, myriad nooks and crannies, and differently sized and shaped rooms. It was idyllic. Already she had earmarked part of the long, low stables as a gymnasium and many of the old workrooms and servants' quarters were almost ready to serve as accommodations or specialised rooms for private study and practice.

Entering through the main doorway and sweeping up the central staircase, Mother Magdalene felt her heart pounding in her breast and realised that she was as giddy as an excited schoolgirl. She smoothed down her crisp new veil and lifted the folds of her black habit clear of the stairs.

To the left of the staircase on the first floor a short corridor opened onto a beautiful library. Mahogany bookshelves, presently only half full, lined three of the walls while the fourth had floor to ceiling mullioned windows with a stunning view of a lush meadow and a pretty pond complete with preening ducks. Mother Magdalene could hear her feet echoing hollowly on the parquet floor, but her ears were tuned to the sound of soft whistling at the far end of the room. Coming to a halt in the middle, she waited with baited breath.

The black cloth and white collar of the priest looked elegant, almost like dinner dress, on the tall figure approaching with long, leisurely strides. Father Lionheart stopped in front of her and, putting one of her hands to his lips, kissed it slowly. 'Welcome home, Mother Magdalene.'

Tears welled in her eyes. 'God bless you, Father.' She reached up and stroked his thick, newly-cropped hair. 'You've cut it. It suits you.'

Father Lionheart smiled in his inimitable, languorous fashion and shrugged. 'It had to go. Spoiled the clerical look. Now, I believe you made me a promise some time ago, Mother, and you know it's wrong to make promises you don't intend to keep, don't you?'

Mother Magdalene grinned up into his twinkling, tawny eyes. 'Who said I didn't intend to keep the promise?' She stepped back from him and slowly lifted the hem of her habit, revealing sheer black stockings and spiky stilettos. 'It's time you said your prayers, Father. Kneel down and prepare to supplicate yourself.'

Groaning with desire, Father Lionheart dropped to his knees and clasped his hands in prayer. 'Dear Lord, for what I am about to receive, make me truly, truly thankful. Amen.'

Mother Magdalene hitched her habit up further to

reveal glimpses of soft white flesh and golden curls above the black stocking line. Stroking his shorn hair, she placed one leg over his shoulder and breathed in sharply as he buried his nose and mouth in her moist flesh. Sucking and probing, he sent hot stabs of pleasure rippling up through her abdomen and down into her thighs. Her legs began to feel weak and she rasped, 'Lie down. Lie down on the floor.'

In one graceful movement his long legs were spread out and he was smiling up at her. Unbuttoning the top of her habit to free her straining breasts, she crouched over his face and sank down onto him with a sigh. Reaching up for her milk-white breasts, he rhythmically circled her nipples with his thumbs until she moaned and writhed on top of him. He seized her clit between his teeth, and sucked and nibbled relentlessly, drinking in the scent of her, loving the wild abandon with which she came, thrashing and shrieking and wrenching his hair.

Pulling her down next to him, he hugged her tightly and murmured, 'Beautiful Mags . . .'

'Ssh,' she chided him, 'that's Mother Magdalene from now on.'

Grinning, he flipped her onto her back. 'Right you are, Mother. Would you be a mother of mercy at all?'

He unzipped his tailored black trousers and yanked them down to his knees, revealing his generously long penis jutting out of a tiny black silk pouch. The thong disappeared into his muscular haunches.

'Is there something I can help you with there, Father?' taunted Mother Magdalene, stroking his hardness through the flimsy fabric. 'I'm with The Compassionate Order for Relief, you know. We wouldn't stand by and watch anyone suffer.'

She spread her legs and pulled back her knees to afford him a better view. He paused for a moment to drink her in – the red-gold curls breaking free from her veil, the white cowl askew, her black-stockinged legs akimbo, revealing more golden curls.

'May God have mercy on your soul!' he cried, plunging himself deeply into her sweet, hot pussy. In a frenzy of excitement they beat against each other, flesh slapping loudly with each fierce thrust. Mother Magdalene cried out in a long shrieking wail as she felt another orgasm begin to rip through her.

'Ri-ch-a-ard!'

'Am I hurting you?' he breathed, pausing to check her face anxiously.

'No, don't stop!' she yelled, tearing away the flimsy cloth of his pouch and raining blows on his bare buttocks. With one last grinding movement, they locked eyes and shared a few moments of exquisitely naked, loving intimacy, while their bodies contorted in heady waves of pleasure. Blissfully happy, they curled into each other and marvelled at this dream made real. The Order had finally found a home.

The first few weeks at The Priory were a chaotic rush of decorating, furnishing and spontaneous eruptions of wanton sex. Mother Magdalene often stopped to pinch herself to see if she was awake. It was hard for her to believe that this place, conceived of so very recently, was now reality, and yet here she was in the heart of a thriving community.

She paused to watch the smiling young faces of some of the volunteers who were splattering each other with lime wash as they whitened the exterior of the old stable buildings. Who would ever guess that these fresh-faced young men and women were becoming expert sexual practitioners and experienced spiritual counsellors? Sister Gabriel had done an excellent job in helping to train new recruits, and she had encouraged them to know when to keep their identity as members of The Order secret. Sensibly, she counselled that there was no need for a beneficiary to know that they were receiving organised charitable favours unless it was likely that they had a calling to be a Brother or Sister. Only a tiny percentage of recruits dedicated themselves to working for The Order full time, the rest were getting on with their careers, performing sexual services in the community, and attending ceremonies and initiations at The Priory.

She felt a little thrill as she imagined The Order's secret lay Brothers and Sisters joyfully servicing a wide range of needy people while indulging their own love of sex. The diversity of recruits had brought a rich supply of talents to The Order, including some adept city traders and international bankers whose financial acumen had allowed the purchase of these incredible premises. Powerful city women seemed to take to The Order's regime like ducks to water and delighted in channelling their adrenaline into sexual pursuits, but many of the men had struggled with loss of face or control. Mother Magdalene grinned as an image of handsome, smartly-suited men popped into her head, but then disintegrated as her eyes travelled down to where their trousers had been replaced by fishnet stockings and patent leather ankle boots.

Some of Sister Gabriel's training methods were highly unorthodox, but then, so was the work out in the 'real' world. Mother Magdalene looked forward with relish to the feedback sessions with field workers, when she could hear more of their various exploits away from the confines of The Priory.

Chapter Four

'*R*oland, I can't wait all bloody night. When is that call coming through?'

Melinda paced up and down the office holding an unlit cigarette between her fingers. A voluptuous, red-haired woman of indeterminate age, her sharp tailored suit, perfectly manicured nails and smooth chignon gave her an air of indestructibility.

'I'm sorry, but we can't leave until the contract confirmation comes through. Sit down, you're driving me nuts.'

Roland shot a glance at his colleague, Geoff, whose floppy blond fringe hung over one eye, making him look like a roguish, shaggy dog. Surreptitiously making a brief sign of the cross to his friend by crossing his index fingers, Geoff flipped the hair out of his eyes and grabbed Melinda's arm as she strode by. 'Why so tense, Mel? Still having hubby trouble?'

Melinda rounded on him fiercely. 'What the hell do you know about my personal life? Do you have any idea how it feels to be a woman with two kids and a no-good husband who has walked out on her?'

Roland and Geoff came to her side and placed an arm each around her. Melinda shrugged off their embrace, looking confused and irritated. Geoff laid a hand on her arm and squeezed gently. 'Hey, steady on. You told us yourself, Mel, that night after the works do – we all went to the Alaska bar?'

'Yes, you did,' nodded Roland, his dark, cropped hair and black, slanted eyes giving him an exotic, oriental appearance. 'You had your sister staying, the religious one. She was giving you a hard time.'

Melinda slumped tearfully against a desk and allowed their solid arms to encircle her. 'I'm sorry, I just don't know where to turn. Eight months struggling on my own, but technically I'm still married. And I'm so lonely!'

Roland dabbed her eyes with his handkerchief and soothed her. 'Of course you are. Who wouldn't be?'

'Once a Catholic, always a Catholic,' spat Melinda. 'My sister never stops reminding me about my responsibilities as a Catholic wife, but what about me, the woman?'

Geoff smoothed back his unruly fringe from his boyishly handsome face and nodded sympathetically. 'I know just what you mean. My family was bloody awful to me when I wanted to live with my first girlfriend. Marriage or nothing, that was their view. But I just wasn't ready. It ruined everything.'

Melinda glanced up at him and smiled half-heartedly. 'You're young, gorgeous. Why should you worry? You can pick and choose. Me, I'm not getting any younger.' She sniffed and dabbed her eyes with the proffered handkerchief.

Roland stepped back and held her at arm's length, raking her body with his appraising sloe eyes. 'You're a fine looking woman to me, Mel.'

Geoff stroked her hair gently, soothing her with his soft touch and sincere voice. 'Me too. I know we're not in your league, but both of us fancy you like mad.'

Melinda blushed scarlet. 'Don't be ridiculous, I'm old enough to –'

28

'Be your mother?' interrupted Roland, grinning wickedly. 'You don't look anything like my mother.'

'Mine either,' assured Geoff, stepping behind her.

'Wait a minute', stuttered Melinda, 'what do you think you're doing?'

Roland moved closer until she could smell the sharp tang of his aftershave and the faint aroma of something like almonds emanating from his skin. 'Please don't say no, Mel. We both think you're absolutely gorgeous and you deserve to feel nice. We'll do anything, anything you want to make you feel good.' Geoff slipped his arms around her waist and she felt a slight thrill as his prominent erection pressed up against her ample behind.

'But, what about –'

Geoff's large soft lips kissed her neck with delicious delicacy. He whispered into her ear, 'I don't believe God put us here to suffer. He knows all about our needs and wants. He made us all perfect. Like you.'

Roland held her face in his hands and slowly kissed the tip of her nose, her eyes, her chin, until she began to feel her resolve weakening. 'You weren't put here to suffer.' His beautifully manicured hands opened each button on her blouse as if it were a precious jewel. She reached a hand out to touch him, but he pushed it away firmly. 'No, please, Mel. Let us do everything. You're a Goddess. We'll worship at your temple.'

Geoff stroked the silk blouse down over her shoulders and began to lick and nibble the nape of her neck and her back, while Roland ran his tongue over her collarbone and down to the creamy mounds of flesh bursting from her bra. As his face buried itself eagerly in her deep cleavage, Melinda sighed loudly, giving herself up to the exquisite sensations. Geoff's hands reached around and tugged her lacy bra down so that her breasts spilled out over it. His long fingers caressed and kneaded the full roundness of them while Roland's hot mouth soon had her large nipples hard and tingling. She groaned and began to writhe against Geoff, loving the swollen promise of his hard cock grinding into her behind. She felt almost faint with pleasure.

'I need to lie down,' she breathed, frightened to go on and equally frightened to stop. Roland effortlessly swept her feet off the floor as Geoff tightened his arms around her waist and backed her into the boardroom.

She giggled nervously as they laid her across the polished wooden surface of the oval table dominating the centre of the room. As they began to resume their caresses, easing off her skirt and panties, but leaving on her hold-up stockings and shoes, Melinda plucked up courage to whisper, 'Wait. I want to see you. Both of you.'

Grinning at each other, they slowly undressed. As they shed their office uniform of jackets, shirts and ties, Melinda gazed in open curiosity at their bodies. Geoff had the tall, lithe frame of an athlete – slim but muscular, and the face of an angel. His long-lashed blue eyes, turned-up nose and full, red mouth made him appear almost girlishly beautiful. Her eyes flicked down to assure herself that there was nothing girlish about his penis, which was standing out from his body as if at attention. Melinda felt a renewed stab of desire as she saw how long and swollen it looked. She licked her lips.

Turning to Roland she was surprised to find how strikingly masculine he looked naked. His handsome, clean-shaven, Eurasian face was in stark contrast to his broad, heavy shoulders and well-developed chest, which was covered in a thatch of dark hair. It was plain that he worked out regularly and her eyes feasted on his powerful arms, rippled abdomen and muscular thighs. The contrast between the two men excited her, and she wondered if they both intended to fuck her. Her eyes widened at the sight of Roland's stocky, impossibly thick cock sticking up almost flat against his abdomen. With a sharp intake of breath, she wondered how it would feel to have it forcing open her tight flesh. As if reading her mind, Roland reached under the table to where he had stashed his briefcase and pulled out a packet of assorted rubbers, which he spread out for her.

'Pick a colour. Geoff's got some others'.

Geoff held his hand up above his head, as if he were a waiter carrying a tray and said in a silly French accent, 'Perhaps Madame would allow me to choose? May I recommend the knobbly rib-tickler? Guaranteed to please Madame.'

Hands shaking with desire, Melinda accepted the condom and gently eased the rough surface over Geoff's long smooth erection. Choosing a cherry-scented package from Roland, she swallowed hard and began to unroll it over his hot, thick cock. She expected it to burst at any moment, but with a final smoothing from her trembling fingers, Roland's glory was encased in vivid red like a horny demon ready to strike.

'OK, that's us ready. Now you.'

Roland's eyes glittered dangerously as he gently pushed her back onto the table and eased her thighs apart. Geoff unpinned her hair and stroked it out around her, then kissed and caressed her shoulders, belly and breasts. Circling her nipples with his tongue, he finally latched on to them with his lips and teeth, sucking and nibbling until Melinda groaned aloud with pleasure.

Roland's strong hands kneaded and squeezed the flesh on her buttocks and hips while his firm lips kissed the backs of her knees then brushed against her inner thighs and pubic hair. Pushing her legs wide apart, he rained kisses down onto her soft hair and swollen pudenda. His nose burrowed between her pussy lips until he found her clit and he began to make sweeping licks from her bottom right up and over the bud. Melinda writhed on the polished wooden surface, but Roland and Geoff held her firmly in place while they sent waves of electric shocks shivering through her.

Geoff rummaged under the table and pulled out something long, shiny and buzzing. With a wicked grin he rolled the smooth, vibrating surface over Melinda's neck and shoulders then down onto her breasts and nipples. 'We brought you a present,' he smiled.

'Mmm,' murmured Roland, still buried in her soaking wet pussy. 'We thought you might like a little toy of your own, something just for you.'

Geoff slid the vibrator from nipple to nipple until Melinda was panting in ecstasy. The soft buzzing vibrations felt like a giant pleasure bee gathering pollen all over her body. As Geoff massaged her abdomen and thighs, Roland concentrated on his efforts with his tongue. Melinda felt as though she might scream as he set her body tingling almost unbearably.

At last, Roland's strong lips glided up over her belly while Geoff slid the vibrator between her pussy lips and over her throbbing clit. When she felt the tip of the vibrator prize her open, Melinda shrieked and bucked her hips to meet it. Roland held back her arms and kissed her softly and deeply on the mouth, stifling her cries. Melinda was almost delirious with pleasure, every nerve in her body seemed to vibrate in time with the new toy and Roland's kisses, faintly scented with her own aroma, were delicious.

'Now you do it,' whispered Roland, guiding her hand down to the toy. Geoff held her fingers over the base and gently slid the vibrator in and out of her until she was moaning loudly and had taken control herself. Any fleeting ideas of shame or embarrassment evaporated in the pure hedonistic pleasure she was now giving to herself. Roland and Geoff watched her solemnly without touching her but whispering endearments and encouragement.

'You're so beautiful, Melinda. Come on, all the way. You're fantastic.'

'Oh darling, you're coming aren't you? That's it, let go. What a woman you are.'

Melinda sat up so that the vibrator was still deep inside her but also stimulating her stretched and throbbing clit. Locking eyes with each of the two beautiful men in turn who had taken her this far, Melinda rocked backwards and forwards until she felt great spasms almost like electric shocks ricochet through her body.

'Oh yes, oh yes!' she cried, pressing down hard and letting wave after wave of incredible sensation ripple through her belly, thighs and breasts. Flushed red and damp with perspiration, she broke into a beaming smile and said, 'Wow! I've never done that by myself before. In fact, I've never felt quite like that before.'

Geoff and Roland embraced her warmly and grinned with delight at her. Geoff kissed her loudly on the cheek. 'You're one powerful woman. Is there any chance at all of a small reward for your lowly servants?' He looked down pointedly at his enormous erection looking ridiculous encased in knobbly latex. Roland also pressed against her leg with his swollen red devil and Melinda felt a renewed pang of desire and nodded.

'Oh absolutely. I always believe in seeing that the help are properly rewarded.'

'Seriously, what would you like?' asked Roland. 'This is supposed to be your treat.'

Melinda sighed. 'Well, what I want, what I have wanted since I first laid eyes on you both undressed, is for you to fuck me. Both of you, one at a time. Please.'

Roland and Geoff exchanged wide-eyed, smiling glances then lifted her from the table and placed her between them. Roland hoisted her up so that Geoff could finally plunge his swollen cock into her. Melinda gasped at the strange feeling of the ribbed condom, but soon she was panting with delight as Geoff thrust himself more deeply and rhythmically inside her. Roland supported her from behind, squeezing her buttocks and pushing her harder against his friend. Geoff sucked greedily on her nipples and increased his tempo until with a loud roar he finally came, jerking roughly against her. Melinda wrapped her arms around his slender body and kissed his fair hair.

'Beautiful man,' she murmured.

Roland reached down and lifted her silk shirt from the floor and spread it on the boardroom table. 'Lie down,' he whispered close to her ear, sending a shiver down her spine. 'On your front.'

Melinda did as she was asked and stretched herself across the narrow end of the oval table. At a signal from Roland, Geoff moved around and took hold of her wrists. Melinda felt Roland's strong hands grasp her ankles and spread her legs wide apart. He began to slide her towards him, kneading and stroking her flesh and brushing his huge erection against her legs and inner thighs. When her spread-eagled pussy was at the edge of the table, he placed his cock up against her. It felt hot and hard and thick, yet her body was screaming for him to be inside her. When Geoff pulled on her arms and slid her further away Melinda almost wept with frustration but, almost immediately, Roland gripped her thighs again, and drew her against him. The two men see-sawed her back and forward, each time allowing her hungry pussy to come a little closer to Roland's deliciously fat cock. Melinda moaned loudly and cried out, 'Please, please fuck me, oh please!'

At last, she felt Roland reach forward and take a firm grip on her hips. With a slow, deliberate thrust, he pulled her aching body down onto his massive shaft. Melinda growled like a lioness on heat as Roland and Geoff resumed sliding her backwards and forwards, for she could now feel every inch of Roland's magnificent cock pulsing in and out of her. As her shrieks became louder, they upped the speed until she was slamming back against Roland with her pussy stretched wide around him and her clit grinding against his groin. Roland spanked her buttocks and pulled her even harder against himself.

'Oh God, Mel, you're fantastic.'

Melinda felt Roland's cock get harder and harder and then his whole body went rigid as hot, pulsing waves

34

signalled his orgasm to her. Melinda's second orgasm had her howling like a banshee in total abandon, as she surrendered to the fire spreading through her loins and washing over her whole body. Writhing upon the polished table, she felt free of all inhibitions for the first time in her life, and marvelled at the incredible capacity her body had to feel. She had never felt so alive.

Later, when Melinda had been safely tucked into a taxi with promises of absolute discretion, Geoff and Roland caught last orders at the local pub and slaked their thirst with pints of cold beer.

'Do you think we should have told her – about The Order, I mean?' Geoff wiped away a frothy moustache and looked at his friend's serious face.

'Absolutely not,' replied Roland. 'The only people we should tell are those we feel certain would like to join us. Do you think she'd want to?'

Geoff shook his head vigorously. 'God, no. She's just lonely and frustrated really, but I felt a bit strange, her not knowing. Maybe it's because we work with her every day, whereas most of the others haven't really been part of our lives.'

Roland patted him on the arm. 'Listen, we've got a feedback session coming up, so let's talk about it then. I think we made her really happy.'

Geoff grinned. 'Too right. And ourselves! Let's drink her a toast. Fancy another pint?'

Chapter Five

S ister Gabriel strolled through the cloistered walkways and mentally checked off a list of things to do in her head. Novice Brothers and Sisters now had their own individualised induction programme, but she felt that a mentoring scheme involving two to four dedicated helpers per novice would speed up and intensify the process. The gym, although beautifully equipped, was still being underused and she made another mental note to discuss putting someone in charge of it with Mother Magdalene and Father Lionheart. She also needed more volunteers to help out at her new homeless project in Waterloo. All too few of the current Brothers and Sisters showed any interest in giving some of their time to a worthy, but hardly erotic cause. Nonetheless, the public face of The Order as a charitable organisation was an important cover for their true calling and a busy, useful charity in the heart of London would almost certainly deflect attention away from the secret goings-on at The Priory.

Turning towards the chapel, Sister Gabriel came upon Brother Darius, one of their earliest recruits, sitting on a bench in earnest conversation with Sister Maria, a tall, beautiful, Hispanic girl who prided herself on initiating inexperienced men. Brother Darius, a muscular African with a dazzling smile, turned to Sister Gabriel and enlisted her help with the argument.

'Sister, please, listen to this. She says that if we are fully aware sexually and able to satisfy our desires then we would have no need for romantic love, only for friendship or companionship. This is rubbish, no? How can good sex and friendship be a substitute for a truly loving relationship?'

Sister Maria slapped him on the arm and jumped up, her long, thick hair swinging out behind her veil. 'I didn't say that! You're misquoting me. What I said was that you could be perfectly content if you had good friendships and a fulfilled sex life, so romantic love would not seem so important. I didn't say one could be a substitute for the other. But you can be happy without romance, can't you, Sister?'

'Whoa there! How come I'm getting dragged into this? Views about love and romance or sex and friendship are down to the individual. We're all entitled to our own opinion. This is between the two of you.'

Brother Darius stood up and stretched himself to his impressive full height and grinned wolfishly at the two women. 'Well, whatever any of you believe, I'm telling you there's no substitute for true love, but it only comes around once in a while, and not to everybody. So I guess, meanwhile, you might as well have wonderful sex with your friends.'

Sister Maria fixed him with an angry glare and stood very close to him, her statuesque body and above average height making her look like an irate Amazon. 'Well, you'd hardly know the difference, would you, Brother?' With a mighty shove, she pushed him out of her path and strode away.

Sister Gabriel watched in bemused silence as she disappeared into the gym. 'What was that all about? I thought you two were the best of friends.'

Brother Darius laughed easily and said, 'Don't worry,

we are. She's just moody, like so many of you women. Maybe it's that time of the moon. Who knows?'

Sister Gabriel shook her head. 'What is the point of becoming sexually enlightened if you're going to carry around all of those rubbishy stereotypes in your head? Moody women? Time of the month? Come off it.'

Brother Darius slapped his thighs and laughed raucously. 'I'm sorry, Sister. But you are all so easy to upset. I'm only fooling.'

'Mmm. Well, maybe it's your fooling that's upsetting Sister Maria so much. Why don't you go and say sorry?'

Looking slightly chastened, Brother Darius glanced towards the gym. 'Maybe you're right, Sister. Anyway, the making up is always the best part.'

With a return of his cheeky grin, Brother Darius loped off in pursuit of Sister Maria. Sister Gabriel called after him, 'Brother Darius! I need to talk to both of you about being mentors for novices. Come and see me in my rooms at about three. OK?' Brother Darius waved, nodded his assent and disappeared into the gym.

Sister Maria was angrily pulling on a Lycra shorts suit when she saw Brother Darius close the gym door behind him. She swiftly pulled her thick, long hair into a loose ponytail and stepped onto one of the new running machines. Setting the speed at a fast walk, she was soon admiring her own fluid movements and swishing ponytail in the mirror. She fought to keep the smile off her face as she watched Brother Darius greedily regarding her pumping thighs and behind, obviously pondering his next move.

'You know I was only teasing you, Sister. I'm sorry if I upset you.' Sister Maria feigned indifference and adjusted the speed up to a light jog. Brother Darius moved closer, raking her lithe body with his eyes. 'In fact, I'm always talking without thinking. It's hard to think when I'm with such a beautiful woman.'

Sister Maria dipped her head and smirked. Raising her head she resumed her forbidding expression and lengthened her stride. 'I can't hear you properly. Either join me, or shut up.'

Brother Darius wasted no time in stripping out of his robes and donning training shoes before joining Sister Maria on the treadmill. Glancing down at his reflection, Sister Maria burst out laughing. 'I see you've got the right footwear on, but what about the rest of you?'

Matching her stride easily, Brother Darius pressed in closer to her so that his prominent erection brushed and jabbed against her bottom. 'A man likes to be free. Besides, I thought after we'd warmed up, we could do some floor exercises.'

Without breaking her stride, Sister Maria lifted her heavy breasts free of the skimpy sports suit and reached behind to grab his hands and place them on her. Switching the speed up so that they were running, she smiled at him maliciously. 'You'll have to work a lot harder to warm me up if you expect me to do floor exercises with you.'

Beads of sweat broke out on Brother Darius's wide forehead and rolled into his eyes, but he ignored the stinging sensation and pressed in hard against Sister Maria's muscular, lean haunches, wedging his cock between her thighs. He cupped her voluptuous breasts, massaging the smooth flesh and lightly brushing her nipples. Watching her face soften in the mirror, he took each nipple in his fingertips and began to twist and rub them until they were proudly erect and a deep rose pink. Sister Maria's breathing became laboured and she wiped away the sweat on her upper lip as she relaxed her body back against Brother Darius, their legs still pumping in time with one another. Before long, the pressure of his cock rubbing and jabbing her tender flesh and his intense manipulation of her nipples made her start to feel weak with desire. Snapping the machine down to a slow walk, she snaked her hands back around his high, hard behind and, grabbing his cheeks firmly, she pulled him against her. Brother Darius nuzzled her shoulders and neck while she slid her hands down lower and slipped her fingers between his thighs, lightly brushing his balls and anus.

Brother Darius reached over and switched the machine off and then turned Sister Maria to face him so that they could devour each other in a deep, hungry kiss. Sister Maria broke away and dragged him over to the floor mats. 'Floor exercises,' she laughed, panting loudly. 'Come on!'

The tension that had been mounting between them exploded in a frenzy of activity on the mats. She kicked off her suit, dropped to her knees and took Brother Darius's iron-hard cock in her mouth and sucked deeply. Within moments, Brother Darius flipped her onto her side so that he could simultaneously bury his head between her legs and, seeking out her swollen clit, he feasted on it hungrily. Sister Maria imbedded her nails into his woolly hair and pressed herself against him, loving the warm, urgent caresses of his lips and tongue. As her excitement mounted and she felt herself roller-coasting towards orgasm, she slid her lips from his massive cock, pulled herself free of his embrace and forced him onto his back. Laughing, Brother Darius admired her strength and determination.

'What, no push-ups for me today? Whatever happened to the missionary position?'

Plunging down onto him, Sister Maria threw her head back and ground her pelvis in a rapid circular motion until his long shaft filled her completely and her clit exploded with sensation, shaking her whole body. Smiling down at him, she arched one eyebrow and regarded him mischievously. 'Maybe the missionaries have modernised.'

Brother Darius heaved himself up and deftly flipped her onto her back, pinning her arms above her head and forcing her thighs wide apart with his hips. 'Not where I come from.'

With eyes locked in feverish delight, they relished the

sound of their sweaty bodies beating a rapid, thumping rhythm onto the mat until Brother Darius finally groaned with relief as he came deep inside Sister Maria's quivering body.

For a few minutes, they slumped comfortably together, lost in companionable, post-coital exhaustion. Raising herself onto one elbow, Sister Maria prodded Brother Darius with her finger. 'Hey! You don't call that a workout, do you?'

Brother Darius's eyes snapped open and regarded her with mock disapproval. 'You're a very hard woman to please, Sister. Can't you see I'm tired now?' Without warning, he sprang up and crouched beside her on all fours, like a great beast ready to strike. Laughing softly, he crawled forward and licked her inner arm, sending a shiver down her spine. 'But I'll have to see what I can do.'

Inside the main building, the large dining room and adjoining salon were humming with activity. Sister Gabriel sought out Sister Ruth, a petite blonde with a sweet, giving nature, and gestured for her to join her at the fireside seats. 'Hello there. How have you been getting on?'

Sister Ruth's cheeks were flushed a rosy pink and her cornflower blue eyes sparkled mischievously. 'Oh, I love it here, Sister. I'm having so much fun.'

Sister Gabriel followed her gaze back over to the plump sofas where Sister Ruth had been cuddled up with a group of friends. Brother Max, a carrotty-haired, slender youth grinned over at them from his reclining position across two Sisters and one novice Brother. Sister Gabriel laughed. 'Brother Max seems very comfortable here. Are you still getting on well?'

Sister Ruth dimpled prettily. 'Oh yes, Sister. But share and share alike, that's what I say.'

Sister Gabriel leaned forward and placed a warm hand on her thigh. 'I couldn't agree more, Sister. You know, I meant to talk to you about mentoring new recruits, but if I were to be completely honest, there are other things I'd rather do with you in my rooms.'

Sister Ruth giggled and placed her own hand over Sister Gabriel's. 'Well, I think you should be honest. Pleasure before business, that's my motto. Shall we invite anyone else?' Her eyes flickered over towards Brother Max and Sister Gabriel nodded her approval.

'Mmm. Do you know, I meant to talk to Brother Max as well, seeing as you two work so well together. But pleasure first. Do you think we could drag him away?'

Sister Ruth planted a wet kiss on her lips and jumped up confidently. 'Don't be silly. Who'd refuse the offer of some quality time with you?' In a flash, she was whispering into Brother Max's ear and he quickly extricated himself from the group on the sofa.

Sister Gabriel led the way out of the salon and up the rear stairs to her set of rooms on the second floor. Wasting no time on formalities, she pushed aside a heavy curtain at the rear of the small sitting room and entered her private inner sanctum. Sister Ruth's cupid lips formed a perfect O as she swivelled around and ogled the décor.

The walls were covered, floor-to-ceiling, with blood-red, crushed velvet and the ceiling was dominated by a circular mirror, which covered most of its surface. In the centre was a black, wrought-iron chandelier lit with hundreds of tiny candles. Their reflection sent a shimmering light over the huge round bed scattered with furs of many hues and natural lambswool rugs. Four ebony statues of naked goddesses stood at the four compass points, but the red cords draped from each of them suggested uses other than aesthetic. One wall displayed a startling array of leather whips, masks, corsets, chains and strange-looking items that Sister Ruth could not identify, but Brother Max hardly spared them a glance and appeared to know his way around.

He seemed instantly at ease and, as he peeled off his

robes to reveal an impressive erection, Sister Gabriel quickly stripped off her habit and veil and went to help Sister Ruth. Catching her eye, Brother Max joined her in slowly divesting Sister Ruth of her nun's garb until she stood between them in her microscopic red bra and tanga. Her breasts were small, pert and overhanging the tiny brassiere like ripe peaches. Sister Gabriel cupped one in her hand and bit into the soft flesh, causing Sister Ruth to gasp aloud. Looking into her face with a raised eyebrow, Sister Gabriel asked, 'Will you let us dress you for the occasion?' Nodding soundlessly, Sister Ruth put herself completely in their hands.

Brother Max took the tiny garment offered by Sister Gabriel, tugged off Sister Ruth's pants and brassiere, and got her to step into it. With a bit of pulling and pushing, Sister Ruth found herself encased in a waist-clinching black leather corset with an open crotch and bra cups that sat under rather than on her breasts. Her rosy nipples stood to attention and she felt a delicious thrill of anticipation, somewhere between fear and desire. Glancing down, she noticed steel rings stitched into the waistband and wondered what use they would be put to.

Looking up, she saw Sister Gabriel standing before her holding a leather hood with tiny slits for eyes and nose. Feeling slightly panicked, she stalled for time.

'I see there's no mouth hole. Is that so I'll be quiet? Shame, because I'm good with my mouth, everyone says so, don't they, Max?'

But Max was engrossed in fitting himself into a truss-like item made of shiny PVC straps and differently sized rings. The straps were very tight and very thin and seemed to be cutting into his flesh above and below his nipples and across his groin. As he turned to select a mask, she saw that one very fine strap was disappearing into the crack between his cheeks. She winced as she imagined how it felt.

'Are you ready, Sister Ruth?' Sister Gabriel regarded

her patiently and Sister Ruth bowed her head and submitted to her ministrations.

The hood pulled against her hair and felt as though it was grazing her skin as it was going on, but when she glanced up at the ceiling mirror, Sister Ruth felt a shock of delight at her own appearance. She looked like a pornographic version of Catwoman – all sinuous leather and accentuated curves. Glancing down at her feet, she saw that Sister Gabriel had guessed her shoe size correctly and she willingly stepped into an impossibly high-heeled pair of black, lace-up thigh boots.

Brother Max touched her lightly on the shoulder and she turned to find his face half-hidden by a highwayman-style mask that left his unusually serious mouth uncovered. About to speak, she suddenly realised that she was now mute and that her thoughts or wishes were to be subsumed in the pleasuring of Sister Gabriel and Brother Max. Again, an electric shock coursed through her body from her exposed pussy up to her bare, protruding nipples.

Sister Gabriel selected a shiny rubber catsuit and stood very still while Brother Max dusted her lightly with talcum powder before helping to pull it over her generous curves. The sound of the long zip being pulled closed set Sister Ruth's teeth on edge, but the sight of Sister Gabriel in neck-to-ankle rubber, complete with imposing, conical breasts and strategically placed zips soon whetted her appetite once more.

Brother Max scooped Sister Gabriel's long ringlets up into a high ponytail and fastened them with a leather thong, and then allowed her to lean on him while she pulled on a pair of high-heeled rubber ankle boots covered in studs. Jumping onto the bed, Sister Gabriel unscrewed a heavy iron fitting at the bottom of the chandelier and lowered a crude steel hook with a clasp on the end of a sturdy-looking chain. Brother Max fitted Sister Ruth with a pair of buckled wristbands and threaded leather ropes through the steel rings on them and then passed the ropes through the rings at her waist. She trusted Brother Max implicitly, but she still felt a pang of fear at having her arms immobilised by her sides and her mouth completely covered. At a signal from Sister Gabriel, Brother Max helped Sister Ruth up onto the bed and passed the ends of her ropes to Sister Gabriel, who threaded them through the ceiling contraption. Passing one rope back to Brother Max, she signalled for him to pull the rope and fix it to a ring on the North goddess. Tugging with all her might, Sister Gabriel fixed her end of the rope to the West goddess, leaving Sister Ruth suspended almost horizontally, face down over the big bed. Sister Gabriel and Brother Max took a few moments to adjust her height until she was just a few feet above the fur-strewn surface.

Although her breathing was not impeded in any way, Sister Ruth felt short of breath and her heart was hammering in her breast. Brother Max rocked her gently for a moment, but Sister Gabriel indicated the red cords on the remaining two goddess statues and, taking one ankle each, they splayed Sister Ruth's legs wide apart and tied them firmly into place. A deep throbbing welled up from Sister Ruth's exposed pussy, which felt stretched wide open and vulnerable. Taking a short, knotted whip from the wall, Sister Gabriel handed it to Brother Max and whispered something in his ear, which she then kissed greedily. Brother Max nimbly undid some zips and fondled Sister Gabriel's pneumatic breasts, easing her around the bed so that Sister Ruth had a clear view if she craned her neck. Turning Sister Gabriel roughly towards the wall, Brother Max spread her legs and lashed her hard with the whip against her buttocks and thighs. Sister Ruth jerked in sympathy in her harness. Reaching between her thighs, he unfastened another concealed zip, exposing her high buttocks and affording Sister Ruth a tantalising glimpse of her dark pussy lips. Again, the lash of the whip sounded loudly in the otherwise silent room and Sister Ruth began to feel hot and afraid.

Brother Max sank to his knees and kissed Sister Gabriel's beautiful bottom, sweeping his tongue over her cheeks and between her widespread thighs. Without warning, Sister Gabriel whipped around and landed a blow on Brother Max's head, knocking him to the ground where she pressed her spiked heel into his abdomen.

'Enough. It is time to begin.'

Brother Max bowed his head and replied humbly, 'Yes, Mistress.' Pulling him up by the hair, Sister Gabriel grabbed a cat-o'-nine-tails from the wall and thrust it into his hand.

Brother Max climbed up onto the bed and disappeared behind Sister Ruth, but for what seemed an eternity, nothing happened. Sister Gabriel crawled underneath Sister Ruth and began to kiss and fondle her breasts, sucking each nipple until they were both hard and erect. As Sister Ruth felt the first delicious pangs of pleasure, she felt the first stinging blow to her behind. The cutaway corset provided no protection as Brother Max delivered a steady stream of burning lashes to her bare bottom and the tops of her thighs. The pain was intense, but Sister Gabriel's ministrations to her breasts were setting up a conflict of pleasurable and painful feelings so that Sister Ruth moaned into her leather hood in confused frustration.

Swapping ends, Brother Max picked up the smaller, single strand whip he had used earlier and dragged it along Sister Ruth's bare shoulders and dangling breasts. Sister Gabriel planted butter-soft kisses up her inner thighs and over her pussy lips, occasionally sucking in a small amount of flesh and rolling it delicately between her teeth. Sister Ruth moaned aloud through her nose as Sister Gabriel traced her tongue up between her labia and into her tight, moist vagina.

Just as Sister Gabriel completed her exploration and

homed in on Sister Ruth's clitoris, another smarting blow landed on her exposed shoulder. The whip wrapped itself around her bare flesh and the tip caught her across her tender breasts. The tight hood stifled her cries so that she made muffled lowing sounds, but no amount of jerking could manoeuvre her away from Brother Max's determined onslaught. Sister Gabriel rapidly flicked her clitoris with her tongue until Sister Ruth could no longer choose where to focus her attention. Burning pain commingled with flashes of intense pleasure and her clit felt as though it would explode but, just when her body seemed ready to release her, everything stopped.

Dangling in the air with stinging breasts and pulsing clit, Sister Ruth felt hot tears of rage and frustration seeping out of the eye slits. Brother Max and Sister Gabriel scrambled directly beneath her and quickly wrapped their legs around one another and began humping furiously. Sister Ruth wished she could block her ears as well as her mouth as their grunts and cries of encouragement signalled their mutual pleasure, but all she could do was weep silently and wait for them to finish.

When at last their frantic coupling came to an end, Sister Ruth had almost given up all hope of ever being released from her bonds or her heightened state of arousal, but Sister Gabriel and Brother Max wasted no time in untying her and gently laying her on the bed. Sister Gabriel peeled off the restrictive hood and kissed Sister Ruth's sweaty, tear-stained face. 'Well done, you're such a good girl, isn't she, Brother Max?'

Brother Max was busily removing her tight wristbands and coiling up the leather ropes, but he smiled warmly and massaged Sister Ruth's reddened arms. 'She's wonderful. My favourite girl in the world.'

As if in a dream, Sister Ruth allowed both of them to release her from her uncomfortable outfit, and then sighed gratefully as she felt Brother Max massage her upper body and gently kiss her sore breasts, while Sister

Gabriel kneaded the tender flesh under her buttocks and on her inner thighs before making thrilling sweeps of her tongue in between her labia and up over her clit. Two pairs of hands and two pairs of lips soothed away her aches and pains and filled her body with hot, lustful desire. Sister Gabriel sucked the whole of her clit into her mouth and then rubbed her tongue hard over it until Sister Ruth began to wriggle and clutch onto her hair. All of the discomfort earlier seemed to have intensified her capacity for pleasure and she cried out as spasms of sexually charged energy rocked her body. Brother Max's lips were clamped onto one of her nipples while his fingers teased the other, sending tingly shivers down to where Sister Gabriel's blessed mouth was eating her alive. The exquisite feelings generated by being so thoroughly pampered finally reached a crescendo, and Sister Ruth found herself thrashing about on the bed screaming, 'Yes! Thank you! Yes!' as wave after wave of electrifying sensation ripped through her.

Brother Max and Sister Gabriel lay either side of Sister Ruth and stroked her gently, until the spasms had subsided, and then all three wrapped their arms around one another and embraced warmly. After a while, Brother Max sat up and grinned, first at Sister Ruth, then at Sister Gabriel.

'Sorry, Sister Gabriel, but what was it you wanted to talk to us about?'

Chapter Six

Set in the heart of one of the poorest areas of the East End of London, the Greendale Sports and Leisure Complex covered a huge tract of land formerly filled with disused warehouses and rubble, but the modern building was now surrounded by football fields, tennis courts and a running track. Carlos Guillory allowed his dark, patrician features to twist into a brief, self-satisfied smile as he recalled the years of fundraising, council management meetings and petty arguments with the adjoining church until he had realised his dream. Never one to back down, he had charmed, manipulated and sometimes bulldozed his way through the mountains of red tape and infuriating objections and proven all of his detractors wrong. The centre served a balanced mix of local, low-income clients on concessions, and an increasing number of well-heeled, fully paid-up members who enjoyed the unrivalled excellence of the facilities and the street credibility of the location.

Throwing a towel around his shoulders to stop his hair dripping onto his black cotton sports shirt, Carlos loped past the squash courts where the satisfying *smack* of balls assured him that the courts were all busy. Pleasantly warm and tired after his own frenetic match, which he had won as usual, he turned gratefully into his private offices where his personal power-shower awaited him.

Just as he dropped his sports bag onto the floor and reached in to turn on the water, a soft knock on his door was followed by the appearance of a young woman in jogging bottoms and sweatshirt, with her face hidden by a large baseball cap. 'I'm – I'm sorry to disturb you, Father, but I wondered if I might have a word?'

Carlos's tall, angular frame jerked to a halt by his desk and he fixed the girl with a cold stare. 'Please don't call me that. I am no longer a priest. It's been four years now.'

The girl took a few tentative steps towards him and hesitated, uncertain how to continue. 'I'm sorry, it's just that I remember how much you helped my family, after the fire. What should I call you?'

'Emily? My God, I didn't recognise you. Carlos. Call me Carlos. Why are you hiding your face?' He strode across the room and pulled the hat from her head, releasing a shimmering wave of auburn hair, but she buried her face in her hands and began to weep.

'Don't look at me. It's awful. The graft didn't take. I – I –'

Carlos put an arm around her shoulders and squeezed her gently. 'Shh. Calm down. It's all right. Come and sit with me.' He led her to a little two-seater sofa in the corner and settled her next to him. 'Now, let me look at you.'

Very slowly, Emily lowered her hands from her face but kept her chin down and her hair forward. Carlos softly swept aside her silky hair and raised her chin until she was facing him. Her forehead, her left eye and all of her left cheek were an angry reddish purple and in places her skin seemed to be contoured with bright pink ridges. Carlos looked into her tearful eyes and saw that they were the same tantalising shade of emerald green that he remembered. 'You have the most beautiful eyes.'

Emily angrily shook off his hand. 'Yes, but look at the rest of me. The scarring does all the way down over my neck and chest. My breast –' Her voice was choked off on a sob. 'Who will want me now?' she wailed, balling her hands into fists and once more hiding her face.

Carlos grabbed her wrists and forced her to look at him. 'Why have you come to me? Is it because you knew that I would want you? And because you still think of me as a priest?'

His tone was angry but his eyes were soft and kind. Emily's lip trembled but she held his gaze. 'Yes, I suppose that is why. I saw the way you looked at me and I know you're a compassionate man. I'm frightened to be touched. Even being looked at is unbearable.'

Carlos sighed and shook his head as his eyes travelled hungrily over the beautiful but scarred girl. 'Me? Of course I want you, I always did. But remember? It wasn't allowed. Don't you realise you would be fulfilling an old dream of mine if you would let me make love to you?'

Emily struggled through her tears to speak, her lower lip quivering uncontrollably. 'You're only saying that because you feel sorry for me.'

'No. I'm sorry you were hurt and you got scarred, but I'm not sorry for you. I'm just going for a shower. Come with me. You can show me the rest of your scars. I'm afraid mine are all on the inside.'

His eyes were steady and clear and Emily decided that she wanted him to see her. She wanted to be touched, to be caressed by a man.

'Did you know I was engaged? But now I can't let him touch me, not even kiss me.'

Carlos stroked her hair and kissed her softly on the cheek, then harder on her neck. 'Come. What will be will be.' Taking her hand, he led her over to the shower

51

cubicle and then switched on the powerful jets of steaming water. 'Let's get these off.'

Obediently, she lifted her arms above her head and allowed him to tug off her sweatshirt. Shivering slightly, she stepped out of her joggers and stood quite still while he undid her bra and pulled down her panties. Carlos nodded as his eyes travelled down over the corded scars on her neck and the particularly dark ridges on her misshapen left breast. 'You're still in great shape. Are you working out?'

Emily glanced down at her slim, toned body. 'Well, yes, but not here. Over at Clancy's.'

Carlos drew her into the steaming water. 'Where's your loyalty? You should come here. After all, we're old friends.'

His long, thin fingers were wonderfully strong as they massaged a zesty-scented gel into her skin and hair. He poured some into her hands and she began to rub his finely muscled arms, enjoying the heat and the wetness and the feeling of skin on skin. She drew in her breath sharply as the tips of Carlos's fingers lingered on her ravaged breast, tracing the angry scars and unnatural hollows, but she submitted herself to his caresses.

Starting with her face, he kissed first her unmarked skin, then her scars, and slowly made his way down her body. Emily found herself comparing the sensations, noticing that in some areas, like the curve of her neck or the edge of her breast, the lightly scarred areas were even more sensitive to his touch than the unharmed skin. But the thickly ridged keloid scars dulled her ability to feel, so that as Carlos's hands and mouth travelled over her flesh she felt as if sensations were coming in tiny waves: on/off/on, strong/faint/strong.

Carlos lowered his head and trailed his tongue over each of her breasts then sucked her scarred nipple into his mouth and nibbled and nipped until Emily gasped with surprised delight as she felt pleasurable pangs radiating out into the rest of her body. Kissing Carlos's neck and shoulders, she relished the sight of water cascading off his gaunt shoulders and falling in streams from his longish black hair.

Feeling bolder, she ran her hands lower over his flat abdomen until her fingers encountered the springy curls of his pubic hair. Hungrily, she grasped his swollen manhood and explored the velvety softness of the bell-shaped head and the corded hardness of his shaft. The thick, ridged veins under her fingertips reminded her of her own scarred skin, but she felt no revulsion, only desire. Strong pangs of lust rippled up through her groin and belly and she began to ache to feel him inside her.

As if sensing her need, Carlos gripped her bottom firmly and hoisted her up against the slippery shower wall until she could wrap her legs around his waist. Emily gasped as he rested the smooth head of his frighteningly large penis at the entrance to her pussy, but when he did not push it all the way in, she clasped her hands around his neck and lowered herself onto him in one strong movement. A sharp, stinging pain made her cry out in shock, but she could not help but relish the tight, fat feeling of being filled up completely. As Carlos began to move very gently inside her she relaxed into his embrace and the burning sensation faded into a thrilling mixture of discomfort and delight. Clinging to his neck, Emily found his mouth and lost herself in a deep, sensual kiss while her body awoke to a host of new sensations.

All too soon, Carlos's breathing became laboured and he quickened his pace, slapping her bare bottom against the tiles and grunting with animal passion. Emily held on tightly, gripping his waist with her slippery thighs and twining her fingers in his hair. Pulling back so that she could look at him, his eyes locked onto her own and he called her name softly, over and over. 'Emily, preciosa, bonita, Emily . . .'

With one last thrust, she felt his body go rigid and, somewhere deep inside her, a hot, pulsing wetness told her that he had come. Smiling with delight at his obvious enjoyment, Emily planted a kiss on the tip of his Roman nose and slid her legs down to the floor. With loving care, he washed away the traces of redness on her inner thighs and allowed her to rinse his now flaccid penis in the warm water.

Carlos shut off the shower and grabbed two fluffy towels, draping them around their shoulders and then leading Emily to the sofa. 'Lie down, I want to finish you off.'

Handing him her towel and slumping into the seat, Emily waited patiently, but with a grin and a shake of his head he dropped to his knees and pulled her legs apart. In awed fascination, Emily watched his hawk-like face hover before her parted pussy lips and then swoop down. She felt his tongue probing and exploring every fold and crevice and she wriggled and jerked about as a kaleidoscopic array of sensations burst upon her. The strongest, ticklish feelings were almost unbearable and Emily tried to push Carlos's head away, but he merely reached up and grabbed her wrists down against her thighs and continued his sensual onslaught. As his tongue found Emily's most sensitive spot, she started to shriek, but he was undeterred. Tightening his grip on her wrists, he forced her legs further apart and licked her firmly and rhythmically until she felt like a skyrocket bursting from its casing and exploding skywards. Laughing and crying hysterically, she allowed the fantastic feelings to rush through and over her until, at last, she lay spent and satiated.

Carlos released her and slipped onto the sofa beside her. Gathering her into a warm embrace he kissed her hair, her eyes and her nose, grinning like a fool. 'I didn't expect to be the first.'

Emily shrugged and smiled. 'That's OK. Somehow, I don't think you'll be the last.'

Laughing, Carlos hugged her hard.

'I'm sure of it, but I hope you'll allow me to indulge a

few of my personal fantasies with you before you disappear off into your own life again.'

Emily snuggled in closer to him. 'I want you to teach me everything. I've got a lot of catching up to do.'

Later that evening, Carlos put his feet up, sipped on a glass of aged red wine and waited patiently with his mobile phone pressed to his ear for an answer to his call. After several minutes, he finally got through.

'Hello, Mother Magdalene, can I help you?'

'Hello, Mother, it's Father Guillory here. Have you got time to give me a little feedback? I was hoping to run through a recent event with you.'

He could hear Mother Magdalene settling herself into her chair before she replied. 'Now's fine, Father, it's good to hear from you. We were disappointed you couldn't make it for the last lot of initiations. Your wealth of experience has been such a great help to us. Not to mention your many other talents.'

Carlos laughed softly and flexed his strong hands. 'You may recall I was somewhat tied up at the time?' His eyes flicked over to an open cupboard crammed with ropes, winches and harnesses. 'I hate leaving anything hanging in the air. I have to finish what I start.'

'I know exactly what you mean, Father, no need to explain. Are you coming down for the next big celebration? I believe you've been asked for specially.'

Carlos rubbed his free hand down over his suddenly erect penis and sucked his breath in through his teeth. 'Oh yes, I wouldn't miss it. I've already started preparing everything in advance.'

'Excellent. Now what was it you wanted to discuss with me?'

'Well, it's about this girl, Mother. She knew me before, in my parish. You know I enjoy being Father Guillory again at The Order, where it's on my terms, but I hate to be referred to that way up here. That part of my life is over. What I'm doing with her, this girl, is exactly what

I wanted to do when I was a priest and couldn't. Yet it also fulfils my role in The Order. It's all very confusing.' He clenched his hand around the phone and took a larger gulp of his wine, wrestling with his thoughts.

'Who is the girl?' Mother Magdalene's voice brought him back to the present.

'Emily. She's the eldest daughter of one of my old parishioners and, to be honest, I always fancied her. She has survived a terrible fire but she's badly scarred and I am hoping I can help her to regain some of her self-respect. But she keeps slipping into calling me Father, and it throws me completely. I *am* Father Guillory, but I'm not, if you see what I mean. If I was still a Catholic priest, this wouldn't be happening.'

There was a lengthy pause before Mother Magdalene replied. 'You know, I think it might be more helpful for you to discuss this with Father Lionheart. Although he never practised as a priest, I believe he's had some problems with the use of the title. Shall I ask him to call you?'

Carlos narrowed his eyes and thought of Father Lionheart's easy-going manner and confident air. 'You surprise me. But yes, please, do ask him. I need to talk to someone.'

'Don't worry, we're all here for you. Would you like Sister Gabriel to pop around too? She usually cheers you up.'

Carlos laughed and felt the tension in his shoulders relax. 'Now that's an excellent idea. She could help me to co-ordinate the layout of my new gymnasium. And she's a sight for sore eyes in a stretch bodysuit.'

Mother Magdalene's gentle laughter was like music to his ears. 'No sooner said than done. I'll get her to call. And, Father?'

'Yes?'

'Cut yourself a little slack. I'll talk to you soon. Peace be with you.'

'And also with you.'

Smiling at the thought of Sister Gabriel's powerful body in skimpy gym wear, he leaned back in his chair and allowed his hand to fall onto his swollen cock once more.

Chapter Seven

*T*he Caddy Shack was the nickname given to The Order's homeless project that occupied a tiny space near the arches by Waterloo station. Although the offices were cramped and shabbily furnished, Sister Gabriel's welcoming smile, together with free teas and coffees and all year round warmth, guaranteed a steady flow of local clients. A week rarely passed without a violent incident or two erupting among the long-term alcoholics, but so far none of The Order's volunteers had ever been attacked.

Wearing a habit to work had proved to be a useful defence against unwanted attention and had helped Sister Gabriel to maintain an aura of sexless efficiency at odds with her true nature. She and her helpers fostered an atmosphere of comfortable acceptance and there was no pressure put on homeless people to be rehabilitated or pushed onto schemes. This encouraged many of them to drop in for a snack or a friendly chat. Once trust had been established, many of them did ask for referrals for help, and The Order had begun to gain the respect of other agencies working in the field.

Sister Gabriel found herself yawning and smoothed down her veil while she checked the clock on the rough brick wall. She had meant to visit Father Guillory again for one of his unique endurance sessions, but the thought of spending some time with the lovely Savannah had been too great a temptation.

It was after six thirty, Savannah was already half an hour late, and Sister Gabriel's mind turned to wondering why her old friend insisted on staying in touch. They no longer had anything much in common, yet both of them seemed to find it impossible to cut the ties. While she still believed that Savannah was basically too selfish for The Order, she was also sure that she had never met anyone so brimful of beauty and sensuality. She and Savannah had been lovers on and off for years, and the thought of all that spun-silk hair and alabaster skin made her shiver with anticipation. Sister Gabriel sighed as she accepted that her bonds with Savannah were a curious mixture of lust for her beautiful body and loathing for her arrogant, little-princess manner.

As if she had been caught in the act of thinking, she was startled by suddenly seeing Savannah framed in the window, staring at her. Rapping on the glass with one of her rings, she mouthed, 'Open the door.'

Rising to let her in, Sister Gabriel was surprised to see that Savannah had a good-looking young man in tow. Opening the door and hugging her old friend, she looked over her shoulder at the handsome newcomer and asked, 'And who might you be?'

Her searching eyes raked over the blonde crop, striking blue eyes and superb muscle tone of the cocky-looking young man slouched against the door-frame. Savannah stepped back a little and giggled.

'Don't be cross, Gabs. This is my pal from the late-night talk show, Joe. He's a runner for the production team, and he's totally fucked up, aren't you, Joey?' She whacked him playfully on the arm, but he remained silent. 'Come on,' said Savannah, grabbing Sister Gabriel's hand, 'let's go and have a drink. Joe here's renting a new pad just up by The Strand and we've chilled some champagne for a little house-warming.'

Seduced once again by Savannah's dazzling beauty and natural sense of command, Sister Gabriel swallowed any protests and quickly locked up the offices. Hooking arms with Savannah, she matched her jaunty stride as they followed Joe over the bridge towards The Strand.

The apartment was on the third floor of a converted office block and access was via a dark, mildewed lane beside a fast food restaurant. The greasy smell of burgers and chips wafted up the narrow stairwell and Sister Gabriel found herself wondering what she was doing here.

One of the numerous, anonymous doorways opened suddenly and a waif-like youth stuck his head out and called, 'All right, Joe? Got a fag?'

Joe sauntered over and shook out a cigarette. The boy looked over at the two women and said 'Blimey! Have you found Jesus or something? Gone straight, have ya?'

Joe gave him a friendly grin and shrugged his muscular shoulders. 'Could be.' He winked broadly, stuck his cigarettes back in his pocket and inserted his key into the lock of number 22.

Inside, Sister Gabriel and Savannah made themselves comfortable on a deep brown leather sofa and watched Joe's lithe form move around the room fetching glasses and the champagne. Despite his obvious unease, he had the graceful movements of a dancer. When he had settled himself between them, they all drank a few toasts and started unwinding to some mellow jazz. Savannah reached over and caressed Sister Gabriel's thigh, fingers seeking and finding her suspender straps and stocking tops.

'Mmm, still know how to dress underneath, don't you, darling? What do you think, Joe? Isn't she tasty?'

Joe slid to the floor and turned to look at the two

beautiful women. 'Yep, she's gorgeous, but she doesn't do a thing for me, as you well know.'

Savannah stroked his smoothly shaven jaw line and purred, 'Don't be so sure. Gabby here and I could raise Lazarus between us, isn't that right Gabs?'

Sliding off her veil and resting her head of black ringlets in her friend's lap, Sister Gabriel laughed loudly. 'And we have! But I think Joe is trying to say he has other preferences. That's his privilege.'

Joe eyed Sister Gabriel suspiciously. 'Aren't you a Catholic nun? You lot believe queers are the spawn of Satan or something, don't you?'

Sister Gabriel smiled and took another sip of her drink. 'If I was, I'd hardly be sitting here like this. Surely Savannah's told you that I'm in a lay order?'

Savannah spat her champagne back into her glass and snorted with laughter. 'A lay order! That's a good one. Is that what you do down there, in your secret location, get laid? She never tells me anything, Joe.'

Sister Gabriel glared at her. 'Savannah. That's enough.'

Savannah pouted and folded her arms. 'Of course it's enough, because it's all I know. How can you all be so mean? I'd look so horny in a little black habit.'

Another warning look from Sister Gabriel made her bite off whatever else she had to say and she swallowed the rest of her drink in one gulp. Turning back to Joe, Sister Gabriel softened her tone. 'I think the Catholic Church's teachings on homosexuality, or sexuality for that matter, are nonsensical. They cause a lot of grief and do a lot of harm. Are your family Catholic, Joe?'

Joe eyed her bitterly. 'Oh, yes. They spent a fortune trying to sort me out. Counsellors, psychiatrists – the lot. When they threatened to put me in some kind of religious reformatory for treatment, I did a runner.'

Sister Gabriel leaned forward sympathetically and asked, 'When was that? How old were you?'

Joe tossed back the last of his champagne and poured

himself another glass. 'Sixteen, and how long ago is my business.'

Savannah wrapped a possessive set of fingers around Sister Gabriel's wrist and drew her back into her lap. She pulled up the long folds of her habit and ran her hand over Sister Gabriel's shapely, stockinged leg, pausing to linger over the smooth flesh on her inner thigh. Sister Gabriel felt the familiar thrill of Savannah's exquisite touch and parted her legs slightly in anticipation.

'I thought you and I could give Joe a taste of something different, Gabs. Show him what a woman can do.'

Sister Gabriel sat bolt upright and shook her head. 'Hang on a minute. You're gay, Joe, right? And you're sick of your own family trying to convert you. Why on earth would you want us to touch you?'

Joe's handsome face looked strained, but he met Sister Gabriel's concerned gaze head on. 'Because I want to know what it's like. And this is my idea, nobody else's. I asked Savannah, but she insisted on both of you.'

Sister Gabriel looked from one to the other and laughed in exasperation. 'Well, of course she did. She's a lesbian.'

Joe stared at Savannah open mouthed for a moment and then asked, 'Why didn't you tell me? You're always out with men. And look at you!'

Savannah sloshed more champagne into her glass and slipped her hand over Sister Gabriel's prominent breasts. Sister Gabriel half closed her eyes and allowed Savannah's strong fingers to send shock waves through her nipples. Savannah raised her eyebrows and looked at Joe with contempt.

'So, you think all dykes are butch bitches with hair on their upper lip, do you? Why should I have told you? You're a worse gossip than all those studio brats put together. Anyway, now we'll have something on each other. Now, are you up for this little experiment or what? I quite like a bit of dick now and again.'

Joe looked affronted. 'For such a stunning girl, you've got a filthy mouth, Savannah.'

Staggering slightly as she rose, Savannah slurred, 'You're right, love, I have, but wait until you see what I can do with it. Let's go in the bedroom.'

Joe got to his feet and pulled Sister Gabriel up by her hand. 'Come on, Sister, let's see if God's own handmaiden can do anything for me. Fancy trying a bit of laying on of your hands?'

Sister Gabriel halted by the bedroom door and searched his face. 'You're sure this is what you want? You can stop any time, you know.'

Joe gave her a determined little shove into the bedroom and replied, 'I'm sure.'

Sister Gabriel gazed around the room as Savannah stripped Joe and told him to lie down on the bed. All four walls and the ceiling were covered with mirror tiles and the bed was a huge gothic affair complete with wrought-iron arches at either end. Underfoot, thick, oatmeal shag-pile carpet muffled their footsteps. Joe's tastes seemed to exceed the low income of most lowly studio runners.

Savannah hitched up her tight, short skirt and began to peel off her hold-up stockings. She grinned over at Sister Gabriel and said, 'Come on. Off with them. We'll need them for lovely Joe here.'

Lifting her own leg up onto the other side of the bed, Sister Gabriel unsnapped her suspender straps and slowly rolled her silky stocking down over her long, athletic leg. Joe found himself admiring the shapely muscle tone and the smooth chocolate skin. When both women were barelegged, they took hold of his limbs and bound them to the ironwork on the bed. Joe's muscular legs and strong arms were spread wide apart by the flimsy bonds, which he looked more than capable of tearing off, but he lay passively, with his penis still flaccid. Savannah joined her friend and they began to undress each other slowly, both of them conscious of their reflections in the mirrors, offering Joe a clear view from every angle.

Joe watched with great curiosity as Savannah's body was revealed. Dressed, she was stunningly beautiful, but naked she was exquisite. He had a fleeting memory of a painting – a Venus in a shell – that he had seen on a school trip to Italy. He recalled how moved he had been by the perfection of the slim girl in the painting, but it was the colossal statue of David that had caused the first stirring in his loins. Scanning Sister Gabriel's meatier, athletic form he felt the first flicker of interest. Her shoulders were square and her upper arms were plump but firm. He liked the full heaviness of her large breasts and the enormous nipples being caressed by Savannah's small white hands; but it was the first glimpse of her magnificent buttocks that caused his limp cock to jerk to attention. Sister Gabriel's waist was slim and her belly, although round, looked toned. Joe's eyes feasted on the dramatic contrast between her narrow waist and her broad hips and arse covered in a layer of plump, dark flesh. He licked his lips and twisted on the bed as he contemplated her impressive buttocks which, despite being quite fat, stood up proudly, revealing a deep cleft between the cheeks.

Spying his reaction, Savannah turned her friend so that her beautiful behind was just out of reach, near Joe's head. Making sure that he could see in the mirror, she began to rain tiny, bird-like kisses all over Sister Gabriel's breasts and belly, sweeping her silky blonde hair over the dusky flesh. Swivelling around behind her, she continued to kiss, nip and lick Sister Gabriel's back, then knelt down and placed her hands on her friend's muscular bottom. Sister Gabriel arched her head back and fondled her own breasts, lost in the sensations caused by Savannah's deft embraces. Joe watched in fascination as Savannah licked the round globes in front of her and then parted the muscular cheeks and burrowed her nose between them. Joe's cock sprang fully into life and he strained against his bonds and writhed, feeling his heartbeat quicken and his cock ache to be touched.

Savannah lifted one of Sister Gabriel's legs up onto the bed and ducked beneath her so that she had easy access to her wet pussy and tight anus. Joe's eyes widened at the lovely sight of the slender blonde girl licking and sucking underneath the Amazonian black woman, and he rubbed himself against the silky bed covering and moaned with desire. Sister Gabriel watched the same spectacle in the mirror and grabbed handfuls of Savannah's hair and rubbed it over her belly and ground her pelvis against her friend's beautiful face. Savannah slurped greedily as she lapped up the juices running onto her chin and sucked her friend's clit between her teeth. Reaching up to Sister Gabriel's pumping bottom, she splayed the cheeks with her fingers and slipped her little finger into the tight flower of her anus.

Joe felt as though he was going to have convulsions as he watched Sister Gabriel bend her knees slightly to allow the finger to push in more deeply and pulled her pussy lips apart so that Savannah could home in on her clit with strong, practised flicks. Groaning loudly, Sister Gabriel felt ribbons of hot pleasure rippling up through her pussy and into her belly and breasts. Her bottom was clamped tightly around her friend's finger and waves of sensation radiated out and joined those from her clit. Pressing Savannah's silky head against her belly, she moaned, 'Oh baby. Oh baby!'

Grinning like a Cheshire cat, Savannah peered at Joe's stiff, long cock and murmured, 'Oh my. Look who's come out to play.'

Sister Gabriel turned to look and teased, 'What a waste, honey. He won't know where to put that thing with two ladies in the house.'

Joe pleaded with them, on fire with lust. 'Please, Savannah, help me out here. Sister, please.'

Sister Gabriel locked eyes with her friend for a moment before saying 'Well, seeing as you asked so nicely and all.'

She began to massage his upper body while Savannah stroked his feet and legs. Joe gasped as Sister Gabriel sucked and nipped his small nipples until they were tight, hard little balls. Savannah's long, silky hair trailed over his skin sending little shivers of pleasure through him. At last, craning his neck so that he could see, Savannah's beautiful, crimson mouth descended onto his swollen cock.

'Wow!' he cried, feeling her hot, smooth flesh sucking him deeper into her throat. Electric shocks jolted his hips off the bed as her tongue flicked against the swollen bell head and then his balls, before her luscious mouth engulfed him again. Sister Gabriel's full lips and pointed tongue assailed his hypersensitive nipples until a fire was raging throughout the whole of his body.

'Oh no you don't.' Savannah withdrew her mouth as she felt the first pulses of orgasm and gripped the base of his penis tightly in her fingers. 'Not yet, lover boy, I need to get mine.' Flicking back her hair she knelt up, straddling him, and then lowered herself down in a single, smooth movement.

Joe felt panic rising at the idea of a woman mounting him, but his cock still felt hot and horny, and as Savannah began to bounce against him, he lost himself in the powerful sensations coursing through his body.

'Come on, baby, fuck me, fuck me good!' yelled Savannah, slapping his hips and thrashing against him with all her might.

In minutes, Joe felt the mounting pressure in his cock begin to peak, and he roared, 'I'm co-ming!'

Savannah leaned over and kissed the tip of his nose, untying the stockings that were beginning to cut into his wrists. As Joe felt the spasms gradually subsiding, Savannah smiled down at him and cooed, 'There, dear. That wasn't too bad was it?'

Sister Gabriel swiftly loosened his legs and then reached over to stroke her friend's hair. 'How about I finish you off, sexy Savannah?'

Savannah threw herself against the bottom of the bed and lifted her knees out of the way. 'Yes please. Maybe Joe could give you a back rub or something. How about it, Joe?'

While Sister Gabriel knelt between her friend's legs, Joe found himself facing her fabulous behind and he speedily accepted. 'Sure. Why not?'

Once again, the two women locked eyes and grinned conspiratorially, then Sister Gabriel bent down and began to wiggle her agile tongue into Savannah's delicate pink pussy. In no time, Sister Gabriel had homed in on Savannah's already aroused clitoris and sent the first early warnings of orgasm pulsing through her friend's slender body.

Joe took a bottle of oil out of his bedside drawer and began to massage Sister Gabriel's shoulders, neck and back. Her beautiful brown skin glistened as he smoothed the oil into it and he felt a renewed flicker of life in his penis as he reached under her arms and gently kneaded her full, heavy breasts. Savannah's face was wreathed in a beatific smile as her friend's mouth clamped itself around her pulsing clit and took her swiftly over the edge. Listening to Savannah's sighs of satisfaction, Joe's eyes kept flicking greedily to the high, plump mounds of Sister Gabriel's bottom. At last, he allowed himself to dribble some warm oil down between her cheeks, followed by his strong fingers. As if she was reading his mind, Sister Gabriel shifted her position so that her body was pressed down against the bed, and her bottom was stuck up invitingly in the air.

Fully aroused again, Joe knelt up closely behind her and massaged her firm flesh until it was slippery with oil. Splaying the cheeks apart, he looked with admiration at the reddish-brown flower of her anus and tentatively pressed his index finger into it. Sister Gabriel groaned happily and pressed back against him. Feeling bolder, Joe poured more oil over her bottom and rested his now stiff cock against her cheeks. Wriggling backwards, Sister Gabriel allowed his erection to slide down between the cleft and come to rest against her anus. Savannah recovered her equilibrium and leaned forward to hold Sister Gabriel's arms down, so that Joe could take things at his own pace. Greedily feasting his eyes on her wonderful buttocks, Joe pushed himself against her and felt her responding. Revelling in the look and the feel of her, he slowly inched his erection inside, loving the sight of his fair-skinned cock sinking into her luscious, black bottom.

Sister Gabriel grinned up at her friend, delighting in this opportunity to indulge one of her own little vices. His cock felt smooth and hard and filled her completely. Wrenching free of Savannah, she met Joe's thrust with vigour. Excited by her obvious enjoyment, Joe speeded up the pace and soon he and Sister Gabriel were slapping against each other and grunting loudly. Savannah grabbed her friend's large nipples and squeezed them hard, causing fierce jolts of pleasure to ricochet through her body.

Joe began to yell, 'All the way, come on, come on!' He started slapping Sister Gabriel's buttocks and pounding against her with all his might. Stroke for stroke, she rode up to meet him until the hot pressure in her behind and the fiery stabs from her nipples exploded in a rush of joyful spasms, rocking her body with pleasure. Joe collapsed against her back, feeling the last pulses in his cock subside, and then hugged her warmly. 'You're one hell of a woman. Both of you!'

Savannah and Sister Gabriel lay down beside him with their arms around each other, giggling like schoolgirls. 'We know!'

Part Three

Testament

Chapter Eight

Sister Cecily's high-pitched voice reverberated around the high ceiling of the small lecture hall in Saint Columba's RC Sixth Form College, sounding vaguely like a droning bee. 'Angela, Angela!' Sister Cecily's agitated tone broke through Angela's dreamy haze, forcing her back to wakefulness.

'Sorry, Sister, I must have dozed off.'

The nun's intelligent face looked more concerned than annoyed as she said, 'Please stay behind at the end – we need to talk.' Some of the other students sniggered and her neighbour, Daphne, smirked and gave her a coy wink.

'In your dreams, honey,' whispered Angela, deriving great pleasure from seeing Daphne's tight mouth snap shut in outrage.

The remainder of the lecture dragged on: geomorphology, topography, human-geographical distribution. Angela struggled to keep her heavy-lidded, deep-brown eyes open. At last, Sister Cecily ground to a halt and Daphne joined a little knot of her chums with darting, malevolent eyes and superior, pointed noses, whispering and sneering as they left the room. Greg Staunton, one of Angela's few allies, leaned over and squeezed her arm, his long, silky hair brushing her cheek as he gave her a sympathetic, lop-sided grin. Angela was too weary to respond.

As the door slammed shut after the last student, Sister Cecily smiled warmly at Angela and patted the chair she had placed beside her own. 'Come and sit here.'

Angela wished she could just leave or, even better, tell the truth; but she could hardly tell a nun that she was worn out from too much fucking around followed by self-torturing bouts of guilt, could she? She toyed with the phrase, 'I'm beset with rampant desires, Sister,' but soon switched her focus back to Sister Cecily, who was already reciting how the other lecturers had noticed something wrong, too, how concerned they all were – the list was endless.

'Angela, I've asked you before to avail of the college's counselling services, but now I'm going to have to insist. As your form and personal tutor, I have responsibility for your personal and spiritual well-being, not just your academic progress. Frankly, I'm very worried about you. I know things are tough for students up from the country, especially here in East London. Are you sure you can't talk to me about it? Or what about the chaplain?' Angela shook her head then turned her face away to avoid the nun's probing stare. Sister Cecily's searchlight gaze took in the dark circles under Angela's eyes and the thinness of her angular frame. 'You're not sleeping well, are you?'

'No, Sister.'

'Or eating properly?'

'No.'

'Very well. I must inform you that the continuation with your studies here is conditional on your attendance at counselling services. You'll need to present yourself at their offices at one o'clock today, where the head counsellor will try and advance book a weekly session for you with one of the new supply staff, when one becomes available. As soon as a regular slot becomes free, it will be offered to you. Their assistance is completely confidential, Angela, and they will not feed anything back to the academic staff. Do you understand?'

'Yes, Sister.'

'Angela, please look at me. There is no shame in seeking help, only in denying that you need it. I just want to see you happy and functioning. There are only a few months left to the end of term, and that's it, your two years are up. I really want you to have something to show for them; you're a bright girl.'

Angela sighed and gave her a watery smile. 'I know, Sister. I'm sorry.'

Sister Cecily put her arm around Angela's shoulder and gave her a friendly squeeze. 'Don't be sorry, be brave, and try to sort this out. Come and see me any time you need to.'

Angela nestled in closer to Sister Cecily's strong, slim body and gazed with undisguised longing into her eyes. The nun coughed uncomfortably and hastily withdrew her arm. 'Well, off you go, you've just got time for a sandwich before your appointment. Let me know how you get on. Good luck.'

Angela smiled to herself as she twitched her hips and slipped provocatively from the room. So, it would be another few weeks before she'd have the fun of trying to turn on a counsellor? Well then, she'd better get busy, so that there was plenty to talk about.

Chapter Nine

Mother Magdalene smoothed down her veil, enjoying the click-clack sound of her spiky heels on the polished floor of her office. Reaching into a deep drawer in her antique desk, she drew out two cones of incense and placed them in a brass dish beneath the portrait of the Sacred Heart over the mantelpiece. She paused to gaze into the soulful eyes of Jesus, remembering why she had taken this name for herself. Praying quietly, she murmured, 'You never cast her aside, my Lord. You kept her always beside you, just like your sainted Mother, so that people would know that God's love extends to the virgin and the whore without discrimination. Let me serve you in the way I love best.'

The jarring ring of the telephone broke into her reverie and she turned to snatch up the receiver. 'Mother Magdalene, how may I help you?'

After a moment's pause a deep, gravelly voice spoke. 'Margaret. I hear you've fallen from grace.'

Mother Magdalene felt her pulse quicken. 'Who is this please?'

She could hear the rasping breath close to her ear. 'You brazen hussy. They should have stoned you last time. This time, they will.'

Mother Magdalene clutched her throat and swallowed hard, struggling to keep the tremor out of her voice. 'I don't know who you are, but this is a private, reclusive order –'

'Save your breath,' spat the menacing voice, 'just say your prayers.' Click.

Mother Magdalene stared at the receiver gripped tightly in her trembling, sweaty hand. There was something gnawingly familiar about the voice, but she could not find a mental image to fit with it. The sudden return of the dialling tone made her conscious of the anonymous and appallingly intrusive nature of the threat. Waves of giddy fear forced her to sit down. Someone knew who she was and what she was doing. But who? And why would they want to frighten her? She began to dial Father Lionheart's extension but slammed down the receiver instead. Why should she give credence to this cowardly act by reporting it? She had always hated bullies, and that was exactly what this was – bullying. If she gave in to fear now, she would go on living in fear indefinitely.

Defiantly, she lifted her legs onto the desk and reached inside her silken panties and began to stroke herself urgently. Her moist flesh came alive with tingling sensations and her mounting desire soon distracted her from the threatening call. She fumbled in her top drawer and brought out a plump, flesh-coloured vibrator, which she slid into herself, loving the thrilling buzz and hum. She quickly became lost in a state of heightened arousal.

Father Lionheart adjusted his collar and smoothed down the black serge folds of his new soutane. He enjoyed the feeling of freedom beneath the loose robe and smiled to himself as he became aware again of his naked buttocks and freely hanging genitals. Tying on a golden rope belt, he turned this way and that before the mirror and patted his smartly styled hair into place.

The room was somewhat austere, with plain white

walls, dark furniture and minimal decorations, but the focal point was undoubtedly the massive bed, a rustic-looking affair with a roughly-hewn wooden headboard and thick, solid posts. Father Lionheart crossed slowly to the bed and knelt down on a prayer mat, leaning his elbows on the plain, white coverlet and covering his face with his hands.

'Dear Father,' he whispered, 'grant me the grace to follow in your footsteps whenever I can and to have the humility to know when I have strayed too far from the path. You are the way, the truth and the light.'

His prayer was interrupted by a soft knock on the door and he bounced up enthusiastically and paused for a beat or two before gliding over and opening the door. His face registered his disappointment as he saw one of the newer novices standing shyly at the door clutching a small, studded whip.

'You said I was to see you about confession, Father,' the girl blurted, thrusting the whip towards him and licking her lips nervously.

Father Lionheart snatched it impatiently from her grasp and threw it to the ground. 'Not now. Please don't come to my room without an appointment, I'm very busy.' The girl's face fell and she stooped to pick up the whip with a tearful expression. Softening, Father Lionheart touched her arm. 'I'm sorry, you've called at a bad time. Forgive me?' The girl looked into his beautiful, tawny eyes and nodded, wishing fervently that it wasn't such a bad time. 'Arrange something with Sister Gabriel, will you? It looks to me that I'll have to take you firmly in hand.'

Grinning with anticipation, the girl stepped away from the door. 'Oh, thank you, that would be wonderful. Goodbye, Father.' Father Lionheart watched as she disappeared down the corridor and then returned hastily to his kneeling position by the bed.

Within a few minutes, there was a smart knock on the door followed by a familiar voice. 'Well, Father, I'm glad to see you on your knees.' Mother Magdalene's sparkling eyes belied her stern tone of voice. 'What a wicked boy you've been. And what vanity is this? New vestments?'

Father Lionheart rose slowly and turned to face her. 'Forgive me, Mother, but I thought you'd approve.'

Mother Margaret advanced, coolly examining him from the tip of his well-polished shoes to the top of his beautifully coifed head. 'Indeed, I do approve of good grooming but, as you know, today I'm here to exact penance. You will be stripped of your office, your title and your garments. And then you must be punished. What do you suggest, you poor excuse for a priest?'

Father Lionheart untied his belt and held it out to her. 'Perhaps you'd care to use this?'

Mother Magdalene took the rope belt from him and turned it over in her hands, considering. 'Perhaps I would. Prepare yourself, please.'

Father Lionheart turned back to the bed and slowly raised the folds of the soutane until his bare cheeks were exposed. Mother Magdalene felt a thrill of desire as she regarded the contrast between his meticulously neat garments and his fuzzy, muscular bottom and long, bare legs.

'Bend over,' she commanded giving him a shove onto the bed.

Father Lionheart lay face down, with his buttocks resting on the very edge of the bed, where they looked pale and vulnerable. Mother Magdalene rubbed her hands down over her breasts and pressed against her crotch for a moment, clutching the belt in her fingers. Strong pulses of sensation radiated out from her groin just at the thought of the delicious time ahead. In one easy movement, she whipped the soutane up higher and brought down the lash hard against his cheeks.

'Repeat after me, "I am heartily sorry to have offended thee." Go on, say it.'

She lashed again with all her might, leaving angry red

stripes across his bare flesh. He cried out in pain and quickly repeated the words. 'I am heartily sorry I have offended thee. Please forgive me, Mother.'

Mother Magdalene paused to take a breath and then began to aim rapid, stinging blows onto his backside and thighs and in between the crack in his cheeks. Father Lionheart yelped involuntarily, but he submitted to the beating without making any effort to escape the forceful blows.

When the thrill of seeing him in an ecstasy of suffering subsided, Mother Magdalene put down the belt and leaned over to whisper in his ear. 'Get onto the bed, you worthless failure. Take off that fancy dress costume and lie on your back.' Father Lionheart followed her instructions without question and prostrated himself on the bed, trying to quell the excited thumping of his heart as he awaited the next phase of the game. 'Spread your arms and legs.' Obediently, he stretched out his arms and legs and thrilled to the roughness of her touch as she quickly tied him to the bedposts, leaving him spread-eagled and helpless. Mother Magdalene climbed onto the bed and stood on his abdomen and chest in her sharp, spiked heels. Father Lionheart gasped, but his face showed only excitement, which increased when Mother Magdalene reached down and slapped him hard on the cheek. 'Tell me what you want now. Go on, ask me.'

Father Lionheart groaned as her heels bit into his tender flesh, but he raised his head and pleaded with her. 'Abase me, Mother. Use me as you will, but allow me to be Father Lionheart again. Sit on my face. Please Mother, I beg you. Sit on my face.'

Mother Magdalene hitched up her habit and watched his eyes become feverish as she snapped her red suspenders against her pale thighs and parted her legs a little to show him her deep pink cleft and her soft, golden curls. She gently pulled herself apart to expose the glistening flesh within and stroked herself slowly.

'What? You want this? My beautiful pussy, on your greedy face?'

Father Lionheart's breathing became ragged and his eyes bulged. 'Yes please, oh please. Let me show you how sorry I am. Please, Mother.'

Mother Magdalene felt the juices beginning to flow down her fingers and she ached for his tongue and lips, but she held out just a little longer. Placing one dangerous heel either side of his head she lowered herself to within a few inches of his face. He strained his neck and stuck out his tongue as far as it would go, but try as he might, he could not reach her. Mother Magdalene rocked backwards and forwards, hovering just out of reach, and felt the delicious tension mounting inside her as she continued to stroke herself. Father Lionheart's face was becoming red with frustration as she taunted him.

'What's the matter? Can't get what you want when you want it? Poor thing. Ashamed because you couldn't go the distance, you poor, failed priest?'

Soon, muffled sighs and groans of satisfaction began escaping from between her thighs, as she lowered her wet pussy onto his desperate lips. Mother Magdalene felt a jolt of electrically-charged pleasure surge through her whole body as his tongue probed greedily into every fold and crevice until she was writhing deliriously on top of him. Holding tight to his hair, she guided his mouth to her clitoris, almost suffocating him in her eagerness to reach orgasm. At last, Mother Magdalene looked down and feasted her eyes on Father Lionheart's buried head as her body exploded into a million tiny volts of pure, sexual energy. Wailing like a banshee, Mother Magdalene kept her throbbing pussy locked into place on Father Lionheart's mouth until the last tremor had fully subsided. She finally collapsed backwards with her head on his belly and her heels resting on the headboard so that her pussy was still just below his face.

Father Lionheart's wheezing gulps and gasps for air

made her laugh uproariously. 'Jesus, Mags, that's not funny. You nearly killed me.'

Mother Magdalene sat up quickly and slapped him hard again on the face before turning onto her belly. 'I'm not finished with you yet, so shut up, or you'll be saying prayers for mercy.'

Writhing snakelike down his body, she flicked at his semi-erect penis with the tip of her tongue until he began to stiffen. Her beautiful, round, white ass had been just inches from his face, and he moaned loudly as he tried to reach her inviting flesh. Settling for her inner thigh and the backs of her knees, he nipped her skin until she began to pant. She sucked harder on his thickening member and then slid the beautifully shaped head to the back of her throat and glided up and down, feeling the veins begin to stand out as the pressure mounted inexorably. As soon as she felt the first spasms of his orgasm, Mother Magdalene deftly backed away and gripped the base of his penis hard with her fingers, cutting off the flow of blood and semen and stopping his orgasm in its tracks.

Father Lionheart thrashed his head from side to side and cried out in desperation, 'Please, please! Enough! Let me come. I've told you I'm sorry. I've done everything you said. Please . . .'

His voice descended to a bare whimper as Mother Magdalene pulled a piece of knotted leather out of her pocket and tied it tightly around the base of his bulging cock and then nimbly bound his balls into a crushingly painful position. Her soft lips and darting tongue resumed their assault on his tender flesh. While his cock jerked in thrilled response, he flinched in acute pain as his bonds tightened. Her relentless mouth kept his excitement mounting and his erection hardening until he felt as though he was about to burst.

Looking down at his reddish-purple cock and his sweaty anguished face, Mother Magdalene crouched astride him and rested her wet cleft against his bulging head. 'Come on, Father Lionheart. You are Father Lionheart, aren't you? Go the distance. No gain without pain.'

Grunting with frustration, Father Lionheart managed to dig his heels into the bed, and straining against the cords at his wrists and ankles, he arched his back and thrust up into her. The pain was excruciating as the knotted cords dug into his swollen flesh, but he heaved a loud sigh of relief to be inside her at last. Mother Magdalene breathed in sharply as the coarse leather grazed against her soft pussy lips and tight vagina, but she lowered herself onto him and welcomed the stinging sensations burning through her. Gripping hard onto his nipples she twisted them viciously and ground herself against him, meeting his feverish glances with little cries of pain and delight.

Father Lionheart struggled harder against his bonds, loving the hot soreness as his wrists, ankles and cock all burned. Bucking like a crazed cowboy, he rode the crest of pain in his engorged, cruelly bound penis and mangled balls until finally, he found release. Yelling and roaring obscenities, he thrashed and writhed until Mother Magdalene had untied him and calmed him with soft kisses all over his face, eyes and lips.

'Ssh. There now. Don't cry out in the wilderness. I am always here for you. Shh.'

Father Lionheart opened his eyes, which looked huge and glittering in his flushed face. 'I'm crazy about you. You know that, don't you, Mags?'

Mother Magdalene smiled down at him serenely and smoothed the damp hair off his forehead. 'Of course I do. But we'd better straighten ourselves up. I promised that we'd lead a training session on how to derive satisfaction from supposedly selfless pleasure giving. It starts in about ten minutes.'

Father Lionheart groaned and pulled her into a tight embrace, breathing in the scent of her flesh and her hair.

'Only if I get to be the selfless giver and you my needy recipient.'

Mother Magdalene laughed and pulled free from his embrace. 'All right, you're on. Now straighten yourself out. You'll give the newest novices a heart attack if you go down like that.'

Glancing down at himself, Father Lionheart joined in her laughter as he observed his shrivelled penis covered in red welts and still loosely bound in the knotted leather like a Bavarian sausage. 'God, you're right. I'd better slap some salve on and pray for a miracle.'

Chapter Ten

Sister Gabriel paced the shiny wooden floor of the gym, twisting her hands and trying to slow her heartbeat. Had she done the right thing? Recruitment to The Order was always a delicate affair, but it was even more precarious when the new novice had a relationship with someone who had not been invited to join. Sister Gabriel thought of Savannah's beautiful but spoiled face and swallowed hard. It was too late to change anything now, and she knew that if there were going to be repercussions, she would just have to deal with them as they arose.

The door to the gym creaked open and her face broke into a smile of relief as she suddenly recalled why she had felt so utterly compelled to make this decision. Joseph stepped through the door looking uncomfortable in his novice's brown robes, but his face was lit by a smile of surprise as he took in the gleaming, state-of-the-art gym equipment and mirrored walls.

'Wow! This is impressive. It's better than the private club I go to, and that costs a fortune.'

Sister Gabriel relaxed and crossed the floor to meet him. 'Welcome, Joe. Believe me, there's a cost here too, but what that is only becomes apparent with time.'

Smiling warmly, she searched his handsome face and sparkling blue eyes, remembering why she had finally agreed to bring him here. There was a raw honesty about Joe that shone through his model looks and arrogant posturing. In her heart, she knew that this new Brother was going to be a great asset to The Order, not least because of his skills in promoting the body beautiful.

'I'll introduce you to your mentors in a while, Joe, but for now, I thought you'd like to familiarise yourself with the gym. Brother Darius will be along shortly to help you explore the more erotic possibilities, although I'm sure you'll have ideas of your own.'

Joe grinned impishly and wandered around the gym checking each piece of equipment thoroughly and occasionally pausing to admire his own blond, muscular reflection in the mirrored walls.

Sister Gabriel sighed. It was almost inevitable that Joe's vanity and arrogance were going to get him into trouble somewhere along the line, but she felt certain that he would work through his problems in time. Their meetings in London had revealed that despite his family's refusal to accept him and the Church's intolerance of his sexuality, Joe had remained essentially unspoiled and almost childlike in his enthusiasm for life. The apartment on The Strand had, as she suspected, been used to entertain paying male clients, but Joe refused to see himself as a cheap 'rent-boy' and he had already finely honed his skills as a male courtesan.

'A penny for them?' Joe broke into her thoughts and she found herself grinning openly.

'Actually, I was thinking about that night with Savannah. We never did discuss how it was for you, we were having too good a time ourselves.'

Joe sat straddling one of the low bench presses and ran his hands through his cropped hair. 'To be honest, I don't think you've managed a conversion or anything, but I had a whale of a time, and I reckon you've given me a bit of a taste for big-breasted, big-arsed women.'

'Hey!' Sister Gabriel swiped at him with a towel and sat down beside him. 'Less of the "big", please. How about "full" or "generous" or "voluptuous"?'

Joe nodded vigorously. 'Mmm. You're quite right. There's a lot to be said for the erotic possibilities in words. I wouldn't want to put someone off. I'll have to add that to my training.'

Sister Gabriel eyed him greedily. He really was a fine-looking young man but, while he was being mentored before initiation, he was out of bounds.

'Joe, how do you feel about being asked to explore your own capacity to give and receive pleasure with women? Once you're initiated you can pretty much do as you like but you are expected to try everything during your training. It's a way of stretching your own limitations.'

Joe sprang to his feet and began to pace up and down. 'Look, I'll do whatever is expected of me. I want to stay here. Everything you've told me makes me believe that I'll feel at home. You know I don't relish the idea of being with a woman. On the other hand, I'd kind of like to know that I could give pleasure to a woman if I wanted to, or if one really wanted or needed me. Does that make sense?'

Sister Gabriel gazed at Joe's earnest face and any last vestige of doubt about him vanished. 'Don't worry about it, Joe, you'll be fine. I have absolute faith in you.'

As Sister Gabriel gave Joe's hand an encouraging squeeze, the door banged open and a tall, powerfully built African man in a long, black robe strode into the gym.

'Good day to you, Sister. You are looking beautiful as ever. Hello, Joseph, I am Brother Darius, your lead mentor.'

He stretched out his long arm and offered his big hand to Joe, who was struck speechless. Whatever he had been expecting, it wasn't this. His family had hated blacks with the same intensity that they had hated homosexuals, so although Joe had often been attracted by a black man, he had always felt doubly dirty and had never given in to the urge. Brother Darius had dazzling white teeth and liquid black eyes. Joe felt weak, and a little scared. He cleared his throat and grasped the warm, strong hand firmly.

'I'm pleased to meet you, Brother. I hope you'll be able to help me get used to things.'

Sister Gabriel rose and smiled at the two attractive men. Poor Joe. He obviously hadn't paid attention during assessment when she'd told him about facing up to any blocks. All of Joe's secrets, fears and desires, that he had told to her over the weeks and months they had spent becoming friends, had been tucked away for future use. His training as a novice would take him into all the areas that he most feared to enter.

'I must leave you, Brothers. The other mentors are awaiting your call, Brother Darius. Good luck, Joe. Make me an instrument of your peace.'

'And I yours, Sister.' Joe swallowed hard as, in a flash of realisation, he saw that Brother Darius was the big, black man that he had always wanted, but was always too frightened to have. As Sister Gabriel reached the door, he called out, 'Thank you, Sister. By their deeds you shall know them.'

Sister Gabriel beamed back at him. 'All things come to those who wait, Joe. Give thanks to the Lord.' She slipped out, quietly closing the door behind her and leaving Joe watching Brother Darius with a glazed expression and a pounding heart.

'Why are you afraid of me?' Brother Darius's booming voice echoed around the gym, startling Joe out of his reverie. He jumped to his feet and paced the wooden floor.

'Look, I don't know what she's told you. But I don't want to be rushed into anything –'

'That's not an answer.' Brother Darius stepped in front of Joe and forced him to a halt. Joe's face was scrunched into a worried frown and he glanced from side to side in agitation rather than look into his mentor's eyes. 'Joseph. Please look at me.'

Joe felt the sweat break out on his brow as he raised his eyes to meet those of Brother Darius. His mentor towered over him by at least five inches and his body was powerfully built, but Joe began to see that his face was as open and friendly as a child's and not in the least threatening.

Brother Darius fixed his kind, sparkling, black eyes on Joe's and rested his hands on his shoulders. 'I want us to be friends. The good Sister speaks so highly of you. Don't hide your feelings from me.'

His broad smile lit up his dark features and Joe found himself feeling suddenly very young and vulnerable. Tears welled in his eyes and he angrily brushed them away, ashamed of this unexpected attack of emotion. Brother Darius took a step forward and enveloped Joe in his arms. 'Face your demons, Joe. They may turn out to be angels.'

Joe allowed himself to be held and comforted and, after a few moments struggling with conflicting emotions, he put on his bravest smile and said, 'I don't know what came over me. I'm sorry.'

Brother Darius looked serious for a moment. 'I think you do know, Joe, but there's no rush. Today, I just want to get a sense of who you are. Wait here. I'll fetch the others.'

As Brother Darius disappeared back through the gym door, Joe felt a pang of frustration and regret. The handsome, dark-skinned man could have stepped straight out of his dreams. Joe was reminded of the crushes he'd had on black athletes in his youth. His interest in sport and bodybuilding had sprung directly from his fascination for watching toned muscles rippling under oiled, ebony skin. Now, faced with the living embodiment of his deepest desires, he blushed with shame to think of his stammering behaviour and his outburst of tears.

'Here he is.' Brother Darius re-entered the gym followed by a slender young man with a cherubic face and reddish hair. 'Joseph, this is Brother Max and this is Sister Ruth.'

Joe looked past Brother Max's carrotty mop and saw a stunningly pretty, petite blonde with corkscrew curls escaping from her black veil. Joe felt slightly disappointed by these new mentors. Brother Max was too slim and plain for Joe's tastes and Sister Ruth, although beautiful, was small and curvy rather than voluptuous.

Brother Darius led the other mentors to one of the bench presses and they all sat down. 'Sister Maria has been unavoidably detained. We will begin without her and she will work with us a little later. Can you take off your clothes please, Joe?'

Joseph felt shocked at the sudden switch to a business-like tone in Brother Darius's voice, but he stood proudly and peeled off his robe and Lycra gym wear until he stood naked before his mentors. Brother Max examined him appreciatively.

'You're very beautiful. You must work out a lot.'

Before Joe could answer, Sister Ruth licked her pouting, red lips and said, 'Mmm. It would be nice to see you exercise, Joe. Will you show us how you use some of the equipment?'

Joe swallowed hard. 'Well, for safety and hygiene, I'd usually wear –'

'I don't think you should worry about that today.' Brother Darius cut through Joe's objections and waited expectantly. Joe searched each of his mentors' faces and saw that while they were friendly and open, they would brook no arguments. Feeling embarrassed, he climbed onto one of the cycling machines and began to pedal slowly.

'I use this to warm up,' he explained, gradually increasing his pace until his legs were pumping hard and a fine sheen of sweat glistened on his handsome face.

'How does it feel, Joe?' asked Sister Ruth, stepping in front of the machine.

Joe looked perplexed for a moment and then replied, 'It feels good. My body feels strong and my muscles are warming up.'

Brother Max joined Sister Ruth and stood at the other side of the machine, just an arm's length from Joe. 'Yes, but what about where you are sitting? How does that feel? Are you uncomfortable?'

'No,' panted Joe, 'I'm fine, but it's a bit hot and sweaty.'

He started to slow down, but Brother Darius called out, 'Don't stop, Joe. And remember, you are here to share everything about yourself. Don't hold back. Trust us.'

Joe leaned forward into racing position and pedalled furiously, as if he could escape the prying eyes and questions. Brother Max leaned towards him and whispered, 'What about the saddle rubbing on your arse, Joe? And your perineum, is that feeling the friction? How do your balls feel?'

Sweat was pouring down Joe's back and trickling through the sparse hair on his bulging pectorals. 'I – I get a rush out of the effort, the speed, sometimes the pain. Right now, my balls are a bit squashed, but they feel big and hot and good.' He started to pant. 'I can feel the muscles in my backside grinding against the saddle, there's no spare flesh on me anywhere. Except my cock, but I like the feeling of it slapping on my thigh.'

'Touch yourself, Joe.' Sister Ruth brushed his cheek with her lips as she added her whispers to those of Max on his other side.

'Yes, keep pedalling, but hold your cock, Joe. It's the only muscle we haven't seen in use yet.'

Joe felt a surge of anger at being told what to do, but he knew he had to go through this so, swallowing his pride, he let go of one handlebar and grasped his limp, but lengthy penis.

'Watch yourself in the mirror, Joe. You're beautiful,' called Brother Darius.

Joe let go of the other handlebar, raised his eyes and confronted his own naked image in the mirrored walls. His blonde, cropped hair was soaked with sweat and sticking up in all directions and his face looked haunted, but as his eyes travelled lower, he couldn't help enjoying the sight of the muscle definition in his chest and abdominals and the powerful pumping of his legs. The close proximity of his watching mentors, that had been so uncomfortable for him up until now, began to take on an erotic aspect, and he realised that he was getting turned on by being watched. Casting his mind back to the performances he had put on for some of his clients, he wondered why this seemed so much harder. He suspected that if there was not a payment involved then he felt that he was giving something of himself away rather than just doing a job.

He looked hard at himself in the mirror and glanced around at his mentors, who appeared to be watching greedily. He decided to give them something to look at. Leaning back so that his behind was pressed firmly into the saddle, Joe began to stroke his own body, rubbing his chest and belly with deep strokes. He cupped his balls in one hand and massaged the length of his cock with the other. The watching eyes were hot on his body and he felt the first twinges of pleasurable pressure in his thickening member.

'Tell us how it feels, Joe.'

Brother Darius was standing with his arm loosely around Brother Max's shoulder and Joe felt an electric jolt of lust course through his loins. Still pedalling furiously, Joe panted, 'My cock's feeling really hard now and my balls are swollen up. I feel like I'm going to ride myself down so hard onto this saddle that it will disappear up my arse.' His face was red and contorted and he seemed to hold his breath as he gripped his fully engorged cock tightly and rubbed jerkily up and down, just below the head. 'Electric shocks – in my cock, my balls, my belly. I'm filling up, like an air balloon. I'm going to explode. I'm coming!' Joe's pulsing cock sent great spurts of white jism shooting up and over the front of the cycling machine, splattering the mirrors in front of him.

Brother Max and Sister Ruth stood either side of him supporting him in a friendly hug, while Brother Darius stood in front of him and took Joe's face in his hands. 'That was beautiful. Thank you, Joe.'

He leaned forward and placed his thick, sensuous lips on Joe's astonished mouth and kissed him softly. Joe responded tentatively, but Brother Darius pulled away and seemed lost in contemplation.

'You know, Joe, I think you're too comfortable here. The gym's your home from home isn't it? I think we'll have to head over to the chapel shortly. Sister Maria has been making some preparations there.'

Joe felt slightly light-headed and a sick feeling began to twist his guts. 'Why the church? I mean, I'm not religious, Sister Gabriel knows that.'

Brother Darius exchanged glances with the other two mentors and guided Joe down off the exercise bike. 'Let me be the judge of that. Come on.' Sister Ruth towelled him off quickly and Brother Max tossed his robe to him.

Still feeling nauseous, Joe followed his mentors out of the gym and across the courtyard to the chapel. Although Joe had been inside briefly on his tour of the grounds, he could not recall any specific details. As a child he had loved going to church. The ritual, the robes and the intense concentration on ceremony had all appealed to him deeply. When he began to realise that the teachings of the church rejected people like him as aberrations, he started to hate going to Mass with a passion. His aversion to a whole hour in the sanctimonious and self-righteous atmosphere led him to feeling physically sick every time his parents made him go with them. He recalled the relief he had felt when he had finally broken away from them and left home. No more lectures, no more 'therapies', no more church. What was he doing here? Joe fought down the feelings of panic and accepted the offer of Brother Darius's hand as he hesitated on the threshold.

'Trust me, Joe. You weren't brought here to suffer, you know.' Brother Darius gave Joe one of his dazzling smiles and led him through the doorway and into the smoky chapel.

The walls were lined with flickering candles and the heady aroma of incense hung in the warm air. Near the altar, a tall, beautiful woman with waist-length brown hair under a short, black veil was standing with her hands together as if praying. A black leather mask concealed her eyes and her powerfully built body was encased in a tightly-laced black corset. Black fishnet stockings outlined the strong curves of her muscular thighs and her high-heeled lace up knee boots accentuated her already impressive height. On either side of her, heavy ropes hung down from fancy ironwork under the ceiling. Joe felt a shiver of fear and anticipation run through his body. Brother Darius led him up to the step before the chancel and indicated that he was to kneel before the woman.

'Joseph, this is Sister Maria, your fourth mentor. You would be wise to follow her instructions to the letter.'

Joe swallowed the bile rising in this throat. He hated bossy women. He had been sick of his mother and sister ruling the household, yet denying him the right to be one of the girls. Their determination to make a real man out of him had made him want to scream, 'I'm a poof! A queer! Leave me alone!' The woman before him looked terrifying, yet he wanted to resist her.

Brother Max and Sister Ruth had disappeared into the

sacristy and just as he was wondering what they could be doing, they reappeared, completely transformed. Cute little Sister Ruth was squeezed into a shiny, latex catsuit and thigh-length leather boots with vicious spiked heels. Her blonde curls were pulled into a tight ponytail on the top of her head and her eyes were ringed in black, menacing makeup. Brother Max, assuming it was he, was clad in head-to-toe black bondage gear with open zips, dangling chains and an assortment of odd, tool-like implements dangling from a low-slung belt. His feet were encased in heavy biker boots with steel studs and reinforced toecaps and he was pulling on thick, black, leather gauntlets. His whole head was encased in a black leather hood with slits for his eyes and nose and an open zipper at the mouth. Any last trace of anticipation Joe had been feeling vanished and was replaced by quaking fear. If they were out to frighten him, they had succeeded.

Brother Darius nodded to Sister Maria and strode away into the sacristy. Brother Max and Sister Ruth stood either side of Joe and gripped his arms firmly. Sister Maria spoke.

'It is important for you to know how to pleasure a woman. You will pleasure me. When you do it well, Brother Max will reward you. When you do not, Sister Ruth will punish you. Follow my instructions.'

Brother Max and Sister Ruth stripped Joe of his robe and forced him into a tight, thong-like contraption that pressed against his perineum and clamped the base of his penis in a tight grip, leaving his flaccid cock jutting out uncomfortably. A thin strip of leather was jammed between his buttocks and the whole affair was fastened with a tight silver chain around his waist. Brother Max produced two tiny silver dragons from one of his pockets and clamped them onto Joe's nipples. He winced in pain as the metallic teeth sank into his tender flesh, but he also felt a responsive twinge and his cock began to harden inside the tight leather ring.

The two mentors dragged him to his feet and supported him in front of Sister Maria.

'First, I want you to kiss my neck, my shoulders and the top of my breasts. Then I want you to take each of my breasts in turn and massage them gently while you lick and suck the nipples.'

Joe gazed at the magnificent woman before him and decided that resistance was probably futile, and that he had better throw himself into the task.

Sister Maria sighed as he swept his sensuous lips over her neck and collarbone, lingering on the nape of her neck so that he could breathe against the damp flesh where he had licked her. Moving around to her breasts he unlaced the bodice so that he could lift her heavy mounds free of the fabric and he kneaded the flesh rhythmically. 'Not so hard!' she snapped, pulling away from him.

Sister Ruth uncoiled a leather leash and whipped hard against Joe's bare arse cheeks. With his flesh smarting from the blows, Joe gingerly resumed stroking Sister Maria's breasts and bent his head to her nipples. They were beautiful, large and rose coloured and Joe revelled in circling them with his tongue and blowing on them until they began to harden. As they formed into cherry-like peaks, Joe clamped his lips around them and began to suck and nip until Sister Maria moaned in pleasure. Brother Max rewarded him by massaging some warm oil into his buttocks and over his swelling cock.

'Now,' panted Sister Maria, 'I want you to open the poppers on the crotch of this corset and then I want you to stroke my pussy and delicately examine each fold. After that you may explore with your tongue. Once you have accomplished this, I want you to concentrate on my clitoris. I like it licked with hard little flicks, not sucked. Begin.'

Joe's fingers shook slightly as he undid the fastenings and was faced with Sister Maria's bushy mound. Joe had never gone down on a woman before and he felt little stabs of apprehension hampering his movements as he fumbled with the press-studs. Breathing deeply, he calmed himself and fondled the bushy mass of pubic hair. It was surprisingly soft and pleasant to touch and Joe combed his fingers through until he managed to part the hair so that he could get a better look at her pussy. The outer lips were soft pink and slightly moist so Joe ran his fingers over them delicately and then prized them slightly apart. Sister Maria opened her legs a little wider and Joe sighed with relief to think he must be doing reasonably well. Once he could see clearly inside, Joe gently probed the deeper pink folds and pressed an exploratory finger inside her.

'Wet your finger, you're hurting me.' Once again, Sister Maria pulled away from Joe and he felt Sister Ruth grind the heel of her boot into his leg and lash his buttocks until they stung.

After dribbling spittle onto his finger, Joe touched Sister Maria's labia again and then slid his finger inside her. Her pussy was tight and hot and Joe felt a renewed flicker of arousal as her muscles clamped onto his probing finger. Using his other hand to part her plump lips, he scanned the alien flesh with his eyes, marvelling at the delicate, oyster-like appearance, while he located her pearl. With soft, sweeping strokes of his tongue, he lapped against her inner lips and over her clit. As her breathing began to sound laboured he homed in and probed it with the tip of his tongue.

He guessed that things were going really well when he felt Brother Max's leather gauntlet encircle his erection and begin to masturbate him strongly. Joe's balls were aching with the pressure of the leather straps and his cock was throbbing and pulsing. Inside Sister Maria, Joe could feel little ripples beginning to form and he gently began to move his finger in a circular motion. Sister Maria grabbed his hair and pressed her pelvis harder against his face. Joe could smell and feel tangy juices wetting his face and he felt his own excitement mounting, as the woman he was pleasuring became more and more responsive. Sister Maria's hips were gyrating and the pulses in her vagina were mounting into stronger spasms. Joe's own penis was throbbing fiercely, but he hung on, determined to give Sister Maria total satisfaction. Forming the end of his tongue into a hard point, Joe thought of her clit as a tiny shellfish that he had to winkle out and he stabbed and flicked until he could feel the hood draw back and the pearl grow larger. After a few more hard, rapid flicks, Joe felt his finger being clamped into a vice-like grip and Sister Maria's body jerked against him as she climaxed and groaned loudly. Joe rained soft kisses all over her beautiful pussy and soft thighs, relieved that he had been able to please her. As the last pulses subsided, Joe looked up to find Sister Maria unmasked and smiling down at him.

'Well done, Joe. That was perfect for me. All women differ of course, but if you are sensitive to their responses like you were with me, you will always be able to give them pleasure. Thank you.'

She grinned broadly and kissed him on each side of his face, like a dear friend.

Just as Joe was about to stand up and take the weight off his knees, Sister Ruth produced a piece of dark cloth and covered his eyes, leaving him feeling bewildered and disorientated. His senses felt heightened and he became acutely aware of his exposed cock, standing out in front of him, and already beginning to feel painful as the leather ring at the base tightened. His nipples were no longer feeling so sore and he could feel an enjoyable pulse running down from them to his stiffened penis. He listened intently, wondering what would happen next.

Rough hands pulled his arms back and tied his wrists together while another pair of hands pulled the silver chain around his waist tighter, yanking upwards so that the thin leather strip lodged itself tightly between his cheeks. The base ring felt as though it was cutting into his flesh, yet Joe found that the increase in his discomfort and the removal of his sight only intensified the sensations coursing through his body.

A rustle of robes from somewhere to his left was followed by Brother Darius's booming voice. 'Make a good confession, Joe. Tell us that which you would rather not tell. Confess your own darkest feelings. Confess how you have sinned against yourself. Begin.'

Joe searched around in his memory and recalled the right words. 'Bless me, Father, for I have sinned –' Joe paused for a moment and realised that reeling off a list of trite misdeeds was not what he was being asked for. He knew what his real sins were, he just had to have the courage to say them. In a tremulous voice, raw with honesty, he began.

'Bless me, Father, for I have sinned against myself by feeling shame about who I am. I have hated myself for being homosexual. I have sold my body rather than share free, loving sex with men.' Joe paused to consider what he had just said and, in a moment of self-revelation, continued in a whisper. 'I have hated men for wanting me. I have hated women for me not wanting them. I have sinned against myself because I have refused to allow myself to be happy and I have been eaten up with self-hatred. I am sorry I have wasted so much of my life feeling bitter.'

A tiny bell chimed three times and Joe smelled strong wafts of incense all around him. Brother Darius spoke again. 'Novice Brother Joseph, you have made a full and true confession and I believe that you are heartily sorry. I therefore absolve you from all your sins and bid you go in peace. Do you wish to share communion with me before you go?' Joe felt momentarily confused, but he nodded his agreement, opened his mouth and stuck out his tongue.

After a few moments of rustling, Joe realised with a shock that he had a huge, warm cock resting against his tongue. Surprised and delighted in equal measure, he explored greedily and then wrapped his lips around the neatly circumcised member. Sucking hard, Joe drew the beautiful, long cock deep into his throat and massaged its length with his lips as he enjoyed the silkiness sweeping up and down his mouth and throat. Behind him, deft fingers untied his hands, allowing him to reach up and stroke the long limbs before him and to explore the firm buttocks still encased in heavy robes. His blindfold fell away and Joe gazed up in mute adoration at Brother Darius's beautiful, smiling face. His ecclesiastic robes were tied clumsily up about his waist, leaving his fabulous cock and muscular legs bare. Joe worked his fingers into the thatch of wiry black hair on his hard flat abdomen and around his huge erection. Pulling his head back for a moment Joe stared at Brother Darius's massive cock. 'It's true what they say then, about black men's cocks?'

Brother Darius laughed loudly and plunged his meaty length back into Joe's eager mouth. 'No, it's only true about mine!'

Brother Max spanked Joe's quivering bottom rhythmically and increased the pressure in his rock-hard erection by massaging him in strong, rapid movements with the tough gauntlet. Joe could feel the pressure in himself mounting, but he strained to watch Brother Darius's handsome face contort in pleasure as he moved his mouth up and down his shaft, stabbing the head with little flicks of his tongue. The big man grabbed Joe's head and aimed himself deeply into his mouth, buttocks grinding backwards and forwards, lost in sensation.

Joe sucked with a vigour bordering on gluttony and moaned in ecstasy as he felt Brother Darius's orgasm explode into his mouth, leaving traces of hot semen spilling from his lips. Able to hold off no longer, he surrendered to his own violent orgasm and sent jism spurting through the air to land on Brother Darius's embroidered robes.

Brother Darius knelt before him and beamed. 'I look forward to getting to know you better. I think you are a man of many talents, no?'

Joe grinned back, unabashed. 'Make me an instrument of your peace, Brother.'

Eyeing him appreciatively, Brother Darius replied, 'And I yours, Brother.'

Chapter Eleven

*S*avannah sat in the dingy late night café sipping weak cappuccinos and half-heartedly scanning *The Stage*. At 3 a.m. Charing Cross looked seedy, rubbish-strewn and mostly deserted. Her fellow café-dwellers were an elderly, shabby man and a hopelessly drunk young couple holding each other up on their stools as they kissed each other wetly. Savannah turned back to her paper in disgust, wondering where that stupid boy had got to. Still putting out for his last greasy client, no doubt.

As she glanced up for the hundredth time to check the doorway opposite, she was rewarded by the sight of a fat middle-aged businessman being shown out by the youth she was seeking. Throwing down some coins for her last tepid drink, Savannah shot across the road and managed to get a foot through the door just as the boy was closing it.

'Hold up there, sunshine, I need to talk to you.'

The boy banged the door aggressively against her shoe and spat, 'Fuck off, you stupid tart. Get your foot out or I'll smash it for you.'

Savannah smirked into his face and pushed forward. 'If you don't want your skinny little arse locked up at the local nick for soliciting, you'd better let me in.'

The boy's face looked white in the glare of the street-lights as he released his hold on the door and grudgingly took a step backwards. 'What do you want?'

Savannah stepped in, shut the door behind her and looked him up and down with contempt. 'Obviously not you, love. Bit underage and underweight, aren't you?'

Banging his fist on the wall by her head, the boy flushed red. 'Don't you come here insulting me! At least my trade's honest. Not spouting cheap gossip about people you don't know and who wouldn't want to know you.'

Savannah laughed harshly and tossed back her silky mane of blonde tresses. 'Tut! Tut! Don't you like our little show? I thought you were Joe's friend. It's not nice to be rude about your friend's job, is it?'

The boy's lip curled in disgust. 'Well, if he liked it so much, why's he left then? Maybe he couldn't stomach working with you, especially after you and that fat so-called nun threw yourselves at him. Mind you, he liked her better, didn't he?'

Savannah's smile vanished and she caught the boy's shirt in her fist and dragged him up close. 'Don't get cocky with me, you little runt. You'll tell me where he is or I'll have the old bill round here before you can say rent boy.'

She slammed his bony frame against the wall and wiped her hands on her skirt. The boy straightened up shakily against the wall. 'I don't know where he is, honest. All I've got is a mobile number, for emergencies like.'

Savannah resumed her cat-like smirk. 'That'll do. Go and get it, there's a good boy. No, no, I won't come up. Thanks all the same.'

Shooting her a murderous look, the boy galloped up the stairs and was back in a flash with a scrap of paper. 'Don't tell him I gave it you. He's all right, is Joe.'

Savannah snatched the number from his hand and turned to open the door. 'Watch yourself, kiddo. All you've got going for you is your youth, and that'll be gone soon enough. Time you took up a computer course or something. Bye.'

Slamming the door behind her, Savannah strode out onto The Strand, tucked the number into her handbag with a self-satisfied pat, and hailed herself a cab.

It was late evening, and Joseph started guiltily as he felt the vibrate function of his mobile phone in the pocket of his robe. Excusing himself from the erotica study group in the library, he hurried along twisting corridors until he found himself in a secluded bay window. Peering outside and then up and down the corridor, he reassured himself that nobody was about and pulled out the tiny telephone.

'Hello?' Joe knew that probationer novices were not supposed to have any outside contact, but he felt that he must defy at least some of the rules. After all, he wasn't a slave.

'Joe, darling! It's like tracking down an incognito superstar. Why haven't you called me?' Savannah's brittle laughter grated on Joe's ears and he felt a gnawing annoyance with himself for having rebelled by bringing the phone.

'Where did you get this number?' he snapped, feeling vaguely threatened by Savannah's uncanny ability to find out whatever she wanted to know.

'Don't be cross, lover boy. You know I have my sources. So, are you being brainwashed? Do you need rescuing?'

Joe sighed in exasperation. 'Savannah, this number is for emergencies only, and no, I don't need help. I'm happy here.' He glanced about, anxious not to be heard.

'Come on, Joe. The least you can do is tell me all about it. I introduced you to Gabby, after all. Fair's fair. So are you in deep sexual training or something? Are you praying with your knickers off?'

Joe fought against his feelings of rage. 'Leave me alone, Savannah. I don't want to talk about it, not now anyway. Look, I'll call you some other time, yeah? I've got to go.'

Savannah brayed with laughter, forcing him to hold the phone away from his ear. 'Scared of being caught, are we? Naughty boy, Joe. You deserve a good spanking and I'm just the girl to give it to you. When can I see you?'

Joe rumpled his hair in frustration. He'd have to say something or she'd never leave him alone. He'd watched Savannah work and she was like a dog with a bone when she thought she was onto something. 'Listen, I've just got another couple of weeks to go and then I'll officially be Brother Joseph. We can celebrate then. I might be helping out at The Caddy Shack up in Waterloo for a while, so we could meet up then. Why don't I call you?'

Savannah's breathing sounded uncomfortably loud, but she quickly agreed. 'Sounds good to me. But don't let me down, will you, Joe? I hate being disappointed.'

Joe swallowed the bile in his throat. 'Don't worry, it would be good to see you. I'll be in touch. Gotta go, bye.'

He snapped the mobile shut and paced the corridor in agitation. How had she got the number? His mother had it, but Savannah wouldn't know where to start looking for her, and he had left it with Eamon, the boy along the landing at home – but like Dracula, he only came out at night. Joe cursed himself. He knew that breaches of security were treated seriously and that he should probably warn Mother Magdalene or Father Lionheart. Still, she only had his mobile number, and there was no chance she'd get any more information out of him, so there was no problem really, was there? Fearing rebukes or even rebuffs, Joe decided to say nothing, at least for the time being. Smoothing down his ruffled hair, he ambled back to the animated whispers and soft laughter in the library.

Joe found Brother Max sitting on a stool watching Brother Darius's long, powerful, naked body stretched over a leather-bound table peering at a large volume. Sister Maria was standing behind him wearing a puzzled expression and nothing else.

'Surely that's not possible?' she cried, lifting one of her legs up beside her ear.

'Here,' laughed Brother Darius, 'I think penetration is supposed to take place from behind, but side on, like this.'

He grasped Sister Maria's fleshy hips, pressed her raised leg up against his shoulder, and aimed his magnificent erection at her exposed pussy. Staggering, he fell away laughing. 'It's no use, I can't stand and deliver at this angle!'

Sister Maria supported herself on his chest as she eased her shapely leg back down and turned to Joe. 'Help us out, Joe. Do you think these poses are meant to be taken literally?'

Joe fought down pangs of jealousy as he observed the easy camaraderie his mentors had with each other. He would have liked Brother Darius to try Tantric poses with him, but since the session in the chapel, he had had no physical contact with Brother Darius at all. His practice sessions with Sister Ruth had gone amazingly well and he now felt confident that he could couple with a woman as easily as with a man, but he still wanted Brother Darius, desperately. Why provide him with a mentor who was the man of his dreams if he was never going to have him?

Abruptly, he made hurried excuses and fled from the library, hurrying along the narrow corridors in a blind rage.

* * *

'Stop right there.' Father Lionheart appeared out of nowhere and placed a restraining hand on Joe's chest. 'I'll take that telephone please, Joseph.' His voice was level and calm, but Joe could sense his anger by the tension showing in his face and body.

'Father, I know I've been foolish but –'

Father Lionheart snatched the phone and quickly scanned the stored numbers. 'Whose are these?'

Joe caught his breath and considered lying, but something in Father Lionheart's stern expression warned him against it. 'My mother, my neighbour in London and – and Savannah.'

Father Lionheart's face registered surprise and disbelief. 'Savannah? Are you aware that she was refused entry into The Order?'

Joe gulped and nodded, wishing the ground would open up and swallow him. 'She doesn't know where we are, Father, I promise you that. I haven't given her any information at all. I don't even know how she got the number.'

Father Lionheart eyed him with distaste. 'You are a surprise and a disappointment to me, Joe. We have already planned an early initiation for you, and I feel honour bound to go ahead with it, but you will be publicly punished for this at a later date. I have also received a complaint from the novice council that you are preying upon new recruits. Is that true?'

Joe felt his face burning with shame and prayed that he would not be threatened with expulsion. He loved living at The Priory and his self-confidence was increasing all the time. 'I'm sorry, Father, but yes, it is true. I've been letting the responsibility of being a senior novice and gym-instructor go to my head. I can't resist the flattery.'

Father Lionheart snorted contemptuously. 'Won't resist it, you mean. You will have to learn to curb your arrogance and selfishness. If you don't, you won't last here very long. Have I made myself clear?'

Joe quelled the shaky feeling in his stomach and gazed earnestly at the priest. 'I will learn to be better, Father. I give you my word.'

Father Lionheart looked hard at Joe for a few moments and then strode away, leaving Joe feeling like a whipped puppy.

Chapter Twelve

*B*rother Joseph patted a gym horse as he addressed his latest batch of novices: four females and two males.

'Now, I know some of you are keen on fitness and you probably associate the gym with somewhere to suffer. But it has other, pleasurable uses, and it is important to be sexually and sensually fit too. So, let's look at some less orthodox uses for all of this equipment.'

Smiling, he sat down on a footstool and looked at each member of the group in turn, allowing them a few moments for their appraisal of him. The novices saw a handsome, muscular young man in brown robes, whose regular features, short blonde hair and striking blue eyes were marred only by his somewhat arrogant expression.

'I am Brother Joseph. If you work with me, I can help you learn how to use this equipment to perfect your bodies and to improve your sexual techniques. I'll start with basic safety.' He slowly stood up and shrugged off his robe to reveal a beautifully toned body clad in a thin Lycra shorts suit. Several of the novices drew their breath in sharply as he effortlessly swung one of his legs up onto the gym horse and pointed at his foot. 'This is a trainer and these –' he smoothed his hands over his hips and buttocks '– are shorts.' The novices laughed at his exaggerated posturing.

Brother Joseph hid his smile as he flaunted himself in front of them. He knew that his studied indifference and Adonis-like looks always wound them up nicely for this early part of their training and, as his own narcissism had to be massaged from time to time, this was as good a way as any to get one hundred per cent attention. He swiftly took the group on a tour of the various pieces of equipment and demonstrated how gorgeous he looked on each of them. His muscular buttocks pumped up and down on the treadmill, his beautifully defined arms and shoulders bulged obligingly on the rowing machine, and his long, shapely thighs moved with the grace of a great cat on the cycling machine. By the time he had finished, he was not the only one to have worked up a sweat. Taking them onto each piece individually, he leaned against their shoulders, rubbed his arms against their bare skin and rested his hand on their thighs, until all of the novices were becoming increasingly eager for the next part of the lesson.

Brother Joseph glistened as tiny drops of perspiration rolled down his arms and chest. Unexpectedly, he broke into a cheeky grin. 'Well done. You've all got the basics now, and those of you who already use a gym have hopefully refreshed your memories, or even learned something new. Now.' He scanned the group appraisingly and began to peel off the Lycra body suit clinging to him like a second skin. 'It's time to find new ways of looking at this room, and to get to know each other a bit better. Everybody strip.'

There was a sudden outbreak of nervous giggles, but the novices began to disrobe as they feasted on Brother Joseph's leisurely striptease revealing glorious abdominal muscles and a limp, but sizeable shaft. One of the male novices groaned aloud as Brother Joseph bent down to untie his laces, affording them all an unrestricted view of his splayed cheeks and magnificent balls.

Looking coyly over his shoulder he laughed, 'You won't be needing trainers for the next bit. Get them off.'

Stretching upwards and massaging his neck he leaned against the gym horse and examined the new recruits. Both of the novice Brothers were over six feet tall, but neither of them, in Brother Joseph's opinion, had much else that was attractive about them. He skimmed over their untoned bodies and scholarly faces and dismissed them with a sniff. Two of the girls were fashionably thin – almost breastless – and one of them had the tall athletic form of a sportswoman. But it was the fourth woman in the group that Brother Joseph lingered on. Despite considering himself to be rampantly and dedicatedly homosexual, he had found that from time to time he had a predilection for a plump, fleshy woman. This novice had a plain, round face and her hair was dark, coarse and unstyled, but he found himself feeling aroused. Although she looked at least ten years older than the others and her thighs and buttocks were dimpled with fat, Brother Joseph felt a lustful twinge in his cock, making it jerk suddenly upwards. Greedily he ogled her heavy breasts and made a mental note to find an opportunity to play with them in private. Her beautiful fat arse, so white and round, would also be on his menu.

Dragging himself back to his present task, he poured oil onto each of their hands and asked the novices to form a circle with him, facing each other's backs. Deftly positioning himself behind the ripe novice's luscious curves, he instructed them all to massage the back of the person in front of them. He noted that the fairer of the two men in the group was behind the dark one, and the athletic young woman was behind him.

'All right, now what we want is just a gentle massage to relax each other.' Brother Joseph breathed deeply as he enjoyed the dual pleasure of feeling strong fingers kneading his back while his own hands were busily roaming over the ample form in front of him. Dragging his eyes away from her plump cheeks, he glanced towards the window where he had a fleeting glimpse of a dark face disappearing from view. Fighting the urge to scream at Darius's retreating form, he brusquely ordered the novices to turn about and massage the person behind them.

After a few minutes, Brother Joseph got the group to sit in a circle on the floor with their feet facing the centre. 'One at a time, you are going to sit in the middle and tell us one thing you don't like about your body. The rest of us are going to try and devise ways of making you feel better about it. OK, who's first?' When nobody volunteered, Brother Joseph looked at the pale, fair-haired male novice and nodded at him. 'Will you sit in the middle, please? Tell us your name and your problem area.'

The young man moved awkwardly to the centre and sat with his knees drawn up to his chin. His face was open and freckled with a snub nose and a big, generous mouth. Brother Joseph decided he was attractive after all, albeit in a Huckleberry Finn kind of way.

'Hello. I'm Jeremy. I don't like my chest – it's like a pigeon's.'

Brother Joseph nodded sympathetically. 'You've got a very slim frame, Jeremy, and you don't seem to have much muscle tone. But it's your posture that is giving you that sunken chest. You need to strengthen your back and shoulders so that your chest is expanded and supported. If you improve your overall fitness and work on your shoulders, you'll notice a dramatic improvement in a very short time.' He stood up and walked towards the rowing machines. 'Follow me.' Jeremy unfolded his gangly legs and shuffled after Brother Joseph. 'I'll show you how to use this, but I think you'll need an incentive. Are you into men, women, or both?'

Jeremy's anguished face turned pink and he coughed as he tried to answer. 'Both, actually.'

Brother Joseph got him to sit on the sliding seat and fit his feet into the footrests. 'Reach forward and take hold of the rowing handles.' Turning to the only other male he asked, 'What's your name, Brother?'

The second novice looked coldly at Brother Joseph and replied, 'I'm Peter.'

Brother Joe grinned, recognising a trace of homophobia in the new recruit. 'Peter the rock. It suits you. Time to soften up a bit, Peter. Come and crouch here.' He indicated the spot just behind Jeremy. 'When Jeremy pulls back, this seat will slide to here and he'll be leaning back. Against you. Each time he comes back, you will embrace him from behind, then let go as he pulls forward again. Do you understand?'

Peter's aristocratic face wrinkled in distaste as he angrily pushed his dark fringe away from his eyes. 'Whatever you say,' he snapped, and lowered himself into position behind Jeremy.

Brother Joseph noticed that for all his thinness and genteel manner, Peter's body was wiry and fit and he held himself with taut determination. As he sat down behind Jeremy, Brother Joseph could see the fine, developed muscles operating in his thighs and guessed that he must do some running.

'Remember that Jeremy feels bad about his chest, so I want you to stroke it and caress it lovingly each time you embrace him. OK, now who's going to sit at the front?' Brother Joseph saw Jeremy's eye's flicker towards the athletic girl, so he turned to her and asked, 'What about you?'

Smiling shyly, the dark-haired, handsome girl stepped forward and touched Jeremy's arm. 'I'm Bernadette. I'd like to help, if I may?'

Brother Joseph nodded his approval and looked admiringly at her impressive physique. 'You're in great shape, Bernadette, I'm sure you'll be able to point him in the right direction. Now, when Jeremy relaxes forward, I want you to reach out and slide your hands up his arms and onto his chest. Your breasts will be brushing against his forearms and your hands will caress his chest and his nipples. Hold him for a few seconds, and then push him away from you. OK?'

Bernadette nodded enthusiastically and knelt eagerly in front of the machine, smiling encouragingly at Jeremy. Brother Joseph led the other recruits to a couple of bench presses nearby and they sat down to watch.

'OK Jeremy, you've seen me use that machine, now let's see you.'

Jeremy leaned forward and twisted his grip on the handlebar until he felt comfortable. Bernadette ran her hands up his arms, allowing her breasts to trail against his flesh, and then kissed him gently on the cheek. She stroked his shoulders and chest and then tweaked his nipples hard. Shocked, Jeremy pulled away from her and slammed backwards into Peter who promptly wrapped his arms around him and held him tightly. Jeremy could feel the warm flesh of his companion pressed against his back and he sighed as Peter's strong hands explored his bony chest, making him want to sit up straighter. Without warning, Peter let go of him and he whizzed towards Bernadette's beautiful face and trim curves. Once again, she slid her hands up his arms and grasped his shoulders, this time, pulling his face towards her breasts. With a wrench, he felt himself being pushed away, but he pulled back eagerly, knowing that Peter's strong embrace awaited him at the other end. Brother Joseph watched carefully until he could see that all three novices were beginning to relish the task and then he called them back to the group. 'That will be enough for now. Come back and sit in the circle.'

The three flushed novices sat together and the rest of the group giggled at the size of Jeremy's erection. Brother Joseph laughed good-naturedly with the novices and said, 'I see at least one of Jeremy's muscles looks in peak condition.' Another gale of laughter rocked the group and Brother Joseph waited for it to subside before continuing. 'Thank you for your generous participation. Perhaps you three would like to make that exercise session a regular thing?' Brother Joseph enjoyed seeing the pink cheeks and eager nods of agreement. Even sourpuss Peter looked keen. 'Good. And remember, don't limit yourself to what I suggest. If you think of a good idea, something that will feel good or that's fun, then do it.' With a last, longing glance at the empty window, he addressed the group again. 'Right. Who's next?'

Part Four

Gospel

Chapter Thirteen

Golden light illuminated motes of dust in the tiny private changing room attached to the sacristy where Mother Magdalene was preparing herself for the evening ahead. Rails of white surplices and black robes lined one wall and a chaise longue was scattered with discarded undergarments. The air was thick with the tang of candle smoke and incense and Mother Magdalene added a pungent, lavender-scented candle to help her relax while she changed.

Just as she finished tugging a severe new habit over her unruly curls, the old Bakelite telephone began to ring shrilly. Snatching up the receiver, she began to brush her hair as she answered. 'Mother Magdalene, hello.'

Deep, raspy breathing sounded close to her ear. 'Is that the whore? You know what happened at Sodom and Gomorrah, don't you? All you whores and blasphemers will be turned into stone. But only after they've finished stoning you to death first. Handmaiden of the devil!'

Mother Magdalene felt shivers of fear working their way up her legs and her hand trembled as she fought to control her voice. 'Why are you doing this? Who are you?'

'Beware the Lord's vengeance, whore. I know where you are.' The sudden rattle as the caller hung up was replaced by a monotonous dialling tone.

Mother Magdalene replaced the receiver and sat down, resting her hands on her chest, where her heart was beating hard against her ribs. Weeks had passed since the last call and nothing untoward had happened. It was obvious that whoever was making these calls intended to frighten her but, so far, they had not acted upon any of the threats. What was it about the voice that was so familiar? It was almost impossible to tell if it was a woman or a man, and she could be certain that the voice was disguised, yet there was something about it – something gnawingly familiar.

Sighing in exasperation, she got to her feet and resumed her preparations. There was no point in worrying anyone else and, as she was the focus for this malicious campaign, she felt that it was her duty to deal with it.

At the old, free-standing mirror, Mother Magdalene added a last touch of gloss to her lips and hastily finished brushing her red-gold curls before donning a short veil. The tight corset under her habit made it a little difficult to breathe, but the thought of the coming event sent a thrill of anticipation through her. Thankfully, there were still a few hours to go and she concentrated on some deep breathing exercises to settle herself.

A soft tap preceded Brother Darius's handsome face, poking around the door. 'May I come in, Mother?' Mother Magdalene smiled warmly and invited him to enter. 'I'm sorry to come so close to the ceremony, Mother, but something is troubling me, and I need to know what to do.'

Mother Magdalene scanned his handsome face and wondered what could be upsetting him. Brother Darius had been with them from the early days, helping to establish the routine for The Priory and taking great care to see that novices were inducted sensitively. She waited patiently for him to go on. Sighing deeply, he began.

'I have always felt fulfilled in my duties here. I have enjoyed pleasuring myself, women, men – it didn't matter whom, as long as I felt they needed or wanted me. But now –' Brother Darius's darkly handsome face creased into a frown '– I think I am in love.'

Mother Magdalene reached forward and touched him on the arm. 'But that's wonderful. Why should that distress you?' She searched his anguished face and saw that he was struggling to communicate something. 'Take your time, Brother Darius.'

After a lengthy pause, he stumbled on. 'Brother Joseph came through his initiation with shining colours, didn't he?' She nodded, confused about where this could be going. 'He has a gift for making people feel special and for helping them believe that they are beautiful in their own way. But I don't think he ever loves anybody, not really.'

Mother Magdalene's face betrayed her astonishment. 'It's Brother Joseph that you are in love with? I'm sorry if I sound surprised, but I thought you were rather attached to Sister Maria.'

He shook his head like a nervy horse tormented by flies and waved his hand in front of her. 'No, not like that. Of course I like her a lot. I like many of the Sisters. But never before have I felt such a strong pull towards a man.'

Mother Magdalene regarded his distress with concern and continued to draw him out gently. 'So it worries you that you love a man, rather than a woman?'

Brother Darius sighed impatiently. 'No, not really. Where I come from it's quite common to fool around with boys before you marry, but this is different. Although there is no shame in having feelings for a boy, you are expected to move on as you mature. Anyway, I am past all of that now. I have chosen my own way. No,

I'm not upset about being in love with a man, I'm upset about being in love with this person, Brother Joseph.'

Mother Magdalene pressed her fingers to her lips and thought hard. 'Why is it a problem, Brother? There is no rule here that says, "thou shalt not love one another", is there?'

Brother Darius stood up abruptly and started to pace around the room. 'I'm just a toy, like a big, black man-doll for him to play with. Sister Gabriel knew that he had fantasies about men like me and she served me up to him on a plate. But I have not allowed him to realise his dream with me. I am not willing to be a token, black, sex toy for him.'

His usually sunny face was contorted in pain and Mother Magdalene swept across the floor and encircled him in her arms. 'Brother Darius, nobody ever intended you as some sort of gift for him. You were chosen as one of his mentors because we knew that he had deep-seated fears relating to his desire for men like you. We wanted him to get over that fear, and it seems he has. Whether you felt it was appropriate to indulge his fantasies was entirely up to you.' She caressed his face and searched his eyes, where tears were beginning to gather.

'But I want him, Mother. I want him with all my heart. I just can't bear his throwaway attitude. I don't want to be with him as anything less than his lover, but to him, I am nothing more than an itch to be scratched, so what's the point?'

Mother Magdalene hugged him hard, enjoying the feel of his heavily muscled torso against her breasts and thighs. 'How do you know that? Have you spoken to him?' Brother Darius shook his head mutely, looking dejected. Mother Magdalene caught his chin in her hand and forced him to meet her eyes. 'You are an incredibly beautiful and desirable man. No one would be capable of treating you as a disposable item. Nobody.' Her level gaze and sparkling blue-grey eyes steadied Brother Darius's nerves and he allowed himself to enjoy the feel of her beautiful, high breasts pressing into his ribcage. Her petite body was packed with luscious curves and her shining Irish face was a feast for the eyes.

'I must take the word of so beautiful a woman, Mother. I am letting the strain affect my good humour, no?'

Mother Magdalene lightly caressed his powerful arms and her cheeks dimpled prettily. 'It would be a terrible waste, Brother, if you were to let the strain affect anything else. To be honest, I've just had a bit of a shock and I've been feeling a little tense myself.'

He drew back from her slightly, clasping her slim waist in his big hands and smiling tentatively. 'Have you, now? That won't do, Mother. Can I be of any assistance? It would give me great pleasure to serve you.'

Mother Magdalene leaned back a little further and ground her pelvis against the growing bulge in his trousers, satisfying herself that he was becoming as aroused as she was. 'Oh, I think we could serve each other. As the good Lord said, "Come to me, all you who labour, and I will give you rest." I think we're both labouring under too much tension and it's time for a little light relief.'

Craning her neck and standing on tiptoes, she reached her arms around his neck and pulled his head down so that their lips could meet. His wide, full mouth enveloped hers, draining away all thoughts of the malicious caller and stirring feelings of lust in her loins. 'There's very little time,' she breathed, pulling away reluctantly, 'so forgive me if I seem hasty.'

With a swift movement, she unzipped his flies and grasped his beautiful, smooth-skinned erection in her tiny hand. Brother Darius grinned in appreciation as she lowered her red, pouting lips and sucked the bulbous, shiny head. Reaching over her back, he began to hitch up the folds of her habit until her shapely, stockinged legs and waspish corset sparked an appreciative glint in his eye. Pulling her back up into a standing position he kissed her deeply and slid two, long fingers inside the crotch of her corset. He stroked her until she began to moan with pleasure and then hoisted her up and wrapped her legs around his waist.

Clasping his handsome face to her chest, Mother Magdalene wriggled and twisted until she could feel his hot, thick cock forcing the tight fabric out of the way and plunging inside her. Brother Darius stood up straight and gripped her hips firmly in his big, strong hands, then began to pump rhythmically until she started to moan, 'Yes, yes!' like a mantra, oblivious of the loud bangs as her back and bottom crashed against the wood-panelled wall. Brother Darius marvelled at the joyful abandon on her face, and felt his own passion intensifying. His cock felt like a rod of iron and Mother Magdalene's beautiful pussy was swallowing him with the strong, controlled spasms of a snake with its prey.

She wrapped her arms tightly around his neck and lifted herself clear of his erection, locking eyes with him as they both struggled to control their breathing. Their lips touched softly and, as they began to explore each other's mouths with their tongues, Mother Magdalene slowly sank down, inch by inch, onto Brother Darius's pulsing cock. All of the tension they had been feeling was focused within this hot, tight embrace and, with a few more slow, deliberate strokes, they both shivered with delight as their strained bodies found release.

Withdrawing from Mother Magdalene's sensual kiss, Brother Darius smiled in wonderment as he watched her beautiful face quivering in post-orgasmic bliss. 'May blessings be heaped upon you, Mother. A friend in need is a friend indeed, no?'

Mother Magdalene laughed breathlessly and squeezed him with her thighs. 'Oh yes! I've always believed that this is what friends are for. Besides, a problem shared is a problem halved.'

Brother Darius grinned back at her. 'Wait, I've got another one – share and share alike.'

Mother Magdalene groaned and slapped him lightly on the shoulder. 'Enough. We've got work to do, so put me down.'

Brother Darius reluctantly placed her back on her feet and turned to leave. 'There was one more thing, Mother.'

Mother Magdalene looked up from wiping herself and smoothing her clothes back into place. 'What is it?'

Brother Darius looked serious again as he rested briefly against the doorway. 'It's about the ceremony today. I don't want to come. I can't watch Brother Joseph go through that ordeal. Not now.'

Mother Magdalene nodded sympathetically. 'All right, Brother, you may not attend if that is your wish, but there is a condition.'

He moved back towards her looking nervous. 'A condition?'

Mother Magdalene nodded again, face thoughtful and stern. 'Yes, I believe you must talk to Brother Joseph at the earliest opportunity about your feelings for him and about the ideas you have about his attitude to you. I want your word.'

Brother Darius's broad shoulders slumped and his handsome face creased in pain. 'I can't do that, Mother. Please don't ask me.' His eyes widened in anguish and he held his hands out, palms up, towards her.

'I do ask you, and I do insist. Give me your word.'

He rubbed his hands over his face and sighed deeply. 'All right. You have my word.' Without pausing to see her warm smile of approval, he swept from the room, closing the door firmly behind him.

Savannah sighed with relief as she heard the words 'That's a wrap, everyone!' and left the stuffy little studio without pausing for the usual chit-chat. Filming sequences for late-night shows on gloomy afternoons like this one made her feel disorientated and out of sorts.

XTV was still in its infancy, and Savannah longed for the comforts of being a celebrity, rather than an anchor girl for a series of post-watershed, tacky cable shows. Her high point in the week was the ten-minute Hot Gossip slot, when she presented her own round-up of the week's celebrity news and scandal. If she was lucky, she managed to get a small-time actor, model or washed up pop-celebrity trying to re-launch their career to join her for a brief chat, but she was bitterly aware that her guests reflected her own status.

In the taxi on the way home she seethed with frustration as she ferreted around in her mind for ways to advance her career. She was beautiful, she was an adequate presenter and she had good ideas for potentially successful shows, so why couldn't she break through to the next level?

At home, she kicked off her shoes, grabbed a bottle of chilled wine and a glass and slumped onto the sofa with a sigh. After a couple of generous glasses, she made herself more comfortable and reached down for her laptop. Quickly skimming through files of ideas, half-written scripts and endless snippets of gossip, she came to a file entitled *Holy Smoke?* and opened it. Scrolling down through the names of the people she had known who seemed to have been involved in setting up The Order, she wondered what they were all up to right now. She let her eyes jump across the questions in bold type that still tormented her. What is their philosophy, if they have one? Where is The Priory and what goes on there? Why be so secretive about it? Why hadn't they asked her to join? She realised with a jolt that this last question was the one that drove her to keep scratching away at the wall of silence. At heart, she knew that she was mostly suffering from a bad case of 'I didn't-get-invited-to-the-party', and she missed those hedonistic days when she had gorged herself on the pick of Richard's latest friends. Nonetheless, the whole thing was intriguing, and the more they insisted on keeping her out, the more determined she was becoming to find a way in. Besides, if there was anything really juicy going on, it would make one hell of a story.

Chapter Fourteen

*T*he pungent smell of incense hung heavily in the crowded chapel, making Susanna feel light headed. Her skin itched where the novice's garb of starched collar and scratchy, grey serge rubbed against her, but her heart was bursting with pride to think she'd finally made it. At forty, she felt far more mature and worldly wise than a lot of the other novices, yet here she was, heart in mouth, terrified of making a fool of herself during her initiation. On either side of her were the two Brothers and two Sisters who had been responsible for her intense training and who had recommended her for ordination as a Sister. She shivered as she realised that soon she would have to show the whole assembled community what she had learned. Thankfully, it was not her turn yet and she could enjoy the surreptitious thrill of watching and listening to others, a private vice she preferred not to talk about.

Near the altar, Father Lionheart was publicly chastising the new Brother who had failed to follow orders. Brother Joseph was bent over the altar rail with his robes hitched up to reveal his muscular bare buttocks. Mother Magdalene and Sister Gabriel held his arms out across the rail so that his face was squashed against the carved

126

wood and two novice Brothers knelt on the floor gripping his ankles and spread-eagling his tanned legs. Father Lionheart swept forward in a long, black soutane and lashed the exposed flesh with the heavy rope from around his waist.

'Repeat after me, Father forgive me for my weakness and my vanity.'

He rained heavy blows on Brother Joseph's flesh in rapid succession until his cries were ringing through the chapel, but Brother Joseph did not repeat the words. Merciless, Father Lionheart splashed water from a chalice over the seared flesh and then proceeded to lash harder.

Susanna felt a thrill as she recalled her own discipline sessions with Father Lionheart, but this was different. Minor misdemeanours, especially when they involved being overly eager sexually, were rewarded with tantalising confessions and penances with the good Father. But flouting the rules or treating The Order with disrespect was another matter entirely. Susanna began to squirm as Brother Joseph's cries grew louder and his flesh grew red and swollen. She wished fervently that he would stop struggling and submit to the beating with humility, but she also found herself twisting in her seat as lustful twinges of desire moistened her habit through her new crotchless panties.

Father Lionheart aimed the rope so that it lashed between Brother Joseph's buttocks and stung his balls. 'The pleasure and the pain. Say it. Welcome it.'

Weeping, Brother Joseph cried out, 'The pleasure and the pain!'

Satisfied, Father Lionheart nodded to Mother Magdalene and Sister Gabriel and they released their hold on Brother Joseph's arms. The two novices supported him back to the pews and lowered him gently onto his knees.

Mother Magdalene stepped forward and took Sister Gabriel by the hand. 'I want all of you to support Brother Joseph in overcoming his insubordination. There is no shame in his chastisement. His pain is our pain. We are here to heal each other. Now, let us move on and share in celebrating the achievements of some of our Sisters and Brothers.'

Sister Gabriel beamed at the assembled throng and squeezed her friend's hand. 'I want to congratulate two of our lay Brothers for their wonderful efforts in their own environment, the city business sphere. Will field workers Brother Roland and Brother Geoff come up here please?'

There was an affectionate bout of backslapping and good-natured teasing as the two friends made their way through the crowd. Roland and Geoff grinned at each other as they stepped up onto the altar, almost tripping on their long robes. Sister Gabrielle continued, 'In feedback sessions with Mother Magdalene and myself, it has become apparent that these two Brothers have a gift for noticing who is needy around them, and then throwing themselves into their work with admirable dedication!' Laughter rippled through the assembly.

Mother Magdalene quietened the crowd and said, 'Let us not forget why we are here. All we have ever aimed to do was to make sure that we could enjoy good, guilt-free sex and share it with others. These two young men have become wonderfully adept sexual practitioners and have been sharing their skills with loving abandon. Now, who would like to give them their reward?'

With great haste, Brothers and Sisters detached themselves from the crowd and made their way to the front. Twenty or more volunteers gazed hopefully at the two handsome young men at the altar. Sister Gabriel led them forward and invited them to choose. 'Brother Roland and Brother Geoff, will you allow some of these volunteers to pleasure you here, today?'

As one, they moved along the row of Brothers and Sisters, glancing at each other for approval as they made their selections. By the time they had examined them all, they had chosen five: four beautiful young women and one tall, sober-looking man in priest's clothing. Roland whispered something to Father Lionheart, who nodded his approval and watched with a smile as Roland stepped down into the pews. Pushing his way along, he reached the spot where Brother Joseph knelt, head bowed. 'Brother, would you join us? I really want you.'

Brother Joseph's troubled, handsome face looked up at Roland's dark, honest eyes, and he rose from the pew, wiping away his tears. 'I'd be honoured.'

A hush fell over the assembled community as the six volunteers talked quietly with Roland and Geoff about what they wanted for their reward. Two of the Sisters disappeared into the sacristy as Brother Joseph and the priest, Father Guillory, brought out long ropes and candles. Father Guillory was unusually tall for a Spaniard, but his narrow face and black eyes seemed to hold echoes of the Inquisition. He deftly fixed the ropes to some attachments already in place on the ornate metalwork above the chancel and secured them with professional-looking knots. Brother Joseph stripped Roland and Geoff of their robes while Sisters Ruth and Clare, two of the youngest, prettiest girls in The Order, began to massage their skin with warm, scented oils. The Sisters hitched up their habits at the front and tucked them into their belts so that an expanse of shapely, stockinged leg and pale, inner thigh was visible.

At a signal from Father Guillory, the two men were led to the centre of the chancel and Geoff was tied standing up, with his arms and legs spread-eagled, facing the community. When he was securely in place, Father Guillory wound and knotted more ropes so that they tightly criss-crossed his chest and waist. Next to him, Roland was strapped into a sling-like body harness and attached to a strong winch rope which was looped through a sturdy-looking ring. When Father Guillory tested his handiwork by drawing down hard on one of the ropes, Roland was hoisted into the air and left hanging in a half-sitting position, a little above waist height, like a baby in a sling.

Sisters Cecilia and Maria, tall, voluptuous women with a wealth of experience between them, re-entered from the sacristy wearing altar boys' white surplices over bare bottoms and legs. Both women had statuesque bodies, but where Sister Cecilia looked pale and ethereal, Sister Maria's dark olive skin shone in the candlelight and contrasted starkly with the snow-white linen surplice. Removing their veils so that their long dark hair was hanging loose and uncovered, they picked up fat white altar candles, which were burning smokily, and went and stood before each of the tied men.

Brother Joseph took one of the candles and positioned himself behind Roland's dangling form while gentle Sister Cecilia poured hot wax onto his bare thighs and abdomen and then brushed his scorched flesh with her long silky hair. Sister Ruth, his third 'reward-giver', smiled girlishly, blonde curls escaping from her wimple, and puckered up her rosy lips to kiss his neck, shoulders, armpits and nipples. Roland groaned in ecstasy, loving the intoxicating combination of caresses and pain. As Sister Cecilia smiled serenely and splashed more wax onto his chest and nipples, Sister Ruth pushed his thighs apart and began to lap at his swollen balls. Behind him, Brother Joseph kissed the nape of his neck and continued to pour hot streams of molten wax down over his neck and shoulders. Roland writhed and twisted as the burning and kissing continued relentlessly.

Turned on by Roland's obvious cries of pleasure, Geoff dragged his eyes away from his friend and watched Sister Maria pull down the front of her surplice and bare her full, firm breasts for him, pressing his face into them. He inhaled the warm, exotic aroma of her skin and nuzzled hungrily on her spicy flesh, marvelling at her Amazonian proportions. Petite Sister Clare knelt on the floor in front of him, smiling shyly and massaging oil into his legs and calves and then reaching up to stroke his balls and buttocks. Pressing against his back, Father Guillory used his long strong fingers to knead Geoff's arms and shoulders and then deeply massage his outstreched arms and thighs. Geoff felt waves of desire ripple through him as one of Father Guillory's strong hands reach around his slim waist to stroke his erect penis. He moaned loudly when Sister Clare joined Father Guillory's hand and clamped her soft lips around the swollen head and began to suck hard on his throbbing flesh. Sister Maria's beautiful face creased into a mischievous grin as she rubbed her breasts down over his smooth chest and then bent her head to his tender nipples.

Geoff jerked against the tight ropes as he felt hot stabs of pleasure and fierce pangs of increased desire. He leaned back and whispered to Father Guillory, who smiled fleetingly, and then came around to join Sister Maria in front of Geoff. Nodding her assent, she turned sideways so that both Geoff and the watching assembly had a clear view. She allowed Father Guillory to bend her over at the waist so that the white surplice rode up, revealing her juicy bare bottom. Smoothing back his damp black hair, Father Guillory loosened his dog collar and licked his thin patrician lips. Standing close behind Sister Maria's supple form, he rubbed his oily hands over her exposed buttocks and then unzipped the flies in his tight black pants. There was an audible intake of breath as his enormous, magenta cock sprang free and rested against Sister Maria's firm, peachy bottom. Behind them, Geoff's face displayed naked hunger as he savoured the scene before him, while jerking like a puppet on a string, with his cock lodged firmly in Sister Clare's ripe mouth. Father Guillory slathered more oil between Sister Maria's splayed cheeks and over the huge bell-shaped head of his massive penis and then, gripping her hips firmly, he began to press himself deep inside her. Geoff tore his eyes away for a second from the fantastic sight before him and glanced at Roland to see if he was watching this too.

Roland's eyes glittered feverishly in the candlelight as he drank in Sister Maria's voluptuous bottom and Father Guillory's plunging cock. At his rear, Brother Joseph had switched from candle wax to warm oil and had lowered him down a little and lengthened the suspending rope so that Roland's exposed buttocks were hovering just in front of Brother Joseph's erect cock. Roland felt himself being swivelled around so that Sister Ruth could simultaneously gorge herself on his fat, throbbing dick, taking him deep down into her throat and then driving him wild with alternate sucking and licking. He glanced hungrily back and forward between her mouth and Father Guillory's greedy cock sinking deeper into Sister Maria's beautiful behind. He began to wriggle and twist desperately with a fire raging in his own arse until Brother Joseph finally pulled him slowly back onto his hot, stiff erection. Roland groaned loudly with relief. His eyes, his arse and his cock were all on fire, and he was loving it.

Geoff swivelled his eyes back away from his friend and returned to watching Father Guillory's iron-hard body ramming against Sister Maria. At a signal from Geoff, Sister Clare moved back out of the way and watched the slim, muscular Father Guillory effortlessly grab Sister Maria under her thighs and hoist her, still impaled on his cock, up and around onto Geoff's waiting erection. The two men locked eyes as they both penetrated the beautiful woman between them. As Sister Maria began to pant loudly and toss her mane of dark tresses into their faces, they slowed themselves down until their cocks were rhythmically stroking her inside and out. Sister Clare wove from side to side, latching onto her nipples and rolling them between her teeth until Sister Maria cried out hoarsely to be touched. Sister Clare poured a generous amount of oil onto her hand then reached down and wedged her fingers between Sister Maria's legs. As Geoff and Father Guillory increased their pace so that Sister Maria was rocked once more between them, Sister Clare increased the pressure on Sister Maria's clitoris until she cried out with pleasure. Stifling her cries with a deep kiss, Sister Clare expertly continued fingering her raw flesh and then reached down under her own habit with her free hand to pleasure herself. Breaking free of the kiss, Sister Maria threw back her head and screeched in delight as her three lovers brought her to a shuddering climax. Both men continued to pump furiously for a few moments until they came, almost simultaneously, and collapsed against her. Geoff craned his neck forward and planted a grateful kiss full on Sister Maria's smiling lips then whooped wildly with joy.

Roland listened to his friend's cries of pleasure and finally relaxed into Brother Joseph's embrace. He loved the feeling of having a long hard cock thrusting deeply into him at the same time as Sister Ruth's sweet juicy mouth was driving him further into wild abandon. 'I love it!' he moaned, 'I love it!' Sister Cecilia nibbled on his nipples giving him sharp shocks of pleasure and deftly stroked his perineum and balls until the pressure building inside him exploded into a kaleidoscope of delicious sensations. Brother Joseph pumped energetically, jerking Roland's flesh against his harness and forcing his cock even deeper into Sister Ruth's sweet, moist mouth. As he approached his climax she pulled him clear of her lips and squashed his tumescent cock between her pert breasts while Sister Cecilia bit down hard on his electrified nipples. Feeling his cheeks slapping hard back against Brother Joseph, he groaned loudly and spurted hot, white jets of come over Sister Ruth's breasts, face and veil, shuddering in delight as Brother Joseph jerked deep inside him.

He lay still, concentrating on the heady combination of sensations coursing through his body, from his nipples, to his cock, and into his anus. 'Thank you,' he panted. 'Thank you so much.' Brother Joseph gently unhooked and unstrapped him, and slipped his robe back over his head, while Father Guillory loosened the knots binding Geoff.

When both men were fully clad, their volunteers solemnly kissed them in turn, murmuring, 'Go in peace,' before returning to their seats, eyes shining with pleasure. Mother Magdalene and Sister Gabriel hugged them both warmly as Father Lionheart thanked them for sharing themselves so freely with the community. Roland and Geoff grinned at each other's sweating faces and glittering eyes.

'No thanks are due, Father,' said Roland, 'except perhaps to the volunteers. We feel blessed. Truly.'

'Yes, bless you all,' beamed Geoff. 'It was absolutely marvellous!'

Chapter Fifteen

*T*he angle-poise lamp cast a small, circular pool of light onto the untidy desk where Savannah sat tapping her nails. An empty wine bottle lay on the floor by the sofa and a second one was half empty beside her. She shuffled bits of paper with phone numbers and addresses as her mind busily tried to make sense of all the snippets of information she had managed to glean about The Order, but they didn't amount to much.

On the surface, The Order had a squeaky-clean image doing good works among the homeless. It was common knowledge that there was a quasi-religious aspect to the 'cult' behind the charitable organisation, but like so many other vaguely mysterious groups, there was no hard evidence to support rumours of mind-bending practices or sexual shenanigans. Sensibly, The Order had simply got on with its good works, stayed quiet, and waited for the attention to wane, which of course it did.

Savannah nibbled at a bit of dry cuticle and wondered how she could find out more. Richard's sexy parties had been legendary and Margaret had slipped into the debauched goings-on with seeming abandon, so why had they gone underground? Leaked or rumoured stories about some of the members' lurid pasts had only served to plant the idea that they were now making up for it by being holier-than-thou. She realised with a twinge that she still missed the delicious freedom she had felt with Richard and his friends; particularly the spectacular choice of gorgeous girls to turn on to female fun. With a sigh, she remembered how sweet and lovely Margaret had been the first time. What a shame they had not been able to explore all the possibilities together before Mags had vanished into the hidden recesses of The Order. And what about Gabby? Sister Gabriel, who was now playing harder and harder to get. What a waste.

Savannah gulped down the last of her wine and allowed her mind to play with the idea of a threesome, with her in the middle. She slipped her shoes off, lifted her feet onto the table and probed inside her panties with a well-licked finger. How delicious to be sandwiched between Margaret's peaches-and-cream skin and red curls and Gabby's chocolate-delight flesh and gypsy eyes. Savannah arched her back and plunged her finger deep inside herself, enjoying the warm sticky juices trailing down her hand. Imagining Margaret's rosebud lips sucking greedily on her, she tugged her skirt higher over her hips and used her other hand to gently massage her silky pubic hair and her swollen pussy lips. Lost in visions of Gabby's wicked grin, voluptuous breasts and edible bottom, Savannah substituted her own finger for Margaret's mouth on her greedy clitoris and rapidly brought herself to an intense but unfulfilling climax.

Reaching for a box of tissues to wipe her hands, Savannah had a sudden flash of inspiration. Gabby had continued to meet up with her for fun and frolics at first, but now she seemed more interested in boring coffees and chats. So what was she doing for fun now? There wasn't a chance in hell that a woman with her sex drive was going without, yet Savannah's usual saucy suggestions had been turned down flat . . . except for helping

Joe with his little experiment. Wasn't that what seemed to turn Gabby and her pals on – helping the needy?

Savannah pinched the bridge of her nose in an attempt to lessen her growing headache. There must be a way to glean more information about how The Order operated. Was there another member of The Order she could target? Savannah banged her head on the desk in frustration. No immediate plan presented itself, but meanwhile she decided to keep a closer watch on Sister Gabriel's movements in London. Who did she meet? Where did she go?

Savannah sighed as she acknowledged that her own bit-part late night TV job and her scrappy pieces of journalism were not enough to keep her occupied. Nor was she satisfied with how her life was turning out on any level. She might look like a dumb blonde, but underneath there was a fairly bright brunette, heavily disguised with make-up and hair bleach, waiting to get out. Glancing down at her golden locks she thought, 'Well, maybe not the hair, but the bright bit sounds good.'

For once, she was going to pursue an idea to its logical conclusion. So, The Order didn't think she should be allowed in? Then she'd get in through the back door and, if necessary, drag them all out.

Less than two miles away, Angela crushed out a cigarette and wiped away the last trace of semen from her face with the back of her hand. She looked down at the tumbled heap of bodies, all strangers, and wondered why she did this. Feeling physically sick, she staggered to the bathroom and held a cold cloth against the bruised, seared flesh of her bottom then gulped water greedily from the tap. As she crept back into the littered room, she saw with satisfaction that the men and women out cold from too much dope and exertion had more than their share of similar welts and swellings. Cold comfort, but better than nothing.

Quietly pulling on her clothes and gathering her things, she checked her watch and sighed. College again tomorrow, with no sleep to speak of, and total satisfaction always another night away. Angela wondered sardonically what on earth a mere counsellor was supposed to do for her, but she was counting the weeks, waiting for an appointment and, despite her cynicism, praying for a miracle.

Chapter Sixteen

*S*usanna swallowed hard as the two smiling men, Roland and Geoff, made their way back into the pews. Her breasts were swollen and her hard nipples ached in the confines of her peephole bra. There was a soggy patch where she was sitting and she could feel beads of perspiration on her upper lip. She felt perilously close to orgasm, but she needed to focus on her initiation, where she would be expected to demonstrate her ability to pleasure others.

Mother Magdalene and Sister Gabriel were murmuring in low voices with Father Lionheart, and then they turned and smiled at Susanna. This was it. Susanna's initiation was scheduled to take place after the reward ceremony, but as she glanced to her left her mentors, Brother John and Brother Daniel, were talking in hushed tones, occasionally glancing at her and breaking into knowing grins. What was going on? On her other side, the remaining members of her team, Sister Martha and Sister Benedict, had risen to their feet and were motioning for her to join them. Smoothing down her habit and taking deep breaths, she fell in behind them.

The two Brothers followed behind her as they all approached the chancel, where Mother Magdalene stepped forward to greet her. 'Dear Susanna. Don't look so anxious – we won't bite.'

Father Lionheart smiled warmly at her then turned to address the assembly. 'As you all know, the initiation of a new Brother or Sister would usually be performed by her mentors. Sisters Martha and Benedict and Brothers Daniel and John are to be commended for their exemplary work with Susanna. However, in view of their great praise and heartfelt recommendations for this particular novice, we have decided to initiate her ourselves.'

Susanna felt her heart lurch as excited babbling broke out among the watchers. Father Lionheart raised his hand. 'Please be quiet. In honour of this auspicious day in the biblical calendar and the truly giving nature of this young woman, by the end of this ceremony we will be welcoming the new Sister Assumpta into our midst.'

Susanna felt as if her bowels had turned to water, but she smiled bravely and stepped forward to receive the new black wimple in Mother Magdalene's hands.

'Sister Gabriel, can you help her with her robes?'

Sister Gabriel approached her and turned briefly to address the assembly. 'Please offer up all your love and prayers for this lovely woman you see before you. As I strip away her noviciate garments, so too will I strip away her old name and her old life. Farewell, Susanna.'

The voices of the community began to chant, 'Farewell, Susanna, farewell, Susanna . . .' as Sister Gabriel unbuttoned the simple grey tunic covering Susanna's Rubenesque body. A cheer of approval greeted her disrobed curves clad in black PVC split-crotch knickers and conical peephole bra, through which her large brown nipples protruded invitingly. Sheer black hold-up stockings defined the roundness of her calves and slim ankles, while the smooth, plump roll of white flesh spilling over her stocking tops looked like a creamy, meringue confection. Tottering on her four-inch stilettos, Susanna followed Sister Gabriel to the centre of the chancel where Mother Magdalene removed her plain grey veil and unpinned her characteristic bun. Multiple gasps and intakes of breath heralded the release of what seemed like yards of silky brown hair, sweeping down over Susanna's voluptuous bosom and brushing the backs of her knees. No one in the assembled crowd had ever seen it loose before, but Mother Magdalene produced an elegant, silver, bristle brush and began to groom the silky tresses with long, sensuous strokes. Susanna felt tingles creep up from her roots and scalp and down along her spine as the brush tugged gently against her hair, but she blushed furiously when she confronted all the eager eyes trained on her.

Father Lionheart reappeared from the sacristy resplendent in his ceremonial robes of heavy ivory silk and gold embroidery. Susanna felt a pang in her exposed nipples as he approached, swinging an ornate incense holder and intoning, 'Make me an instrument of your peace.'

The assembly took up the chant and Susanna felt a thrill of fear and desire as Father Lionheart circled around her, waving the incense over her flesh. The chapel went quiet as he stopped before her and said, 'Susanna, repeat after me. I will give all that I am.'

Tearfully, she replied, 'I will give all that I am.'

He swung the censor and continued, 'I will accept all that I am.'

'I will accept all that I am.'

He made another sweep with the heady incense. 'I will deny nothing.'

Swallowing hard, Susanna looked deep into his eyes and promised, 'I will deny nothing.'

Mother Magdalene stood beside Susanna and addressed the assembly. 'Those of you who have been ordained will know what these promises mean. For those of you who do not, listen well. To give all that you are means that there is no holding back. You are promising to do everything that is within your power to help others achieve sexual satisfaction. Everything. Likewise,

141

when you agree to accept all that you are, you are vowing to experience everything that you desire. If you can conceive of it, or if you can dream of it, then it must be done. You must receive it, you must allow it, you must accept it. You will deny nothing, to yourself, or to others.'

Sister Gabriel joined Mother Magdalene on the other side of Susanna and gave her an encouraging smile. 'In a little while, Sister, we may be asking you to pleasure us, but first, we have decided to honour you with a demonstration of how well we've come to know you during your training.'

Father Lionheart stepped behind her and spoke over her shoulder. 'Yes, and we want you to show us if you've become as adept at giving yourself pleasure as we know you are at giving it. Can you do that for us, Sister?'

Susanna fought down the feelings of panic and stammered, 'Y-yes, Father. I b-believe so.' This wasn't what she had been expecting. Usually, a novice performed all sorts of things on her mentors and then there would be a friendly return of service. This was all topsy-turvy, and Susanna cringed to think she'd have to endure all those greedy watching eyes while she allowed the three most senior members of The Order to try and turn her on.

Susanna's mentors busied themselves placing a padded chair high up on the altar, facing the whole assembly, and produced an array of bottles and sex toys from the sacristy. Their tasks complete, they genuflected before the altar and returned to their pews.

Sister Gabriel approached Susanna and pinned the new black veil loosely over her shimmering hair. 'Farewell, Susanna, welcome Sister Assumpta. Susanna would not wish to share her secrets with us, but Sister Assumpta is stronger. Please sit in the chair.' She indicated the red velvet seat perched on the altar and

Susanna dutifully clambered up onto the altar and sat facing the crowd, pink with embarrassment.

Mother Magdalene stepped up to her and asked, 'Sister, will you hear my secret wishes? Will you witness my desires?'

Bewildered, Susanna tucked strands of hair behind her ears and sat forward. 'Of course, I will do whatever you ask, Mother.'

Father Lionheart swept forward and said, 'But there is a price, Sister. We ask to know you. We wish you to share your responses to our desires, openly, with this community. Will you do that for us?'

Susanna reddened and scratched and rubbed uncomfortably at the trickles of sweat creeping down her neck and chest. 'What exactly do you mean, Father?'

He fixed her with an icy stare. 'Give yourself to God, Sister. God is pleasure. Come in the name of the Lord. Treat your bodily satisfaction as a gift, and share it, like the loaves and the fishes, with the throng.' He swept his arm to indicate the watching crowd.

Susanna began to shake as she felt the mass of hot, greedy eyes upon her, but she battled down nauseous waves of fear and replied, 'I give myself freely and completely, Father. All that I am, I will give.'

Smiling gravely, Father Lionheart joined Mother Magdalene in thanking her and then went to stand against the altar rail. Sister Gabriel prepared a little silver tray of oils and pleasure aids and rested them on the floor at Susanna's feet. 'Make me an instrument of your peace, Sister.'

Susanna's eyes rested for a moment on Sister Gabriel's darkly beautiful face and liquid eyes then, squaring her shoulders, she tossed her hair back, baring her deep cleavage and hard nipples. 'And I yours, Sister.'

Sister Gabriel walked slowly towards Mother Magdalene and began to open the buttons running down the front of her habit. In a husky voice, she addressed Father

Lionheart. 'Father, I want to confess some of my deepest desires. Can you help me with them?'

Father Lionheart smiled wickedly and replied, 'Mother Magdalene and I are your willing vessels, Sister. Speak freely and boldly and we will serve you as best we can.'

Susanna felt prickles of recognition in the scenario unfolding before her. The spoken word was such a turn on for her, and watching was more thrilling to her than taking part. But how could they know? Her face burned with shame at being asked to allow the whole community to witness her arousal, but with a sinking feeling, she realised that her ordination depended on her ability to share this secret.

Sister Gabriel's voice cut through her thoughts. 'Bless me, Father, for I have sinned in my selfish efforts to hide my secret craving. Just thinking about it makes me feel hot and wet and I need to touch myself to relieve the excitement that talking about this is creating.' Her habit fell away from her gleaming, ebony shoulders and deep cleavage.

As the cloth slipped down over her full hips, Susanna felt a jolt of pleasurable surprise at seeing the skimpy, black teddy stretched over Sister Gabriel's luscious curves. Mother Magdalene looked at Susanna piercingly then reassured Sister Gabriel, 'One must first learn to love oneself, Sister. Give yourself what you need.'

Sister Gabriel slipped a hand under the lacy fabric covering her chest and lifted one full breast out and began to massage her own flesh.

'Father, Mother, I know what I want to do, but it is so hard for me to admit it.' Her fingers tightened on her nipple and her hips began to gyrate.

Mother Magdalene encouraged her. 'Let go of all resistance. Let the body control the mind.'

Father Lionheart untied the golden cord from around his robes and flicked it against Sister Gabriel's buttocks. 'Confess, Sister, confess everything.'

Mother Magdalene pulled off her veil, letting her golden curls tumble over her shoulders, and hastily stripped off her habit. Squeezed into a tightly laced corset, her snowy white breasts looked in danger of spilling out over the top, while her shapely legs gleamed through fishnet stockings. Her metal-tipped stiletto boots clattered on the marble floor of the chancel as she sashayed over to Sister Gabriel. Dropping to her knees, she roughly pulled the crotch of the teddy to one side and buried her face in Sister Gabriel's pussy.

From her high chair on the altar, Susanna watched in frozen fascination as the most senior members of The Order performed for her pleasure. Her long tresses were beginning to stick to her flesh and an insistent throbbing in her clitoris and nipples demanded attention. Scrabbling around on the tray, she found a pair of heavy, silver nipple clamps and fixed them onto her swollen buds with a sigh of relief. As the tightening and pressure in her nipples increased, she poured musky-smelling oil over her abdomen and massaged it into her belly, breasts and thighs, groaning as her fingers strayed to caress the hungry slit between her legs.

Sister Gabriel tore off her veil, allowing black glossy ringlets to bounce around her face as she jiggled her hips and pressed herself hard against Mother Magdalene's greedy mouth.

'Go on', intoned Father Lionheart, snapping the cord against her pumping bottom, 'tell us everything.'

Sister Gabriel held both her own breasts in her hands, squeezing the nipples roughly, while her head arched back and her face grimaced in pleasure and pain. 'I see myself moving through the whole assembly here today, pausing in front of each one, allowing them to choose to touch me or not. And as I am passed from person to person, I submit completely to whatever they wish to do to me. If they want to squeeze my breasts or plunge a finger inside me, that's all right. If they want to force me to my knees and stick their cocks in my mouth, that's fine. Fuck me, bugger me, I don't care. I just want to be a vessel for everybody else's desire.'

Susanna felt the heat beginning to burn in her pussy and she thrust the fingers of one hand inside herself while with the other, she rubbed urgently against her aching clitoris.

Father Lionheart locked eyes with her and commanded, 'Open your legs wide for everybody, Sister. Share yourself.'

Susanna obeyed without question and, snatching up a flesh-coloured dildo from the tray, she spread her legs wide apart, resting her knees on the arms of the chair. Through half-closed eyes she surveyed the front row in the church and felt a tiny thrill to find that although they were all looking at her closely, and at the same time enjoying the spectacle of Sister Gabriel and Mother Magdalene, they were also touching themselves and each other, obviously as turned on as she was. Tossing her magnificent hair back from her face and shiny PVC-clad breasts, she eased the huge dildo into her tight pussy and moaned with relief as she felt her muscles clamp onto it. Stroking herself with her thumb, she manipulated the dildo in and out until she felt the first pangs of orgasm begin to ripple through her.

Father Lionheart lifted his heavy robes and freed his large erection from the tight black leather thong he was wearing. Tying the robes out of the way, he signalled to Mother Magdalene and they lifted Sister Gabriel so that her bottom was balanced precariously over the altar rail with her head hanging down towards the altar. Mother Magdalene strode around to the front of the rail and, gripping Sister Gabriel by the hips, resumed her deep exploration of Sister Gabriel's pussy with her tongue. On the altar side of the rail, Father Lionheart positioned himself behind Sister Gabriel's head, tilted it back, and slipped the fat head of his penis into her mouth.

'Let us serve Sister Gabriel's needs, Brothers and

Sisters and, by so doing, initiate Sister Assumpta into our Order.'

Susanna twisted in the chair with frustration. Hearing and watching Sister Gabriel had driven her to the peak of excitement, but she could not let herself go in front of all these people. She could imagine herself in their eyes: spread-eagled legs, crotchless knickers, peephole bra – she felt utterly exposed and wanton.

Sister Gabriel was grunting now as Father Lionheart pressed himself even deeper into her throat and Mother Magdalene slurped noisily on her clitoris. A high-pitched whining signified the tumultuous orgasm that was rocking Sister Gabriel's body, and her hair thrashed against the rail in a disjointed, then gradually slower, rhythm. Gently, Father Lionheart withdrew from her mouth and kissed her. Sitting up, Sister Gabriel broke into a huge, shining grin and leaned forward to kiss Mother Magdalene. Susanna felt red hot flushes of shame flood her cheeks and neck, as she saw all three turn to look at her. Father Lionheart took Sister Gabriel by the hand and led her to the end of the first pew.

'Brothers and Sisters, you have heard the brave and humble confession of Sister Gabriel. Serve her with love and gentleness. Sister Assumpta will want to hear what it is you wish to do, so be sure to tell Sister Gabriel. Go in peace.'

The first Brother in the front pew smiled shyly and said, 'I'd like to kiss you, Sister,' and Sister Gabriel puckered up her lips and offered them to him. The Sister beside him gasped, 'Let me suck your nipples,' quickly bent her head and, one after the other, took each of Sister Gabriel's huge nipples in her mouth. As she passed along the row, Sister Gabriel listened to the desires of her fellow Brothers and Sisters, and willingly offered her body to each in turn. Her breasts were aching from so many caresses and she began to feel sore from being penetrated front and back, but desire raged through her like a fire out of control. By the time she was half way through the crowd she was almost delirious with sensation. Two Brothers were penetrating her, one in her mouth, one in her tender pussy, while two Sisters were sucking and biting hard on her nipples, so that she felt faint with pleasure. Sister Gabriel heard good-natured cheering as several Sisters and Brothers called out, 'Let's pass her over our heads! Let's lay hands on her.'

Susanna watched like a mongoose fascinated by a snake as dozens of hands began to lift Sister Gabriel's beautiful body up and pass her around the congregation. Mouths and hands touched, licked and caressed every inch of her flesh, until she was crying out incoherently in the throws of passion. Susanna forgot about her embarrassment and slathered more oil over her tight flesh and then plunged the dildo deep inside herself. She watched hungrily as, yelling and shrieking, Sister Gabriel came and came for what seemed an eternity. The sound of her cries pushed Susanna over the edge and she began to moan loudly, tossing her hair about until she looked like a whirling dervish.

Gently placing Sister Gabriel on to her feet and embracing her warmly, the crowd turned to watch Susanna high up in her chair. Susanna's legs were still spread wide apart and hooked over the arms of the chair so that everybody was afforded a clear view of her mouse-brown fuzz and deep pink pudenda. She slid the dildo in and out of her damp cleft with long, slow strokes while stretching her pussy lips wide and circling her clitoris with her thumb. Her breasts and nipples were jutting through the tight holes in the peephole bra and the silver nipple clamps tinkled noisily as Susanna's fleshy form bounced on the velvet seat. Opening her eyes wider, Susanna scanned the watching faces and saw only communal love and lust. Temporarily freed from her fear of being watched, she allowed the first waves of pleasure to break over her body as she fully enjoyed the thrill of the tight nipple clamps and her own thumb sending shock waves into her belly and thighs. Plunging the dildo deeply inside herself one last time, she felt her muscles go into spasm and her clit explode with delicious sensations. 'I'm coming,' she shrieked, 'I'm coming now!' With a banshee wail and another toss of her magnificent hair, Susanna's body went rigid and she slumped into the seat wearing a tearful, beatific smile. Eyes shining, she allowed the spontaneous burst of applause to wash over her and met each generous face in turn, until she had acknowledged every person in the chapel.

Mother Magdalene and Father Lionheart helped her down as Sister Gabriel rejoined them in front of the altar.

'Welcome, Sister Assumpta,' beamed Sister Gabriel.

'Yes, welcome, Sister!' Father Lionheart and Mother Magdalene joined Sister Gabriel in smothering the newly ordained Sister Assumpta in kisses and warm strokes, then stepped back while she began to make her way through the assembly.

'Sister Assumpta! Sister Assumpta!' roared the crowd, parting to allow their newest member to pass through them, but showering her with friendly pats and kisses.

'I've made it,' thought Sister Assumpta, 'I've finally made it.'

Chapter Seventeen

*B*rother Darius's pectoral muscles and biceps bulged as he heaved himself into another push-up. Sweat streamed into his eyes as he forced himself beyond his own limits. '101, 102 –' The sudden sound behind him broke his stride and he collapsed onto his stomach, grimacing in pain. Wiping the perspiration from his face with a towel, he glanced up to see Father Lionheart sitting watching him from a bench.

'How long have you been here?' Brother Darius found himself scowling at the idea of someone having seen the way he had just punished his body.

'Long enough. What's bothering you? You look like you're being pursued by demons.' Father Lionheart's face looked impassive, but Brother Darius thought he could sense a trace of irritation in his voice. 'Having a hard time?'

Brother Darius searched Father Lionheart's expression and wondered why his words were tinged with irony. Sitting up and towelling off his shoulders and arms, Brother Darius took his time in replying. 'I think you know I'm having a hard time. Mother Magdalene was very kind to me yesterday, but my problems remain the same. How was the ceremony?'

Father Lionheart cracked his knuckles and stretched out his legs. 'It was wonderful. You were missed.'

Brother Darius snorted. 'I doubt that. Did Brother Joseph repent?'

'Oh yes.' Father Lionheart smiled thinly. 'He resisted at first, of course, but then that's his way, isn't it?'

Brother Darius rose uncertainly and found himself circling the man he had always loved and respected. 'Did you enjoy punishing him? Did it take a lot of blows to make him sorry?'

Father Lionheart remained impassive but laughed softly. 'Of course it took a lot of effort, and haven't I always enjoyed it? Why should that bother you now? I thought Mother Magdalene would have taken your mind off Brother Joe for a while.'

Brother Darius came to a halt in front of the faintly sneering priest and felt a flash of realisation. 'You're jealous. Of her and me. How can that be, in The Order?'

Father Lionheart's veneer of indifference cracked and he pushed Brother Darius hard on the chest, shoving him backwards. 'What? You think I don't have feelings, like anybody else? Like you do about Brother Joe?'

Brother Darius threw himself against Father Lionheart's much slimmer frame and caught him in a fierce bear hug. 'At least I admit it! Yes, I love him, and you sicken me with your desire to hurt him and everybody else.' Father Lionheart struggled against his grip but Brother Darius grappled him to the floor. 'You're a coward, Father. Does she know you love her? Like this?' Brother Darius was spitting into his face with rage and had him pinned to the floor, but Father Lionheart met his eyes without fear.

'How do you love an institution?' The hopelessness in his voice struck a chord in Brother Darius and he loosened his hold so that Father Lionheart could catch his breath. 'I'm sorry if my jealousy has tainted my relationship with you, Brother. I wasn't aware of it myself, until now. As for Brother Joseph, I promise you I was no

151

harder on him than anybody else and, despite what you think, my personal pleasure in punishment depends on the experience being enjoyed by the recipient. Formal chastisements hold no thrill for me.'

Brother Darius heard the ring of truth in the words and released Father Lionheart. He sat hugging his knees while the priest straightened his clothing and swept his fingers through his rumpled hair. 'I'm sorry, Father. I misjudged you.'

Father Lionheart shook his head. 'No, you don't owe me an apology. Both of us seem to be struggling with feelings that we are finding hard to reconcile. We should be helping each other, not wanting to take a swing.'

Brother Darius looked up and grinned in relief. 'I wouldn't want to fight you, Father.'

'No,' mused Father Lionheart, staring openly at Brother Darius's powerful body, 'I don't think I'd like that much either. How about we get into some jeans and sneak off to the village pub instead?'

Brother Darius got up and offered a hand to Father Lionheart, pulling him to his feet. 'Most excellent idea, Father. We will put the world to rights over a pint of best, yes?'

Father Lionheart grinned back at him. 'Yes!'

Mother Magdalene and Sister Gabriel lay either end of a big, comfortable sofa in front of a crackling fire, massaging each other's toes and reviewing the previous day's events. Mother Magdalene's homely little sitting room had been created out of a walk-in clothes closet and tiny dressing area that had probably once housed an abbot's or bishop's ecclesiastical wardrobe. It amused her to think of the shock that would have registered on their faces if one of them had walked in now and found two women, naked but for see-through cotton shifts, being so blatantly intimate. Then again, maybe they would have been more pleased than astonished?

The door in question opened suddenly, giving Mother

Magdalene a start, and she laughed with relief when Father Guillory sauntered in carrying a decanter of brandy and three crystal glasses.

'I was told I'd find you here. I'm not disturbing you, I hope?'

Mother Magdalene and Sister Gabriel exchanged wide-eyed glances and grinned at him in obvious welcome. 'Not a bit of it,' assured Mother Magdalene, 'come and join us. We'll make room.' They moved their legs just long enough for him to settle himself between them and then lay them across his lap and resumed massaging each other's feet.

Father Guillory stretched his fingers to hold all three glasses steady in one hand and poured a generous measure of brandy into each.

'Your good health, Father,' toasted Sister Gabriel, 'you were wonderful yesterday. That's quite some equipment you've got there.'

She wiggled her thighs to indicate the equipment she had in mind, but he smiled suavely and smoothed back a greasy lock of black hair and regarded her with half-hooded eyes. 'Ah yes, my skills with ropes and bindings is improving with time.'

Mother Magdalene laughed raucously and dug her elbow into his bony ribs. 'Cut it out, Father, you know perfectly well that your best bit of equipment is the one that God gave you. Tell me, how is the lovely Emily coming along?'

Father Guillory's dark face broke into a warm smile. 'Alas, the bird is now fully-fledged and has flown. She's getting married. I needn't have worried about her calling me Father for too long. In her eyes, I am nearly old enough to be her father and, if it hadn't been for my change of career, she'd have been asking me to wed them.'

Sister Gabriel snuggled down harder against him. 'That can't be true. You're the one who restored her to

153

herself, sexually, right? So if you'd still been a priest, she might not be getting married at all.'

Father Guillory yawned and stretched, then took a big gulp of his brandy and sighed deeply. 'I'm too tired for philosophical discussion, and anyway, I'm very happy for her. Besides, it wasn't restoring so much as unleashing.'

Mother Magdalene pinched the tight flesh of his arm through his thin black shirt. 'You old dog! You never told me she was a virgin.'

He closed his eyes and smiled thinly, pulling the skin tight across his noble nose and looking as righteous as a Jesuit. 'Well, she wasn't by the time I called you. And now I think she could teach you both a thing or two.'

As one, Sister Gabriel and Mother Magdalene rose up, snatched the decanter and glass away from him and pinned him beneath them.

Mother Magdalene was panting with exertion and excitement. 'Is that a challenge, Father? Or should we call you Carlos? I like Carlos, what do you think, Sister?'

Father Guillory struggled to free his arms and pulled both women down on top of him and fondled their bottoms through the thin fabric of the shifts. 'Call me anything you like. Father Lionheart tells me you have the perfect cure for any nonsense about names.'

Mother Magdalene laughed as Sister Gabriel caught her eye and then bounded off and returned with a set of long, fine leather straps and a black silk scarf. Rolling it into a blindfold, Sister Gabriel slipped it around Father Guillory's head and fastened it tightly over his eyes. 'Father?' she whispered into one of his ears, brushing his cheek with her thick, sensuous lips while she pulled his hands behind him and tied them. 'May I call you Father?'

'Carlos, Carlos,' whispered Mother Magdalene into his other ear, as she stroked his rapidly stiffening member. 'Now, now, Father Carlos, what are we going to do with you?'

Part Five

Nemesis

Chapter Eighteen

*S*ister Assumpta was not at all as Angela had
expected. There was nothing pious about her robust
physique or her shining, round, jolly face. She bustled
over to the doorway where Angela hovered uncertainly,
crying, 'Come in, come in, my dear. It's Angela isn't it?
How lovely to see you, would you like a cup of tea? No?
Well never mind, pick a seat that looks comfy and we'll
get acquainted. That's all we'll do for today, if you like.
All right?'

Angela looked around the cosily furnished little room
and marvelled at how different it was from the bland
functionalism of the rest of the college. Chintzy little
two-seater sofas clustered randomly around a variety of
differently shaped coffee tables, and there were two or
three overstuffed wing-backed armchairs that looked
like they belonged in someone's private study. One of
them was at right angles to a dark, mahogany bookcase,
brimming with leather-bound, serious looking volumes,
together with paperback novels, journals and magazines,
all in a jumble of disorderly heaps. Angela sank into the
chair, enjoying the intimate informality of the room.

Sister Assumpta sprawled casually on one of the sofas,
sipping from a steaming mug of tea. 'Will you think me

wicked, dear, if I tell you what I believe can be interpreted from the choice of a seat? You needn't take any notice of it, it's only my little whimsy, but I did an MA in psychology many years ago and some of it stuck, I just can't escape it. Do you mind?'

'No, not at all,' replied Angela, surprised to find that she meant it.

'Well,' continued Sister Assumpta, 'that spot you've chosen there is what I call the "sensualist's corner". You see, the chair has a lovely crushed velvet covering that feels terribly nice on the skin, and it's a deep, rich red, which is the colour of sexual heat. But those bookshelves appeal to an unconventional, imaginative mind, to a person for whom the status quo holds no appeal – a traveller if you like, on a voyage of discovery.'

Angela's eyebrows crept upwards as the tiny hairs on the back of her neck tingled in recognition of herself in the nun's description. 'But isn't it sinful, Sister, to feel like that?'

'Gracious no, child, whyever should you think that? You're a Catholic I suppose?'

Angela nodded. 'You are too, aren't you?'

'Oh no, dear, I'm a Sister in a lay order; we have no religious denomination as such, although you could say the principles are Christian, even Catholic in the main. Many of the Sisters and Brothers were raised as Catholics, which is a great help when dealing with problems concerning guilt, or sexual uncertainties. I like to think that counsellors from my Order can adapt to the needs of any troubled soul, or body for that matter.' She beamed. Her charming, apple-pie cheeks looked so wholesome it was impossible to believe she could be discussing such delicate matters without a trace of embarrassment.

'What if I'd sat in that leather wing-back by the standard lamp?'

Sister Assumpta waved a finger in the air and cried, 'Aha! Couldn't be more different. I'll bet you chose that

158

because you know you don't like it. That would signify a strong desire for conformity, a reactionary, conservative leaning, a need for order and discipline.'

'But I like discipline,' blurted Angela.

Sister Assumpta gave Angela a long, thoughtful look. 'Do you now? Well, that's very common, you know, especially among Catholics. Do you want to tell me about it?'

Angela wriggled uncomfortably in the chair, the crushed velvet leaving pretty, abstract patterns on her skin. Tentatively, she decided to try and gauge what would be acceptable as subject matter for these counselling sessions.

'Sister, the troubles I've been having are of such a deeply personal nature I don't know how to speak about them. I even feel some of them are unspeakable.'

Sister Assumpta nodded sympathetically and slipped off her shoes, then lay back on the little couch and closed her eyes. 'My dear, we are all God's creatures and every last one of us was made in His image. So there is no thought or feeling or desire that God will not recognise, and not one urge or compunction that He will fail to understand. If it helps, why not think of this as a confessional? I have no desire to judge you, Angela, merely to hear you and to support, help and guide you. Remember what Jesus said, "Come to me, all you who seek comfort, and I will give you rest."'

Tears welled up in Angela's eyes and spilled down over her cheeks. She so desperately wanted to reconcile her strange desires with her faith, yet the two seemed incompatible. Falteringly, she began. 'When I was a little girl, there was nothing I wanted more than to be a nun . . .'

Admiring her own reflection in the stylish King's Road windows, Savannah flicked her long blonde hair over her shoulder and checked the effect on the faces of passers by. Lengthening her stride, she smiled smugly in the knowledge that several people swivelled their eyes and craned their necks for a better look at her. The pungent aroma of freshly brewed coffee signalled her arrival at Starlight's, where hordes of harassed shoppers were sipping their cappuccinos and rifling through carrier bags stuffed with impulse buys.

'Savannah! Over here.' Searching the crowded tables, Savannah's eyes eventually lit upon the chocolate cream complexion of her old pal, looking more radiant than ever.

'Hi! Long time no see.' Savannah squeezed in beside Sister Gabriel and searched her old friend's face. 'You look amazing. How're things?'

Sister Gabriel dimpled prettily and queried, 'You mean I don't usually?'

Susannah stretched out her long legs and slumped into her seat. 'How would I know? I hardly ever see you. I miss you, Gabby.'

Sister Gabriel squeezed her hand and said, 'Look, you know I love you, but our paths have gone off in different directions, that's all.'

Savannah pouted and said, 'Just because I've got into a bit of writing and broadcasting doesn't mean I haven't got time for you, does it?'

Sister Gabriel twisted uncomfortably in her seat, wondering what to say. 'I'm really proud of you, Savannah – you know that. And you can see me when I'm working at the homeless project. It's just that when I'm busy with The Order, there's so little time left over, and I do have to abide by the rules. We all do. They're not negotiable.'

'Yes, but why?' whined Savannah. 'Why did you all get so secretive? I mean, what is Richard doing – and Mags – what's happened to her? Everyone's disappeared.'

Gabrielle looked hard at Savannah's petulant face and felt relieved that she'd kept things quiet around her.

'Savannah – Richard, Margaret and I shared a kind of spiritual angst that we needed to work through. I'm sorry if you feel left out, but you know that's not your kind of thing.'

Savannah tossed her hair back impatiently. 'OK, no it's not, but why can't I visit? What harm can that do?'

Sister Gabriel grinned. 'Quite a lot, actually. Besides, although it's a secular order, it's reclusive.'

'Meaning what exactly?' sneered Savannah.

'Meaning,' sighed Sister Gabriel, 'that we have chosen to have a base where we can separate ourselves from mainstream society and focus inwards. It's a private place, Savannah. We don't entertain visits from anybody outside The Order. I'm sorry.'

Savannah jumped up from the table, knocking Sister Gabriel's coffee flying. 'Like hell you are!' she spat. 'And what about Joe? Why has he up and vanished? I'm sick of you, with your holier-than-thou charity work, and those two with their bloody secret club. Knowing Richard, it's probably a home for retired perverts. I'll find out, don't you worry.'

Flushed scarlet with anger, Savannah shoved her way out of the coffee bar leaving Sister Gabriel feeling as if she'd just been hit by a tornado. Finishing her coffee with a sigh, she made a mental note to bring up Savannah's behaviour with Mother Magdalene at the next opportunity but, in the meantime, she might as well get back to work.

Outside, she checked her watch and realised that she wasn't due back for almost an hour and a half. Savannah's hasty departure had left her with a lunch break to fill. Checking the time again, she remembered that Sister Assumpta usually popped into her college café about now, so she quickly strode towards the underground entrance and flashed her pass. As she alighted at Whitechapel, a flash of blonde hair further down the station briefly caught her eye, but when she looked again it was gone. She chided herself for being melodramatic and hurried out of the station.

As Sister Gabriel strode confidently along the road

161

and into the crowded little café, Savannah fell back and stepped into a bar with a convenient window on the opposite side of the road. Smiling coldly, she settled herself down to wait.

Angela found that her whole week seemed to be one long wait until her next appointment with Sister Assumpta. She felt deeply peaceful in the big, soft chair, with Sister Assumpta sprawled out on her couch like a great black and white cat.

'I can't believe, Sister, how fervent I was as a child. I remember praying, "Oh please God, please God, let me win – I promise, I'll do anything if you let me win. I'll be a nun!" I know it was only a silly bride doll, and there were hundreds of raffle tickets being sold, but I wanted that doll so badly.'

Sister Assumpta smiled and nodded. 'But did you win the doll?'

Angela smiled ruefully. 'No, of course I didn't, and I forgot my promise at once too. But the idea of being a nun had definitely started to appeal to me, I even liked the clothes. I wanted to be good, to do something to help people and I liked the way nuns were dedicated to their work. I thought they wore their robes like a badge of honour – a declaration of intent.'

Sister Assumpta folded her hands in her lap and closed her eyes. 'It's not an uncommon fantasy, Angela. Did you ever think you seriously had a vocation?'

Angela looked wistful. 'Oh yes. I was quite a sweet little girl really, and I had absolute faith in Jesus – he was like a special invisible friend, my reassurance that no matter what else went wrong, He loved me. The trouble was, by the time I was twelve, I was already getting these big crushes on older boys. I couldn't wait to get caught in a clinch with one of them.'

Sister Assumpta interrupted her. 'But surely that's normal? Every girl has crushes, just like many of them think they'd like to be nuns.'

162

'But I wanted them to touch me – I ached for it. Then I started to feel bad, because the Church says that sex before marriage is a sin.'

Sister Assumpta felt her pulse quicken and sensed the approach of more intimate details. 'So what did you do? How did you cope?'

'Well, no amount of praying seemed to help and, as I got older, I started seeing how far I could go without actually going all the way, if you know what I mean.' Sister Assumpta nodded sympathetically. 'The boys I chose were always older than I was, because they seemed to know what they were doing, but I stayed in control of what they were allowed to do, and how far they could go. Maybe believing that God didn't allow penetrative sex heightened all the other sensations, because when they petted me, I was on fire – absolutely consumed with sensation and craving.'

Sister Assumpta felt a throbbing sensation in her own loins and asked, 'What actually happened?'

Angela leaned her head back into the seat and closed her eyes. 'My neck being kissed or bitten sent electric shocks right through me. My ears being nibbled or licked had me writhing in ecstasy. Even a deep, sensual kiss made me feel like I was drowning in pleasure. Can you imagine what even the suggestion of having my breasts touched did to me?'

Sister Assumpta fought the impulse to touch her own breasts and pressed her hands against her quivering stomach instead. 'Oh yes, dear, I can imagine. Do go on.'

'Well, I eventually progressed onto more intimate things. I craved the shuddering thrills from having my breasts stroked and my nipples bitten, and of course it was inevitable, sooner or later, that I just had to let a hand stray under my skirt and up into my knickers.'

Sister Assumpta stifled a moan as Angela's words worked their magic on her body just as efficiently as the hands in Angela's stories. She could feel that her panties were starting to get wet and her nipples were hard beneath the rough serge of her habit.

'How did that make you feel, Angela?'

Angela kept her eyes tightly closed as her head twisted from side to side. 'I would be soaking wet, and the feel of a long, probing finger inside me made me moan with delight – it was like coming home. So, it had to happen. One night, I just opened my legs and went with the flow. It was like finally scratching an old, unreachable itch. I absolutely loved it. I couldn't get enough.'

Sister Assumpta's body jerked convulsively and she felt the familiar first hot pangs of orgasm shimmying up into her belly and down into her trembling thighs. Clutching a pillow to conceal her responses, she waited until she felt able to control her voice before continuing. Flooded with relief, she asked, 'Didn't that make you happy? Or was it hard to reconcile your feelings with your faith?'

Angela sighed loudly, opened her eyes and looked into the bright, kindly gaze before her. 'For a while, I had incredibly strong feelings of guilt and I decided to try and be pure. No kissing, no touching, nothing. I felt quite sad because I knew I'd already spoiled everything and I could never be a nun. I even thought that no decent man would marry me.'

'Guilt is a terrible thing. So destructive. But how are things now, Angela?'

'Oh, everything changed again when I came up to college. I couldn't believe how many lovely boys and girls there were. All of us away from home, all of us free to do as we chose, except in the sight of God, of course.'

'Sorry to interrupt, but did you say girls, Angela?'

Angela coughed, reddened and finally replied, 'Yes, Sister, but I'd rather not get into that right now, if that's OK?'

Sister Assumpta sat up, smiling and stretching. 'Not at all, dear, we're nearly out of time anyway. You've a lovely way with words, you know. It's a pleasure to listen to you.'

Blushing furiously, Angela replied, 'Thank you, Sister, it's been much easier than I'd expected.'

Sister Assumpta slipped back into her shoes and guided Angela towards the door. 'I feel it's very important for you to be heard, Angela, so unless you want to ask me for feedback on anything, I'll just be here to listen. All right?'

Angela squared her shoulders, surprised to find that she felt a little better, even lighter somehow. She looked straight into Sister Assumpta's open, warm face and said, 'I really think you've helped me. Maybe, over time, I'll find some peace. Same time next week then?'

Sister Assumpta smoothed her veil and wiped a tiny slick of sweat from her upper lip. 'As I said, it really is a pleasure to listen to you. You've obviously got a lot to give. Yes, dear, same time.' Angela held her hand out awkwardly to shake on it, but Sister Assumpta took her proffered hand in both of her own and said, 'In my Order, Angela, we believe in the principle of helping each other to find peace. As Jesus once said, make me an instrument of your peace, Angela.'

Tentatively, Angela replied, 'And I yours, Sister.'

Father Lionheart felt ill at ease in civilian clothing. He tugged uncomfortably at the collar of his shirt and readjusted his jacket for the tenth time. Brother Joseph looked up from the flowerbed he was weeding and wolf-whistled mockingly as he passed by on his way to the gate.

'Where are you off to Father, anywhere nice?'

Father Lionheart paused and rubbed at his sleeves awkwardly. 'I've promised to give a talk at Sister Assumpta's college as part of a cultural and religious diversity week. I used to teach philosophy, for my sins.'

Brother Joseph whistled again and pointed at the brown loafers that Father Lionheart was wearing with his tweedy jacket. 'That would explain the shoes. Only a philosopher could be seen out in daylight in them. But why the mufti?'

Father Lionheart laughed good-naturedly, feeling a little tense. 'I know. I used to fancy myself as a French philosopher-poet or something so they're a remnant of my attempts to scorn the footwear of the bourgeoisie. I'm not wearing the collar because I don't want to have the students making religious assumptions about me. I want to talk about universal spirituality.'

Brother Joseph grinned and waved his hand. 'All right, all right. Save your lecture for when you get there. Actually, I think you look quite tasty. Very casual-intellectual.'

'Thanks. I'll remember that if they start to heckle me. Casual-intellectual. I like it.'

Smiling to himself, he carried on down the drive and disappeared from view.

Chapter Nineteen

Mother Magdalene's heart pounded as she heard the first rasping words of her anonymous caller begin to torment her again.

'Well, whore? Thought the eye of God had turned away from you and left you to do Satan's work after all, did you? Missed me?'

The voice had a gloating tone and Mother Magdalene felt the bitter bile of fear wash into the back of her throat.

'What do you want? Why are you calling me?' Even with her supreme effort to sound unconcerned, she could still hear the tremor in her own voice echoing down the line.

'Just to remind you that you're all going to burn in hell, every last one of you. Oh Margaret, Margaret, why have you forsaken me?'

Gathering her courage, Mother Magdalene placed her lips close to the telephone and let herself get spitting angry. 'How dare you use my given name and be cowardly enough to conceal your own? You get a kick out of this don't you, you whinging hypocrite? Call me again and I'll set the police on you.'

She slammed down the telephone and lay back, shaken, on her bed. Breathing deeply to slow her heartbeat down a little, she waited long enough to convince herself that they would not call back, and then she dialled a number and waited anxiously.

'Sister Assumpta? Thank heavens. I need to talk. Urgently.'

The little coffee shop adjacent to the college was just starting to fill up as Mother Magdalene shook the raindrops from her umbrella and smiled warmly at the corner table where Sister Assumpta was tucking into a plate of cream cakes. Catching her eye, Sister Assumpta called out, 'I've got to look after my figure, Mother. You can't maintain all these voluptuous curves without a cake or two. Would you like one?' She offered the plate as Mother Magdalene settled herself into the seat beside her.

Mother Magdalene shook her head ruefully. 'No, I don't think so. I like them, but they don't like me. As a Geordie woman once said to me, "You might as well strap that straight to your thighs." More's the pity, she was right. I've only got to think about cream cakes to put on weight. No sign of Sister Gabriel yet?'

Sister Assumpta wiped a fleck of cream from the corner of her mouth with a satisfied smile. 'No, she rang to say she's running late. The Caddy Shack is oversubscribed and understaffed, apparently.'

Mother Magdalene nodded sympathetically. 'Yes, I think it's time we allocated a few more members to the project, although it doesn't appeal to those who prefer to be more active sexually. How are you getting on?' She quickly placed an order for coffee with a harassed looking waitress and gave Sister Assumpta her full attention.

'Oh, I love it at the college. My background in counselling is put to good use, and of course there's the opportunity for a lot of listening, which you know I like.'

Mother Magdalene grinned widely. 'Indeed I do. And

your expert skills have identified many new members for The Order. You have a gift, Sister.'

Sister Assumpta coloured prettily and took a noisy slurp of tea. 'Actually, I've come across the most incredible girl. Face of an angel, so her name suits her. Angela. But she's got the most natural, delightful sexuality I've ever come across and, without realising it, she's already one of us, if you know what I mean.'

Mother Magdalene smiled and nodded encouragingly. 'She sounds wonderful. You should invite her down. Anyway, you know I trust your judgement, so go ahead and set up her training if you like. I'm sure you can pick an appropriate team of mentors for her.'

Sister Assumpta sighed contentedly and then looked sharply at Mother Magdalene's strained features. 'How are you getting on, Mother? You seem to be terribly busy most of the time.'

Mother Magdalene shrugged. 'Well, I am very busy – it's an increasingly large organisation. But I do find time for a little light relief from time to time you know.'

Sister Assumpta returned her knowing look and scanned the beautiful face and unruly hair escaping from under the veil. She wondered if Mother Magdalene really ever took a break from The Order. It seemed impossible to imagine her doing anything else, yet her looks and vibrant personality would assure her a place in any number of alternative careers. Refusing to be distracted by the tempting reference to Mother Magdalene's sex life, Sister Assumpta continued to probe gently. 'But are you happy, Mother?'

Mother Magdalene looked wistful for a moment and impatiently brushed stray strands of hair from her forehead. 'I'm content. I'm satisfied. I like to be busy.'

Sister Assumpta raised an eyebrow. 'But that's not happiness is it? Did you ever want anything else for yourself?'

Mother Magdalene snorted mirthlessly. 'I could hardly have *wanted* The Order could I? It would have been inconceivable. That's the funny thing about it. Everything I believed then made even imagining something like this impossible, yet here we are, a pair of lay Sisters in The Compassionate Order for Relief. This is where my struggle with my faith and my sex drive took me. It's a compromise.'

Sister Assumpta felt as though some important piece of a puzzle was eluding her. 'All right, I understand what you're saying – but before the idea for The Order appeared, what then? What did you expect from your life?'

Mother Magdalene sighed and gazed through the steamy windows into the bustling street outside. 'Not much. A home, a career, maybe a family. I had a bit of a crush on Richard. I thought we might even settle down together, eventually. Oh, I don't know. Look, can we leave it? I'm not really in the mood to talk about this.' She sat up straighter and busied herself with pouring coffee from a little silver pot.

Sister Assumpta looked baffled. 'But I thought you wanted to see me to talk, because you were worried about something? You sounded so – well, almost frightened.'

Mother Magdalene dropped sweeteners into her coffee with military precision. 'Did I? Yes, I suppose I was a bit stressed out, but really, there's nothing to worry about. Let's just drop it. I want to have a wander around the West End and do a bit of window-shopping. What do you think the Soho sex shops are going to make of a nun rummaging through their goods?'

Sister Assumpta spurted a mouthful of tea across the table and coughed violently as she choked on the hastily swallowed liquid. 'You wouldn't!'

Mother Magdalene beamed and settled back into her seat. 'Stop looking so scandalised. Of course I would. If anyone asks, I'll claim that I'm on an educational foray on behalf of my lost flock, so that I can relate to them better.' She grinned broadly and said, 'Ah, here comes Sister Gabriel. Let's see what she thinks.'

Sister Assumpta turned towards the door where the tall, impressive figure of Sister Gabriel was pushing her way through the throng of lunchtime sandwich buyers.

'Hi! Sorry I'm so late. Have we still got time for this chat?' She quickly looked from Mother Magdalene to Sister Assumpta and sensed that something was amiss. Mother Magdalene quickly took control of the situation.

'Let me order something for you, and then we can catch up. No, whatever it was, it's not bothering me now, so let's just enjoy a girlie lunch, shall we?'

She smiled brightly and ordered more teas and coffees and a selection of sandwiches and cakes, chatting gaily all the while. Sister Gabriel was soon engaged in a heated debate about the merits of gym training with Mother Magdalene, while Sister Assumpta looked on in quiet reflection. Clearly, something was bothering Mother Magdalene, but this was not the day when she would find out what it was. Perhaps they could all spend an hour diverting their energies elsewhere?

When the last crumb of cake had been swept up and eaten, Sister Assumpta checked her watch and said, 'Look, it's still an hour to my next appointment, so shall we pop back to my apartment for a little break?'

Sister Gabriel and Mother Magdalene exchanged glances and then smiled widely at Sister Assumpta.

'I'd love to,' declared Mother Magdalene, 'I could do with some dessert that's not fattening.'

Sister Gabriel grinned broadly. 'All right! Sounds like my cup of afternoon tea too. What time's that appointment, Sister?'

Sister Assumpta snatched up the bill from the table and emptied some money from her purse. 'Two, so let's go now. Be a shame to rush.'

* * *

Within minutes, the three women, clad in demure nuns' habits, had swept from the café and were walking swiftly to the terraced Georgian house where Sister Assumpta rented the whole of the ground floor and garden. As she unlocked the front door, a pair of mottled tortoiseshell cats wove between their legs meowing a welcome.

'Hello, darlings.'

Sister Assumpta led her two friends into her plushly furnished living room and began to shed her veil and habit in a purposeful manner. Sister Gabriel whipped off her own veil and greedily nuzzled Sister Assumpta's soft, fleshy shoulders and white, plump neck.

Amidst a whirl of tugs and impatient moans they stripped each other of their outer vestments to reveal an appetising array of erotic underwear. Mother Magdalene's creamy flesh was a vision in scarlet lace and fishnets, while Sister Gabriel's chocolate-toned skin was shown off to flattering effect by a microscopic gold satin bra and tanga set. Sister Assumpta tugged the band from her hair and let it cascade down over her ripe curves, which were clad in a raspberry, crushed velvet corset with black, criss-cross lacing.

As if by telepathic agreement, all three women lay down on the carpet and formed a circle with their bodies. Mother Magdalene burrowed between Sister Gabriel's athletic thighs and started lapping greedily on her plump pudenda and moist inner lips. Sighing with pleasure, Sister Gabriel tugged on Sister Assumpta's shapely legs until she could rest her head on her inner thighs and snap open the poppers at her crotch. Wasting no time, she homed in on Sister Assumpta's cherry-like clitoris, forcing the plump pussy lips apart with her tongue. Sister Assumpta felt a thrill of erotic delight as waves of pleasure rippled through her own body at the same time as she began kissing her way up towards Mother Magdalene's peaches-and-cream pussy. Breathing in the faintly sea-salt aroma of her juices, she caressed the golden pubic hairs with the tips of her fingers and swept her tongue between the pink lips in long, slow strokes. Mother Magdalene gasped with pleasure and briefly relinquished her hold on Sister Gabriel's swollen clit, but soon returned to her task with joyous determination, egged on by Sister Assumpta's delicious ministrations.

The quiet of the afternoon in suburbia was broken by cries, moans and occasional shrieks as the three women focused all their energies on giving and receiving pleasure. Sister Gabriel was the first to reach a climax as Mother Magdalene deftly slipped her little finger into her anus and attacked her clitoris with rapid, relentless flicking motions.

'Oh God!' Sister Gabriel cried out, and pressed her own finger deep into Sister Assumpta's tight little pussy. But Sister Assumpta was busy devouring Mother Magdalene, lost in the soft flesh and wild abandon of her. Sucking mercilessly on her hard, erect bud, she was rewarded with Mother Magdalene's uninhibited moans and the sudden jerking of her hips as she came.

Sister Gabriel raised her head for a moment and shared a beatific grin with Mother Magdalene, and then both of them turned their attentions to Sister Assumpta. Mother Magdalene took hold of her arms and pinned her down while she let her mouth wander over Sister Assumpta's shoulders and neck, finally reaching down to nuzzle her voluptuous breasts. Sister Gabriel resumed her assault on her now soaking pussy. Within minutes, Sister Assumpta felt a surge of energy course through her body, electrifying her skin from her toes up to her scalp. Hot pulses of pleasure radiated out from her nipples and her clitoris making her feel as if someone had switched on the Blackpool illuminations.

'Alleluia!' she cried, tossing her mane of hair into the faces of her pleasurable tormentors. Giggling like schoolgirls, the three women sat on the floor with their arms wrapped around each other, exchanging soft kisses.

With a sigh, Sister Assumpta glanced at the carriage clock on the mantelpiece and said, 'Alas, it's time to go.' Mother Magdalene rose and pulled on her habit and veil and then cradled Sister Assumpta's face in her hands and kissed her hard on the mouth. 'Thank you, Sister. That was much more refreshing than a chat!'

Sister Assumpta smiled warmly, but placed her hand on Mother Magdalene's arm and looked deeply into her eyes. 'I'm here if you need me. Any time.'

Mother Magdalene placed her own hand over Sister Assumpta's. 'I know. Thank you.'

Sister Gabriel strode over and hugged them both roughly. 'Come on, you two. Time to go.' Sister Assumpta gathered up her things and followed them to the door. 'Back to work,' sighed Sister Gabriel, as she kissed Mother Magdalene, then Sister Assumpta, in turn. 'I do hope we can do this again. It was great.'

Sister Assumpta's eyes twinkled mischievously as she replied, 'Ask and thou shalt receive, knock and the door shall be opened.'

In the phone box across the road from the house, Savannah finished scribbling down the address and then dialled her message service. No word from Joe, then. Two-faced creep. He'd said he'd ring her but, so far, not a word. Damn him to hell. Damn them all. She noted the time on her little pad and then quickly snatched up the receiver again and turned her face away as the door opened and Sister Gabriel came out, followed by Mother Magdalene. As they sauntered off up the street in one direction, the plump nun they'd gone in with came out and hurried off the other way. Giving her a few moments to get well ahead, Savannah dropped into step behind her.

Chapter Twenty

Angela felt the hot tears welling up in her eyes just before they spilled over onto her cheeks and ran down her freshly made-up face. Too late to stem the flow, she started frantically dabbing at herself with a tissue, desperately trying to control her overwhelming feelings as she approached the altar, but small sobs escaped from her mouth and her lower lip trembled uncontrollably. Her beautiful, crisp new habit and starched veil rustled with each step she took, and her heart lurched when her eyes met those of Sister Assumpta and Mother Magdalene, who were waiting for her beside Father Lionheart and Sister Gabriel.

For her, this was a dream come true, a moment that she had wished for since she was a little girl, the way some had wished for a white wedding dress. Pride and a sense of achievement made her straighten her shoulders and tilt her chin up, so that, despite her tears, her face was creased into a huge smile. Mother Magdalene held out a hand and led her to a spot directly between herself and Sister Assumpta. Squeezing Angela's hand, she turned to address the assembly.

'Brothers and Sisters, today we have come together for a very special initiation. Most of you will know what an intense and sometimes trying experience your training can be, and I'm sure that you were glad to have the devotion of your mentors to help you through.' Bursts of knowing laughter broke out among the assembled community. Mother Magdalene smiled and waited for the noise to subside, then continued. 'Once in a blue moon, along comes a novice who seems to have been a fully ordained member before they even got here. In this very special case, I believe that our new Sister may have been sent to teach us something about remembering our dreams, and believing we can fulfil them. A few short weeks ago, a girl called Angela joined us here at The Priory, and I know that many of you have already had the pleasure of meeting her and working with her.' Another round of guffaws and giggles confirmed Mother Magdalene's words. 'Today, I have no hesitation in presenting her to you as Sister Evangeline, our newest member.'

A surge of applause filled the chapel as Sister Evangeline was warmly embraced and kissed, but there was also a murmuring of surprise at the unusual sequence of events. Sister Assumpta raised her hands to signal that they should be quiet.

'No, Sister Evangeline will not be going through the usual initiation ceremony because we have already decided to give her the full status of Sister. I can assure you that Mother Magdalene, Sister Gabriel and I were very thorough in assisting Sister Evangeline with her new robes, and Father Lionheart has already heard a very full confession.' Spontaneous applause and raucous laughter filled the little chapel and Sister Assumpta had to wave her hands to quell the uproar. 'Thank you, thank you. Now, in lieu of the usual initiation we would like to invite some of you to share in a celebration of Sister Evangeline's successful transition from novice to Sister.'

Father Lionheart looked very dashing in his latest altar robes of pale silk and gold embroidery as he stepped forward to speak. 'Sister Evangeline, we would be honoured if you would select some of our Brothers and Sisters to share in this celebration with you. Who would like to volunteer?'

Excited laughter and exaggerated stage whispers were followed by several Brothers and Sisters detaching themselves from the crowd and assembling in front of the altar. Sister Evangeline's eyes widened as the group of volunteers continued to swell. Ten, sixteen, twenty, twenty-five. By the time the rest of the community had settled back down, thirty-one volunteers were lined up before her.

Smiling broadly, Father Lionheart raised his eyebrows. 'Well, Sister, quite a turnout! Please make your selection.'

Sister Evangeline scanned the faces and bodies of the willing men and women before her and her heart swelled with pride. 'All of them, please, Father. I want them all.' Sister Evangeline's cheeks were flushed scarlet and her eyes shone with mischievous anticipation. 'Could we go outside? It's such a lovely day and it would be much nicer to be out in the air.'

Father Lionheart looked over questioningly at Mother Magdalene who shrugged and smiled indulgently. 'All right, why not? Everybody outside, please. Sister Evangeline, lead the way with your volunteers.'

Gathering up the folds of her habit, Sister Evangeline stepped proudly forward and made her way along the central aisle and out into the sunshine. Packed closely behind her were Brother Joseph, Sister Maria, Brother Darius and the rest of the group of increasingly ribald volunteers, pinching and poking each other lewdly.

The balmy, late summer air was a welcome relief after the stuffy heat of the chapel, and soon the entire community was spread out around the central quadrangle, sitting on the cloister walls or lounging on the edge of the grass. In the centre, Sister Evangeline's whispered consultation with her volunteers was punctuated by giggles, snorts of laughter and nods of assent. At her signal, the volunteers spread themselves out into a circle and assumed postures of prayer and humility. Brother Darius looked positively angelic with his hands clasped in front of his chest and his eyes turned skyward. Beside him, Sister Maria was the image of demure modesty with her eyes and head lowered and her hands joined in prayer. A slight breeze stirred the brown robes, black habits and veils, but otherwise, they all stayed perfectly still.

Sister Evangeline took what looked like a rosary from her pocket and wound it about her hands before walking in small circles, whispering under her breath. She too had the air of prayerful contemplation, and her eyes were fixed on her hands as she twisted the beads through her fingers. Spiralling outwards, she began to walk in a circle just inside the ring of volunteers and, without warning, some of them reached out and touched her breast or felt her bottom. Whispered comments and giggles broke out from the onlookers but the volunteers and Sister Evangeline all remained eerily silent.

As she continued her slow walk, more hands began to reach out and lift her habit or rub against her crotch, but she continued to walk with her head down. Brother Darius, Brother Joseph and two or three other Brothers throughout the circle stripped off their robes and underwear and stood naked in the glorious sunshine. As Sister Evangeline's circuit took her past Brother Darius, he reached out and grabbed her hand and rubbed it swiftly over his chest and down onto his cock. Snatching it back, she resumed her walk.

All of the Brothers and Sisters increased the pace and intrusiveness of their embraces, until Sister Evangeline began to feel her body starting to hum with excitement. Keeping her eyes down, she could not see clearly who her delicious tormentors were, but she could feel a host of strong, massaging hands and myriad probing fingers through the starchy newness of her habit. She started to gasp with pleasure as her own hand was pulled onto a naked muscled thigh or a rigid cock, and she was delighted to find that pretending to ignore the fingers tweaking her nipples or slipping up under her habit only intensified the pleasurable sensations.

Sister Maria nodded imperceptibly to some other Sisters and they too hastily disrobed. Now, as Sister Evangeline struggled on through a blizzard of exciting, groping hands, she was thrilled by the occasional encounter with a soft breast or a moist pussy. Time and again her circuit was briefly interrupted as her hand was grabbed and guided onto another tantalising erection or into an equally inviting cleft.

Then Brother Joseph clapped his hands loudly and Sister Evangeline stopped in her tracks. Sister Maria stepped out from the circle, her thick, dark hair swinging against the small of her back. She approached Sister Evangeline and deftly tied a blindfold over her eyes and around her veil. Leading her to the centre, she spun her around and gave her a gentle shove before resuming her place in the ring.

Sister Evangeline put her hands out before her and walked uncertainly forwards until she encountered a body. Strong hands rent her gown and she felt the sun and breeze on her shoulder and the top of her breast. Once more she was spun around and pushed away into the arms of another volunteer who tore off a strip of her habit, leaving her breasts exposed. Throughout the circle, Brothers and Sisters divested themselves of their robes so that Sister Evangeline increasingly encountered naked flesh as she crashed around the ring, which was closing in on her, little by little.

Among the onlookers, the heat was also rising, and many Brothers and Sisters began to slip out of their clothing and lay sprawled in an appetising array of underwear and bare skin. Sister Evangeline felt a heightened sense of awareness as more pieces of her habit were ripped away and her bare flesh was explored by what felt like thousands of unseen fingers. When at last she was stripped completely naked, Brother Joseph untangled the rosary from around her left hand and held it up so that the crowd could see that it was actually a rudimentary whip made of strips of knotted leather.

Sister Maria and Brother Darius took one of her arms each and forced her down onto her hands and knees and then joined the other volunteers who had lain down on their backs in a ring around Sister Evangeline. Brother Joseph lashed her bare buttocks and drove her forward until she encountered a pair of dainty feet. Moving over the body, she searched with her fingers and found a plump pair of juicy thighs and a warm, moist pussy. A stinging blow on her rear increased her appetite and she guzzled greedily on the fuzzy lips and soft flesh until she felt a pair of hands pull her sideways and, instead of eating, she was being eaten. Sister Evangeline sat astride a greedy mouth, unsure and uncaring about whose mouth it was as long as she could enjoy the thrill of feeling her clitoris being sucked so hard and her pussy lips being nibbled delicately.

Just as she started to moan loudly with pleasure, another lash across her back signalled her to move on. Sister Evangeline began to lose all sense of time as she felt her whole being subsumed by lust and desire. Crawling, rolling and being pulled from one body to the next, she feasted on a cornucopia of breasts and cocks and pussies while her own body was licked and probed until she was delirious with pleasure. Stinging blows from the whip spurred her on to greater excesses and she spread her legs wide to allow more tongues and fingers to stimulate her throbbing flesh. It seemed as though even the act of breathing had become orgasmic and she cried, panted and wailed as a succession of explosive surges rippled up and down her groin and belly, only to begin another climb to yet another crescendo.

The onlookers had long since ceased to be able to play

the part of audience and, turned on by the orgiastic sight before them, they fell upon each other in a flurry of Bacchanalian delight. In the ring, Sister Evangeline felt her bruised lips being pulled away from another delicious cock and she cried out, 'Someone fuck me, now!' Brother Darius disengaged himself from a sweaty tangle of bodies and lifted her free of the writhing mass. He placed her arms around his neck and waited while she hoisted herself up over his hips and wrapped her legs tightly around his waist. Without preamble he impaled her on his rock solid shaft and grunted with pleasure as he felt her tight pussy swallowing the full length of him.

Sister Evangeline bounced herself up and down and slapped herself against him, devouring him greedily. She twisted and turned her hips to ensure that every aching hot spot within her was massaged to her satisfaction. Even though most of her volunteers were by now a tangle of limbs and thrusting genitalia, they roared their encouragement and approval as she rode him with abandon, and the rest of the community soon took up the chant and egged her on. 'Go, Sister! Go, Sister!'

For a moment, Sister Evangeline felt as though she had been transported to the Colosseum in Rome and she imagined herself battling for her life in order to please a merciless crowd. She plunged down onto the fat cock inside her and pounded her flesh into submission until at last, she rose up like a rider in the saddle and let out a piercing shriek of victory. As her body was rocked by a violent and overwhelming orgasm, hot jism spurted in great gushes up into her shivering flesh and she collapsed against the warm, strong chest of her deliverer, feeling spent and complete.

Very gently, Brother Darius removed her blindfold and she sat still wrapped around him, blinking into the sunlight like a blinded rabbit. Delighted to find out the identity of her lover, she kissed him loudly on the mouth, prompting a burst of applause. Brother Joseph then came up beside her, gave her a hug while he dangled her whip from his fingers and smiled like a Cheshire cat. Sister Maria crept up behind her and pressed her heavy breasts into her back and snaked her hands around to cup Sister Evangeline's glistening breasts. Sister Evangeline grinned wickedly at them all and then whooped for joy as she finally broke free of their embraces and moved among the crowd to share kisses, squeezes and pats of thanks.

From his vantage point at the top end of the quadrangle, Father Lionheart straightened his robes and wiped away the slick of pussy juice from his lips. Sister Gabriel flopped down beside him and leaned over to kiss Mother Magdalene and Sister Assumpta, who were just back from their foray into the crowd. Mother Magdalene's red-gold curls were frizzed up into a halo around her shining face and Father Lionheart thought she looked as though she had just stepped out of an ancient painting of nymphs and shepherds. Her pale breasts and rosy nipples were tinged with gold by the setting sun and her luscious lips were puckered into an inviting cupid's bow.

Beaming at the happy throng, she sat down beside him and squeezed his arm. 'Isn't she wonderful?'

He followed her gaze to where Sister Evangeline lay surrounded by her friends and admirers, pumping new blood into the community. 'Oh yes', he replied, 'wonderful.'

Chapter Twenty-One

S ister Evangeline struggled into the tight rubber sheath, muttering, 'Damn, damn! I'm going to be late!'

Her intensive training sessions had finally gained her the role of field worker, along with about eight pounds, in as many weeks. She had come to the conclusion that semen was more fattening than chocolate. The red, rubber tube dress was a nightmare to get into, even with half a tin of talcum powder smothered over her.

The feel of her slightly fuller breasts and buttocks encased in tight scarlet latex provoked the first darting pangs of arousal. The dress barely covered the cheeks of her bottom, but ended in a high chaste collar, which was all that would show under her long black coat. After pulling on a pair of wet-look thigh boots to complete her outfit she dragged her long fair hair into a severe top-knot and rolled up a home-made whip of thin, knotted strips of leather, which she hid in her pocket. Fastening the buttons of the voluminous coat, Sister Evangeline laughed with glee at how plain, almost frumpish, she looked, and decided to add a thin slick of red lipstick – just the merest suggestion of her hidden delights. Over-joyed to be back in town and on the prowl again as not-so-angelic Angela, she couldn't wait to try out her new skills on her first victim.

'Beneficiary, Angela!' she murmured to herself, 'Your first official charity-fuck. All right!'

Travelling on the top of the bus, Angela felt the eyes of a miserable-looking middle-aged to elderly man in the seat across the aisle staring intently at her lower body. Glancing down, she saw that the front of her coat had parted slightly, revealing a flash of bare flesh between shiny black boot top and red micro-mini. Feigning ignorance, Angela leaned back into her seat, half closed her eyes and parted her legs a fraction, affording her admirer an even more revealing view. Through her lashes, she saw him glance furtively around before stuffing his hand deep into his pocket.

Angela spread her legs a little wider, but by the time his breathing became laboured, it was time to get off. She wrapped her coat modestly around her, gave him a surreptitious wink and disembarked. Looking up, she saw his face glued to the window, his eyes pleading and desperate as a trace of his saliva dribbled onto the pane of glass.

Angela suddenly felt deeply sorry for him; he was probably lonely and isolated, cut off from human contact like so many people in this big city. Angela put her finger to her lips, miming 'Shh', opened her coat, and held the long folds away from her body. Ignoring the gaze of everybody but him, she pirouetted slowly, just for him, showing off her beautiful young body in the red rubber dress, enjoying the feeling of freedom and *joie de vivre*. She came to a halt as the bus drove away and grinned back at the man who was now smiling and blowing kisses. Angela waited until she could just see his waving hand disappear, before turning and hurrying to her appointment with Toby.

* * *

'I th-thought you weren't coming', stammered Toby as Angela stood, smiling serenely outside his door.

'I promised, didn't I?' Angela stepped over the threshold, giving Toby a brief kiss on the cheek, before flopping into a deep, soft sofa.

She looked admiringly around Toby's apartment and found that, once again, she was completely wrong about someone's home. Toby was very plump, always dressed in outsize faded jeans and check shirts, and wore his hair in what she thought of as a Mummy's boy short back and sides, but with a floppy fringe. She had imagined a grungy bedsit, perhaps with tacky posters, and certainly a mess. Instead, she found herself in a spacious room with high ceilings, furnished in delicate shades of cream and mint green, carpeted in deep, earthy terracotta. Framed prints by Hockney and Matisse added splashes of colour, and there were a surprising number of exotic plants, adding a leafy elegance to the atmosphere.

Toby hovered anxiously near the plush, cream velvet sofa, asking, 'D-do you like it? Can I get you a drink? Shall I take your coat?'

Angela reached up and took his hand, smiled warmly at him, and gave him a gentle pull. 'Come and sit down a minute, you're making me nervous.'

As Toby lowered his bulk beside her, he laughed, 'I'm making you nervous? That's good. H-how can that be right, when it's me who hasn't, who c-can't –'

Angela kissed him firmly on the lips to shut him up, held his dear, pudgy face in her hands and said quietly, 'I really like you, Toby, you're lovely.'

Anxiety changed to puzzlement as he looked into her eyes, searching for a lie. 'Why? Why would you? You're so b-beautiful.'

She smoothed his hair out of his eyes and spoke earnestly. 'Toby, I won't pretend to love you or even to find you passionately attractive, but I like you a lot, and I've become fond of you. You've told me so much about

185

yourself and, well, I want to help. Not like charity – but just to be nice to you. Because I can, and because I want to. Because I think you'll really enjoy it, and so will I.'

Tiny beads of sweat began to form on Toby's upper lip as Angela massaged the back of his neck and placed one hand on his meaty thigh. 'W-will you be my girl-friend?' he stammered, glancing furtively at the black coat which had slid open enough to reveal a tiny patch of red.

Angela opened the first few buttons of his shirt and answered honestly, 'No, but I'll be your lover, for a while at least. Would you like that?' Toby replied by clasping her tightly to him and fumbling with the buttons on her coat. 'No', she murmured, 'let me.' Pushing free of him she stood up and slowly slipped out of her coat. 'Let me do everything.'

Toby's eyes widened with surprise and desire as he saw the thigh boots and impossibly tight dress. He nervously licked his lips as she let down her long silky hair and stood astride him, straddling his knees.

'Feel it', she invited, guiding his hands over the red sheath.

'Rubber,' he moaned. 'Y-you remembered.'

Toby needed no further encouragement before he began to slide his large hands all over Angela's cur-vaceous hips and up onto her prominent breasts, which were moulded to perfection by the thin, stretchy latex. Grabbing him by the hair, she pulled his face into her crotch, where he rubbed and sniffed like an eager hound. Angela took hold of his hands and wrapped them around her until he understood what she wanted and gripped her firm buttocks. Toby moaned as his hands slid lower, coming into contact with the line where tight rubber ended and naked flesh began. He whimpered with delight when Evangeline sank lower, pressing her pert bottom harder against his hands and enabling him to nuzzle her breasts.

'Kiss them', she whispered, beginning to writhe so

that her breasts rubbed back and forward over his ravenous mouth, intensifying the delightful feeling of his strong, damp hands kneading her buttocks. Toby began to plant strong, hungry kisses all around each breast in turn, then tentatively took a rubberised nipple into his mouth.

'Suck hard,' breathed Evangeline, aware that she was becoming increasingly turned on as Toby's mouth clamped itself onto her erect nipple, while his hands had begun to explore between her cheeky bottom and down into the damp warm crevice between her legs. Toby moved onto the other breast as he slid a searching finger into Angela's hot, tight pussy. She bent her knees a little to allow him greater depth of entry.

'Bite me,' she moaned. 'Go on, bite my nipples!'

Toby had reached deep inside her and was circling and probing with his finger, causing Angela's juices to flow over his hand and onto her thighs. He nipped and sucked at her nipples, delighted with the taste and smell of rubber coupled with the heady excitement of exploring the real flesh of a real woman.

Angela gently withdrew from his ministrations, enjoying the thrill of keeping her sensations under control, then cupped his flushed face in her hands, saying, 'Now it's your turn.' Toby's eyes were wide and shining, his usually tidy hair dishevelled. Angela felt a surge of affection for him and promised, 'I'm going to make you feel so good. You'll never regret this. Never.' Glancing around the room she spied a pretty, full-length mirror near the entrance to the hall. 'Come over here,' she invited, turning away from him so that he could enjoy the view of her rear as she sashayed over to it. Angela stood Toby a few feet from the mirror, but placed herself between the glass and him, so that he could mostly see the back of her. 'Just watch', she whispered into his ear, 'and relax.'

Opening his shirt buttons one by one, Angela planted warm, soft kisses down his neck and throat and over his

187

chest. When the shirt was fully open, she slipped it off his shoulders and down onto his arms but, instead of taking it off, she reached behind him and bound his arms with it.

In the mirror, Toby was transfixed by the sight of himself being made love to by this incredible-looking girl with blonde hair and outrageous clothes. His penis, already stiff, gave a jolt, aching to be freed from the confines of his coarse denim jeans. Bending over further from the waist and spreading her legs so that Toby would see even more of her naked, pale flesh, Angela's soft mouth and moist tongue continued their meandering descent. With teeth and hands, she tugged open his button and teased down his zip with little jerking motions. Dropping to her knees, bottom still artfully splayed in front of the mirror, Angela grabbed hold of the waistband of Toby's voluminous jeans and yanked them down to his ankles.

'Oh God,' moaned Toby.

'Oh God indeed,' purred Angela, rubbing her silky head against his legs and up onto his thighs. Toby was overweight, but his skin was soft and peachy and his flesh was firm and juicy. Once again, she had guessed wrong about his cock. It was longer than she had expected and, although it was slim, with a slight bend, the shaft was a beautiful shade of walnut and the head was large and plum-coloured, just waiting to be eaten.

Angela buried her face in his great thighs, inhaling the warm, clean, soapy smell of him. 'Mmm, yummy,' she mumbled.

As she concentrated on his inner thighs and nuzzled closer to his balls, Toby giggled hysterically, crying, 'No, wait, it's too much – I can't.'

Angela sat back on her heels for a moment and beamed up at him. 'I see you've lost your stammer', she smirked, and leaned in to concentrate on kissing and licking his groin.

Toby gaped at the spectacle in the mirror and focused

on his own hugely dilated pupils as Angela began to rain soft kisses onto the head of his cock, then made great, sweeping strokes with her tongue from down below his balls, right up to the swollen tip.

Angela wriggled her hips and pushed down onto the back of her boot heel, rocking gently back and forward, as her own excitement increased with Toby's. Toby closed his eyes and moaned loudly when Angela finally took his eager cock deep into her hot, sucking mouth. Grabbing his meaty buttocks, she moved her head back until the barest tip of his cock was resting on her full, red lips. Toby looked down and felt dizzy at the sheer, erotic beauty of the sight. Angela's hands guided his hips back and forward so that he was sliding and gliding in and out of her mouth. When he was moving of his own volition, she cupped his balls with one hand and slid the little finger of the other up onto his anus and then, just inside.

Toby was beginning to thrust frantically in Angela's mouth, but she pulled away and said, 'Hold on, Toby, just hold on a second.' She shuffled both of them around so that they were side-on to the mirror and Toby could drink in the image of Angela's kneeling, horny posture and his own half-naked, bulky body, proud at last. Sure that he was watching, Angela knelt with her legs spread more widely apart and hoisted the red rubber sheath up to her waist.

'Watch me for a moment,' she breathed hoarsely, parting her golden-fleeced labia and pulling her skin gently upwards so that the hood of her clitoris was stretched back, revealing her swollen pink bud. 'This is what I'll be doing to myself,' she explained, putting a generous helping of saliva onto her middle finger and beginning to gently rub it onto her hard little pleasure spot with obvious satisfaction.

Toby watched in the mirror like a hypnotised snake as Angela's blonde head came closer to his rock-hard dick and began to lap at the plummy head. Glancing down, he saw her hand sliding quickly between her legs, adding to the excitement of the scene. Feeling adventurous, he wrestled his hands free of the shirt, clasped a handful of her hair and pulled her mouth slowly onto his shaft, causing shudders of pleasure to ripple through his body. Cautious of causing her discomfort, he went only as far as he could comfortably push without meeting any resistance and revelled in the combined pleasures of feeling himself in her delicious mouth and seeing the pair of them in the mirror.

Angela, however, was gorging herself on his lovely cock, wanting more and more. Her own mounting excitement was being set alight by the simultaneous pleasures of her own finger hitting exquisitely upon the right spot, and the satisfaction of feeling Toby sliding deeper and deeper into her throat. Only when she was almost gagging from the feel of it bumping into the back of her throat and pulsing with the beginning of his orgasm did she allow the fiery spasms in her loins to ripple up through her shaking body. She was drowning in the delicious, dual sensation of having a juicy, fat cock between her teeth and the explosive pleasure of her self-induced orgasm. Withdrawing her mouth at just the right moment, she felt Toby's come pump and spurt onto her face, dress and hair. Laughing in the joy of her own afterglow, she shrieked, 'April showers!' then pulled Toby down onto the carpet where he enveloped her in a great, bear hug.

His eyes were sparkling as he said, 'Wow! That was amazing.'

Angela snuggled in close to him and after a few moments said coyly, 'But I've been a naughty girl, I shouldn't have made you come yet. You'll have to punish me.'

Toby leaned on one arm and looked intently into her face, swallowing hard. 'D-do you mean sp-spank you?'

Angela rolled onto her belly, massaged her own bot-

190

tom and grinned at him over her shoulder. 'I most certainly do.'

'W-where did you get this?' Toby's eyes widened in surprise as he pulled the knotted strips of leather from Angela's coat pocket.

Sprawled on the deep pile of his carpet, her rubber dress riding high over the bare cheeks of her bottom, she laughed wickedly and replied, 'I made it. It's my very own cat-o'-nine-tails, but with a twist. Each knot is to remind me of something I'd rather forget. Come back over here, I've been naughty, remember? You've got to punish me.'

Toby groaned as his eyes swept over her luscious bare bottom and imagined it being marked with stripes. 'No. I c-can't do that. I don't want to h-hurt you.'

Angela looked back at him with a frown. 'Why are you arguing with me? I really like it. Come on, smack me.'

Toby took a step backwards and let the whip dangle from his hand. 'S-sorry, but I don't w-want to.'

In a flash, Angela was on her feet and snatching the whip from him. 'Don't want to?' she snarled. 'After what I just did for you?' She raised the whip and brought it down with force across his bare chest.

Toby's eyes were wide with shock as the stinging sensation deepened on his abused flesh. 'I th-thought you liked it.'

Angela's face was red and sullen and she twitched the whip in irritation. 'How can you judge what I like? If you won't lash me, then I'll have to lash you. Turn around and bend over.'

Toby shook his head. 'W-wait a minute. You're supposed to b-be my friend.'

Angela slapped the whip against her thigh. 'Oh, I am your friend, but are you mine? I do what you want, but you won't please me. So, either you let me lash you, or I'm out of here, and I'm not coming back.'

Toby's face crumpled into a childish, bewildered expression. 'B-but –'

'No buts. Yes or no?'

Toby rubbed his chest for a moment and then silently turned around and lay face down over the edge of an armchair with his huge bottom and thighs up in the air. As Angela approached with the whip he bit into the cushion and braced himself for the first of many blows, which he knew would soon come.

Later, Angela smiled with satisfaction as she smoothed some vaseline over the raw flesh and then took Toby in her arms and kissed him tenderly. 'There's a good boy, that wasn't so bad now, was it? You will do that for me next time, won't you?'

Toby dried his tearstained face and struggled to comprehend the incredible pleasure and then the awful pain of the evening. He wasn't sure if he liked it, but Angela was so beautiful and he'd never had the opportunity before to do any of these things.

'Toby? You will, won't you?'

'W-will you dress up for me again?'

Angela smiled and stroked his cheek. 'Of course I will. What do you want me to wear?'

Toby brooded for a moment and thought of the conversations he'd had with Angela about childhood and figures who had influenced them both. The image of a nun sprang into his mind. The last serious beating he could remember had been administered by a sadistic nun who loved to wield the cane and who saw something obscene and ungodly in a frightened, obese little boy. He had hoped that prep school would offer some respite from his mother's cloying attentions, but he'd soon learned that a wealthy, fat kid was shown no mercy by his peers, or the nuns. Small wonder he had kept running home to Mummy. He felt the blood begin to course through his veins and his penis began to flicker with life.

'I'd love to f-fuck a nun. Not a real one. Just you d-dressed up.'

Angela beamed at him and kissed him more warmly. 'What a wonderful idea! I've even got a habit already, but I'll be the dirtiest nun you've ever seen.'

Toby's eyes lit up with excitement and he bounced up and grabbed a couple of glasses and some wine. Sitting back down with a grin he said, 'I think I c-could spank you if y-you were a nun.'

Part Six

Apocalypse

Chapter Twenty-Two

*B*rother Joseph flexed his considerable biceps and ran his hands over the exquisitely defined muscles of his abdomen. He mimed a boyish grin in the mirror, admiring his own blonde, blue-eyed good looks, turning from side to side to gain a better view of himself from all angles. He reached for a small bottle and began to oil his body slowly, enjoying the sensation of his own strong hands as they produced a glistening sheen on his perfect torso.

'Aren't we supposed to wait for the Sisters to do that?'

Brother Joseph tore his eyes away from his own reflection and smirked at the novice Brother who had just arrived, no doubt a new contender for initiation into the ways of the Brotherhood. He turned back and resumed oiling his chest and arms.

'I'm Gregory, in Father Lionheart's new group – he said I'm rooming with you. You are Brother Joseph, aren't you?'

Sizing up the handsome newcomer in the mirror, Brother Joseph felt a flicker of interest. 'Call me Brother Joe,' he urged, 'and yes, the Sisters will include a good rub down in their programme. But I like to look after myself too, know what I mean? Keep them keen!' He laughed as he lifted the thin straps of his silky, black thong high over his hips so that he could oil his thighs, and bending lower, his calf muscles and feet. Suddenly, he threw the bottle of oil to Gregory, strode over to him, and turned to face the other way. 'Do my back,' he ordered.

'I'm – I'm not sure . . .' mumbled Gregory, shocked by the sudden thrill of sexual desire as his eyes took in the tanned, flawless back and firm, muscular buttocks before him.

'Don't be so wet, just do it.'

Gregory quickly whipped off his lightweight jacket and rolled up the sleeves of his shirt. As he poured some oil onto his hands and began to massage it onto Brother Joe's shoulders, upper arms and back, he caught sight of his own reflection in the mirror. At six feet four, he was a full head taller than Brother Joseph and he couldn't help noticing the attractive contrast between his companion's shorter, muscular, blond good looks and his own rangy, olive-skinned frame and black shoulder-length hair. His green, cat-like eyes met the blue stare of Brother Joe, who reached up behind him, grasped Gregory's wrists and guided his hands down onto his haunches.

Gregory closed his eyes for a few seconds and, having made a swift prayer, began to knead and stroke the golden flesh of Brother Joe's muscular behind, using deeper and stronger movements, until Brother Joe began to moan. With one hand, Gregory pulled his shirt over his head while with the other he reached through Brother Joe's glistening thighs and cupped his warm, heavy balls. Sliding his own hairless chest over the smooth skin of Brother Joe's back, he began to lick and nip at his neck and ears, inciting louder moans of pleasure and writhing hips.

In the mirror, he smiled with satisfaction at the naked surprise on Brother Joe's face. He let his long hair caress Brother Joseph's flesh, while his hot tongue traced a moist line down his companion's arching spine. One of Gregory's hands reached around to massage Brother Joseph's engorged, stocky penis, while the other parted his cheeks and deftly caressed his anus. He spied a tall stool covered with discarded clothes and, keeping one arm firmly around his lover, he reached for the stool and placed it in front of the mirror.

'Lean over,' he breathed into Brother Joseph's ear as he unbuttoned the flies of his dark jeans.

In the mirror, Brother Joe's eyes widened with a mixture of anticipation and fear as he saw Gregory's impossibly long, smooth shaft slip free of his jeans. With his perfect white teeth, Gregory slowly ripped open a small packet and Brother Joe started in surprise and delight as he heard the rubber sheath being rolled and snapped into place.

Standing astride behind him, Gregory poured some more oil into his hands and generously lathered it over Brother Joe's buttocks, anus and thighs. Pushing Brother Joe's body lower onto the stool, Gregory held his cheeks wide apart and began to circle his pulsing anus with the tip of his penis. Brother Joe gripped his own penis tightly and began to masturbate furiously. Gregory continued to slide his cock over Brother Joseph's aching balls and up and down between his cheeks, skirting the swollen flower of his anus.

'Please, please,' Brother Joseph begged, pushing back with all his might.

Gregory shoved him back onto the stool with surprising strength, then practically lifted him into the air as he took a firm hold of his hips. Splaying the buttocks wide apart, he plunged deep inside him. Brother Joseph shrieked with pain, but Gregory stuffed the fabric of a shirt into his mouth and continued to thrust into the burning channel, his pelvis making loud thwacks against Brother Joseph's stinging buttocks. Within moments, Brother Joseph began to relax and return the thrusts, eagerly wiggling his bottom to afford greater depth of entry. With sobbing grunts of pleasure, he resumed massaging his own cock, watching for the crucial moment in the telltale mirror.

Gregory had thrown back his head and closed his eyes, his long, smooth neck streaming with sweat. Opening his eyes, he locked onto Brother Joseph's wild-eyed stare in the mirror and began to control his efforts, starting with slow, delicious sliding strokes, then increasing speed to rapid, strong thrusts, reaching a crescendo as both men battered against each other's bodies in a frenzy of orgasmic tension. As Brother Joseph felt Gregory's cock pulsing deep inside him, he felt his own jism spurting and pulsing into the air, spraying his face and arms.

The Brothers' eyes met again in the mirror and as they took in the unholy spectacle, they launched themselves into hysterical laughter, falling onto the nearest bed. Gregory lay back with one arm behind his head, turned to look at his blissfully relaxed companion and said, 'Next time, you'd better ask me nicely, Brother Joe.'

Brother Joseph grinned wickedly and replied, 'Oh, that I will, I most certainly will. Make me an instrument of your peace, Brother.'

Gregory licked him on the cheek, grinned back and said, 'And I yours, Brother. Oh, and call me Greg.'

The evening air felt balmy and exotic as Brother Joseph swept up his sports bag and left the gym, but a gust of cooler breeze made him glad that he had thrown on his warm brown robe. Wiping the sweat roughly from his face with a towel, he whistled tunelessly as he made his way back to his rooms where he was looking forward to a steaming hot shower and a quiet hour to complete his meticulous grooming.

He jumped in fright as a pair of arms shot out from the bushes and dragged him off the path. Blind terror seized him as his attacker, who was holding him from behind, kept one hand clamped over his mouth and began to pull up his robe. Brother Joseph thought of knives, guns, injury and death. He trembled with fear and decided that a struggle would only increase his chances of getting killed. Bile rose in his throat as a hand forced its way inside his gym shorts and roughly groped his shrivelled cock.

'What's the matter? Isn't this the way you boys like it? In the bushes, in the dark, with strangers?'

Brother Joe's mind froze as he recognised the voice. All fear left him, and he felt incandescent rage flood through his blood stream. Jabbing hard backwards with his elbow, he landed a painful blow in the ribs of his attacker and then spun round and pummelled at his face and chest, knocking the man backwards.

'Brother Darius! What are you doing? You must be fucking insane!'

Brother Darius responded by fending off his blows and grabbing him by the wrists. His teeth gleamed white in the gloom of the trees. 'All right, stop hitting me. I've made my point.'

'Your point?' Brother Joe tore his hands free and stepped back in disgust. 'What kind of point is this? That you could rape me if you wanted to? Because you're bigger and stronger than me?' His voice broke and he started to tremble. 'Why didn't you just ask?'

'Why didn't you?' Brother Darius's words hung in the air between them as Brother Joseph tried to understand why this man he admired so much was behaving in such an uncharacteristic manner.

'Do you mean, why didn't I ask you to have sex with me?'

'Yes. Why do you flirt with me, and then go straight to others? Why do you show me in your eyes that you want me, but do nothing?'

Brother Joe moved restlessly from foot to foot while Brother Darius stood like granite watching him. 'That doesn't give you the right to pounce on me out of nowhere. Even gay men in a park wait for consent.

Besides, I assumed that if you wanted me, you'd have made a move by now, and because you haven't, I've been hurt and wanting to get back at you.'

Brother Darius remained immobile and regarded Brother Joe gravely. 'What I just did to you, you are doing to me all the time. It feels the same. Because I've been in The Order for some time, you take it for granted that everything will always be direct and easy with me. But it isn't. A heart is still a heart, even if it's inside a free body. If I make the same assumptions about you, as a gay man, I can expect you to like a quick fuck in the dark, can't I? But you don't want it like that with me, do you? Any more than I do with you, in one of those training session free-for-alls.'

Brother Joseph swallowed hard, his cheeks burning, as he realised that Brother Darius was right and that they had been violating each other emotionally. Tears stung his eyes and he needed to take several deep breaths before he could speak. 'I'm sorry. I thought you were playing with me, because once I'd got over my fear of letting go with you, you seemed to lose interest. By then, I was already in love with you.'

Brother Darius took a step forward and halted abruptly so that he could check what he had just heard against the expression on Brother Joe's face. 'Love?'

'Yes, I love you, but I'm so scared. My heart and body have done a good job of working independently until now.'

Tears were streaming down over his handsome features but he made no attempt to hide them, and his eyes were dark pools of longing. Brother Darius felt his pulse quicken and could hear his own blood pounding in his ears as he drank in the words he hadn't even dared to hope for. He closed the space between them and enfolded Brother Joe in his arms.

'Forgive me,' he whispered into his hair, 'I've been sort of crazy. Wanting you has been like a sickness in my head. I couldn't bear to be no more than another conquest for you to strike off your list. My eyes eat you. My body is starving for you. My heart is already yours.'

Brother Joseph reached up and silenced him with his finger, his heart pounding with sudden, giddy joy.

They stood very still for a few moments gazing into each other's eyes before Brother Darius bent his neck and tentatively kissed Brother Joe's mouth with his thick, velvety lips and then traced the edge of his teeth with the tip of his tongue. Brother Joe felt a shiver of pure, unadulterated delight and responded by sucking Brother Darius's bottom lip into his mouth before greedily exploring with his tongue. A slight breeze rustled the leaves around the two men as all of their pent-up passion became unravelled and unleashed.

Brother Joe broke free of the voluptuous kiss and pulled Brother Darius hard against him. 'I'd like it just fine with you, here. Now.' He slipped his hand between their hot bodies and moaned aloud as he found Brother Darius's massive cock straining against the fabric of his robe. 'Let's take these off.'

Brother Joe allowed Brother Darius to lift his robe over his head and he quickly peeled off his gym wear and stood naked in the cooling air. Brother Darius wasted no time in dragging off his own robe and laughed as his huge cock sprang to attention.

'Someone's pleased to see you!'

Brother Joe leaned back against a tree and looked straight into Brother Darius's eyes. 'Don't mess about. I want you in me. I've waited long enough.'

In a single stride, Brother Darius stood in front of Brother Joe and grabbed his fat erection in his hand. He kissed his lover hard and deep and roughly cupped his balls in his hand. Brother Joe felt his breathing becoming erratic, and he parted his legs so that Brother Darius could reach under his balls and stroke his anus. Reaching up, he clung onto Brother Darius's broad shoulders and hoisted himself up and wrapped his legs around his waist.

'I want to see you,' he breathed.

Brother Darius smeared some saliva over the head of his penis and gripped Brother Joe's buttocks, splaying them apart. He rested the bulbous head against the puckered flesh and they both paused and smiled into each other's eyes with anticipation. Brother Joe waited a few more moments until he felt himself open up, and then, with his eyes staring in wonder at Brother Darius's beautiful, black face, he lowered himself onto his huge shaft.

Brother Joe cried out in pain as the massive member stretched his tender flesh and slowly penetrated him to an impossible depth, but soon, he felt hot waves of pleasure begin to flow up into his belly and cock and down into his balls and legs. Brother Darius watched him carefully and grinned with delight when he could see that Brother Joseph was way past the stage of discomfort. As if somebody had speeded up the film, the two men's bodies began to move against each other in increasingly rapid thrusts. Brother Joe grunted with sheer animal passion as he impaled himself on Brother Darius's demon weapon, while he bit and scratched at his back and shoulders. Brother Darius drank in Brother Joe's beautiful face and body and his big heart felt as though it would come pumping out through his chest.

Supporting Brother Joe with one hand, he reached down between them and gripped his swollen cock and began to massage it furiously, in time with the thrusts of their bodies. His own erection was now painfully large and lost deep within Brother Joe, who juddered and shivered with each renewed plunge.

'Oh Darius,' moaned Brother Joe, whose body was on fire and filled to overflowing, while his own cock was on the verge of exploding. 'I'm going to come! I'm coming now!'

Brother Joe threw his head back against the tree and surrendered to the dizzy waves of pleasure that shook him from head to toe as he showered Brother Darius's belly and chest with hot jism. Panting with relief, he watched Brother Darius take a firmer hold on his buttocks and begin to pump hard and deep, crushing Brother Joe against the rough bark of the tree. With a loud groan, Brother Darius's face contorted and his hips bucked erratically as a huge orgasm rocketed through him, leaving him shaking and trembling with exertion. Brother Joe slid his legs down and stood, pressed tightly against his lover, revelling in the look and smell and taste of him. Brother Darius recovered his breath and kissed Brother Joe tenderly. 'How about we go to my rooms now, and try this my way?'

Brother Joe laughed and looked back at him with shining eyes. 'I have been known to do it indoors, you know! But I'll do it any way you like, love, so long as it's with you.'

Chapter Twenty-Three

S tretching out her back and gently easing the muscles in her neck, Sister Gabriel scanned the untidy piles of paper in front of her and snapped off the angle-poise lamp. Stuffing a couple of files into her voluminous leather bag, she decided to head for home. The day had been long and troublesome, with a steady stream of unusually aggressive clients making impossible demands upon her. Feeling weary, she wandered about the room, plumping cushions and switching off lights. To her surprise, when she opened the door a fair-haired, striking looking man in a wheelchair was blocking her path.

'Sister Gabriel?' She nodded her assent as the man stared at her intently with large, pale blue eyes. 'Will you have a drink with me?'

Sister Gabriel began to feel irritated. 'I've just finished work and I'm very tired. Who are you?'

The man leaned forward and held out his hand. 'David Goodman. I work in the ad agency around the corner. I'm always passing by and I couldn't help but notice you. One of your clients told me your name. Are you really a nun?'

Sister Gabriel smiled despite herself and returned his

warm grip, enjoying the feeling of his strong fingers wrapped firmly around her own. 'A lay nun. I'm not attached to a religious order.'

His unusual eyes searched her face as he increased his grip on her hand. 'You're beautiful. Do you always wear that?'

Sister Gabriel laughed and pulled her hand free. 'No, not always. Why?' She quickly scanned his slim, muscular frame and found that questions about whether everything below his waist was dysfunctional, or just his legs, leapt unbidden into her mind.

'I'd just like to see you in something else, that's all. So. Will you come for a drink with me, or am I going solo?'

He backed his wheelchair out of her path and Sister Gabriel's eyes surreptitiously wandered over his broad shoulders and strong hands. Feeling a little thrill of anticipation she nodded her assent. 'OK. Let me go home and change first. Where shall we meet?'

His serious face lit up with a dazzling smile displaying a set of even white teeth with slightly wolfish incisors. 'All right! What about Blakes? That's nice and cosy.'

Sister Gabriel thought of the dark, padded alcoves, soft jazz music and comfortable décor and found herself beginning to relax. 'Yeah, that would be good. I like jazz. Say about half an hour – David?'

'Suits me. By the way, do I have to call you "Sister", or do you have anything a little easier on the tongue?'

Sister Gabriel grinned, as another unbidden thought popped into her head. 'You can call me anything you like, honey, but Gabrielle's my given name.'

David wheeled around in a rapid circle before zooming off down the road chanting her name. 'Gabrielle, Gabrielle! See you there then, Gabrielle.' Sister Gabriel stood feeling dazed and confused.

Shaking her head, she hurriedly made her way home and found herself agonising over what to wear. Feeling angry with herself for acting like a teenager on a first date, she pulled off the clingy sweater dress she had on and threw on a comfortable pair of jeans and a worn, baggy sweatshirt. A slick of neutral lipstick and a quick scrunch of gel into her unruly curls and she was ready. Pausing for a moment to check her reflection in the hall mirror, she nodded slowly as if agreeing with herself about something. 'Gabrielle,' she breathed. 'Gabrielle.'

From about a block away Gabrielle could just make out the low strains of music from Blakes. Peering through the curtained doorway she was relieved to see that it was not yet too busy and she could see David's handsome profile as he chatted easily with one of the bar staff.

Turning to her, he held her gaze for what seemed an eternity and then beckoned her over. Gabrielle felt her heart skip a beat as she slipped past him into a booth, where the staff had removed the end seat so that David's wheelchair fitted snugly. Noting her glance he said, 'Yes, they're very accommodating here. Pity more places aren't like it.'

Gabrielle caught the bitter tone in his voice. 'I take it you have a lot of problems with access and getting around?'

He smiled grimly. 'Oh, yes. The underground wasn't designed with wheels in mind. Ask any mother of young children. But at least they get helped on and off buses. They're a no-go area for me. I'm afraid we wheelchair users are like a breed apart. Still, it's getting better. Anyway, what would you like to drink?'

Gabrielle agreed to share a bottle of red wine with him and then returned to her attempt to understand him better. 'Have you always – I mean – how long have you used the chair?'

David grinned at her discomfort. 'It's all right. Five years now. I had a motorbike accident. Broke my back. And yes, I am completely paralysed from the waist down. Intact, but no feeling whatsoever.'

Gabrielle grabbed his hand. 'I didn't – that's not what I –'

'Please.' David pulled his hand away. 'I don't need your pity. And, yes, you did. Every woman wants to know, it's just that most can't ask. Tell me it hadn't occurred to you?'

Gabrielle smiled shyly. 'Well yes, it did sort of pop into my head, but only because I find you so attractive.' She took a huge gulp of her wine and peered over the top of her glass.

David chinked her glass with his own and leaned across the table to look deeply into her warm brown eyes. 'Cheers. Well I think you're gorgeous. You've been inspiring my copywriting for weeks now.'

Gabrielle grinned broadly. 'That's a bit sneaky, isn't it? You could have said hello sooner.'

David shook his head vehemently. 'Oh no, I couldn't. It took me this long to pluck up the courage. And no, not because I'm in a wheelchair – you'd be surprised how often the sympathy vote helps me pull a woman. It was you. The veil and everything. I thought I'd fallen for a nun.'

Gabrielle choked on her wine. 'Well you have!' she spluttered. 'But not the kind you thought. No, don't ask. I'll tell you some other time. Look, can we just be on a date please? Let's leave my Order and your disorder out of this.'

David kissed her softly by the side of her mouth, sending a tiny electric charge through her body. 'It's a deal.'

Gabrielle abandoned any ideas of cautious pretence and reached hungrily for his lips, losing herself in a deep, exploratory kiss.

The evening disappeared in a warm, hazy blur of strong red wine, seductive music and stolen kisses, although David insisted on limiting himself to one glass because he was driving. They pulled apart like guilty adolescents every time a waiter approached the table, and then resumed their intoxicating embraces. By closing time, Gabrielle had planted herself on David's lap and he twirled her around while they laughed uproariously. Holding her beautiful face in his hands, David whispered, 'Will you come home with me?'

Gabrielle leaned against his neck and gently nibbled his ear lobe. 'Try and stop me.'

Together, they negotiated the thinning crowd and made their way to David's car. Gabrielle watched in admiring stupefaction as he lifted himself into the car and neatly folded and stowed away his chair.

A short drive later they arrived at David's beautifully modified ground floor apartment where he confidently wheeled about and fixed them drinks and a late supper of bread and cheese. Wiping crumbs from the corner of her mouth, Gabrielle wondered idly where the bedroom was. Not that she wanted to go to bed. Not yet, anyway. Her imagination was fired by the erotic possibilities of the wheelchair.

As if reading her thoughts, David glided into place beside her and began to fondle her heavy breasts. 'Will you stand up, please?' His pale eyes raked her athletic body with greedy intent.

Gabrielle stood in front of him, forcing her legs between his knees so that she could get closer. With slow, deliberate movements, David stroked her torso, her breasts and her thighs. Tugging on the sweatshirt, he pulled her down so that he could lift it over her head and then reached behind her to unhook her brassière. As her voluptuous mounds swung free, David buried his face in them, squeezing and kneading with his hands and then sucking each nipple lovingly.

Gabrielle was on fire with desire for this man, loving his looks, his touch, and his sardonic humour. She rained kisses down onto his head, neck and ears, allowing her tongue to worm its way into one of them until

David moaned softly. Unzipping her jeans, he tugged them down over her hips and used his tongue to trace lines from her navel down to the flimsy band of her thong and then on down to the delicate flesh of her inner thighs.

'Wait,' gasped Gabrielle, 'I have to get out of these.' Once she was standing in all her naked, chocolate-skinned glory before him, she put her head on one side and looked at him quizzically. 'Can that chair bear me standing on it?'

David smiled in delighted anticipation. 'Oh yes, it could take more than twice my weight. Wait while I put the brake locks on.'

Gabrielle leaned over him and unbuttoned his shirt, pulling it off to reveal beautifully developed chest and arm muscles, and a smattering of dark-brown moles. 'Mmm,' she sighed, 'just let me lick these first.'

Sitting astride his legs, she alternated between big, greedy kisses and flicking stabs of her tongue all over his neck, shoulders and chest, finally homing in on his nipples. David's eyes feasted on the sight of her full, plum-coloured lips against his own pale flesh. As the intense licking and sucking on his nipples became more urgent, David grabbed handfuls of her hair and cried out, 'Oh yes! That's good, that's so good!'

Gabriel broke away laughing breathlessly. 'But what was that you said earlier about "something easier on the tongue?" Was that just about my name, or could you do anything for me?'

David grinned wolfishly and licked his lips with a loud smacking noise. 'You know what happens to blind or deaf people's other senses? How they become more acute – stronger?'

He licked his lips again. Gabrielle's eyes widened as she caught his drift and she hastily crawled up over his body and balanced herself precariously on the arms of his wheelchair, bending her knees a little so that her pussy was poised enticingly just above David's self-satisfied smile. 'Show me,' she breathed, lowering herself nearer to his mouth.

David reached around her and grabbed her plump bottom, pulling her hard against him. Gabrielle felt him nuzzling and sniffing like a hungry hound into each fold and crevice, and then she gasped as his incredibly long, strong tongue swept up between her pussy lips and began to lap at her. She held onto his head and felt her knees weaken as he changed tack and began to burrow inside her and tickle her perineum. Gabrielle bit her lip, trying not to scream as he continued to electrify every inch of her body with the wicked ministrations of his outrageously gifted tongue. Within minutes, she felt powerful waves of pleasure rock her body, and hot, ecstatic rushes began radiating out from where David was buried between her legs. As her rapid orgasm reached its exquisite peak, Gabrielle almost tore David's hair from its roots and collapsed onto his lap, her legs no longer able to hold her.

'Oh my Lord. I just entered the land of milk and honey.'

David kissed the curls on the top of her head. 'No, it was I who drank the nectar of the Gods. You are pure ambrosia.'

Gabrielle lifted her head and gazed into his luminous eyes. 'Easy to tell you're in advertising. Where's your bed, by the way? You do have one don't you?'

He grinned good-naturedly and unlocked the brakes on his wheelchair. 'Of course I do. Watch this.'

Wheeling over to a console of switches, he pressed one and a soft whirring noise signalled the descent of a huge bed from the wall. When it was fully in place, David wheeled them both over to it and, removing the side arm of his chair, tipped Gabrielle onto the plush cream coverlet. In a simple swinging movement, he joined her on the bed and tugged off his shoes.

'No, let me.' Gabrielle lovingly peeled off his socks, pulled down his trousers and slid her hand inside his boxer shorts. 'Ooh, what a waste.' Kneeling up so that she could experiment more easily, she kissed and sucked his flesh from his throat down to the boxers. 'Tell me where you can feel it,' she mumbled.

David obligingly whispered, 'Yes, oh yes!' as she worked her way down his body. Once she strayed below his navel, his cries of delight petered out. 'Gabrielle, don't waste your time, I can't feel a thing.'

Gabrielle pulled his boxers down with her teeth and planted a noisy kiss on his flaccid penis. 'I know. But I bet it looks good.'

It did indeed look good, thought David, and he enjoyed a feeling of growing pressure in his belly and chest as Gabrielle's black curls fanned out over his skin. Gradually she returned to his stomach and upper body, stroking, kissing and nipping until he was writhing in lustful anticipation of her reaching his nipples.

'Turn over.'

David swallowed his disappointment and rolled onto his stomach, explaining, 'I can get an erection, you know, if I use a vacuum pump, but it's not a pretty sight.'

Gabrielle sat astride his lower back, pressing her hot pussy into him. 'Shut up. I want to give you a massage.'

Her hands rode up and over his back like healing rain and he sighed blissfully as she moved rhythmically over his skin. Her strong fingers kneaded every inch of his arms, shoulders and neck and then swept in powerful strokes down over his back sending surges of pleasurable sensation coursing through him. Where her hands had been, her tongue soon followed, trailing cool saliva onto his hot flesh.

Flipping him back over with a rapid shove, Gabriel straddled his slim hips and massaged his chest and arms in a sweeping circular motion, brushing over his nipples with each stroke. David caught his breath as she rolled each nipple in turn between her finger and thumb, squeezing harder until he winced. She lowered her head and took mouthfuls of flesh between her teeth and sucked and nibbled until he felt as though he would explode. Finally, her hot, moist mouth clamped onto one of his nipples while her fingers rapidly rubbed and tweaked the other. David's head thrashed from side to side as Gabrielle's relentless assault pushed him close to delirium. Steeling himself for the usual letdown of being unable to achieve orgasm, David suddenly jerked up into a sitting position as he felt tiny electrical charges radiating out from his nipples into his belly and chest.

'Wow!' he moaned, open-mouthed at the astonishing feelings mounting in him. The first flickers of almost orgasmic pleasure grew and grew until he shrieked aloud, 'It's like I'm coming! Like I'm bloody coming!'

Clutching Gabrielle's head to his chest, he felt hot tears of relief spill down his cheeks onto her hair. Suffused with a warm glow, he flopped back onto the bed and roughly wiped his face with the back of his hand.

Gabrielle kept her cheek snuggled against his chest and peered up at him. 'You are an incredibly beautiful man. I can't wait to get to know you better.'

David kissed the tip of her nose and smiled broadly. 'It feels like you know me better than most already. That's never happened before. Are you something of a miracle worker?'

Gabrielle nestled under his chin and wrapped a leg over him possessively. 'Don't be silly. That wasn't an act of God, just an act of lustful will. I so wanted to make you feel good, like you did me. That tongue of yours should be registered as a dangerous weapon.'

David laughed loudly and hugged her tightly to him. 'Never mind my tongue, you can have all of me if you like. I wish I could keep you forever.'

Gabrielle giggled and squeezed him back. 'Careful what you wish for – you just might get it.'

214

Chapter Twenty-Four

*F*ather Lionheart poured two generous brandies into balloon glasses and brought them over to the sofa before the fire where Mother Magdalene lay with her feet up. Her golden red curls glistened in the firelight and tiny reflections of flames lit her eyes.

'You look beautiful, Mags.'

Swirling the amber liquid around the glass she gazed at him thoughtfully. 'You're the only person who calls me that. Why do you still use it?'

He lifted her legs onto his lap and snuggled in beside her. 'Because I like to remember you as you were when you first came to England. You were so innocent – so girlish.'

She walloped him playfully with a cushion. 'Oh and I'm an old hag now, am I? Too serious for you?'

Father Lionheart loosened his white collar and took a swig of his brandy. 'It's not that. It's just that sometimes I miss that girl – the free spirit. You were the most wanton wench I'd ever met, yet you were good as gold. There was a sweetness about you. Oh, I don't know.' He shrugged and took another gulp of brandy. Leaning his head back and closing his eyes, he kicked off his shoes and sighed as he stretched out his long legs.

Mother Magdalene stared into the fire and wondered if she had become harder somehow. It had never been her intention to create a large organisation, but The Order kept expanding, and someone had to run it. They now had fifty full time Brothers and Sisters at The Priory and another hundred or so out in the community. The chapel was almost too small for the full meetings, which were hugely popular with everyone. Certainly, she felt more grown up and responsible, but harder?

She gazed wistfully at Father Lionheart's ruggedly handsome face that had also gained a few lines. His beautifully thick wavy hair was cropped close to his well-formed head and she recalled with a smile the long mane that had first attracted her. They had all changed. Even Sister Gabriel, who prided herself on her harsh fitness regime, had grown a little broader in the beam, although this was more than compensated for by the proportionate growth of her magnificent breasts. Mother Magdalene smiled to think of how much the three of them had changed, how much they had grown up.

Father Lionheart interrupted her musings. 'I bumped into an old friend the other day. Do you remember Savannah?'

Mother Magdalene spluttered and choked on her brandy. 'Remember her? How could I forget her? But I thought she and Sister Gabriel had fallen out or something. I understood that she was annoyed about not being invited to join The Order.'

Father Lionheart shrugged and took another sip of his brandy. 'She seemed fine with me. Nice as pie. Said she'd been feeling a bit down, though. I thought I might pop up and see her some time. Would you come? She'd really love to see you.'

Mother Magdalene thought for a moment and then said, 'Look, hang on a second. Where did you meet her?

'Well, that was quite a coincidence. She was near the college where Sister Assumpta is counselling. She walked into me as I came out.'

Mother Magdalene looked sceptical. 'Savannah, in the East End? Don't you think that's odd?'

Father Lionheart rubbed her thigh soothingly and laid his hand against her cheek. 'Don't get paranoid, Mags, she's an old pal, and I thought she looked lonely. Will you come?'

Mother Magdalene shook her head. 'I don't think so. Let me think about it. Listen, I feel a bit restless. Do you fancy a stroll in the grounds?'

Stretching out, Father Lionheart sighed and murmured, 'The things I do for love. Come on, then.'

They wrapped two long cloaks around themselves and stepped out into the frosty night air.

The moon was almost full and cast a luminescent glow on the old buildings. Here and there, a lighted window created a little pool of warmth in the darkness and Mother Magdalene found herself drawn to observe the activities within. Grabbing Father Lionheart's hand, she signalled him to be quiet and crept over to one of the windows.

The gym, as always, was occupied and through the slightly steamy window, they could see Brother Joseph hanging face forwards from the climbing frame against one of the walls. His wrists and ankles were tied with ropes and a plump, female novice was rubbing her enormous breasts against his face and chest. She turned away from him, jiggling her considerable haunches at him, and then sank back against him, grinding her fat bottom against his pelvis.

Mother Magdalene greedily drank in the erotic scenario. Brother Joseph's body was superbly toned and his face was boyishly handsome, yet here he was, at the mercy of a plain, plump woman.

Father Lionheart whispered into Mother Magdalene's ear, 'Isn't he supposed to be gay?'

Mother Magdalene smiled. 'Oh, he's a man of many talents.'

217

Crouching behind her, Father Lionheart began to feel aroused, and he lifted Mother Magdalene's habit and caressed the smooth skin of her bottom. Kneeling down, he bit her softly and ran his tongue up the crack in her cheeks. Moaning quietly, Mother Magdalene leaned forward and rested her elbows on the window ledge, eagerly watching Brother Joseph sucking again on the novice's huge, brown nipples. She rose up onto her toes as Father Lionheart swept his tongue under her damp pussy lips and began to probe and prod inside her.

Inside the gym, the novice fetched a footstool and climbed up onto it, facing away from Brother Joseph. She bent forward so that her pendulous breasts hung near her knees and spread out her ample bum cheeks with her fingers. Mother Magdalene felt a double thrill as Father Lionheart's tongue lapped at her while she watched Brother Joseph's hungry face contort in pleasure when the novice sank back onto his cock.

Pulling Father Lionheart to his feet, Mother Magdalene unzipped his flies and released his delicious cock from his pants. Resuming her position leaning on the ledge, she wiggled her bottom provocatively and waited. Father Lionheart took in the scene inside the gym and wasted no time in positioning himself behind Mother Magdalene. As the novice plunged herself backwards again onto Brother Joseph's cock, he sank his own throbbing erection into Mother Magdalene's tight bottom, lifting her feet off the ground. Reaching around to squeeze her breasts, he circled inside her, and then wet a finger and caressed her clit until she was panting loudly.

Eyes locked onto the lovers in the gym, they ground against each other, matching their movements to those of the other couple. Father Lionheart's finger flicked relentlessly against Mother Magdalene's clit until she felt hot stabs of pleasure shooting up into her belly and bottom. Moaning, she slapped back against him until she felt an answering release as he came in electrifying pulses within her.

After a few moments wallowing in delicious sensations, they turned to face each other and kissed deeply. Father Lionheart held her tightly to him as though he feared losing her. 'I love you with all my heart. You know that, don't you?'

Mother Magdalene drew gently away from him. 'Of course I know. I love you too, and I always will. Come on, let's go back. I don't want to be caught snooping! And you've got early confessions.'

She slipped her arm into his and turned back towards the main house, smiling to herself. Father Lionheart cast an anxious glance at her and looked as if he was about to say more, but as Mother Magdalene began to hum in a carefree manner, he sighed bitterly, and looked away.

Sister Evangeline pressed her lips closer to the grille in the dark confessional box and whispered, 'I tried not to – it just happened.'

Her heart beat a fast, throbbing rhythm against her ribs as she swallowed hard in a vain attempt to alleviate the dryness of her mouth. After a short, silent pause, the smoky voice of the priest responded menacingly, 'You know the punishment – assume the position.'

The grille made a harsh, grating sound as it slid away. Sister Evangeline lifted her habit with shaking fingers and climbed onto the confessional kneeler. As she turned, exposing her bare, plump cheeks to the priest, he barked, 'Push further!'

The hard edges of the window cut into her flesh, but she penitently bit down into the crisp white cowl of her surplice and then mumbled, 'Forgive me, Father.'

Thin knotted strips of leather beat against Sister Evangeline's quivering buttocks, each lash causing her to cry out. She stuffed more of her surplice into her mouth as the blows rained down onto her flesh.

'The pleasure and the pain', intoned the priest. 'The pleasure and the pain,' cried Sister Evangeline.

When the criss-cross patterns on her cheeks had deepened into angry red welts, the priest leaned in closely and planted delicate, butterfly-soft kisses on each sore spot. 'Are you truly sorry?'

'Oh yes, Father, yes.'

His tongue swept over the swollen flesh leaving a cooling trail of saliva. 'Then make a good act of contrition.'

Sister Evangeline shivered with pleasure and struggled to say the words. 'Bless me, Father, for I have sinned, and will sin again, and again, and again . . .'

The priest nuzzled into her soft, firm flesh, alternately nipping gently and licking in deep, strong strokes. Her breathing came hard and fast as his hand reached through her thighs and up into her warm, moist pussy. 'Do you give yourself to God?'

'I do, I do,' she panted.

'Is your body an instrument of His pleasure?'

'Yes, oh yes, yes it is.'

'Then come, in the name of the Lord.'

Sister Evangeline squeezed her own nipples roughly through the folds of her habit and humped frantically against the priest's soft, manicured fingers, grunting with relief as spasm after spasm of hot stinging pleasure rippled through her loins and up into her belly. The priest sat back into the darkness, pushing the button to slide the grille back into place. 'You may kneel, Sister.'

'Thank you, Father,' she panted, as she straightened her habit and resumed her kneeling position.

'Now, Sister, if these impure thoughts press you to consort with novices again, you must come and see me at once. Redouble your efforts to channel those urges into your work. Have you anything else to confess?'

'No, Father, I'm truly sorry now, Father.'

The priest intoned the words of absolution, as the sensual glow began to subside in Sister Evangeline's

body. Stepping outside the confessional, Sister Evangeline came to face to face with Father Lionheart's handsome, austere face.

'You realise that you can't get away with your abuses
as a field worker so easily? Sister Assumpta felt compelled to share some of the details of your feedback
session with us. Your penance, Sister, will be to help
Mother Magdalene with the novice Brothers – all field-
work is temporarily suspended. Go and see her now.'

Sister Evangeline wanted to cry out in protest, but she
bit her lip until she tasted the first tang of blood and
then answered humbly, 'Yes, Father. Thank you, Father.'

'Make me an instrument of your peace, Sister.'

'And I, yours, Father.'

Chapter Twenty-Five

*T*he offices of Linden Tree Advertising occupied the top three floors of a stylish fifteen-storey block just a stone's throw from Waterloo Station. Oscar Linden Senior, who founded the agency in the sixties, had made a shrewd guess about the future of the area and coaxed his backers into buying the whole building. Consequently, the Linden Tree agency had reaped huge dividends, especially with the opening of Eurostar, which had been pumped back into the expanding business until it joined the top five agencies in the world. David Goodman had been one of their most respected junior copywriters before his accident and had continued his steady rise in the company after his return to work. No expense had been spared in modifying the offices for him so that he could continue to feed on the 'buzz' generated by being part of a team. People said that he was a nicer character since his accident and he had to agree that his arrogant, goal-orientated, former self was nothing to be proud of. Now, he could still do the same quality of work, but without trampling over people to get it done.

From what he could tell, women still found him attractive too, although he was weary of the thinly veiled pity and the inevitable questioning glances that asked, but didn't ask, if he was still virile. Picking up the telephone, he allowed warm memories of his night with Gabrielle to flood through his mind, fixing his face into a silly grin. 'Hello, David Goodman.' He tapped his pen on the desk, lost in steamy thoughts.

'Hello, yourself. I know you're a good man, but I was just wondering when are you going to be good for me again?'

David laughed loudly. 'Gabrielle! I know this is a cliché, but I was just this second thinking about you.'

'That's all right then, because I was just thinking about you too, which is why I rang. Why haven't you called me?'

David adjusted his wheelchair and glanced around to make sure he wasn't being overheard. 'Because I wanted to see if you'd call me. We all know what a great time I had. I thought I'd suffer without you for a little while and see if you missed me at all.'

Her laughter sounded like music to his ears. 'Oh I missed you all right. Enough to come get you. I've got the afternoon off and I'm in the foyer. Wanna come out to play?'

David's heart did a strange lurch in his chest and he felt himself flushing hot and pink. 'Come up and get me. You can see where I work. Fourteenth floor, turn left. You can't miss me.'

Gabrielle laughed breathily into the mouthpiece. 'I told you already, I am missing you. I'm on my way up, lover boy.'

Grinning from ear to ear, David swivelled around and cast a cursory glance over the mess that was his desk. The view from his window calmed him down a little, so he focused on the sluggish Thames and tried not to listen for the 'ping' of the lift. When it came, David jumped in his seat and tried to look busy at his iMac.

Turning to greet Gabrielle, he was momentarily struck dumb by a vision in red. Gabrielle's voluptuous figure was elegantly clad in a beautifully cut suit with a short, but not too short, skirt, and a waist-hugging, tailored jacket. She was carrying a soft leather document holder in charcoal grey, which matched her high-heeled, pointy-toed shoes, and her unruly ringlets were piled up into a smart chignon, softened by a few loose curls around her beaming face.

'David! I'm so glad you could see me.' Gabrielle turned every head in the open-plan office as she walked purposefully to his desk, but slowly enough to give everyone a generous, all-round view of her undulating curves. Leaning over to kiss him, she revealed an enticing flash of scarlet-lace-edged cleavage and David's pulse quickened when he thought he could just make out the faint bulge of suspenders through her skirt.

'You look incredible,' he breathed.

Wiping a smear of red lipstick from his cheek, Gabriel rested her bottom against his desk and gazed out of the window. 'Nice view up here.'

David's eyes roamed hungrily over her. 'Nice view from down here too.'

Gabrielle swivelled around and her warm, brown eyes locked onto his. 'I didn't come for the view. Let's go.' As they headed back towards the lift Gabrielle had arrived in, she lowered her voice and asked, 'Isn't there another lift? You mentioned something about the penthouse one, and that you've got a key?'

David paused and searched her mischievous face before answering, 'Do you want to go up?'

Gabrielle grinned and followed him to the rear of the offices where the other lift arrived almost immediately.

Once inside, Gabrielle pushed G for ground, but hit the stop button after a few seconds.

'I told you, I'm not here for the view. Switch off the alarm, quickly.'

David flipped open a panel and hit a switch just as a bell started to sound. Laughing breathlessly he said,

'You know they're in conference up there today, the directors?'

Gabrielle reached into her document holder and pulled out two tiny contraptions and started to unbutton his shirt. 'So are we.'

Silencing him with a kiss, she sat on his lap and stroked his body then rained greedy kisses over his exposed flesh. Sucking hard on his nipples until they were erect, she placed the tiny clamps onto each nipple in turn and then activated them. David felt a tingling, buzzing sensation and looked down in surprise. 'Vibrating nipple clamps! Where did you find these?'

Gabrielle tore herself away from nuzzling his neck and grinned at him. 'Seek and you shall find, knock and the door shall be opened! Actually, I asked in a sex shop. We really should go together some time. They've got some wonderful toys.'

David snatched up her bag and pulled out a curious collection of gadgets and underwear, but his eyes lit up when he found a penis-like vibrator with a rotating head. 'This looks just like me. Come on, get up here.'

Gabrielle obligingly snapped on his brakes and stood astride the arms of his chair, hiking up her skirt to reveal a delicious display of chocolate flesh in scarlet suspenders. Lowering herself into position, she spread her legs a little wider so that David could begin his magic work with his tongue.

David sat and watched for a few moments, drinking in the glorious sight of the beautiful, sexy woman before him and relaxing enough to allow the nipple clamps to start to turn him on. Without warning, he plunged between her legs and voraciously kissed, licked and sucked her bare inner thighs, her moist pussy lips and her tight vagina until Gabrielle was crying out for him to suck her clit. Placing the head of the penis-vibrator just inside her, he switched it on and began to move it a fraction further with each cry of delight.

Gabrielle grabbed onto his hair, broke free of his

hungry mouth and forced herself down into a sitting position, legs akimbo. She ran her hands all over his face and body and then focused her attention on the tender flesh of his midriff, just above his navel.

'Isn't this where you said you sometimes feel everything more deeply?'

David's voice sounded deep and husky as he gasped, 'Yes. And isn't this where you want me to touch you?'

He licked his middle finger and slipped it between her legs until he found her swollen clit and then began to circle rapidly. Gabrielle groaned with pleasure as she felt the combined forces of the vibrator and David's fingers driving her rapidly towards orgasm. Kissing him deeply, Gabrielle felt as though her heart would burst, she felt so happy. Keeping up the pressure on his abdomen, she slipped her other hand around to the back of his neck and then plunged her tongue into his ear.

David moaned and writhed, revelling in wave after wave of acute sensation, from his hypersensitive ears, to his humming nipples and on down to his pulsing belly. Throwing back his head, he laughed loudly and redoubled his efforts with Gabrielle. Leaving the vibrator wedged inside her, he yanked open her jacket and pushed aside the flimsy lace until he could gorge himself on her fabulous breasts. Biting down on a nipple, he met her frenzied rocking motions with deliberate flicks from the end of his finger, until Gabrielle started whooping for joy.

'Who-hoo! Alleluia! Here I come!' Gabrielle clutched David's head to her bosom and thanked God, the universe, whoever, for this wonderful man. 'I love you. I really love you.'

David pulled back and searched her beautiful face, hardly daring to believe that this woman could really want him. Swallowing hard, he murmured, 'Me too.'

Gabrielle laughed and tossed clumps of escaped curls off her face. 'What, you love yourself as well? Wait, what's that noise?'

David's eyebrows shot up into his hairline as he registered the insistent buzzing. 'Shit! I thought that was these.' He pulled off the tiny nipple clamps and dropped them back into her bag. 'That's the call bell. It's been going for ages. Must be one of the directors trying to get down, or someone down below. We'd better get out of here.'

Hastily tidying their clothes, they descended to the foyer, where the receptionist and two security men were arguing about the malfunctioning lift. David and Gabrielle smiled broadly and made a hasty exit as three pairs of eyes regarded them in open-mouthed disbelief.

Romeo's Brasserie was heaving with people when Gabrielle and David arrived, but he felt relieved when he saw that she had booked ahead, and he was grateful for the attentive waitress who walked in front of his chair, clearing a path to their corner table.

As David reached for the menu, Gabrielle laid her hand over his and shook her head. 'I've already ordered for us. It's my treat.'

David replaced the menu and looked up in surprise as the waitress returned with a bottle of champagne in an ice bucket.

'What are we celebrating? I haven't missed your birthday, have I?'

Gabrielle leaned over and kissed him full on the mouth. 'I'm celebrating you. It's exactly one week since I met you and I'm goofy with happiness. Happy anniversary.'

David picked up his glass and chinked hers. 'I'll drink to that. And to many more to come?'

His face was impassive, but Gabrielle could sense the tension beneath the surface. 'Many, many more to come.' She held his gaze and then downed her champagne in one gulp. 'Refill please, I told you, this is a celebration.'

Laughing, David refilled both their glasses and waited to see what foods would arrive. It soon became apparent that Gabrielle knew about the aphrodisiac qualities of shellfish, because each course contained a tantalising array. 'So, you remembered I like seafood then?' teased David, sucking a juicy mussel from its shell.

Gabrielle swallowed another Dublin oyster and swigged back another gulp of champagne. 'I can see why you'd think that, but no, it's just that I heard they're good for you.'

David dribbled champagne from the corner of his mouth as he coughed. 'Good for what, exactly?'

Gabrielle smiled smugly and munched on another stalk of asparagus dipped in shrimp sauce. 'You know perfectly well what for. We'll have to test the theory, don't you think? Can you get a few hours off?'

David looked at her huge, merry eyes and pushed aside thoughts of the new aftershave campaign he'd been working on. 'Well, a certain couture company will be deprived of my awesome slogan for their new scent, but they can wait.' Gabrielle beamed at him and squeezed his arm, loving the fresh smell of him and the sight of those pale, hypnotic eyes. David emptied the last of the champagne into their glasses and raised his in a toast. 'To you. My inspiration. Hey, you know it's another anniversary today. My accident. It's five years exactly. Unbelievable.'

Gabrielle looked puzzled and sat back in her seat. She regarded David suspiciously. 'Do you mean this is the actual day? It can't be. Anyway, you haven't even told me anything about it, so I couldn't have known.'

David shook his head and grabbed her hand, holding it tightly. 'Of course not. It's just coincidence, or synchronicity, depending on which way you look at it.'

Gabrielle looked upset, and her eyes seemed slightly teary. 'But that ruins everything. I wanted this to be a happy occasion.'

'It is. Don't be silly. Look, I'll tell you what happened. It was all my own fault. I had to have the best of everything. These Harleys I collected – I'd pay almost anything, go almost anywhere. The one I came off was really special. Only forty-four were ever imported. They were really flash.'

Gabrielle sat closer to him and began to relax. 'What did it look like?'

'The Heritage Nostalgia? Great big 50s-looking thing with beautiful red pinstriped paintwork and black and white cowhide trimmings. It was nicknamed the "Moo-glide" because of that. Anyway, I saw one advertised about two years after they came out and because I'd missed them first time, I went racing off to buy this one. I was a bit suspicious about the low mileage, but the guy said it was a collector's bike. I fell for that, because I'm one myself.'

Gabrielle began to see where the story was going and nervously picked at the fabric on his shirt. 'You mean there was something wrong with it? Is that what caused the accident?'

David nodded and took a thoughtful sip of his drink. 'I was paying nearly twelve grand. I should have had it checked, but I was so greedy for that bike I just brushed aside any reservations I had and decided to ride it home.' He paused, lost in thought, his eyes distant and unfocused. Gabrielle waited patiently for him to resume, cursing herself for choosing this day, but glad that at last she would know what had happened.

'I was only thirty miles out of Birmingham when the back wheel of the bike locked and I went into a sudden skid. It was all so fast. I hit the central reservation and got thrown over onto the northbound carriageway, where two cars swerved to avoid me, but a third bounced off one of them and hit me. Anyway, it was the fall that probably broke my back.'

Gabrielle felt tears stinging her eyes and she squeezed his hand hard. 'What was wrong with the bike?'

David reached forward to dab away the tears with a napkin. 'Hey, don't be sad. I'm alive, aren't I? It turns out that the bike was a ringer, a stolen one adapted to

229

look like the Moo-glide, but poorly assembled. It looks like the pipes from the oil tank to the engine vibrated loose when I was at top speed and all the oil was dumped out. After that, the engine seizes up and the rear wheel locks. Hey presto! Rider is ejected.'

Gabrielle shook her head in bewilderment. 'How can you be so calm about it? Whoever sold you that bike nearly killed you. Did the police get them?'

David raised one eyebrow and looked at her sardonically. 'What do you think? By the time I was scraped off the road and the bike bits were examined, it was too late. The police came and told me it was a ringer, but the place I bought it from had already been cleared out. Gabrielle, what matters is that I thought I was going to die. I still can't believe I didn't. I'm glad to be here at all, it's like being given a reprieve. Can you understand that?'

Gabrielle sniffed loudly and swallowed the rest of her protests. Nothing could take David back to before the accident happened and punishing someone for their part in it was not going to give him back the use of his legs.

'All right, tell me one thing about recovering that made you sure you were going to live.'

David thought for a moment and then his handsome face lit up. 'The nurses! No, not what you think. You see, I'd been on a lot of morphine so I slept a lot and when I was awake I was still groggy. Anyway, this one day, I woke up and found four nurses holding up the sheets so that they could get a good look at my great big stiffy.'

Gabrielle's face showed her incredulity. 'What? What on earth were they doing? And anyway, what great big stiffy?'

David laughed loudly, enjoying her outrage. 'It's caused by nerve damage in the lower back. Priapus. I had this enormous dick for a while, but when I saw all those nurses gathered round me giggling and whispering, I just knew that I couldn't be dying.'

Gabriel shook her head in wonder. 'The little trollops. Still, it sounds like they cheered you up, so we'd better have a drink to them.' She caught the eye of the waitress and took delivery of another bottle of champagne, then shoved a glass into David's hand. Raising her own, she stood and saluted him. 'Come on, beautiful man. Help me drink this and then we'll both be legless.'

David's face briefly registered astonishment at her crude joke before he folded over in his chair, and guffawed loudly. Slurping his champagne, he grinned up at Gabrielle. 'My grandfather used to say, "we're all the same length lying down." When you're good and legless, we'll have to pop back to my place in a taxi and see if he was right. Perhaps I'll have to immobilise you a little to even out the odds.'

Gabrielle sat down quickly and leaned across to kiss him. 'Is that a promise?'

David kissed her back, long and deeply. 'You betcha.'

'Well then, maybe we'd better go back to mine. Access is no problem and I think I may have a few more toys than you, especially the immobilising variety.'

David's eyebrows shot up. 'Really? Fancy that. Well if you show me yours, I'll show you mine.'

Gabrielle's mouth dropped open for a moment. 'You have toys? Big boy's toys?'

David smirked and shook his head. 'Uh, uh. No deal. You show me yours first, remember? Shall we go?'

Gabrielle felt an overpowering urge to rip open her shirt and press his face into her breasts, but realising that this might put some of the other diners off their food, she settled for a greedy kiss instead. 'There's no need for a cab, we can walk it easily from here.'

David pushed himself away from the chair unsteadily and reached out to save a glass that he had knocked from the table. 'I'm not sure I'm in a fit state to drive myself.'

Gabrielle stepped up and bowed. 'May I?' Knowing how much he hated being pushed, she half expected a refusal, but instead, he rested his head backwards and gestured her on.

'Drive on, Madam, drive on. I haven't got all day.'

Gabrielle slipped in behind his chair and started to weave him through the crowd. Leaning down close to his ear she whispered, 'You'd better have all day, if you're coming home with me.'

Chapter Twenty-Six

'*D*amn, damn, damn!' Sister Evangeline strode angrily across the green quadrangle and realised that she would have to compose herself before seeing Mother Magdalene, who did not look kindly on ill-tempered behaviour. But the Brothers? Damn. And no field work? It was the centre of her being, the reason that she had known she had to join The Order. The opportunities to pour oneself like a soothing unguent over another's body, to fulfil every desire, every lonely, sad craving. Her vocation was to offer succour to the lonely, the spotty, the fat, the shy; all the varieties of men and women who were eaten up with need, the need to feel the warmth of her loving body offered freely, and with grace. At a price. Now she would be stuck with those strutting cocks-of-the-walk, seeing that they were pampered and petted. Oh, God, and no more novices. Sister Evangeline felt a strong twinge in her abdomen and clamped her buttocks together as the thought of all that young, girlish flesh flashed through her mind. Quickly checking her watch, she realised Mother Magdalene would be in the final stages of her morning session with the fresh batch of female novices, and she simultaneously thought of an excellent way to purge herself of her anger.

She dashed to the chapel and slipped into one of the side entrances leading up to the cloisters. As she emerged from the winding stairwell, she crept forward and sat on the floor between the pews. Peering over the ornate carved balustrade, she saw Mother Magdalene addressing a group of giggling, shy girls in long, grey habits, but with their hair loose and uncovered. The novices formed a circle with Mother Magdalene, and Sister Evangeline feasted her eyes on the delicious sight below.

Mother Magdalene was the most full-bodied of the women; her high, thrusting breasts formed a mountainous region of blackness capped by the snow-white crispness of her cowl. Her full, red lips opened and closed like an anemone in the milky whiteness of her face. She slowly, seductively began to pull the skirt of her habit up, revealing high, spiky-heeled shoes and slender, black-stockinged legs. When the ruched, black fabric bared her knees and thighs, it became apparent that apart from stockings and shiny black suspenders, she wore no other underwear. Her soft, white thighs were plump yet firm, and contrasted beautifully with her curly, ginger hair, fleshy pudenda, and enticing black straps. An alluring tableau.

Sister Evangeline slipped her hand up under her own habit and slid a finger into her silky wet folds. With her thumb, she caressed herself, breathing in short, sharp gasps. Down below, each novice in turn lifted the skirt of her habit, revealing a cornucopia of feminine flesh and hair and sex. Sister Evangeline moaned softly as the novices mimicked Mother Magdalene's seductive motions. One by one, they took a step, opening their legs wide apart, revealing their plump, juicy labia.

Sister Evangeline hoisted her own habit higher so that she could pinch a throbbing, erect nipple with one hand, while sliding her finger in and out of her hot pussy and rubbing more firmly over her bruised clitoris with her thumb. The sight of the novices parting their own lips and licking a finger before plunging it between the folds of their warm flesh, which was covered with an array of golden, brown and black pubic hair, sent Sister Evangeline into spasms of delight. With a deep intake of breath, she felt her muscles clamp tightly onto her finger as the pressure from her thumb caused her clitoris to mushroom, sending electric shocks of pleasure running up into her abdomen and down into her thighs.

For a few moments of complete abandon, Sister Evangeline closed her eyes and lay spread-eagled on the hard floor, nipple locked in a vice-like grip, knees akimbo, body jerking against her wet, aching hand. Mother Magdalene's voice drifted up to the cloisters, melodious and matter-of-fact. 'God wants you to love your own body . . . to give, one must first learn to receive . . . enough for today. Make me an instrument of your peace . . .'

'And I yours, Mother,' intoned the novices, whispering and giggling as they left the church.

Sister Evangeline straightened her robe, smoothed her cowl, then stopped to sniff the pungent aroma from her fingers, casting her mind back to her own initiation.

She was startled out of her reverie by a hand on her shoulder. Her eyes flew open and she stumbled to her feet as Mother Magdalene chided her, 'What are we going to do with you, Sister?' Her smile, however, was warm and friendly as she gripped Sister Evangeline's elbow and led her out of the church. 'Come along, I have an important job for you.'

Sister Evangeline began to mumble an apology but Mother Magdalene strode along briskly saying, 'I don't have time for this now, Sister Evangeline, I know you are more tormented than most, but then, God has also gifted you with an inordinately high number of talents. So! We'll make the best use of them, won't we?' She linked arms with the young nun and gave her an affectionate squeeze. 'There's a new Brother that needs lots of help and I know you're just the girl.'

Sister Evangeline pulled free and pleaded, 'But it's only throwing away my skills, sending me to him. Can't I go back to the community, Mother, please?'

Mother Magdalene stopped sharply and said, 'I think it's time you developed some discipline, Sister Evangeline, and I don't mean Father Lionheart's variety. You must learn to put the needs of others before your own, at least some of the time. So – no training female novices, no field work. Residential duties with Brothers only. Is that clear?'

Sister Evangeline sighed and nodded. 'I'm sorry, Mother. It's just that I can get so, well, involved. I feel safer when I know I'm in control.'

Mother Magdalene put her arm around her waist and admonished her. 'Trust me. It's your need to be in control that we've been trying to subsume, remember? Now, Father Lionheart believes this Brother may be troubled about his sexuality, although he's very confident with females and as far as we know, he gave Brother Joseph something of a surprise when he first got here. He's got a lovely, gentle, caring personality and he's a fine-looking fellow, so he's model Brother material, with the potential to be a field worker, rather than a resident. You're one of the team that will be helping to prepare him for field work. He's in the sacristy gym, waiting for you.'

Sister Evangeline resigned herself to her task and entered the sacristy through a rear door, enjoying the coolness and the dark, hushed atmosphere. She knelt for a moment and prayed for the strength to do her duty, and no more. The pungent aroma of incense lingered in the air as she divested herself of her habit and stepped into the small cubicle where Brothers and Sisters could shower after services.

Stepping out feeling clean and refreshed, she bent this way and that in order to glimpse sections of her body in the old, ornate, dressing mirror. The round, soft fullness of her breasts pleased her, as did her gently curving belly and generous buttocks. She had once thought that being whippet thin was essential to feeling attractive, whereas now she felt like a woman, not a girl.

A perverse notion made her snatch one of the altar boys' cassocks and pull it over her head. The deep, square neck allowed an outrageous amount of her breasts to be seen, barely covering her suddenly hard nipples, while the lace trim at the bottom brushed silkily against her downy pubic hair and plump buttocks. Standing on tiptoe and swivelling around, she laughed aloud with delight at the sight of the lower half of her cheeks protruding below the lace hem. Leaning forward so that her pudenda peeped invitingly between her cheeks and thighs, she could see what a tantalising aspect was in store for the novice Brother. Straightening up, she took one last look at herself in the mirror. With her liquid brown eyes and beautiful, angelic face framed by long, silky, hair, she knew that he would not be disappointed.

Entering the gym, she heard the grunts and groans of someone working out and quietly climbed up onto the gym horse for a better view. A pair of long, well-defined, masculine legs were braced, knees bent, against the floor. His elbows obscured his face as he did rapid sit-ups, with his breath sounding harsh and laboured. Sister Evangeline sat astride the gym horse, carefully arranging the cassock to afford an inviting glimpse of her bottom, leaned forward with her breasts perilously close to popping out of the neckline, and purred, 'Aren't you expecting me?'

The novice Brother stopped exercising, wiped the sweat from his forehead with the back of his arm, and stood up quickly, saying, 'God, I'm sorry, I didn't know you were here.'

As he straightened to his full height he freed his dark hair from his ponytail and shook it loose until it cascaded over his shoulders. Their eyes met and, with a sudden shock of recognition, Sister Evangeline gasped, 'Greg!'

His incredibly green eyes searched her face in puzzlement for a moment and then realisation dawned. 'Angela? But you're ... You look amazing. Angela!' In two strides he crossed the gym to her and swept her into a great bear hug. 'It's unbelievable. We were told you'd moved abroad after your studies.'

Sister Evangeline struggled free and firmly took hold of Greg's wrists. 'Listen to me. I really appreciate you being pleased to see me, but I'm on duty now, and so are you. We can talk later if you like, but that's not what I'm here for now. Let me introduce myself. I am Sister Evangeline and I am here today to assess your potential and begin to develop your skills for your role as a field worker. With your permission, I will take full responsibility for today's session.'

With a hurt expression, Greg withdrew his arms and stood with them limply by his sides. 'As you wish, Sister.'

Sister Evangeline's heart was beating rapidly as she struggled to regain her composure. She had never encountered someone she already knew in The Order before, although she had always known it was possible. But Greg Staunton of all people, the desirable college friend she had not dared to become involved with for fear of him judging her or exposing her perverted lifestyle to the other students. She fought the sudden desire to punish him for reappearing like this and unsettling her – however, his beautiful green eyes compelled her to smile at him instead, and she whispered, 'Make me an instrument of your peace.'

He eyed her hopefully, and answered, 'And I yours, Sister.'

Sister Evangeline swung her shapely legs over the gym horse so that she could face Greg and parted her thighs to reveal her soft downy pubis. His wide, hungry eyes were fixed on her unashamed display with apparent relish, causing a shiver of pleasure to charge through her body. She spread her legs wider along the battered leather and eased her breasts into full view over the starched white neck of the cassock. Licking one of her forefingers she circled each of her dark pink nipples until they were erect, then gently stroked her silky pubic hair and demanded, 'Are you ready to worship at the temple of the Lord, novice?'

His voice sounded thick and husky as he replied, 'I'd be honoured.'

Sister Evangeline's clitoris began to ache deliciously and she parted her moist pussy lips to afford him a better view. 'Then get down on your knees and pray.'

Brother Gregory sank to his knees with a soft moan and crawled towards her on the floor. Feasting his eyes he murmured, 'Beautiful,' then leaned forward and nuzzled into her flesh, inhaling deeply before kissing her inner thighs and delicately licking the soft inner lips of her fragrant pussy.

For what seemed an eternity, he lapped and nibbled, until Sister Evangeline gripped his hair tightly, writhing and groaning as her pleasure mounted. With the point of his tongue he began to aim rapid, flicking motions into her crevice until she raised her hips higher, allowing him full access to her clit.

As the first touch sent shocks of delight coursing through her body, Sister Evangeline pulled handfuls of his soft, silky hair up onto her belly and over her thighs, crying out, 'Yes, oh God, yes!' Her body was on fire, gripped by a glowing, incandescent heat so strong that she momentarily lost all sense of where she was, or whom she was with.

Greg's lips fastened themselves to her engorged clitoris like a barnacle to the hull of a beautiful boat – the more she pulled away, the more tightly he sucked and held on, casting her sensations adrift in a stormy sea. Her orgasm, when it finally came, crashed through her body with great waves of dizzyingly powerful pleasure as she grabbed fistfuls of his hair and clutched his fantastic mouth tightly to her.

She opened her eyes dreamily and smiled in blissful relaxation. She felt heavy-limbed and languorous. Greg raised himself up, slid his smooth body over hers and softly took her lower lip into his mouth, stroking her damp hair fondly. As the kiss deepened, Sister Evangeline suddenly pushed him away angrily, yelling, 'Get off me!'

Startled, Greg stood back and asked in bewilderment, 'What's wrong? I don't understand –'

'You don't need to understand,' she spat, 'you just need to learn that I'm in charge here, not you.' Struggling to her feet, she smoothed down her hair and fixed him with a cool, controlled stare. 'Come here,' she commanded, 'and bend over this.' She indicated the gym horse with an angry flick of her hand.

Greg's handsome face was creased into a puzzled frown as he followed her orders. Seizing a piece of skipping rope, Sister Evangeline roughly bound his wrists to the horse so that his face was pressed into the leather and his arms stretched out painfully on either side of him. In what seemed like seconds, she had grasped each of his ankles in turn and spread his legs wide open, tying him firmly to the legs of the gym horse. Greg felt naked and vulnerable, but was also aware of the thrilling ache of sexual arousal, which grew stronger as he became more fully aware of his precarious position.

Sister Evangeline, meanwhile, was pacing the gym in an agitated fashion, furious with herself for having been so instantly susceptible to his ministrations. She snatched a collection of items from around the gym and returned to Greg's prone, helpless form.

'I understand you have impure thoughts towards men, Brother.'

Greg jerked against his restraints and felt the first

tingling sensations as the blood began to reach his fingers again. 'Impure is hardly the word. Confused would be more like it. I don't desire them, but I get turned on if they want me, so then I fuck them.'

A small change in position offered temporary respite, but the tight cords cutting into his wrists and ankles, together with the painfully wide span of his legs, caused him deep discomfort. So why was he so turned on? Sister Evangeline surprised him by switching from her rough gestures and angry tones to suddenly grabbing a bottle of oil and smoothing it delicately all over his back in long sensuous strokes. His tentative erection began to feel hot and tight and, somehow, his confusion and feelings of vulnerability only served to heighten his arousal.

'Now, Gregory, how do you feel?'

Sister Evangeline moved in front of the gym horse and uncurled some knotted pieces of leather, which she stretched and snapped between her hands. Gregory answered hoarsely, 'Everything's new to me, I don't know what I'm supposed to do, or feel.'

He raised his head a little and watched in fascination as Sister Evangeline slipped the leather strips between her legs and rocked gently back and forth so that they rubbed deeply between the folds of her flesh.

'Novice Brothers are tested to the limits of their sexual and sensual endurance, you must have been told that? During the assessment, a Sister may uncover preferences or aversions. Everything should be revealed. Your capacity to give and receive pleasure and, where appropriate, pain, gives an indication of the kind of work you are best suited to. I'm going to inflict some pain on you, and you are going to tell me all about yourself. No holds barred. How's that?'

The leather had become deeper brown, moistened with her juices, and her eyes looked dangerously dark and unfathomable. Gregory felt his heartbeat accelerating as he said submissively, 'Make me an instrument of your peace, Sister.'

Sister Evangeline hated his kind, subservient tone of voice and her feelings of irritation mounted. 'And I, yours, Brother.'

She yanked the leather strips from her pink-lipped pudenda, causing a sore but satisfying sting that whet her appetite for the task in hand. She knew that it was wrong to let her personal feelings overtake her duty like this, but the vague memories of tenderness she had once felt for this man and his sudden appearance, as handsome and loveable as ever, made her crazy with anger.

Her eyes scanned his lean, muscular arms and legs, stretched over the gym horse in a powerless parody of gymnastic prowess, and in two swift strides she stood behind his naked, vulnerable buttocks and lashed him hard.

'What do you like to do with women?'

Greg's body jerked in pain as he gasped, 'Everything, everything.'

The leather cut into his buttocks again. 'Tell me.'

Again his flesh stung and burned as the thin, knotted strips whipped against his thighs and into the crevice of his cheeks.

'I love to lick them, to suckle their breasts, to smell their perfume on my fingers.'

Sister Evangeline appeared in front of him, thrusting her bared breasts against his face. 'Show me.' When he had managed to suck one of her hard, warm nipples into his mouth, she reached over his back and lashed him again, with ferocious energy. 'Bite me, come on, bite me.'

The pleasure of her sweet, tantalising flesh pressed against his face contrasted with the pain spreading through Greg's buttocks and perineum, which felt like fire as the wickedly thin strips of leather began to curl around under his bottom and snap against his testicles.

Sister Evangeline suppressed a moan as the tingling

sensations in her breasts rippled down through her body and set her clit throbbing in sympathy. She crouched down under the gym horse and whipped him from underneath, her lips agonisingly close to his throbbing cock.

'What else?' she demanded, flicking the head of his penis with her tongue in time with the light, stinging blows to his jerking rear.

'To be in their mouth,' cried Greg, 'to feel myself, hard, and pushing and thrusting in their mouth, or in their hot pussy, or their tight behind.'

Sister Evangeline slid her tongue along the underside of his penis, over his swollen balls, and up to his semi-exposed anus. 'You like to take them from behind?' murmured Sister Evangeline. 'In here?'

Her hands pressed his cheeks wide apart and her hot, pointed tongue swivelled around his tender flesh and, intermittently, stabbed into his anal flower. Greg struggled against his bonds. 'No, please no. No! Don't do that. Please.' A note of panic had entered his voice, but Sister Evangeline merely promised, 'I won't hurt you,' and continued to probe with her tongue, then her finger.

Sweat streamed into Greg's eyes as he felt more oil being poured onto his bottom and smoothed over his anus, while the hard shaft of his penis was gripped in a slithering hand. His feelings veered between revulsion and excitement as Sister Evangeline expertly massaged his cock until it was rock hard and throbbing with intense pleasure. With a shock he realised that Sister Evangeline's probing finger had been replaced with something much fatter, harder and cold.

'What is that?' he shrieked. 'Stop it! I-I don't like it!'

Sister Evangeline shivered with anticipation, her absolute control and his total helplessness a heady drug, urging her to further excess. She continued to massage his penis and kissed his back and buttocks softly.

'I promise I won't hurt you. It's just a dildo, a play

243

penis with lots and lots of oil. Feel – I've stopped, it's just inside.'

Greg felt a slight burning sensation in his bottom, but the delicious strokes of Sister Evangeline's long fingers on the tip of his penis were driving him to distraction and forcing his anal muscles to relax, letting the dildo slip further into his body. Sister Evangeline leaned back just enough to drink in the sight of Greg's strong, lusty buttocks with the black rubber dildo protruding from his increasingly receptive anus. Feeling his shaft pulsing perilously close to orgasm, she withdrew her hand and reached down to pleasure herself.

'I want you to give in to me, Brother, to open yourself and let me in.'

She began to inch the dildo a little deeper, drinking in the sight of his pale, tender flesh impaled on thick, black rubber. Greg could no longer stand the tension in his swollen, straining cock and he began to rock back and forward, his head spinning with desire. Each movement backwards swallowed a little more of the dildo, and despite his protests, Greg found himself grunting and pressing backwards, his tension mounting beyond endurance.

Sister Evangeline felt her own juices making her fingers wonderfully slippery and rubbed herself furiously as she revelled in the sight of Brother Gregory's buttocks finally rising to swallow the long, black dildo. Great surges of pleasure ricocheted through her loins, belly and breasts as she moaned aloud in relief. Reaching for her leather whip she flicked the tip against Brother Gregory's reddened cheeks and growled, 'All the way, Brother, come on, all the way.'

Brother Gregory became frantic, and screamed, 'Yes, yes! I want it all, all of it.'

He pumped his hips back against the dildo, feeling lost on a sea of pleasure and pain. As if reading his mind, Sister Evangeline lashed him harder, intoning, 'The pleasure and the pain – say it.'

Brother Gregory felt as if his insides were about to explode, but he obeyed, sweat streaming from his body, and cried, 'The pleasure and the pain.'

Finally, the relentless stinging blows from the whip and the hot, pulsing pressure somewhere deep inside him was channelled up into his painfully tight penis. With one last thrust against the shaft of the dildo, his sperm coursed out of the bulging head of his cock in wave after wave of pleasurable relief, matched only by the spasmodic pulsing of the muscles in his rear.

Gregory barely noticed as Sister Evangeline gently removed the dildo and quickly untied the ropes around his aching wrists and ankles. She adopted a businesslike manner, trying to conceal her embarrassment in having, once again, gone too far, but she stopped picking things up and generally fussing about when she heard a strange sound from Greg.

He had not risen from his face-down position on the gym horse, and his body was shaking and trembling. The sound came again, louder, and Sister Evangeline realised with a shock that it was the sound of weeping. Pushing the long strands of hair away from his face she saw with astonishment that his handsome features were contorted in misery and giving vent to his feelings, he sobbed loudly, taking great gulps of air. Sister Evangeline felt as if she had been given a cold shower and quickly put her arms about his trembling shoulders.

'I'm so sorry,' she whispered, 'I'm really so sorry.'

Pulling him down onto the floor, she held him in a tight embrace, rocking him gently as though he were a child. His heartbreaking sobs gradually diminished into occasional whimpers, then finally petered out. Sister Evangeline raised his chin and looked with dismay into his eyes. 'What is it, did I hurt you? Was it because you didn't like it?'

Greg's quivering face cracked into a watery smile as he shook his head and said, 'No. It's because I liked it.'

Part Seven

Revelation

Chapter Twenty-Seven

Mother Magdalene looked grave, her usually soft, friendly features pulled into a grimace of distaste. She looked from Sister Evangeline to Gregory and addressed the shame-faced Sister.

'Am I to understand that you inflicted distressful practices on this novice Brother – not in the loving manner you have been trained to, but out of self-indulgence and spite?' Brother Gregory tried to interject, but Mother Magdalene fixed him with a warning glare and said through clenched teeth, 'Let her speak.'

Sister Evangeline twisted her hands in anguish and replied, 'I don't know what came over me, Mother, I've managed to control my temper up until now. It's no excuse, I know, but I'm so sorry.'

Mother Magdalene remained impassive. 'Control. That word again. When are you going to learn to relinquish control, Sister – to give yourself completely to God and his works, as you once promised to do? How can I continue to entrust you with the delicate, loving approach required for sexual healing, if you allow yourself to be consumed with this desire for control?'

A great tear rolled down Sister Evangeline's cheek

and splashed onto her shaking hands. 'Please don't make me leave, Mother, please don't send me away.'

Turning to Greg, Mother Magdalene placed her hand over his and said, 'Thank you, Brother, for your compassion in accompanying Sister Evangeline here to confess to this undisciplined behaviour. You played no part in this loveless charade other than as a victim, and your account of events will not be required. Please go and rest, I will come and see you later.'

Gregory began to protest, 'But Mother, it wasn't all her fault –' but on seeing Mother Magdalene's stony expression and Sister Evangeline's mute appeal for him to stop, he bade them farewell, and hurried from the room.

As the door closed, a sob escaped from Sister Evangeline's trembling body and she pleaded once again, 'Please, Mother, don't reject me. Punish me any way you see fit, but don't send me away.'

Mother Magdalene sat stiffly in her chair. 'Oh, punishment. Yes, you like punishment, at least of the flesh, don't you, Sister? I do not intend to reward your outrageous behaviour. True punishment requires the recipient to suffer and repent. What is there left for me to do but order your excommunication?'

Sister Evangeline's gaze wandered hungrily around the familiar surroundings and came to rest upon Mother Magdalene's wise, beautiful face. 'Could you think of something appropriate, Mother – something that would both punish me and help me to give up my desires for absolute dominance and control?'

Her breaking voice exposed both the misery of her situation and her willingness to try and change. After what seemed like an unbearably long pause for reflection, Mother Magdalene spoke. 'I need time to pray for guidance on this matter – I feel it would be wrong of me to make a hasty judgement. For now, the most appropriate punishment is isolation, where you will have time to reflect upon the likelihood of your banishment from this

Order. You will go to your room, and remain there for an indefinite period. You will see no one, speak to no one, and consort with no one. If the Lord directs me to find an alternative, you will find out in due course. You may go now, Sister.'

Tears streamed down Sister Evangeline's face as she unfolded herself from her seat and stood blinking in distress. 'Make me an instrument of your peace, Mother,' she sobbed.

'And I, yours, Sister.'

Feeling as if her heart would break, Sister Evangeline left the room, fearing that she may never enter it again.

Sunday morning in the refectory was unusually quiet as Sister Evangeline made her way to one of the long tables. Every eye in the room seemed to follow her – surely they couldn't all know about her imminent expulsion? Finding a spot vacant next to Brother Joseph, she slid in beside him and kept her head down over her porridge. A sharp dig in the ribs from his elbow prompted her to meet his eye.

'Look at this!' he hissed, shoving a folded newspaper onto her lap. Glancing down, Sister Evangeline reddened as her eyes scanned the banner headline over a grainy black and white photograph of a nun. *NIGHT SISTER IN SEX SCANDAL* shrieked the headline, but it was the photograph that made it impossible for her to breathe. The nun, in full habit, was clearly flashing a pair of slim, mesh-stockinged ankles and shiny four-inch stilettos. The sultry, heavily made up face was easily recognisable as hers.

'Oh Christ,' she muttered.

'Christ is right, love, they'll definitely crucify you over this. Whose doorway's that anyway?'

Sister Evangeline quickly scanned the photograph again and banged the table angrily as she spat, 'Bloody Toby! How could he? But he wouldn't dare –' Her angry outburst was cut short by the arrival of both Father

251

Lionheart and Mother Magdalene, scurrying in with pale faces and rapid steps.

'Sister,' breathed Mother Magdalene, 'come with us at once.'

Brother Joseph gave her hand a little squeeze as Sister Evangeline got to her feet.

'I – I didn't . . .'

'Please, Sister,' hissed Father Lionheart, 'not here.'

With the air of someone approaching the gallows, Sister Evangeline followed them from the suddenly humming room.

In Mother Magdalene's office, Sister Evangeline gazed with pleading eyes at the picture of the Saviour on the wall, but felt in her heart that no one was going to save her this time. On Mother Magdalene's desk, Father Lionheart was busy laying out a photo special from the centre spread of the offending Sunday paper. Mother Magdalene guided her to a chair and ordered her to sit.

'When do you believe these were taken, Sister?' Mother Magdalene looked surprisingly calm, if a little pale.

Sister Evangeline swallowed hard. 'Very recently, Mother. I've been seeing Toby in my capacity as a lay worker over the last few weeks, but he really wanted to see me in my habit, so I wore it for him the last time I saw him.'

Father Lionheart snorted. 'And how would he know you had one? Lay field workers don't usually keep robes outside of The Priory, do they?'

Sister Evangeline shook her head and bit hard on her lip to stop it trembling. 'I'm so sorry, Father, but I only told Toby I could dress as a nun if he really liked the idea. It was a fantasy of his. I thought it was just another costume to him – I mean, the time before, I went there in red rubber.'

Mother Magdalene's anxious face creased into a brief

252

smile. 'Do you mean to say that Toby didn't know about The Order?'

'Absolutely not. I know I struggle with the rules sometimes, but I take my vows very seriously. I'd never knowingly compromise everybody.'

Father Lionheart rose from the table and began to pace about the room. 'Your behaviour in general threatens to compromise us all of the time. If he knew nothing, what was the press doing there? Two consenting adults having a bit of fun is hardly news, is it? And the paper states quite clearly that you are believed to be a member of a "secret cult" mingling religion and sex. Where the hell did they get that?'

Mother Magdalene jumped up and caught his arm, bringing him to a standstill. 'Stop browbeating the girl. Why are you assuming she had anything more to do with this than being foolish enough to dress up for someone? Surely we should be finding out if anyone in the community knows of anyone with a particular grudge against us. The article is very poorly informed.'

Father Lionheart shrugged off her hand angrily. 'When are you going to stop defending her? First the novices, then Brother Gregory, now this. Why are you so sure she hasn't done this herself?'

Sister Evangeline sprang to her feet. 'Don't you say that about me. I'm as upset as you are, but there's no way that I would do anything like this intentionally. Toby didn't know enough to make an issue out of it, so it had to be someone else.'

Mother Magdalene put a friendly arm around her shoulder. 'It's all right. You may be misguided, but I know you don't have it in you to be so calculating. Can you call your friend and find out if he knows anything about it at all?'

Sister Evangeline nodded. 'There is always his mother. She's a bit of a control freak, but then, how would she know anything about us?'

Mother Magdalene led her gently to the door, patting

her back as though she were a colicky child. 'Please don't fret over it. Find out what you can, and we'll do the same. Let's all get together here this evening at seven.'

After ushering the distressed Sister Evangeline out of the door, Mother Magdalene closed and locked it, and turned to face Father Lionheart. 'There's something I have to tell you. You'd better sit down.'

Father Lionheart searched her face anxiously and pulled a chair up close to her. 'What is it? You look awful.'

Mother Magdalene pressed her fingers against her lips and scrunched up her face as though she were about to cry. With an audible sigh she squared her shoulders and placed her hands in her lap. 'I've been getting threatening phone calls – anonymous, of course.'

'What? How many? How often? Why haven't you told me before?'

Mother Magdalene's eyes filled with tears as Father Lionheart bombarded her with questions. 'Please, Richard. I didn't want to worry anybody, especially as they were directed primarily at me, not The Order. When nothing actually happened, I just decided to ignore them. Until now.'

Father Lionheart rubbed his hands over his face and hair. 'I can't believe you'd keep a secret like this from me. So do you think they're connected – these calls and this story?' He indicated the sordid newspaper article spread across her desk.

She shook her head. 'I don't know, but it's possible. Whoever made those calls knew my telephone number, my real name, my chosen name and something about what we do here. But there was nothing very specific in the newspaper article, so I doubt if it's someone from here. Still, they must have some inside information. Look, I think we should call an emergency meeting of The Priory's key team – ourselves, Sister Gabriel, Brother

254

Joe, and maybe get Sister Assumpta to come along too. Perhaps she can diffuse some of the tension.'

Father Lionheart got up and resumed his pacing. 'We'll have to consider the implications. There could be more of this to come. Where will that leave us?'

Mother Magdalene could not fathom his strange expression, but she imagined that he must be feeling as though the world they had so carefully created for themselves was about to crumble.

'I'm going to my rooms to think this through. Will you telephone Sister Gabriel and Sister Assumpta and ask them to come down from London?'

Accepting his curt nod as an affirmative, she unlocked the door and left him to his own thoughts. Still feeling strangely calm, she allowed herself to consider the idea that The Order was possibly coming to an end, and found that she felt oddly relieved, as though a burden that had finally become too much for her was going to be removed.

Chapter Twenty-Eight

A light tapping on the door brought Mother Magdalene back out of her reverie and she realised that her bath water was almost cold. Wrapping a thick towel around herself, she hurried to the door to find a grim-faced Brother Joseph leaning against the frame.

'May I come in, Mother? I really need to talk to you.'

Mother Magdalene saw the deep anxiety lurking in his startlingly blue eyes and ushered him straight into her bedroom, where she lay down and closed her eyes for a moment.

'Forgive me, Brother Joseph, but I got out of the bath too quickly and I feel a little giddy.'

Brother Joseph approached the bed and touched her arm. 'Stress can do that too. Would you like me to give you a back rub? Massage is my secret speciality.'

Mother Magdalene opened her eyes and found herself meeting his cheeky grin with a vigorous nod. 'Wonderful idea. I never was one for big dramas, unless they're on the stage.'

She turned over and allowed Brother Joseph to pull the towel down until it was just skirting her bottom, and then sighed with relief as his strong, supple fingers began to sweep over her back in a succession of slow, deep strokes.

'Do you have any oil?'

Mother Magdalene nodded and pointed to the drawer in her bedside cabinet. Opening it, Brother Joseph whistled his appreciation as his eyes fell upon a wide array of lotions and creams and a host of aromatic oils. Selecting a bottle of rosemary and camomile massage oil, he pushed the drawer closed and poured some into his hands.

'That's quite a collection you have there. I take it you like to look after your skin?'

Mother Magdalene gave a muffled laugh. 'And the rest! I'm a bit of a self-pampering junkie. That cupboard could tell you a lot about the other bits of myself I like to care for, but I don't think you'd really want to know too much about that.'

Brother Joseph resumed his delicious massage, gliding his warmly oiled fingers all over her skin and kneading her tense shoulder and neck muscles. 'You shouldn't really go making assumptions about people, Mother. It's most uncharitable. You'd be surprised what interests me from time to time.' His hands slid down lower and kneaded her pert bottom before focusing on her hips and thighs with rhythmic side-to-side strokes. Mother Magdalene felt a hot surge of desire flow up from his hands over her thighs and into her pussy and groin.

'Nothing much surprises me about you, Brother. Any chance of a full massage? Your hands are doing wonders for me.'

Brother Joseph paused for a moment with his fingers resting on her inner thigh just below her aching pudenda. 'As long as you don't mind waiting for what I have to tell you. It's about this newspaper thing.'

Mother Magdalene groaned loudly and buried her face in her pillow. After a moment, she raised her head and looked hard at Brother Joseph's handsome, worried face. 'Tell me later. No point in rushing bad news is there? Besides, nothing can change what's already happened, and we're all meeting later anyway. Stop looking so hounded.'

Brother Joseph let out a long breath and smiled hesitantly. 'Why don't you turn over? I'll do your front.'

As Mother Magdalene made herself comfortable on her back, Brother Joseph helped to smooth out the towel under her. 'I'd be happier if I could get out of these robes. I don't want to get oil on them.'

Mother Magdalene's eyes lit up at the thought of his perfectly toned body. 'Please, be my guest. You're always a sight for sore eyes, Brother, I'm sure you know that.'

Delighted with the compliments, Brother Joseph made a slow striptease of removing his outer garments and then bent over to take off his footwear, affording Mother Magdalene a prime view of his muscled buttocks and microscopic red g-string. As he straightened and turned around, Mother Magdalene saw that the pouch of the G-string was far from microscopic and she felt another pang of lust as she ogled his impressive bulge.

Brother Joseph's whole manner seemed to grow in confidence once he was out of his robes, and he quickly climbed onto the bed and then sat astride Mother Magdalene with his strong thighs gripping her tiny waist. Warming more oil between his hands, Brother Joseph basked in her greedy, admiring gaze and then set to work, massaging her face, her neck and then her shoulders, until she was writhing with pleasure. She strained her breasts upwards, aching for his touch and, before long, she was rewarded by the feeling of his hands gently kneading her tender mounds and then circling her sensitive nipples. With his fingers and thumbs, he rolled and tweaked them until they were hard and alive with sensation. Lowering his head, he took first one, then the other, in his mouth and made her feel dizzy with pleasure as he expertly sucked and nipped until she was moaning loudly.

Sliding back down her body so that he could gain

access to her golden-haired pussy, Brother Joseph continued his massage down over her flat stomach and on to her slender thighs. As his fingers began to dig into the flesh of her inner thighs, brushing her labia and almost tickling her bottom, she began to thrash around on the bed, stuffing some of the towel into her mouth so that she did not scream. He knelt between her legs and pushed her thighs wide apart and then began to lick her groin and her pussy lips, occasionally flicking his tongue between them and dipping into her.

Mother Magdalene arched her back and thrust herself towards him, desperate for more of his sensuous, sinuous tongue. At last, she felt a sharp, electric thrill course through her as he homed in on her throbbing clitoris and massaged it deliciously. Abandoning all efforts to control her noise levels, Mother Magdalene reached down and tried to clasp Brother Joseph's closely-cropped hair and began to shriek with delight as he relentlessly probed her super-charged flesh. Gaining purchase on his ears, she pressed herself against his face and roared, 'Yes! Yes! Here I come!'

She bucked and shivered for what seemed like an eternity, and when at last her feelings had subsided to a warm glow, she looked down wonderingly at Brother Joseph's face between her legs, pink from exertion. He beamed at her, chin glistening with juices.

'Do you think I could have my ears back now, Mother? Only I can't hear a thing.'

Laughing with delight and relief from all her worries, Mother Magdalene let go of his ears and reached down to pull him up onto her so that she could hug and kiss him.

'That was so wonderful. Where did you learn to do that?' Brother Joseph propped himself up on one elbow and laughed. 'Where do you think? Here, of course. Sister Maria's a dedicated teacher.'

Mother Magdalene smiled and nodded, thinking of how many men, well-trained in cunnilingus, Sister Maria had turned out by now. 'Ah yes. Sister Maria. That explains it. But what about you, Brother Joe? What can I do for you?'

Brother Joseph shook his head and kissed the tip of her nose. 'If it's all the same to you, Mother, I'm happy as I am for now. Saving myself for later, if you know what I mean?'

Mother Magdalene cocked her head on one side like an inquisitive bird. 'Oh? And who would that be with? I know I'm not really your type anyway, although I gather you do dabble with women sometimes.'

Brother Joseph laughed loudly and pinned her to the bed, kissing her roughly. 'You're right. Gorgeous as you are, you're far too skinny for me. I used to think I was solely gay until I discovered an occasional taste for big women. What does that make me?'

'Sexual, just like the rest of us. I don't know why we all love labels so much. You still haven't told me who you're seeing later.'

Brother Joseph rolled onto his back and looked up at the ceiling. 'Brother Darius. He's someone really special, you know? Kinda makes me nervous. I can't explain it, but the last thing I was looking for here was love.'

Mother Magdalene sat up and placed her hand on Brother Joseph's forehead, smoothing away the tiny furrow that was forming there. 'John said, "There is no fear in love, for perfect love casteth out fear." In other words, I think you'll both be fine if there's enough love between you.'

Brother Joseph sat up and clasped his hands together. 'I need to tell you about Savannah.'

Mother Magdalene rose from the bed and began assembling her garments for the evening. 'Savannah? What about her? Are you still in touch?'

Brother Joseph pulled on his socks. 'Not now, but we were until recently. She got mad at me for not telling her more about this place. And somehow she got hold of my mobile number and called me here.'

Mother Magdalene came to a standstill in front of him, stockings in one hand. 'Your mobile? Here?'

Brother Joseph kept his head down while he fastened his shoes. 'Yes. I'm sorry, Mother, it was foolish of me. I got rid of it straight after Father Lionheart caught me.'

Mother Magdalene sat on the edge of the bed and began to roll on her stockings. 'That's odd, he didn't mention it to me. So what did Savannah want? Father Lionheart bumped into her in London recently, but he didn't notice anything amiss.'

Brother Joseph pulled on his robes and began to fasten his belt, smoothing down the fabric for a more svelte line. 'Well she was pretty bitchy to me. Seemed to feel kind of left out and a bit annoyed by all the secrecy. Why wasn't she asked to join?'

Mother Magdalene's manner became brusque. 'I'm sorry, but I don't want to go into that now. But thank you for talking to me. We'll need to raise this with the others this evening. Now, if you don't mind, I need a little time to rest and get ready.' She steered him towards the door and swung it open. 'Goodbye, Brother Joe. Thank you for everything.'

Somewhat mollified by the warmth of her smile, Brother Joseph bade her farewell and headed for the dining room. He suddenly felt ravenously hungry.

Chapter Twenty-Nine

Mother Magdalene looked around the library and felt proud of the densely packed shelves, the huge leather- and gold-embossed study table and the comfortable selection of chairs, tables and sofas. She recalled the hollow ring of the floor the first time she had walked over it and realised that she was unconsciously making an inventory of all the good times she had enjoyed here at The Priory. All of her instincts told her that the end was at hand.

Brother Joseph threw a log onto the fire and poured everybody another glass of wine, unable to sit still. Sister Assumpta's calming voice poured over them like oil on troubled waters.

'Why is there such emphasis on finding a culprit? Is that really going to help? What we need to decide now is how to respond to the attention that will be focused on us. We need a strategy.'

Father Lionheart sprang from his seat and started pacing in agitation. 'That's very noble of you, Sister, but what about the implications of this meeting? You're asking us to pull together as a team when it's just become obvious that we don't know how. Mother Magdalene has wilfully kept quiet about threatening telephone calls, Brother Joseph has smuggled a mobile phone in here and had Savannah trying to track him down, and now Sister Gabriel "forgot" to tell us that Savannah has already threatened to expose us.'

'Steady on.' Sister Gabriel interrupted his speech by banging on the table. 'I didn't say that. I just said that she was angry at being kept out and that she was going to try and find out more about us. She was upset. Why shouldn't she be? You're the one that excluded her in the first place. She might be a bit selfish, but aren't we all?'

Brother Joe and Sister Assumpta exchanged curious glances, but stayed quiet. Father Lionheart's handsome face became ugly with anger.

'I refuse to be drawn into a debate on why perpetrators of mischief act the way they do. That's how murderers end up being treated as victims. Savannah is a professional gossip merchant and would have every reason to want to make a buck out of this. And as for that sadistic little control freak, Sister Evangeline, she's probably living up to her name by being Savannah's avenging angel.'

Mother Magdalene stood up and touched his arm. 'Stop working yourself up. You just sound pompous. Come and sit down, there's something I need to say.'

Father Lionheart looked with anguish into her serene face and allowed himself to be led back to his seat.

Mother Magdalene looked at each face in turn. Father Lionheart, whom she had loved from the moment she first saw him, and who had helped her to make this dream come true; Sister Gabriel, the laughing, dashing-eyed black girl who had become like a real sister to her; Brother Joseph and his Adonis-like looks, who graced every situation with his beauty and made them laugh with his vanity, but whose heart shone through like gold; and dear Sister Assumpta, who had somehow moved seamlessly from novice to Sister, to mother of them all – a truly beautiful, cornucopia of a woman.

Mother Magdalene felt choked with emotion but swallowed hard, and addressed them in a clear, thoughtful voice.

'Whatever happens next, there is no way that The Order can continue.' She waved aside protests from Brother Joseph and Sister Assumpta and went doggedly on. 'I'm sorry that those of you who have joined us most recently will not be able to walk away with as many fond memories as the rest of us, but we simply cannot go on. I have no wish to continue.'

Father Lionheart looked puzzled and took her hand. 'So you think the publicity will finish us?'

Mother Magdalene shrugged. 'It may, it may not, but we can never be the same once our secret is out. That's been half the fun, hasn't it? The secrecy? Besides, I don't want to carry on. We've become too worthy by half. I'm tired of all this order and purpose. I want some frivolity.'

Father Lionheart and Sister Gabriel exchanged astonished glances, but it was Sister Assumpta who voiced their thoughts. 'We all thought that this was your life, what you'd always wanted.'

Mother Magdalene nodded and smiled as she caught Brother Joseph's admiring glance, urging her to go on. 'So it was. But it's not now. Whoever decided to expose us did me a favour. I just hope I was right in thinking we've done nothing illegal. There are sure to be all sorts of accusations flying and I've no wish to pay for my sins.'

Father Lionheart looked ashen. 'How long?' he croaked. 'How long have you known you wanted to stop?'

Mother Magdalene considered for a moment before answering. 'Months. Months and months. I think I only acknowledged it to myself when this scandal broke. I felt so relieved.'

Sister Gabriel clapped her hands in delight and nodded furiously. 'Alleluia! Lord only knows how good it is to hear you say that. I've been so worried about how to tell you all that I've been thinking about moving on.'

'You too?' Father Lionheart's face seemed to be frozen into an expression of disbelief.

'Well, yes. It's not that I don't love The Order and all, but most of the fun seems to have gone out of it. That was partly what it was about, wasn't it? Having fun?' She slowly removed her veil and ran her fingers through her lustrous black curls. 'I've met someone really beautiful. Someone I prefer to be Gabrielle with. I guess I'm just tired of being Sister Gabriel. The game's up. And it's like Mother Magdalene said, if what we do isn't secret, we can't even do it.'

Brother Joseph's face was flushed and shining with happiness. 'Don't you see? This is a great opportunity for all of us to move on. The field workers who were never very involved with The Priory will be fine, so it's up to the rest of us to decide what to do with all the publicity we're going to get. All news is good news if it's handled right. Believe it or not, the best person to help us is Savannah!'

Mother Magdalene laughed and Gabrielle threw back her head and whooped. 'Whoo-oo! That girl is going to go ape if she only gets to come here after it's all over. But it's true, she's got a media head on her shoulders, and if we've already been rumbled, we need someone in the know on our side.'

Sister Assumpta nodded thoughtfully. 'That's certainly an option, but what are we going to do now? I mean, the story was very scant. Have you considered just riding it out? They might just get bored and go away.'

Mother Magdalene shook her head and poured herself another generous glass of wine before passing the bottle around. 'No, it may take a few weeks, but it will blow. I for one have no intention of waiting for the axe to fall and then being forced into public mourning. Let's finish this thing with a bang. We'll have a party.'

Father Lionheart stood up slowly looking lost and bewildered. 'I don't understand you. Not at all. I thought you'd be heartbroken, inconsolable.'

Mother Magdalene went to him and wrapped her arms around his waist. Looking tenderly into his face, she said, 'It's all right, Richard. I'm fine. Maybe we don't know each other as well as we thought we did. Or perhaps we've lost sight of Mags and Richard somewhere along the way. Come on, help me arrange a big party for everybody. We'll let all the field workers know and then afterwards, anyone who wants to slip away quietly from The Order can go ahead, and the rest of us will face the music. What do you say?'

Father Lionheart touched her face and gazed wistfully at her for several moments before breaking away and staring into the fire. 'What's the point? This whole thing was created for you and now it turns out you didn't need it after all. I thought you needed me too, but you don't, do you? I've been an idiot.' With a sigh, he stepped back, pulling the white collar from his throat and throwing it to the ground at her feet. 'I'm out now. I can do without becoming part of some media circus. I thought you'd be sad, want to hide, need my support. Ha!' His bitter laugh matched his cold, ugly expression as he turned on his heel and stalked from the room. Nobody made a move to stop or follow him.

At precisely this moment, Savannah was discovering the joys of being installed in her very own secret location, courtesy of the first quality newspaper she had ever had dealings with.

'Are you sure you're comfortable Savannah? Is there anything else I can get you?'

The features editor was a well-kept woman in her late forties with a large expense account and a "seen-it-all-before" look in her world-weary eyes. Savannah glanced around at the sumptuous furnishings, the well-stocked mini-bar and the sunken spa and smiled cheekily.

'Oh, I think I'll manage. Some champagne would be nice. Cristal?'

Flopping down on the over-stuffed, oatmeal sofa, Savannah watched Katherine appraisingly as she ordered the champagne, and some coffee for herself. She envied the other woman's self-assurance, but felt confident that her own status was about to take an upward turn. Katherine came and sat down on the other end of the sofa, kicked off her shoes and tucked her feet up under her, looking instantly at home.

'So, let's run through this one last time. You get the cash lump sum, a by-line on the feature and a favourable photo and biography. We've also agreed with your agent to follow and publish all developments relating to you and your career for a minimum of the next three months. In return, we have the exclusive rights to all of your information about The Order and you will hand over to us your notes, photographs, computer and laptop. You agree not to give interviews with any other newspaper or magazine for a minimum period of four weeks and we get first refusal on any other material you turn up. Fair deal?'

Savannah widened her eyes. 'How would I know? I'm just doing what my agent tells me. Besides, I've already signed, so why are we doing this?'

Katherine took a pack of cigarettes from her bag and lit one, blowing a stream of blue smoke into the air between them. 'What would you rather be doing? As you said, the deal's done. I don't have to be nice to you any more.'

Savannah shook back her silky hair and smiled provocatively. 'But you wouldn't mind, right? Being nice to me? I'm getting in that hot tub. You can do what you like.'

Without preamble, Savannah stood up and started to peel off her clothes, dropping them all over the floor as she explored the open-plan suite. Bending down to turn on the taps, she glanced over to Katherine who was still sitting comfortably, watching her every move. A tap at the door announced the arrival of the drinks and Savannah was pleased to see Katherine move to the door swiftly and intercept the waiter with the words, 'I'll take that.' She slipped a note out of her bag and handed it through the doorway before wheeling in the trolley.

Savannah strolled back over in her gossamer underwear and popped the champagne herself, then took a slow slug from the bottle, allowing some to dribble down over her chin onto her breasts. Seeing a flicker of desire light up Katherine's eyes, she wiped her mouth with the back of her hand and trailed her fingers through the glistening champagne on her breasts.

'Want some?' Smiling like a sphinx, she snatched up two glasses and the bottle and sashayed back over to the tub. Acutely aware of Katherine's hard, blue eyes on her naked flesh, she carelessly shrugged off her underwear and stepped down into the steaming water, still holding the champagne and glasses. 'Come and get it.'

Katherine coolly stubbed out her cigarette and added cream to her coffee. Stirring in a some sugar, she sauntered over to the hot tub and gave Savannah a smile, with her mouth in a thin line, that failed to reach her eyes.

'You've got a lot to learn, sugar. You can start by being a lot nicer to me, because I'm the one with editorial control, remember?'

Savannah laughed softly and reached her hand out to stroke Katherine's shapely ankle. 'Why don't you just get in here, and we'll worry about who's being nice to whom later?'

This time, Katherine's smile brought a sparkle to her eyes and a faint tinge of colour to her cheeks. She pulled off her silk polo-neck, ruffling her short, dark hair and revealing an ample, freckled bosom in a sporty, low-cut, black cotton bra. Savannah whistled appreciatively as she kicked off her tailored slacks, showing off her trim waist and beautifully toned thighs. As she turned to reach for her coffee, Savannah admired her smooth buttocks and flat stomach, wondering idly what this woman must spend on self-maintenance.

Katherine put aside the coffee cup and peeled off her briefs and bra and joined Savannah in the tub. Without a moment's hesitation, she pulled Savannah to her and kissed her deeply while she fondled one of her pert breasts. Catching her breath, Savannah lifted both of Katherine's heavy breasts in her hands and buried her face in them, nuzzling and licking hungrily. Katherine wrapped her strong thighs around Savannah's waist and massaged her back while Savannah sought out each of Katherine's large nipples in turn. She sucked and licked them both until they were hard and then bit down on one, causing Katherine to gasp in her ear. Katherine tightened her grip on Savannah's waist so that she let go of her nipple and they regarded each other with interest. Katherine laughed quietly and gently stroked Savannah's pert breasts.

'How about we get out and share that champagne with some strawberries?' She eyed Savannah's hardening nipples with undisguised lust and Savannah's eyes grew round as she felt a sharp twinge of excitement run from her breasts down into her groin.

Helping Savannah out of the tub, Katherine shook up the bottle of champagne and sprayed it all over her. Savannah shrieked with delight and snatched the bottle back so that she could soak Katherine's body too. They fell on each other as if they were starving, with a flurry of greedy hands and mouths, and in seconds they were rolling together on the shag pile carpet, slurping the champagne from each other's skin. Turning top to tail, they sucked each other's toes, licked each other's shins and calves and nibbled the backs of each other's knees until they were both in a sweat of anticipation.

Savannah lay flat on the floor and giggled as Katherine sat beside her pouring more champagne over her breasts and into her navel. She wallowed in the sensation of Katherine's mouth travelling down over her breasts and guzzling on her stomach, but she ached to taste her pussy.

'Katherine, turn around. Kneel over me, I want you to straddle my face.'

Katherine grinned and ran her hand over Savannah's midriff and down onto her mound. 'As long as you let at me at that sweet little pussy of yours too.' She knelt over Savannah's face and rested her voluptuous breasts on her belly while she peeled open the labia and gazed admiringly at the delicate pink flesh and hooded clitoris. 'My, but you're a pretty girl.'

Savannah laughed and reached up to grab Katherine's hips and bottom. 'People usually say that about my face!'

Katherine slid her finger over the folds and slipped it into Savannah's moist slit. 'Faces are ten a penny. This is a work of art.'

Soon, Savannah felt unable to make any more quips, as Katherine expertly used her tongue and her fingers to waken every nerve in her body. Savannah felt a raging hunger begin to burn in her loins and her mouth puckered up towards the inviting, darkly fringed cleft just above her. She pulled Katherine down onto her face and breathed in the sharp sea smell before plunging her tongue into the crack and lapping at the hard little clit.

Savannah was in pussy heaven, with a mouth full of responsive, quivering flesh, while at the same time, she was being eaten alive by an obvious epicure. Her clit felt as though it had swollen to the size of an acorn and she kept feeling her grip on Katherine slipping as she lost herself on waves of heady pleasure. All too soon, she felt a rush of pure bliss begin to emanate from between her legs and then wash up and over her whole body, leaving her shaking and moaning in semi-delirium.

Collecting her thoughts in the haze of her afterglow, she homed in on Katherine's clitoris and applied her tongue with rapid flicking motions until she was rewarded by hearing Katherine's panting turn to cries of, 'That's it! Yes, right there. God, yes!'

She sucked hard and held on until Katherine's body stopped jerking against her face. Then Katherine pulled away from her mouth and turned around so that she was lying on top, grinding against her with her pelvis. Savannah pulled Katherine's head down and they kissed deeply, allowing their juices to mingle while their tongues danced a tango.

Coming up for air, Savannah grinned at Katherine in delight and surprise. 'Wow! I hope you're not going anywhere in a hurry! You were so nice to me.'

Katherine kissed the end of her nose and smiled slyly. 'Ah, but seeing as you were quite nice to me too, I was thinking of getting back in the tub. Coming?'

Savannah beamed her most dazzling smile and allowed Katherine to pull her up from the floor and they sank back into the swirling water with a sigh.

Chapter Thirty

*I*n the library at The Priory, all eyes were on Mother Magdalene, who stood by the fire with round, sad eyes and pale, waxen cheeks, like a rabbit caught in headlights. Gabrielle rose slowly and took her friend's hand.

'Are you all right?' Mother Magdalene seemed to have difficulty in focusing on her face, so she gently led her back to the table where Brother Joseph held a glass of wine to her lips and Sister Assumpta rubbed her hands vigorously between her own.

'There, dear, a bit of a shock for you, that's all. How are you feeling now?'

Sister Assumpta's kind expression and Brother Joe and Gabrielle's concern unlocked a torrent of tears and she rocked backwards and forwards, keening like a recently bereaved widow. When she finally seemed to have vented her grief, Gabrielle and Brother Joe squashed in beside her while Sister Assumpta slipped off her shoes and massaged her feet.

Brother Joe looked at her questioningly. 'He's taking it very badly. It sounds as though he was expecting a very different reaction from you. Pity he's not still here to see the results of his outburst.'

Mother Magdalene accepted a handkerchief from Sister Assumpta and blew her nose loudly before answering. 'I'm not crying over that, or The Order. It's Richard. I've just realised something that I'd rather not know. And no, it isn't that he loves me, because I've always known that, the way he's known I love him.'

Sister Assumpta looked up at her from the floor. 'What is it then, that would break your heart like that?'

Mother Magdalene shook her head. 'I need to talk to him about it first.'

Sister Assumpta's intention to draw her out was scuppered by the timely arrival of Sister Evangeline, looking suitably chastened. 'Sorry I'm late, but it took ages tracking Toby down. His place is under siege. All the gutter press are staking out his workplace, his home and his mother's. Fortunately, we had a little code via a friend's mobile and I managed to talk to him.'

Mother Magdalene waved her over to a chair. 'Sit down. Have a drink.'

Sister Evangeline did as she was told but kept stealing glances at Mother Magdalene's tear-stained face. Catching sight of her worried expression, Mother Magdalene smiled encouragingly at her. 'No, dear, don't worry about me. Unrelated misery, I assure you. Do go on.'

Sister Evangeline coughed and cleared her throat. 'I don't think he's going to say much to the press because he doesn't want his mother to find out, but he is upset about it being public knowledge that I was seeing him charitably. He's quite mad at me as well for, well, for some spanking that got a bit out of hand.' Mother Magdalene's face hardened. 'He didn't want to spank me, so I made him let me hit him, and then I got him to agree for the next time. That's how I came to be in my habit, because he felt quite enthusiastic about spanking a nun. So he didn't mind that time.'

Mother Magdalene shook her head and looked with revulsion at the selfish, spoilt girl before her. 'Sister Evangeline, how could I have been so wrong about you?

Where's your compassion? Where's your understanding of the concept of consent? You are a beautiful, likeable girl, but this vicious, controlling behaviour revolts me. I'm glad The Order is ending if we've failed to help someone like you.'

'Ending?' Sister Evangeline's voice was hardly a whisper.

'Yes. There will be an announcement, and we're planning a big party. It's the end of days.' Mother Magdalene looked at Sister Gabriel, Sister Assumpta and Brother Joe and felt heartened by the sight of their dear faces. 'You may tell Brother Gregory as he's as much of a friend as you allow yourself, but please refrain from discussing this with anyone else until I've had a chance to let everybody know.'

'But where will I go? What will I do?'

Mother Magdalene raised an eyebrow sardonically. 'You're very resourceful. I'm sure you'll think of something. Look, we're all in the same boat. Come to the party and help us to celebrate what we've had. We'll worry about what happens next after that. All right? Why don't you go and find Brother Gregory now. We need time to discuss things.'

She nodded towards her companions. Sister Evangeline stood up looking tearful and reluctantly made her way to the door. 'Do you know how the press found out?'

Mother Magdalene opened the door for her and guided her through it. 'Does it matter? Don't worry, no one holds you responsible. Go in peace, Sister.'

'And you, Mother.'

The next evening Gabrielle lay on her bed looking at the sumptuous rooms that she would soon be leaving. She found it impossible to feel any sorrow, for this room belonged to Sister Gabriel, whereas she was now happy to be Gabrielle once more, especially if she could share her life with someone as wonderful as David.

Her heart gave a lurch as she thought of what she was going to say to him. The papers had been in a feeding frenzy looking for information about The Order, and some very damaging things had been said about them. Mother Magdalene had promised her that she was going to make sure that mitigating information was released to offset the sleazy allegations currently doing the rounds, but Gabrielle knew that you could never really undo what was said or written. Summoning her courage, she decided to ring David and invite him to the party. She desperately needed him to know how much she loved and needed him.

Dialling his home number, she held her breath and waited for a reply. Just as she was about to hang up, she heard his beautiful, deep voice in her ear. 'Hello?'

Gabrielle's heart was pounding so loudly she could hardly think. 'David, it's Gabrielle, I really need to talk to you.'

'You've got some nerve.' David's voice was cold and level.

'No please, listen, about those press stories –'

'Gabrielle, or Sister Gabriel, or whoever the hell you are, I don't want to hear it. I didn't ask to be a charity-fuck and I'm not grateful. Go and play with someone else's emotions. Just because I'm in a wheelchair doesn't give you the right to patronise me.'

'But David, I –' Click. Gabrielle listened to the dialling tone in dawning horror, as she realised she had lost David for good.

Chapter Thirty-One

*F*or the first time in its long and varied history, Mount Olive Priory was bedecked with fairy lights and vibrating with thumping music. The entrance hall, the cloisters and the quadrangle were thronged with people wearing an eye-popping array of clerical wear, party clothes and underwear. Brother Joe bounded up the entrance stairs clad in tiny gold shorts, hotly pursued by Brother Darius in a clerical collar and sober black shirt over a black leather thong and biker boots. Inside the main hall, Sister Maria was up on a table performing a Salomé-style dance of the seven veils with a specially modified habit which she was deftly peeling off, bit by bit. Around her, Brothers and Sisters in various stages of undress were cheering her on and calling out lewd propositions or volunteering their services. Under the table, a tangle of limbs made it impossible to tell who was under there or what exactly they were doing, but sporadic sighs, groans and giggles made it sound like a lot of fun.

Mother Magdalene pushed her way through the throng searching for Father Lionheart. Since the second story had hit the headlines with further and more accurate details about some of the members and founders, he had withdrawn into his rooms and refused to see anyone. She had slipped a note under his door saying she was hoping that he would join the party and say goodbye to their loyal members, but so far he had failed to appear.

As she reached the first floor library she stopped to check her outfit. For the first time she had decided to modify the usual nun's garb that she wore and the sight of herself in the long landing mirror made her glad that she had gone ahead and ordered something different. Her hair was pulled tightly into two little bunches on the top of her head, which she had wound around until they were like little horns. Instead of a wimple, her face was framed by a sparkly white hairband, with a tiny PVC veil hanging from it between her bunches down over the back of her head. Glancing round to check that she was unobserved, she reached into her black PVC bustier and lifted her breasts higher so that they were spilling out provocatively and then she rearranged the shiny folds of her matching short skirt and smoothed her long, PVC evening gloves. A quick twist straightened her seamed stockings and she turned her ankles this way and that, admiring the way her spiky-heeled ankle boots emphasised the curve of her calves.

Pushing open the library door, she was surprised to see Father Lionheart standing before the fire with his trousers around his ankles and Sister Evangeline in a red rubber dress on her knees with his cock in her mouth. As he started to say something, Mother Magdalene quickly put her finger to her lips and quietly slipped into a chair to watch.

From her vantage point near the door, she had a clear view of Sister Evangeline's expert ministrations and Father Lionheart's handsome, engrossed face. Mother Magdalene watched him closely she lifted the folds of her skirt up to expose her creamy white thighs and her golden-haired pussy. Spreading her legs apart she ran her hands down over her inviting cleavage and stroked her thighs and soft pubic hair. Father Lionheart groaned, prompting Sister Evangeline to guzzle harder on his iron hard shaft and she too reached under her tight, rubber dress and began to rub herself vigorously.

Mother Magdalene parted the fleshy lips of her pudenda and smiled wickedly as Father Lionheart's eyes became locked on her moist, glistening pussy. Pulling off one of her gloves with her teeth, she slid her middle finger into her cleft and probed gently inside herself. Still holding her pink pussy lips apart with her gloved hand, she stuck her tangy finger into her heavily lipsticked mouth and withdrew it slowly, puckering up her pretty red lips. Father Lionheart grabbed a handful of Sister Evangeline's blonde hair and angled himself more deeply into her mouth, glancing back and forward between Mother Magdalene's beautiful pussy and exquisite face and Sister Evangeline's silky hair and greedy lips.

Mother Magdalene eased her finger from her mouth and reached down to her parted cleft and stroked the soft folds of flesh before homing in on her hard nubbin. As she began to circle and flick the engorged flesh, Father Lionheart's face reddened and his breathing became more rapid. Sister Evangeline tilted her head back to allow him deeper access to her throat and bounced her bottom up and down as she massaged herself more furiously. Mother Magdalene felt a laugh about to escape unbidden from her mouth so she clamped her hand over it and kept up the pressure on her clitoris with her bare finger. Father Lionheart's eyes became glazed and he grunted with relief as his cock spurted hot semen into Sister Evangeline's throat.

Mother Magdalene shot out of the chair and crossed the floor to where Sister Evangeline was approaching climax. Grabbing her by the wrist, Mother Magdalene pulled her to her feet. 'Not so fast, Sister. We have other plans for you this evening.'

Sister Evangeline's brow creased. 'Plans? It's a party, and I was just about to come.'

Mother Magdalene smiled but her eyes were steely. 'To the party, yes, but orgasm, no. You seem to have forgotten that you have yet to be punished for your recent misdemeanours.'

Father Lionheart coughed. 'You do know she had nothing to do with the press don't you?'

'Oh yes. I know all about that. I've been waiting to see if you'd come and talk to me. Savannah's coming.'

Father Lionheart's face went ashen. 'I see. I take it you've already spoken to her?'

Mother Magdalene shot him a withering look. 'Of course. Oh, and I've also spoken to Toby, *Angela*. He's here already.'

Sister Evangeline pulled free of Mother Magdalene and stood staring at her, aghast. 'Toby? What on earth is he doing here?'

Mother Magdalene looked at her coolly and pulled her long glove back on. 'He's my guest. It seems he has a lot in common with some of the other men and women who have experienced your peculiar brand of loving. Like Brother Gregory. They've all agreed on a suitable punishment for you.'

Sister Evangeline's eyes started to sparkle at the idea of punishment and she smoothed down the rubber dress, shivering in anticipation. 'What will I have to do?'

Mother Magdalene's face was impenetrable. 'I need to talk to Father Lionheart, so you'd better see Sister Assumpta down in the old pantry.'

Sister Evangeline shook her head and looked questioningly at Father Lionheart.

'I'm sorry', he muttered, 'I don't know anything about it.'

Sister Evangeline turned back to Mother Magdalene. 'The old pantry, at the back of the ground-floor kitchens, right? What a weird place. Why there?'

'Because that's where they're waiting for you. Now,

off you go. I'll be down shortly.' Sister Evangeline hurried from the room, hoping the punishment was going to be suitably vicious and delicious.

Mother Magdalene sat against the big table and hoisted up her skirt. 'Could you do one last thing for me? For old time's sake?'

Father Lionheart dropped to his knees and clamped his arms around her legs, pressing his face into her thighs. 'Please forgive me, Mags. Please.'

Mother Magdalene parted her thighs and presented her throbbing pussy to him. 'Don't talk now, Richard. Just do it.'

She lay back on the table, enjoying the feeling of her flesh being stretched as she opened her legs wider to afford him easier access. Father Lionheart reverently kissed her inner thighs and the curve of her buttocks and then buried his lips in her inviting cleft. Mother Magdalene cried out as his tongue found all her special places and then began to circle her swollen clitoris. He placed his lips over it and sucked gently while his tongue attacked the tip with rapid, delicious little flicks. In minutes, Mother Magdalene was gripping onto his hair and writhing in pleasure. Her breathing came in ragged gasps and as her climax reached its peak, she shrieked aloud, tossing her head from side to side and grinding her pussy into his face. As the spasms subsided, Father Lionheart stood up and leaned over her, brushing her thighs and mound with his rejuvenated penis. Looking imploringly into her flushed face, he kissed her nose, her eyelids and her chin.

Pushing him away, Mother Magdalene sat up and spat at him. 'Get off me, you traitor. You snake in the grass. Judas!' She placed her spiked heels against his chest and shoved with all her might, sending him crashing back into one of the chairs and then leapt from the table and stood glowering over him. 'Why? Why for

God's sake? Even the phone calls – yes, I finally recognised your voice. It was you, all of it. Why?'

Father Lionheart wiped the sweat from his brow with the back of his hand. 'Because I loved you. Because I was jealous of the way The Order took you over. I thought the phone calls would scare you into dropping it. When that didn't work, I came up with letting the press find out.'

Mother Magdalene shook her head in bewilderment and sat down abruptly in another chair. 'Well, it's all backfired, hasn't it? And you backed the wrong horse with Savannah. She wouldn't sell us out after all, would she? Why the hell did you talk us all into keeping her out anyway?'

Father Lionheart put his face in his hands for a moment and then sighed deeply. 'Jealousy again. She gave you your first orgasm. I hated her because of that, and because she's so beautiful. All of you seemed to buzz around her like bees at a honeypot. But no, she wouldn't hurt any of you. When I met her, I thought she'd be useful for passing information to the press, but even though she'd found out a lot already, she wouldn't use it. Said she was saving it up for a rainy day or something.'

Mother Magdalene stood up unsteadily and tidied herself. 'Well, she's benefiting from that rainy day now. I gave her the go-ahead to release all of her information along with some additional things that I've told her. So far, it's looking favourable. The prosecution service have dropped all charges and agreed that there's no case to answer, as money didn't change hands. But you, Richard, you have charges to answer. You betrayed me. Your actions are unforgiveable.' She paused by the doorway and looked at him in the flickering glow of the fire. 'I loved you once, Richard, but the ends do not justify the means. Goodbye.'

* * *

'No, not so tightly, she'll enjoy that. Fix it here.'

Father Guillory took over from Sister Assumpta and loosened the wristband on Sister Evangeline's harness, then deftly slipped the straps back through the steel loops on the wire mesh of the cage. Sister Evangeline widened her eyes in mute appeal, but the team responsible for trussing her up inside the cage were under strict instructions to ignore her completely. Brother Gregory checked the black gag and slipped his finger under the knot to make sure it was tight enough, but not too tight.

Sister Evangeline was sitting down in a rectangular wire mesh cage with her legs tied straight out in front of her and her arms comfortably down by her sides, but securely fixed to the cage. A loose blanket covered up most of her red latex dress and there was nothing erotic to be seen in her bondage, which pressed uncomfortably on her clitoris but succeeded in making her look like a trussed lamb on its way to market. In sheer frustration, she tried screaming down her nose, but the pumping party music drowned her out and her tormentors continued to ignore her. Toby tucked the blanket around her feet and smiled shyly at Father Guillory, who then snapped the cage door shut and turned a small key in the padlock.

'That should do it.' He smiled, evidently pleased with his handiwork, and began to pull the cage on rollers through the entrance hall and into the main hall where the party was in full swing.

By the time they reached the centre of the hall the cage had attracted a large group of followers and a big crowd gathered round to see what would happen. Father Guillory signalled to Brother Gregory who loosened a rope at the side of the hall. A strong hook and clamp descended on a rope from the middle of the ceiling near the chandelier.

'Brothers and Sisters, ladies and gentlemen, I have been asked to create a suitable punishment for a young lady who likes too well to be punished. So! In this lovely cage, she can see our wonderful party, but she can't join in, and we can't touch her. Under that dull little blanket is an ugly looking body harness that should keep her wonderfully excited but with no hope of release. In any sense of the word! Now, anybody who has suffered unwanted or uninvited attention from Sister Evangeline, please join us in hoisting her out of the way, so that we can get on with enjoying ourselves.'

Once Father Guillory had securely attached the hook and clamp to the top of Sister Evangeline's cage he joined the growing group holding onto the rope with Brother Gregory and Toby. On the count of three they heaved together, and Sister Evangeline's cage rose into the air and was left suspended just below the high ceiling. After a few minutes of clapping and cheering, jeering and laughter, the crowd resumed their frantic party-making and Sister Evangeline, high above them all, was soon forgotten.

Chapter Thirty-Two

*B*y dawn, the party was still in full swing but Mother Magdalene was struggling to keep her eyes open. Despite the frenetic atmosphere, generated by the knowledge that this would be the last call for The Order, she was beginning to feel the effects of a whole night of uninhibited revelry. Her new bodice had been ripped open to the waist during one of Father Guillory's improvised bondage tableaux and, somewhere along the way, she had given away her spiky new boots, so her stockings were now in tatters. During an outrageous tango sandwiched between Brothers Joe and Darius, her unruly curls had burst free from the devilish little bunches, but the glittery white hairband still framed her smudged and mascara-streaked face. The overall effect was that of a debauched Alice in Wonderland in search of the white rabbit. Gamely snatching up a two-thirds full bottle of champagne, she set out for a last tour of her beloved Priory.

Bacchanalian scenes met her eye everywhere she looked. Staggering out of the main hall – where Sister Maria was being feasted upon by a group of at least ten men directly under the cage holding the bulging-eyed Sister Evangeline – Mother Magdalene passed through the darkened entrance hall. All around her she could hear the soft sighs, moans and groans of a host of lovers in the dark.

Outside in the crisp early-morning air, she took a long swig from the bottle and laughed to see the jumble of bodies and clothing scattered all over the quadrangle. She turned into the cloisters and slowly made her way around to the gym. Peering through the window, she saw the black, muscular haunches of Brother Darius bent over a gym horse while Brother Joe, looking almost translucent by comparison in the ethereal morning light, knelt at his ankles and was kissing and licking his way up those long, athletic legs. Raising her bottle to them in silent salute, she smiled to herself and went on her way.

After a full circuit of the cloistered walkways, which also harboured little groups of lovers and party casualties, she reached the beautiful little chapel that she had loved from the outset. Feeling a sudden rush of emotion, she stepped through the doorway and closed her eyes for a moment so that she could breathe in the familiar scent of incense and candle smoke and old wood.

A touch on her arm startled her out of her reverie and she opened her eyes to find Savannah's beautiful face smiling at her. Mother Magdalene blinked and tried to take in the Madonna-like vision in gold gossamer underwear before her.

'Hey, Mags. You look all partied out. Have you come for a little rest and prayer? Everyone said you'd end up here.'

'Savannah! God it's good to see you, I thought you hadn't come. But *Mags*? Do you know, I've almost forgotten ever being called Margaret or Maggy?'

Savannah baldly cast her eyes all over Margaret's tattered outfit and bared breasts. 'Well I certainly haven't. I've been feeling deprived. Come and meet Katherine; she's the editor I told you about.'

Mother Magdalene followed Savannah's almost

naked, beautiful body over to the altar steps, where a handsome, short-haired woman in a tiny black leather boob tube and hotpants was sprawled, looking completely at home. She sat up and stretched out her hand as the two women approached.

'Hello at last. Do I call you Mother Magdalene? I'm Katherine Lloyd, I did the feature on The Order with Savannah. I hope you liked it.'

Mother Magdalene smiled and shook her hand warmly. 'You can call me Margaret, or Margaret Dempsey, after this party, but as it's my last night in The Order, I'm still Mother Magdalene. Yes, I thought the article was very fair, it did a lot to mitigate all that rubbish the gutter press was printing. Thank you.'

Katherine shook her head and slipped her arm around Savannah's waist. 'Don't thank me. It was Savannah who negotiated the deal on the angle. She's a hard bargainer.'

Mother Magdalene laughed and sat down on the steps. 'I can imagine. I take it you've also agreed to keep this party off the record?'

Savannah smiled smugly and laid her hand on Katherine's thigh. 'Of course she has, you silly goose.'

Katherine looked coolly at Mother Magdalene and leaned back on the steps. 'I've always been dying to get asked to a party like this. I would have sold my soul, never mind kept quiet. We've had a whale of a time, and you might not have seen us, but we've certainly seen you. You're an amazing woman.'

Mother Magdalene took another slug from the bottle and realised how drunk she must have been for most of the night. 'What the hell,' she said aloud, 'it's my last night as Mother Magdalene, founder and head of The Order. Here's to me!' She poured some more champagne into her mouth, spilling some over her breasts, and handed the bottle to Katherine, who toasted her.

'To the inimitable Mother Magdalene, and to the one and only Margaret Dempsey. Health, wealth and happiness!' Katherine took a generous gulp from the bottle and passed it on to Savannah who smiled lewdly and held the bottle to her lips.

'Cheers, Mags. To the girl with peaches and cream between her thighs!' Savannah sucked on the bottle, slurping noisily, and then coughed and spluttered as another voice called out, 'I'll drink to that!'

Looking like an extra from a horror movie in a shredded black evening gown, with her hair in knots and black mascara rings around her eyes, Sister Gabriel strode up the aisle and snatched the bottle from Savannah's hands. Savannah and Mother Magdalene sprang to their feet and embraced Sister Gabriel roughly.

'What a reunion!' shrieked Savannah 'My two favourite women in the world, apart from you Kate.' Savannah shot an apologetic glance at Katherine who stretched nonchalantly and rose to join them.

'Mind if I join in? I'm Katherine, Sister Gabriel, and have I heard a lot about you.'

Sister Gabriel grinned and broke free of Savannah to allow Katherine into the group, giving her an appreciative once over. 'Likewise.'

Mother Magdalene gave Sister Gabriel a deep kiss and asked, 'Where the hell did you get to? One minute you were hanging from one of Carlos's spinning contraptions and the next you were gone.'

Sister Gabriel shrugged her shoulders. 'I don't know, it's all a bit of a blur. Brother Max used me in his magic show and I guess I must have disappeared. I've been looking for Savannah since then.' She glanced at Mother Magdalene and then Savannah before addressing Katherine. 'So how do you feel about sharing, Katherine? You know, in the spirit of The Order and all? I mean sharing Savannah? It's just that some of us will find it hard to let go, unless you wean us off gently.'

Savannah's eyes were huge as she watched the interplay between the other women. 'Mmm,' purred Mother Magdalene, 'and I haven't seen her for so long I'm like a starving wench at the banquet, just looking at her makes my mouth water.'

Katherine laughed good-naturedly and reached out to touch Mother Magdalene's exposed bosom. She looked boldly into her eyes as she slowly ran her fingertips down over the creamy breasts and gently fondled both rosebud nipples.

'The thing is, Mother, we have all gathered here to pay homage to you, the infamous Mother Magdalene. So why don't we three ladies, including the highly desired Savannah, of course, give you a decent send off? We can worry about the future when it arrives.'

Savannah and Sister Gabriel beamed with delight and wasted no time in leading Mother Magdalene up the altar steps.

The church door creaked open and Father Guillory walked towards them holding some lengths of rope. 'Can I help you with anything, ladies? I heard I might be needed, isn't that right, Sister Gabriel?'

Mother Magdalene shot a questioning glance at Sister Gabriel who grinned unabashed. 'You're a bit early, Father, but you could watch for a while if you like.'

Father Guillory sat down in the front pews and stretched out his long legs. 'Don't mind if I do.'

Sister Gabriel and Savannah stood either side of Mother Magdalene and took a breast each to hold and nip and suck. Mother Magdalene felt almost giddy with exhaustion, but Savannah's beauty and Sister Gabriel's loving touch were working miracles. They pulled off her dishevelled little skirt and gently prized her legs apart so that they could explore her with their probing fingertips. Katherine knelt down in front of her and massaged her aching legs and then softly kissed the exposed flesh just above her shredded stockings. Mother Magdalene heaved a sigh of relief as Katherine's lips reached her golden-fleeced pussy and rained hungry kisses all over it. Savannah swooped onto her neck and throat and then kissed her mouth voraciously, leaving her feeling breathless but even more excited. Sister Gabriel sucked noisily on her nipples until they were painfully hard and super-sensitive, so that each subsequent nibble left her buzzing with electric energy.

She opened her legs wider and pressed herself against Katherine's face so that she could feel her sweeping licks more intensely. Savannah's tongue disappeared into her ear at the same moment that Katherine's began to circle her clitoris, and she moaned loudly as strong feelings of unadulterated passion washed over her. As she felt her climax building, Savannah's voice whispered in her ear. 'Hang in there Mags, you deserve better than a quickie.'

Mother Magdalene opened her eyes to see Father Guillory approaching with his ropes and a shadowy figure taking a seat in the pews. 'Who is that?'

Father Guillory turned to look and smiled at her conspiratorially. 'Just one of your many admirers. Why don't we save him for later?'

Sister Gabriel and Savannah held out her arms while Father Guillory constructed some rope nooses and then slipped them over her wrists and ankles. Katherine sat back on her heels and watched with interest as Mother Magdalene's ropes were tightened and fixed to the chancel above her and the altar rail below. By the time Father Guillory had finished she was securely bound and resting against the altar like a crucified Madonna. Katherine, Savannah and Sister Gabriel took it in turns to stroke, kiss and lick tiny portions of her flesh until she was panting with desire. Father Guillory joined the women and buried his fine nose into her cleft like a perfumier with a prized bouquet of jasmine. As his nimble tongue began to delve and probe, all three women continued to caress her until she felt so aroused that she started to scream. The delicious torments continued unabated until her shrieks became deafening.

'Here's your present,' whispered Sister Gabriel. Mother Magdalene shook the sweat from her face and peered at the man approaching from the pews.

'It's only me, Mother. You kind of left me high and dry.'

Brother Gregory shrugged off the hooded cloak he was wearing and stood before her in all his naked glory. She glanced down at his rod-like member standing stiffly out from his beautifully toned body and laughed hoarsely.

'I see what you mean. Sorry about trussing up your favourite girl, but she really had it coming. I'm quite fond of her myself you know.'

Brother Gregory approached and looked hungrily at Mother Magdalene's white flesh already reddened in places where the ropes had begun to burn. 'Well you're both trussed up now but, fortunately, I can get to you.'

Mother Magdalene felt a piercing little thrill shoot up from her loins into her belly. 'Be my guest, if you can.'

Brother Gregory prised her legs apart a little and slipped his long fingers between the folds of moist flesh. Mother Magdalene shivered and twisted against her bonds as her heightened state of arousal kicked back in with a vengeance. She moaned and tossed her head as Father Guillory loosened the ropes holding her feet and handed one to Katherine, who helped him pull them apart, spreading her legs wide. Sister Gabriel and Savannah supported her hips and held her up to Brother Gregory, who was stroking his engorged cock and probing her delicate flesh in anticipation. Carefully positioning himself so that the head of his penis was resting at her entrance, he plunged deeply into her and launched into powerful, rhythmic strokes that soon had Mother Magdalene grunting and yelling with pleasure. 'Oh yes! Yes! Fuck me hard! Harder! Yes!'

Mother Magdalene felt herself soaring into a higher stratosphere as wave after wave of intense sensation broke over her body. Her arms were tingling from being tied outstretched for so long and her legs ached from being held so far apart. As she felt all of her friends' hands and tongues descend on her body, she slipped into semi-delirium. Brother Gregory's fabulous cock rocked her to her core and, as his luscious young body slapped against hers in a frenzy of passion, she drank in his handsome features, contorted with effort. Finally surrendering herself to the rollercoaster ride of super-arousal, she rocked, keened and ground her teeth until the enormous pressure building within her finally reached its peak. With a huge rush, her long-delayed orgasm crashed through her whole body and left her feeling as though she was floating far above them all, near the ceiling of the chapel. She made a silent prayer of thanks for having been allowed to experience every scrap of feeling a human body and heart could enjoy or endure.

Gradually, life returned to her aching limbs and rav-aged flesh, and she felt herself slowly coming back down to earth. As her beloved friends untied her bonds and showered her with kisses and caresses, she wept copious tears of joy tinged with sorrow, for she knew, in her heart, that this phase of her life had finally come to an end.

Epilogue

Epilogue

The live audience in the cramped television studio was getting hot and restless. The warm-up comedian had stoked them into a raucous, jolly mood, but delay after delay had left them feeling irritable. At last, a loud piece of organ music signalled the start of the show and, as the stage manager stepped back holding up her 'applaud' sign, a gravelly male voice-over boomed out, 'Ladies and gentlemen, saints and sinners, welcome to tonight's celebrity edition of DI-LEMMA! And now, here's our resident angel, the lovely SA-VANNAH!'

The restive crowd burst into thunderous applause and whistles, relieved to finally have something to do. The front of the set was shrouded in heavy purple velvet drapes embroidered with big gold crosses and, as they parted, the audience gave a collective 'ooh!' and clapped even harder. Savannah's white-gold hair was shimmering in a mixture of candlelight and artfully placed spot lights as she wiggled her way down a golden spiral staircase wearing a flimsy, transparent bit of white cloth, wings and a halo.

'Good evening, mortals, and welcome to this week's DI-LEMMA! Let's get cosy on the couch and see which mystery guest has got a problem to share with us this week.' She sashayed over to a huge, blood red chaise lounge and sprawled herself provocatively on it. 'Now, for those of you who don't already know, here on XTV each week we invite a special guest to set our team one of your dilemmas. And thank you all you wonderful worriers who've phoned the hotline with suggestions. Keep watching and maybe one week soon it will be the turn of your very own DI-LEMMA! But this week, we've got a juicy celebrity guest for you with a hot problem, so stay tuned to DI-LEMMA!'

Savannah basked in the thunderous applause and then signalled for silence. 'For all of you sad sinners who aren't sure what is or isn't by The Book, now's your chance to find out. So let's meet our saintly adjudicator, the one, the only, MO-THER MAG-DALENE!'

Off stage to the right, there was a flurry of powder and a last slick of lipstick before Margaret was pushed towards the set.

'Are you sure this purple eyeshadow isn't too much?' She twisted anxiously for a final look in the mirror, but Joe slapped her on the rump and pushed her forward.

'You look gorgeous, Mags, now get on there.'

Smiling sweetly, she slipped between the gold curtains and pressed her hands together in the attitude of prayer, bowing to the audience. Feet thrummed on the floor and whoops and catcalls deafened her but, as far as she could tell, they were all good-natured. Raising her hands, she signalled for quiet.

'Thank you, Savannah, and hello, my lovely flock.' She beamed with delight at the raucous laughter that followed her greeting and felt the urge to camp it up even more. 'I'm Mother Magdalene and I want to thank you all for joining us on this week's DI-LEMMA! And I do hope you'll all give us a helping hand by voting for a solution at the end of the show. That's if you've got one free of course.'

More cheers and applause. She slipped up onto the

high stool near a golden lectern and her purple habit slid open to reveal a tantalising glimpse of red, fishnet stockings. As she leaned forward, a flash of crimson lace accentuated her deep, creamy cleavage. A roar of approval from the audience prompted her to cross her legs, making the habit ride even higher, showing off her sparkly gold suspenders.

'In a moment, Savannah will bring in tonight's mystery guest who will set this week's DI-LEMMA!' Entering into the spirit of things, the audience began to join in every time the show's name was mentioned. Margaret laughed and waited for the roar to subside. 'But first, let's meet the team who will act out this week's DI-LEMMA!'

To crashing applause, hoots and whoops, four young people clad in body-hugging black Lycra ran onto the set, took their bows and stood either side of the lectern. Margaret tucked a stray red curl behind her ear and smoothed her veil before quietening the audience and turning to the couple on her left.

'Over here, to my left, meet this week's SUPER SAINTS, Ruth and Max!' The petite blonde and the gangly, ginger-haired young man placed their hands together as if praying and bowed solemnly to the audience. A mixture of cheers, boos and laughter filled the air. 'And on my right, this week's SAUCY SINNERS, Greg and Angela!' The crowd roared, wolf-whistled and hissed as the slim, blonde girl with big brown eyes and the tall, muscular, dark-haired man, writhed against each other suggestively and pretended to lick and bite. Margaret gave them a playful slap with a tasselled rope and turned towards the couch. 'Savannah, my lovely angel, who have you got for us this week?'

Savannah uncurled herself and went to stand before another set of gold curtains at the far side of the set. Beaming at the audience, she stood up on tiptoes and peeked through, leaving her bottom poking out delightfully, causing another rash of stomping and cheering from the crowd. Turning to the audience but leaving one arm through the drapes, she opened her mouth wide and feigned astonishment.

'Bless my soul! You'll never guess who I've got here. What an unholy old rock and roller! Shall I drag him in?' The crowd erupted with calls of 'Yes!' and 'DI-LEMMA! DI-LEMMA!' until Savannah finally yanked the tall, bony frame and famous grin of Rick Savage through the curtains.

Amidst thunderous applause and foot-stamping, Savannah led the grinning rock star to her couch, where she lay down with her head in his lap and wallowed in her new-found celebrity status. Catching Margaret's eye, she burst out laughing as 'Mother Magdalene' gave her a wink and then lewdly hoisted her cleavage up higher in the cutaway habit and snapped the straps on her suspenders.

'There, that's better,' she cooed to the audience, 'now let's see what kind of sticky little poser our guest has got for us on this week's DI-LEMMA! Be an angel and find out, for us, will you Savannah?'

The audience erupted into roars of 'DI-LEMMA' and jeers of 'Out with it, Rick!' while Savannah oozed smiling sex appeal and prepared to encourage her star guest to reveal all.

Almost thirty minutes later, Margaret was beginning to perspire under all the heavy make-up and felt relieved when she saw the stage manager hold up three fingers to her, signalling that it was time to wind up the show.

'Well!' exclaimed Mother Magdalene, 'what a close call! Of course, if we went by The Book, I'm afraid it would have been "til death do us part", but the studio audience have voted by a majority of seventy-six per cent for the married man to become a filling in that sexual sandwich, as long as his wife gets to choose the other slice! Viewers at home, you have until midnight to register your vote on this issue, so keep watching for the

298

numbers on screen, coming up now. That's it for this series, blessings on you all. Give a big hand to the most angelic angel of them all, SA-VANNAH!' Thunderous applause shook the studio.

'And a special thank you to the delightfully wicked – don't we just love him? – RICK SAVAGE!' The audience erupted into shouts, whistles and footstomping. Margaret did her best to calm them down. 'I'm Mother Magdalene, and I'm afraid that's the end of this series, but we'll be back soon. God bless, good bye!'

Savannah, Rick, the Saints and the Sinners and Mother Magdalene all took their bows to riotous applause and, arms about each other's waists, made their way off stage.

As the final bits of applause diminished into ragged clapping and finally petered out, Margaret breathed a sigh of relief and sank gratefully into a back-stage chair. Savannah came over and threw her arms around her, knocking her veil askew and smearing her heavy makeup.

'You were brilliant! I told you it would work! The producer's over the moon. He's talking about another ten weeks. I've finally got my break! And it's all thanks to you.'

Margaret took Savannah's head in her hands and kissed her on the nose. 'Don't be silly. This was your idea, and you were right, it really does make fun television. I'd never have believed it possible, to do this kind of thing on TV.'

Savannah sprang up and began to cream off her makeup. 'Anything's possible on TV, that's the culture we live in. But you're a natural, Mags, I'd never have guessed it. Did Joe talk to you about the Internet site? We want to start offering online chats direct with Mother Magdalene after the show. Oh, and Breakaway, the company who do all kinds of talk shows, want to know if you'd be interested in doing a more serious sex programme, kind of like a Doctor Ruth sex guru type thing. You need an agent, Mags!'

Margaret stared at her own face in the mirror, still reeling from the dizzy speed with which she had been changed from vilified press villainess into television's own sex darling. Public opinion was fickle, and she had decided to make the most of it while it was in her favour.

'Shall I try Max Shilling? He's been after me since the newspaper story first broke.'

Savannah laughed as she changed into a simple black dress and stylish strappy black shoes. 'That old rogue? Actually, you could do worse. He's made quite a few people's fortunes over the years, especially if there's a sex angle! Yes, why not?'

Margaret finished taking off her makeup and acknowledged lots of 'well done' and 'great show' comments from the crew as they packed up for the evening. Nimbly she stripped off her habit and stepped into a glimmering, off the shoulder, emerald-green gown and she was giving her hair a final sweep of the brush when Joe came up behind her and planted a warm kiss on her cheek.

'How's it feel to be a "sex goddess"?'

Margaret laughed and turned to give him a hug. 'Don't start. Next week I could be a nobody again. You know what they're like.'

Joe hugged her back and gave her a stern look. 'Not likely, darling. You're beautiful, you're sexy, and you're incredibly talented. In more ways than one.'

Margaret gave him a playful shove and wrapped a colourful pashmina around her shoulders. 'All right, leave off. Are you coming on to Sachs for the party?'

He shook his head and paused in front of the mirror to ruffle his cropped hair into boyish tufts. 'Uh-uh. I've got a date.'

Margaret looked surprised. 'But it's the post-production party. It's the last time we'll all get together until the next series.'

Before she could cajole him further, a runner stuck her head around the corner of the door and caught Joe's eye. 'There's someone here for you. Shall I –?'

Joe sprang towards the door and flung it open. Margaret's eyes lit up with delight as she saw the tall, dark figure standing there.

'Darius!' she cried, as Joe threw himself into his arms. Darius grinned at Margaret over Joe's shoulder.

'Hello there, Mother Margaret. Nice to see you again.'

Margaret swept over to him and embraced him warmly. 'Where on earth have you sprung from? I thought you were off visiting your folks.'

Darius grinned and stepped back to look at her. 'So I was, but this spoiled young man claimed he was missing me and convinced me that I ought to come and stay with him in London for a while, so here I am.'

Margaret looked from Joe's shining face to Darius's broad grin and felt a pang of envy. 'Listen, I know you two have some catching up to do, but how about coming to my place later, for a sort of post-post party? There'll be quite a few old faces. What do you say?'

Darius and Joe exchanged questioning glances and then both nodded. 'Sounds good,' said Joe, 'I'll call you if we get too tied up elsewhere.'

Margaret smiled wryly. 'Carlos will be there. Why not get tied up with us instead?'

Darius's eyebrows shot up and he and Joe both burst out laughing. Greg and Angela came and tugged on her arm. 'Come on, you. We can't have an end of the series party without the star of the show.'

Margaret allowed herself to be hustled from the room, but called over her shoulder, 'Please try and come, guys. We won't have the same fun without you.'

Joe and Darius laughed. 'Don't worry,' boomed Darius, 'we'll be coming all right. Oh, and we'll try and make it to your party, too!'

* * *

Margaret's new apartment was on the seventh floor of a brand-new Docklands development that Roland and Geoff had recommended to her. Her sitting room opened onto a huge balcony and Margaret loved the views of the ever-changing Thames and the lonesome call of seagulls, which reminded her of home. Feeling more than a little drunk, she staggered out onto the terrace, wearing her high heels and nothing else, and took a few deep breaths of air. Carlos trailed after her carrying another bottle of champagne and wiping chocolate smears from his smiling lips.

'Wait!' he cried. 'I haven't finished with you yet.'

Margaret cupped a hand over her chocolate-streaked mound and backed against the rail. 'No more, I swear I'll be sick. Look.'

She pointed back into the dishevelled room, littered with bodies, chocolate wrappers and sex toys. Joe and Darius were slumped in a heap with Susanna, whose ripe curves and long hair made her look like a sleeping Rubens model. Next to them, still handcuffed to the coffee table, were Max and Ruth, both dressed as French maids, and under the table lay Greg, holding onto Angela protectively, his biceps bulging under her pretty, blonde head.

'Everybody's had it, Carlos, even me. Well, almost everybody.' Beside her, the faint glow of a cigarette lit up Katherine's face in the dark. Savannah's silky blonde head was resting in her lap, but she was snoring softly and her pretty red mouth was hanging open. 'You've worn her out!' laughed Margaret, happy to be among so many of her friends, who clearly still enjoyed being around her.

Carlos draped his arm around her shoulder, brushing her goose-pimpled breast with his fingertips, and looked shrewdly at her. 'Do you miss it? The Order?'

Margaret shook her head. 'No, I'm glad it's finished. "To every thing there is a season." Anyway, it would be impossible to do it again. It's over.'

In the first traces of dawn light, she began to see more clearly. In the far corner, David's wheelchair was bumping rhythmically back into the wall with Gabrielle balanced precariously on the arms while David feasted on her pussy.

Katherine smiled indulgently and carried on watching with hungry eyes. 'That's quite a reunion they've got going. How did you manage it?'

Margaret leaned on the railing and gazed into the swirling waters below. 'I prayed for them, of course. Oh, and I went to see David and told him that if he didn't do something about my broken-hearted friend he wouldn't be needing that wheelchair much longer, because I'd kill him. That seemed to help. They're both very stubborn.'

Katherine snorted with laughter. 'They're certainly very determined, judging by what I've seen tonight. Mmm, mmm. And have you noticed – look – they've got the brakes off?'

Margaret glanced over just in time to see Gabrielle sink down onto David's lap and kiss his bare chest and nipples, before pushing against the wall with her bare feet so that they zoomed across the balcony and crashed into the table, laughing manically.

Margaret felt Carlos's arm tighten around her and she cast her eyes over all of her beautiful, guilt-free pals and her stunning new home. She shrugged and beamed at Katherine. 'It's not a bad philosophy for life!'

The loud silly tune on the mobile phone made several other early-morning commuters look up in either amusement or annoyance before returning to their newspapers and checking their watches as the train pulled out of the station.

'Hello?'

The hiss of static distorted a gravelly voice. 'God moves in mysterious ways.'

'His wonders to perform?'

'Tonight, eight o'clock. Make me an instrument of your peace.'

'And I yours.'

BLACK LACE NEW BOOKS

Published in October

ALL THE TRIMMINGS
Tesni Morgan
£6.99

Cheryl and Laura, two fast friends, have recently become divorced. When the women find out that each secretly harbours a desire to be a whorehouse madam, there's nothing to stop them. On the surface their establishment is a five-star hotel, but to a select clientele it's a bawdy fun house for both sexes, where fantasies – from the mild to the increasingly perverse – are indulged.

**Humorous and sexy, this is a fabulous yarn of women
behaving badly and loving it!**

ISBN 0 352 33641 2

WICKED WORDS 5
A Black Lace short story collection
£6.99

Black Lace short story collections are a showcase of the finest contemporary women's erotica anywhere in the world. With contributions from the UK, USA and Australia, the settings and stories are deliciously daring. Fresh, cheeky and upbeat, only the most arousing fiction makes it into a *Wicked Words* anthology.

By popular demand, another cutting-edge Black Lace anthology.

ISBN 0 352 33642 0

PLEASURE'S DAUGHTER
Sedalia Johnson
£6.99

It's 1750. Orphaned Amelia, headstrong and voluptuous, goes to live with wealthy relatives. During the journey she meets the exciting, untrustworthy Marquis of Beechwood. She manages to escape his clutches only to find he is a good friend of her aunt and uncle. Although aroused by him, she flees his relentless pursuit, taking up residence in a Covent Garden establishment dedicated to pleasure. When the Marquis catches up with her, Amelia is only too happy to demonstrate her new-found disciplinary skills.

**Find out what our naughty ancestors got up to in this
Black Lace special reprint.**

ISBN 0 352 33237 9

Published in November

THE ORDER
Dee Kelly
£6.99

Margaret Dempsey is an Irish Catholic girl who discovers sexual freedom in London but is racked with guilt – until, with the help of Richard Dalbeny, a failed priest, she sets up The Compassionate Order for Relief – where sexual pleasure is seen as Heaven-sent. Through sharing their fantasies they learn to shed their inhibitions, and to dispense their alms to those in sexual need. Through The Order, Margaret learns that the only sin is self-denial, and that to err is divine!

**An unusual and highly entertaining story of forbidden lusts and
religious transgressions.**

ISBN 0 352 33652 8

PLAYING WITH STARS
Jan Hunter
£6.99

Mariella, like her father before her, is an astrologer. Before she can inherit his fortune, she must fulfil the terms of his will. He wants her to write a *very* true-to-life book about the male sexual habits of the twelve star signs. Mariella's only too happy to oblige, but she has her work cut out: she has only one year to complete the book and must sleep with each sign during the month of their birth. As she sets about her task with enthusiastic abandon, which sign will she rate the highest?

A sizzling, fun story of astrology and sexual adventure.

ISBN 0 352 33653 6

THE GIFT OF SHAME
Sara Hope-Walker
£6.99

Jeffery is no more than a stranger to Helen when he tells her to do things no other man has even hinted at. He likes to play games of master and servant. In the secrecy of a London apartment, in the debauched opulence of a Parisian retreat, they become partners in obsession, given to the pleasures of perversity and shame.

This is a Black Lace special reprint of a sophisticated erotic novel of extreme desires and shameful secrets.

ISBN 0 352 32935 1

Published in December

GOING TOO FAR
Laura Hamilton
£6.99

Spirited adventurer Bliss van Bon is set for three months' travelling around South America. When her travelling partner breaks her leg, she must begin her journey alone. Along the way, there's no shortage of company. From flirting on the plane to being tied up in Peru; from sex on snowy mountain peaks to finding herself out of her depth with local crooks, Bliss doesn't have time to miss her original companion one bit. And when brawny Australians Red and Robbie are happy to share their tent and their gorgeous bodies with her, she's spoiled for choice.

An exciting, topical adventure of a young woman caught up in sexual intrigue and global politics.

ISBN 0 352 33657 9

COMING UP ROSES
Crystalle Valentino
£6.99

Rosie Cooper, landscape gardener, is fired from her job by an over-fussy client. Although it's unprofessional, she decides to visit the woman a few days later, to contest her dismissal. She arrives to find a rugged, male replacement behaving even more unprofessionally by having sex with the client in the back garden! It seems she's got competition – a rival firm of fit, good-looking men are targeting single well-off women in West London. When the competition's this unfair, Rosie will need all her sexual skills to level the playing field.

A fun, sexy story of lust and rivalry ... and landscape gardening!

ISBN 0 352 33658 7

THE STALLION
Georgina Brown
£6.99

Ambitious young horse rider Penny Bennett intends to gain the sponsorship and the very personal attention of showjumping's biggest impresario, Alistair Beaumont. The prize is a thoroughbred stallion, guaranteed to bring her money and success. Beaumont's riding school is not all it seems, however. Firstly there's the weird relationship between Alistair and his cigar-smoking sister. Then the bizarre clothes they want Penny to wear. In an atmosphere of unbridled kinkiness, Penny is determined to discover the truth about Beaumont's strange hobbies.

Sexual jealousy, bizarre hi-jinks and very unsporting behaviour in this Black Lace special reprint.

ISBN 0 352 33005 8

BLACK LACE BOOKLIST

Information is correct at time of printing. To avoid disappointment check availability before ordering. Go to www.blacklace-books.co.uk

All books are priced £5.99 unless another price is given.

Black Lace books with a contemporary setting

------ ✄ ------------------

Please send me the books I have ticked above.

Name   ....

Address   ....

               ....

               ....

         .... Post Code ....

Send to: **Cash Sales, Black Lace Books, Thames Wharf Studios, Rainville Road, London W6 9HA.**

US customers: for prices and details of how to order books for delivery by mail, call 1-800-805-1083.

Please enclose a cheque or postal order, made payable to **Virgin Publishing Ltd**, to the value of the books you have ordered plus postage and packing costs as follows:

    UK and BFPO – £1.00 for the first book, 50p for each subsequent book.

    Overseas (including Republic of Ireland) – £2.00 for the first book, £1.00 for each subsequent book.

If you would prefer to pay by VISA, ACCESS/MASTER-CARD, DINERS CLUB, AMEX or SWITCH, please write your card number and expiry date here:

....

Please allow up to 28 days for delivery.

Signature ....

------ ✄ ------------------